Perfectly Criminal

WITHDRAWN

A novel by

Celeste Marsella

A Dell Book

PERFECTLY CRIMINAL
A Dell Book / April 2009

Published by
Bantam Dell
A Division of Random House, Inc.
New York, New York

ISBN 978-0-440-24467-7

Printed in the United States of America
Published simultaneously in Canada

www.bantamdell.com

OPM 10 9 8 7 6 5 4 3 2 1

For my daughter, Stacy Clair Sahagian

Perfectly Criminal

GUNK

JEFF KENDALL LOUNGED AT THE DEFENSE TABLE, one arm slung casually behind him in an attitude that made his hard wooden chair look like an overstuffed Barcalounger. I can barely spell *haute couture,* but I'd swear on a stack of gambling chits that his dandified three-button suit was Italian hand-tailored. All that aside, though, it was those ballet-sized feet of his, peeking out from under the table in argyle socks and tasseled loafers, that gave me a familiar malodorous taste in the back of my throat like I'd just slurped down a bad raw oyster. What a freaking weasel Jeff was. A rodent when we were on the same side—prosecutors at the Rhode Island Attorney General's Office—he had devolved into a slug when he left the AG's to ooze into the pond scum of criminal defense.

Jeff's courtroom antics, alas, had neither evolved nor degenerated. Today he was defending the guy I was prosecuting, a creepy dude accused of shotgunning his wife

to death in their posh Dean Estates mansion. Jeff was
still conjuring up the same tired tricks to make up for his
lousy legal skills—twirling his pen in the air like an autis-
tic child or an idiot savant, trying to distract the jury from
my impending closing argument. No need to overwork
yourself, Jeff old boy, I thought. My case was built on a
house of cards and I had nothing magical up my sleeve.

I unfolded to my gangly six-foot height and, clicking
across the room toward Jeff in metal-tipped stilettos, I
watched his raccoon eyes ratchet open in quaking anticipation of an early death. He stared up at me and fumbled his cheap courtroom Bic to the floor. I waited. My
timing was always top-notch. When the pen clattered to
rest between my black-stockinged legs, I turned to the
jury and pointed, my arm completely outstretched and
held high, like I was denouncing a Nazi war criminal.

"In a few minutes this man will stop twirling his ba-
ton and stand before you. He will try to convince you
that the defendant, Micah Cohen, is a tortured and mis-
understood soul whom the state is trying to crucify—
Jesus Christ of Nazareth—"

Jeff bolted to his feet. "Objection, your honor!"

Judge Ragusta raised both hands in fatigued surrender. He was used to my courtroom drama and the curtain had just opened on my finale.

"She's only *just begun*, Mr. Kendall. Let's allow her a
little more...rope."

The jury was confused. They looked worried, non-
plussed. Had there been evidence involving *rope* at trial?
A lasso perhaps? A noose? A garrote?

"What the judge is *suggesting*," I explained, "is that I

might eventually get myself in trouble by saying something I'm not supposed to say, like telling you things the defendant *doesn't want you to know.*"

The judge rolled his eyes. Jeff clamped his shut. And I continued without objection.

"But I will gladly get myself in trouble with this court if it means that Micah Cohen will be punished for murdering his wife. I'll gladly sacrifice myself on a cross right next to his gallows."

"As if," Jeff whined in this incredibly teensy voice.

"Mr. Kendall," the judge warned.

I nodded a sweet smile at the judge. "Thank you, your honor," I said, sighing deeply. "I do tend to become overemotional when a defenseless woman's *brains* are splattered all over her bedroom ceiling and have to be scraped off by a local cleaning crew."

The jury sucked air into its collective lungs. A united choral gasp. I really wanted to bow, but I knew my limits. They were gobbling up my soap-opera slop. Not an easy performance, might I add. Juries, by nature, are a resentful group—captivity is a bitch. My job was to make these twelve people feel like righteous avenging angels of a dead woman's soul—to make them *exult* as they were herded into a stifling hot courtroom every day to listen to grisly blood-spatter evidence, when instead they could have been enjoying a breakfast bagel melt at their local Burger King. Christ, even *I* was bitchy at eight-thirty in the morning, and I was paid to be there.

I clicked my ruby red spikes at the heels and bellied up to the jury box. "My friends, that man—who has resumed his baton-twirling act to distract your attention—

will come before you momentarily and tell you that the
State of Rhode Island has no direct evidence against the
defendant. He will tell you the evidence we have is *circumstantial.* He will explain that circumstantial evidence
means that no one actually *saw* Micah Cohen put the
gun to his wife's sleeping head—"

"Objection!" Jeff was back on his feet again. "There is
no evidence that Mrs. Cohen was asleep before she died."

"Well, a gun blast to the head would certainly wake
me out of a sound sleep," I remarked to the jury.

"Quiet!" yelled the judge.

The jury's attention shot to the judge, but I kept mine
on them.

"Objection overruled. Mr. Kendall, your own expert
testified under cross that she *could* have been asleep
when the gun was fired. Miss Lynch, continue, and let's
try to get through this before the end of the lunar year."

The jury's eyes returned to me. They cracked a few
cautious smiles at the judge's humor. And even though
the last damn thing I felt like doing was smiling, I smiled
back at them and continued my Oscar-worthy performance.

"The baton-twirling defense attorney will also tell
you that Micah Cohen *adored* his wife. That he doted on
her. Depended on her like a child does its mother." I
cupped my hands over the railing dividing us and leaned
into the jury box. I was entering their space. Their heads
drew closer to me, as if we were going to share some se-
crets. "And let's assume that it's true. That Micah Cohen's
feelings for his wife were those of a child for its mother."
I straightened, raised my head high, and let my voice sing

across the room. "Because they certainly weren't the feelings of a man for a woman in the traditional sense of a marital relationship." I paused, and lowered my head again. "Micah Cohen is gay. Charlene Cohen discovered her husband's homosexuality *three weeks* before she died. *Three weeks* before she died, Charlene Cohen retained an attorney to end her marriage. And three weeks later, she was shot dead."

I waited for that fact to sink in, because it was the rusted linchpin for my whole rotten circumstantial case.

"My heart goes out to Micah Cohen," I said with Meryl Streep sincerity. "Our society remains so tragically reluctant to accept homosexuality as natural that men like Mr. Cohen feel they have to bind themselves in disingenuous relationships with women in order to cloak their true natures. Micah Cohen wanted to continue the charade of a happy marriage." I shook a few spiky platinum strands of hair into one eye. I was trying for the seductive look, but I may have looked the madwoman, which wouldn't have been too bad either—maybe I could *scare* them into a guilty verdict. "But Charlene Cohen said no to her husband. 'No, I will not continue this charade,' she said."

I breathed deeply again, to coax the jury into following suit. They were by now hanging on my every word, and the poor souls looked faint.

"Charlene Cohen said no to her husband. She said, 'I don't want a pretend life. I won't live with the lies anymore.' She told her sister that she wanted another chance at *love*."

On silenced heels, I tiptoed to the water pitcher at

my table. The cheap lunchroom glass looked smudged and full of prints. And was that red glop at the edge lipstick? I poured, raised the filthy glass to my lips. A few feet away Jeff Kendall had called his Bic back into action and was sketching figures of evil-looking women with short bristling hair and protruding horns.

Setting the disgusting glass down on the table, I turned back to the jury as their collective stare shot from my legs to my face. " *'I want another chance at love,'* " I said in the ethereal voice of a dead woman. "You heard Charlene's sister testify that Charlene said this. That Charlene told her sister she finally realized why her marriage had been so frigid. *'I want another chance at love.'* I ask you, ladies and gentlemen, are those the words of a woman who wants to die?"

The jurors' eyes were fixed on me like a classroom of grade-schoolers worried that the teacher would call on them. *"No,"* I answered for them. "Charlene Cohen didn't want to die. Ask yourselves this: Why did Charlene Cohen hire a lawyer if she intended to kill herself? Because Charlene Cohen wanted freedom, not death. But three weeks after she said no to her marriage, Micah Cohen bought a gun and shot her. Three weeks after she said, 'This sham of a marriage is over,' she was dead."

I let those words linger, hoping I wasn't overdoing it. The twelve men and women in the box might have been enjoying the show, but they weren't as dumb as I liked them to be. One repetition too many and I'd offend them.

At my silence, their dozen heads pivoted from me to Jeff, waiting for him to stand, object, or show any sign of life, but he merely sat there doodling, while next to him, the defendant had buried his face in his hands. If Micah Cohen had been my client, I would have kicked him under the table, or passed him a note: *Hold your head up, you idiot, and look shocked. You look guilty as hell.*

I returned to my chair, dragged it noisily back against the stone floor, and sat.

Judge Ragusta looked up at the clock on the back wall. Jeff Kendall glanced at his watch.

"Mr. Kendall," the judge said, "I'll let you go now if you want, or you can wait until we reconvene. It's up to you."

Jeff decided to wait until Monday. Smart choice, of course. Over the weekend the force of my closing argument, weak as it was, would become but a dim memory in the jury's mind.

The judge dismissed the jurors, and when the last one had disappeared, Jeff ambled over to me as I packed up my briefcase. "What's all this saccharine hypocrisy you're spewing these days?" he asked. "Religious allusions? Christ on a cross? Shannon, you're a bloodless misanthrope. Have you no pride?"

I leaned in close to Jeff's white face. "Where's your *gold* Montblanc? You trying to appeal to the dirty unwashed by hiding your silver spoon behind a Bic ballpoint?"

I strode out of the courtroom, Jeff following at my heels to tell me he might not even give a closing argument. "You have no case, why should I even waste the court's time?"

I forwent the elevator and bolted down the stairs two at a time trying to lose him, but the little nit stuck to me like flypaper. One would think, given our hostile history at the AG's office, he'd want to escape from me as soon as the judge gaveled his final hammer, but he kept buzzing in my ear. "You're a shark who'd prosecute a shih tzu puppy for pooping in the street if Vince Piganno told you to. This case is going to ruin your sterling trial record."

"I put *people* in jail, Jeff, not *puppies*. People who rape, murder, and perpetrate various and sundry acts of mayhem on innocent victims."

"You know," he said, "I've often wondered if someone like you could even *be* a victim. I mean, if you were raped, wouldn't it qualify as just another one of your dates—your payback for saying 'Fuck you' to the wrong guy in the wrong alley too late at night after too many vodka martinis?"

"Scotch neat," I corrected him. Out through the rotunda and down the steep courthouse steps, he followed me. "And unfortunately, raped or not, I'd be duty-bound to deliver my *bad date* to the local cops."

"While you'd no doubt be fantasizing about a time- and cost-efficient bullet through his skull. You still carry that Colt Defender in your purse?"

I stopped a few feet from my car parked on the street. "I do, as a matter of fact. So why are you still stalking me?"

My three-inch heels gave me the height advantage. He looked up into my eyes and smiled. "My car's right up there." He glanced toward a shiny, gunmetal gray BMW farther down the street, and then back at me. "Are those dark roots I see? Don't let your hair grow. The sharp spiky look is more in character with your icy and unforgiving nature. Falling in your eyes like that? It gives guys the wrong idea...like you're approachable or something."

"As long as *you* keep the wrong idea zipped in your pants."

"No problem there. I like the insecure type. How *is* Marianna, by the way?"

His wink looked more like a twitch, and he walked off toward his car still cocksure of himself, not caring if he won or lost or whether the prize was a woman or a trial. For Jeff Kendall and his spoiled clan, the daily game of life began with a coming-out party at birth, cruised through the sweet-teen years, and sailed on a breeze to vested middle age. And Jeff had nothing resembling a conscience to bump him from that first-class nonstop flight to his gold-watch-retirement gala at the family estate.

I was still fumbling with my rusty car lock when Jeff zoomed up with his head out the window. "Speaking of Marianna, how's the rest of your crew?" he asked.

"I'm meeting them now. I'd invite you, but Marianna still has her laser sight pointed at where your dick would be if you had one."

Jeff cackled and waved an arm in the air, driving off as I sighed in relief. I boarded my giant SUV and headed to Fox Point and then into the parking lot at Al Forno, where I assumed my closest friends and coworkers, attorneys Marianna Melone and Laurie Stein and paralegal Beth Earles, were already upstairs at the bar decanting my scotch.

Straddling two steps at a time, I sprinted up to the second-floor bar and shimmied onto the stool they'd held for me. "I friggin' hate August. One hell of a scorcher, huh?"

Laurie's head swayed toward me. "Hey," she said, then looked down at my glass. "Glenlivet, right?"

I raised my drink in affirmation.

Marianna stuck her hand in the air in a tired hello, and Beth leaned over her and Laurie. "We're waiting for a table, Shannon. But I know you like the bar, so we can stay here if you want."

I shrugged, noncommittal. The drinks were always a more generous pour at the bar.

We were at Al Forno to commemorate our sixth year at the AG's office, but being gravely jaded about the stinking death and violence we dealt with daily at work, the atmosphere was more like a memorial service. It always seemed to be my job to hoist the jolly flag on our mast, but I was fresh from court on a losing case and I was beat to shit. Not wanting to disappoint, I downed my scotch in two gulps and held the empty glass up to the bartender. "Another round for everyone—and make 'em doubles."

A fresh pour of potent drinks later, Beth announced, with a toast, that she was leaving in the fall for law school.

"Beth, that's superior news!" Laurie exclaimed, finally coming to life. "Education is independence."

"And stress," Marianna added cynically, three shots of Grey Goose notwithstanding. "So how's the trial going?" she asked me.

"Losing," I said. "Not a speck of evidence. Vince should have let this one go."

Beth was still chirping, bouncing on her bar stool like a baby chick. "Wait! Can I talk first? I've been holding all this in, and I'm ready to burst."

I pulled out a fresh pack of Camels. I couldn't smoke inside, but just fondling the little cellophane package in my cupped hands would assuage a jittery nicotine withdrawal. "All right, sweetkins," I said to Beth. "Talk. But omit the chintz-covered adjectives and redundant conjunctions, huh? I spent the better part of my day with prepster Jeff Kendall, and I'm all choked up on proper nouns."

"Leave her alone, Shannon," Laurie said, pushing my drink closer to me. "This is big news. Remember when you got your law school acceptance letter?"

"Frankly, no. I've successfully nuked my life before the age of six."

"Shit!"

We turned to Marianna, who was all lit up with the high-watt bulb that had just gone off in her head. "Beth is quitting. That must be why Vince hired Brooke Stanford." She turned to Beth. "When did you tell him you were leaving?"

Beth nodded. "In May when I got the acceptance."

Our chauvinist boss, AG Vince Piganno, or "the Pig" as we called him behind his back (and to his face when I was in a particularly pissy mood), had hired the new girl in July, a month ago. Go figure why. He was generally disgusted with employees who got menstrual cramps. I swore if the fat pig dared make another crack about women lawyers, I was going to shove juicy Brooke down his throat—whole.

"Brooke seems very nice," Beth offered. "Well behaved and very quiet."

"That's an understatement," Laurie said. "She hasn't peeped a syllable since her first day. But then, maybe we just weren't listening. Jesus, I'm hungry," she added without a breath.

"She's a Stepford mutant," Marianna said. "And in the general fabric of human worth, she's a piece of lint."

Marianna was the first of us to blackball Brooke as a potential addition to our little group. In my opinion, Marianna was clinically depressed. But what the hell do I know? She kept refusing to consider her need for megadoses of SSRIs and so far so good. She hadn't jumped off any bridges.

At Marianna's criticism, Beth shook her Grace Kelly mane, releasing a curtain of platinum hair over one eye. "Mari, dropping a comment like that is so far beneath you...that even Shannon has to stoop to pick up on it."

I choked on my own laughter. Beth was too saccharine for a tart like me, but I respected her homespun attempt to keep the dirty lot of us laughing. And I'll take all the credit—she'd been hanging around me so long even her usually classy barbs were ripening to raunch.

"And what's with those outfits of hers?" Marianna sniped. "Her skirts are so tight you can see her thong outline when she bends over."

"And who," I added, "wears thongs anymore? I mean, the point of them is what?"

"Truthfully," Marianna said, "I think men find thongs more enticing than no underwear at all. They get off on the sadism of sexy clothes."

"Masochism," Laurie corrected. "Men don't *force* women to walk around all day with a glob of fabric in their asses."

"Then why do we do it?" Beth asked.

All eyes spun to Beth.

"Are you shitting me?" I said to her. Laurie and Marianna looked at her in silent accusation. Beth's mouth fell open, the deceit of denial caught in her throat.

"*We* don't," Mari answered. "And if we *do*, then we shall, *forthwith*, gather all such garments up in a Goodwill box and drop them at Brooke Stanford's office first thing in the morning. Okay, Beth?"

Marianna's gut reaction to Brooke Stanford was nothing more than her normal paranoia hiked up a notch by some healthy old-fashioned competitive jealousy. (You don't get ahead by cutting the new guy slack.) And since Marianna was our resident beauty—Italian in all the right places—she saw Brooke Stanford as a threat. And yeah, I guess Brooke was pretty if you like that finely-toned-racehorse look. I only know that our receptionist, Andrew (don't-frigging-ask-me-how-to-pronounce-it) Lavigne, had to wear a neck brace for a week every time Brooke blew past him. And Andy was a born-again, dyed-in-the-wool homosexual. He'd come so far out of the closet that I'd carved his name on the last stall in the girls' room.

My lack of trust in *Mayflower*-inspired Brooke was based on more substantial things like the fact that she was Beth without a soul. Beth understood the privileges she'd been born into and the flimsiness of their shelf life in a rotting society. Brooke, on the other hand, seemed pissed that she actually had to *work* for a living. Suck it up, Brooke baby. Life is no oak barrel of laughs and eventually we all get a taste of those bottom dregs.

Beth's excitement over her law school acceptance having been damned to the hereafter, we all returned to our drinks until the oppressively sweet whiff of "Miss Dior Chérie" came wafting our way. I raised my nose to the air like a vulture sensing fresh kill. Sneaking a look over my left shoulder, I watched none other than Brooke flip-flop into the room wearing gold sandals (Jack Rogers flats, signifying a summered Southampton pedigree, so Beth informed us). Brooke paused at the entrance, looked around, and registered her own scent of danger— the phalanx we'd set up at the bar.

Since she hadn't been invited to our celebratory soiree, I wondered just how the hell Brooke happened to find us.

Marianna began lamenting her existential fate. "Oh, just shoot me," she said. "Here's the bane of my waning existence. Why does that broad feel the need to torment us with her glaring presence? As if I need to see the light of my fading youth reflected in the glow of her twenty-five-year-old complexion."

Beth rolled her periwinkle eyes to the ceiling. "Mari, thirty-five years hardly constitutes a waning life."

Beth tirelessly fell for Marianna's depression act. Laurie, however, was Jewish. She knew all about mental health or the lack thereof, but she figured that if her great-grandmother could survive Auschwitz, she could manage a cushy life in twenty-first-century America with a few off-color jokes and a Dewar's on the rocks. Laurie and Beth had remained sentries to the cause of hoisting Marianna's soul out of the dump, but I was ready to start lacing her vodka with powdered Prozac.

"Hey, Mari," Laurie snapped. "What's your alternative to old age? Huh? Tell me! What is it?"

"Here comes the bride," Marianna muttered.

As if Maudlin Mari didn't have enough on her already bleak plate, Brooke Stanford was inching toward us along the bar—slowly, proudly, like a Clydesdale horse getting ready for a ringside prance, except this horse had giraffe-length legs. Her flaming red hair was pulled back in a low bun, sloppy but insouciantly sexy, with just the right amount of tendril escaping into her palm-frond green eyes. I regarded her curvaceous lips that seemed to be always puckered, yet invitingly open for business—ready for the next blow job—lips through which one was blindly drawn to a dazzling display of naturally pearlescent teeth that captured the overhead pendant lights and reflected them back at higher voltage.

The crystal gears of Brooke's transparent brain working away, she was smartly wondering whether we'd acknowledge her as she watched the four of us stare at her without so much as a nod. I hoped she wasn't expecting a high five, because I was lifting my middle finger to her when Beth rolled off her bar stool and blocked me. Of course at five-four, Beth's halo hovered somewhere beneath my chin.

"Hello, Brooke," Beth said sweetly. "Would you like to join—"

"Private party," I snapped over Beth's head. "Six years

together at the AG's. But hey, Brooke, since you're already here, I've been wondering. Why did you want to work at the crappy AG's office? I hear Edwards & Angell is always looking for class acts like you. Air-conditioned offices. Lots of available young associates to hook up with. And unlike Vince, your boss at E&A won't throw a chair at you when he's pissed."

She tilted her head, too unsure of me to laugh. Of course, there was always the possibility she didn't think I was funny. More likely she was scared shitless that I'd bite her tongue out if she laughed with an open mouth.

"Many great politicians begin their careers as prosecutors," she recited rote like a schoolgirl. "Hillary Clinton is my hero—"

I heard Laurie gag in the background.

"—and actually Mr. Piganno was very persuasive," Brooke continued unabated. She looked at Beth and smiled. "He said Beth was the only *real* female in the office and he wanted to replace her with someone...well... likewise feminine."

Well, that's all 36C Mari had to hear. Not that she ever showed off her fatty milk glands. She harnessed her boobs into high-buttoned oxford shirts, always trying to hide her Mediterranean heritage, afraid that no one would take her seriously if they suspected a gene pool that included Carmela Soprano.

She hopped off her stool and into the fray. "Did Vince really say that, Miss Brooke?"

Brooke stepped back. I think she feared a rumble. An actual fistfight. Was she too stupid to realize the implications of what she'd said, or was she so smart that she'd auto-blasted the three of us in one sentence? Shit if I knew or even cared. But I watched in jaded amusement as Laurie twirled around to face Brooke, who was paling to the color of skim milk.

"Miss Stanford," she said, "do you know how tough it is to deal with hardened criminals every day?" Laurie turned her cheek, giving Brooke a clear view of the scar she wore thanks to a defendant who'd managed to smuggle a knife into court. "This was carved by one of the fine young men I prosecuted a few years ago. He thought I was a little too *feminine* looking, so wasn't he surprised when I judo-chopped him in the balls as my face spattered blood all over his polyester shirt."

I loved Laurie when she was mad. Religiously cool under pressure, she was a zealot on ice.

"So, *Brooke*," Laurie continued, "let me sum up: I don't know what swill the Pig fed you at your interview, but *femininity* is best left at the office doorstep and he knows that better than anyone."

I had begun a slide off my bar stool when Laurie started her tirade. I had implicit faith in her ability to finish Brooke off and leave her for dead, so I smiled at Laurie's salvo and headed for the unisex bathroom off the hall outside the bar. I was pushing on the door when it abruptly opened and I fell through the threshold into the all-encompassing arms of a tall, suited gentleman. Bleary-eyed and teetering on shaky legs, he wrapped his arms around me and for a moment we held each other, neither of us sure who was supporting who, but neither of us letting go either.

It was love at first sight.

2

DRAWING BLANKS

"HEY, PARTNER," I SAID. "ROUGH DAY AT THE office?"

His head fell into my chest and he gasped for a lungful of air. He raised his head and looked at me with the hollowed-out eyes of a preteen rape victim who was learning about sex with a filthy hand clamped over her mouth.

"My God...so sorry," he stuttered, still holding on to my forearms. "It's hot in here, no?" His forehead was beaded with sweat.

With my heel, I kicked the door closed behind me. "What's up, buddy? You in trouble?"

I expected him to stumble past me, out the door, back into the bar, but he dropped his arms to his side and fell back against the wall, looking down at his hands as if wondering why they were still attached.

He was late forties; his hair, gray-flecked, was the color of beach sand and shorn short in one of those metrosexual styles that improved when mussed. A broad face and strong jaw were set in a slightly anemic pallor begging for a tropical vacation. His suit was sweat-wrinkled and his tie missing. He seemed the quintessential gentleman after a bit of bad news (a dip in the stock market lightening the load on his investment portfolio?), but definitely not the kind of guy in any real trouble—the kind of trouble the girls and I were used to seeing at the AG's office every day—murder, armed robbery, and the occasional aforementioned child rape.

With watery gray eyes just ready to overflow, he said, "One too many martinis."

"No shit," I said calmly. "We've all had those days."

I eyed him a bit closer as I waited for another few words, but he remained mute—shaking like a sweaty kid who'd been looking for his lost dog all day and hadn't found him. He didn't seem drunk; his words weren't slurred and his eyes were keenly focused on mine—actually too keenly focused, like he was asking me for an explanation. But melodrama aside, it was, after all, still hovering around 100 degrees outside, so maybe he was just hot. I nodded my head a few times to keep him calm in case he was having a little heart attack in addition to a seasonal hot flash.

"Maybe I should call 911?" I asked. "You here with anyone?"

He shook his head and started to say something, but before he could push the first syllable out, he frigging fainted—fell into my arms—all roughly 230 muscular pounds of him—dragging us both down to the black and white tile floor.

And that's where Brooke Stanford found us seconds later—his head, cheek to the floor, burrowed between my thighs, his legs splayed out on the floor in front of me.

Her glance went from me to him. She walked slowly around to see his face, recognition widening her eyes. "Scott? Is that you?"

"Shut up, Stanford," I said, "and splash some water on his face."

She didn't move. "Is it a heart attack? How disgusting! What were you doing in here?"

I forgot I wasn't talking to one of the girls, my buddies still outside at the bar, any one of whom would have ripped a toilet from the floor at my request because we had an act-first-ask-later kind of trust. Brooke Stanford, on the other hand, reacted to my command like a typical broad when another female barks an order at her: She bristled and then joyously ignored me with a smirk on her puss.

"Get the fuck out of my way," I said, pushing myself away from the still-unconscious deadweight and standing up.

In fear (I hoped) she backed up a few steps against the bathroom door and watched as I cupped water in my hands from the sink and threw it down on the guy's face. Within seconds his eyes fluttered open.

Brooke came forward and knelt by him, suddenly his guardian angel. "Scott, omigod, Scott! Are you okay?"

I stood back, waiting for Scott's reaction. "Get out of here, Brooke. Get out now," he moaned.

Satisfied that she wasn't his long-lost daughter or someone equally precious, I yanked her up by the shoulders and twirled her toward the door. "You heard the man. And if you breathe a word of this anywhere but in the priest's confessional, I'll rip your tongue out."

"I'm not *Catholic*," she sneered. "But I would never say anything. Scott and I are ... old friends."

"Yeah, well, your old friend is toasted."

"Scott doesn't drink," she said proprietarily.

He tried to sit up, apparently tired of hearing us talk about him as if he were a helpless six-year-old. "Brooke, please leave us alone," he said.

I cracked a smile, or what I thought was a smile, and because I didn't do it often, I tried to make it look sincere. Showing my teeth was probably a mistake.

Brooke did her version of a toothy smile back and curtsied out the door.

"Get up," I said to the hulk on the floor. "People are going to start needing to pee in here, so you've got about another minute to pull yourself together—or I'm out of here."

He began pulling himself up by the sink. It was time for him to do some of the work, so I let him grapple by himself.

"I'm meeting my ... a business associate here. I've got to get outside to the bar."

"Your *girlfriend* said you don't drink."

He looked at me, possibly too jaded by now to even dispute the Brooke-as-girlfriend remark. "*Tonight* I do. Tonight's a whole new ball game for me."

"Yeah. I can see how drinking yourself into oblivion and then fainting in a public bathroom could topple one's value system."

He stumbled to the sink and splashed more water on his face, then began scrubbing his hands like Lady Macbeth. Few of my male friends even washed their hands, so a germophobe did not augur well for a long-term relationship with someone like me, who lived and died by the five-second rule. He was drying up with a paper towel when Marianna walked in.

She looked at him, then at me. "You've been in here *fifteen minutes*, Shannon. Long *date* for you, no?" She looked at him hard. "Hey, you look familiar."

"Wrong guy," he said ruefully, and stumbled by her out the door.

I slapped Mari on the back. "I'm leaving. I think I'm in love."

"*You* know you're a lunatic, Shannon, so I won't bother saying it, but—"

"He seems to need a shoulder to cry on. A bad day at work, I think. Sweet Jesus, he's wearing a Brioni suit! How the fuck dangerous can he be?"

" 'A shoulder to cry on'? He's using the oldest pick-up ploy in the book. That guy is pulling your leg so hard you're going to be walking with a limp."

"Maybe so, pal, but he's giving me heart flutters, so I want to finish what we started in here before his wife incarnates."

"He's fucking *married*?"

"Married? Who knows? Fucking her? Probably not or he wouldn't be so quick to fall for my charms—as difficult as they are to resist. Anyway, Mar, I just met him. I don't have the particulars yet but I don't need his Social Security number to get laid."

I walked out and Marianna followed. We found my inamorato at the bar with a virile-looking scotch rocks already pressed to his hot lips. I typically fell for bad boys. Falling for a stranger who'd collapsed in a bathroom was definitely stretching the limit, but there was something about *this* alcoholic that wasn't ringing true. I eased in next to him and ordered my heart to stop pounding—along with another Glenlivet.

"Forgive me for sounding like a wife, but are you married?"

"Not anymore."

"Okay, good...whatever...but should you be having another *drink*?"

He turned to me, looking a bit more relaxed now that some ninety-proof was coursing through his veins. He rubbed his already bloodshot eyes until they flamed even brighter. "I started drinking again tonight. For me it's poison."

"Is he still drinking?" whispered Marianna, who was to my left, on the edge of her bar stool, almost in my lap.

To Marianna's left was Laurie, leaning forward over the bar to get a better glimpse of my rumored bluebeard. Beth just figuratively said, *What the fuck,* and came over to stand behind us, eavesdropping on our conversation while sucking on some prissy pink drink sporting an umbrella swizzle stick.

Brooke Stanford, thank Christ, had left the immediate premises.

I tried to ignore the girls as they hovered over me like flies to garbage. Leaning close to the Scott-man, I said, "Either you drop your plum Amex card on the bar and pay your tab or I'm taking my marbles and going home. I've had enough of your self-indulgence."

Secure enough, he cracked a half-assed smile at my assumption of control over him. He saluted me like a damned prisoner of war and shoved his hands in his pants pocket, extracting a wad of bills. Wrapped around a hundred-dollar bill, the roughened cuticles of his fingers were caked in a reddish dirt, despite the hand-washing. He graciously offered to pay for my drink, but I gave the bartender a no-can-do sign and then nodded toward Marianna. He blinked once in understanding, and when I beamed back to Scotty, he was sneaking down the last of his scotch.

He shrugged and I said, "Let's go."

Marianna's head popped up. "Where you going?" she hissed.

"Cancel my reservation. I've got a date."

As I turned to leave, she pulled me back by the arm. "Don't you take him home. You're going to get yourself killed one of these days."

Marianna would be the first to admit that when she fell in love she morphed into an airhead. She became an emotional wimp with men she was falling for, whereas I just pulled down the sheets for them. Something about my towering stature fooled me into thinking I was more a man's equal—a champ in the same weight category. But unlike Marianna, who kept her gun stored in the top shelf of her closet, I kept mine handily in my bag 24/7.

Scott, whose last name was still a mystery, followed me through the steamy night in a white Chrysler Sebring. His car choice was already making me think we might never get to surname familiarity. I drove to the underground garage of my Downcity loft and motioned him into the guest spot next to mine. He exited his car and followed me to the elevator, in which we zoomed up to my fifth-floor aerie with nary a word. Once inside he walked straight over to my floor-to-ceiling windows through which Providence at night was lit up like a Christmas miniature of the big city it was trying to be. The Independent Man statue, once triumphant atop the State House, now stood emasculated by the new glassy skyscrapers that had been popping up around him like the new kids on the block.

My bathroom stranger and I stood there together, swallowing the view. I wondered anew why anyone would actually move to Providence if they hadn't been born here. My excuse was an escape from an alcoholic father in South Boston. Providence was far enough away that he couldn't, or wouldn't bother to, reach me.

Scott's arms lay limp by his sides. I expected something clever or witty—a prelude to the dance to bed—but I wasn't disappointed when he simply reached his arms out and pulled me to him, smothering my face, shoulders, and neck with surprisingly expert kisses.

"It can't just be my perfume," I managed to gasp.

"I need this. I need *you*," he said. "I'm so damn lost."

And then—I swear on my dead mother's soul—he swooped his arms under my legs and lifted me off my feet, and as if he'd been living there his whole life, he carried me to the bed hidden in the far corner of the room behind a mirrored screen. Strong dude, I thought briefly.

As he fumbled with buttons and zippers, he asked me

if I was *okay with this,* "this" meaning sex, and "okay" meaning he would stop if I wanted him to. That was all the go-ahead I needed: one more chance to say no—considered and rejected—and then I opened the floodgates, helping him with the all the troublesome fasteners keeping us apart. And then he seemed to calm down, as if just knowing I was willing and wanted him as much as he wanted me was enough for him. He stopped and buried his head into my chest.

"Are *you* okay with this?" I asked him. And then I swear I felt a dampness, the trickle of water roll down between my breasts—and at a cool 68 degrees inside the air-conditioned 1000-square-foot open space of my apartment, it wasn't sweat.

"I'm sorry." His bloodshot eyes were staring deep into mine. "I seem to be apologizing a lot tonight."

I waited for additional information, or another tear-fest, but I got nothing.

"Look, buddy," I said. "I don't mean to kill the moment, but are you crying or do I need a HEPA filter on my vacuum cleaner?"

He placed both his palms flat against my cheeks. "You're so different from anyone I've ever been with." His hands ran up my face and through my hair. He smiled ruefully. "I'm going to say something, and you may not like it, but I think it's a compliment."

I remained silent, staring into his sad eyes.

"You are the most sexy yet unfeminine woman I've ever met. How in the world do you do it?"

"Dial soap."

His eyes narrowed in a soft smile. "I bet you were a

real tomboy when you were a kid. You wore your hair in braids? Or was it always a bed-messed mop?" He took an enormous breath, and his eyes went blank again. He had already jumped ahead in his mind—on to something else—the same thoughts that had brought the initial swell of tears to his eyes.

"What's wrong, man-named-Scott who I've still not formally met? Something's really out of whack in your life, isn't it?"

If he didn't answer, I wouldn't ask again. It was a prosecutorial handicap even in personal relationships—I wouldn't interrogate him unless he was under oath, so I waited for a noncustodial confession. "I'm not holding you here," I advised. "You're free to leave if you've changed your mind about this."

He kissed me gently on the forehead and then pulled away, lying next to me. "I'm in trouble," he said.

"Yeah, well, I knew that when I first laid eyes on you."

He rolled to the side of the bed and sat up, grabbing for his pants and rifling through the pockets, where he found what he was looking for. Feeling at home already, he didn't ask my permission to smoke as he lit his Marlboro Light and threw the match into the ashtray on my bed table.

"I guess we're going to skip the good part," I said, taking his pack from him and popping out a cigarette of my own. "Was it good for you? Because I've got to tell you, I've had better."

"I may have killed my wife tonight."

Certain now that our moment of passion was over, I grabbed my pants from the floor. "You *think* you killed her?" I pulled on my pants, sans underwear, which I rarely wore anyway, and then, bare-chested, moved toward him for a light.

"I blacked out," he said, holding the match to me. "I took some pills. I'm not supposed to drink with them. I blacked out and when I came to, she was dead."

I should have been having second thoughts by then, but I wasn't afraid. If he'd just killed someone, it hadn't been premeditated. Hell, I wasn't even sure anyone was dead. He looked like the kind of screwed-up, tightly wound guy who could convince himself that cutting off his wife's Saks charge was tantamount to grievous bodily assault. So I figured they'd had a fight, albeit a bad one, and maybe he even whacked her, and she fell. But I didn't see any cuts or defensive wounds on him. And he was stark naked, so I could see everything there was to see. So a fight that ended in one of them dead? Nah.

I nodded my head a few times to keep him calm. "So, um, where's your wife now?" I asked.

"A friend's boat in the Newport harbor."

"You sure she's *dead* dead?"

He looked at me with owlish eyes and blew smoke out of his trembling lips. With a falsetto crack in his baritone voice, he said, "She's dead all right. They're *both* dead."

"Both?"

He nodded slowly.

With each additional detail the evidence was mounting exponentially, and I was building an airtight case against him at Mach speed: Husband finds his wife with another guy. Testosterone-powered jealousy turns an otherwise docile guy into a murderer. Happens all the time. But with the right sleazy defense lawyer, he could go with an insanity defense. Plead temporary insanity that prevented him from understanding right and wrong, or even a heat-of-passion type thing to get his charges reduced from murder to some lesser manslaughter offense. With good behavior, he'd be out in maybe two and a half years...

What the hell was I thinking?

Better question: Why was I thinking like a defense lawyer when I should have been handcuffing him to the bed and dialing the cops?

"Let me get this straight," I said. "You actually murdered your wife because you found out she was cheating on you? Because I've got to tell you, if I find a guy cheating on me, I just go tell him to have a ball. Believe me, it's not half as much fun to cheat if you have permission. 'Go fuck her, and then go fuck yourself,' I say to him, and he usually responds by taking me out for a nice dinner. I mean, jealousy is a real waste of time, and the fallout from it, which in your case was murder, is a real bitch."

He turned to me, delving into my eyes as if he were seeing me for the first time. I could see the pain in his eyes as they kept drifting away into the smoke from his cigarette. Maybe he was wondering what sane female would sit around chatting with some nude dude who just confessed to murder, or maybe he was sobering up and he didn't like my hair....

"Who *are* you?" he said.

I stuck my hand out to him. "Assistant Attorney

General Shannon Lynch. Homicide's my specialty. You've certainly come to the right place."

He didn't shake my hand. I guess we were beyond that, he and I. We'd already bonded at a much starker level.

"You're a prosecutor?"

"Yup. I incarcerate scumbags for a living. And I can usually sniff 'em out by their stink. So I gotta tell you, you're smelling pretty sweet to me right now, despite your earlier nap on the toilet floor."

He went calmly back to the butt of his Light, taking his last hit deep, like it was the extinguishing roach of expensive pot. He blew the smoke from his mouth and stabbed the cigarette into the ashtray until it broke apart. "My wife was having an affair," he explained.

I nodded. We'd been through this part before.

"With a woman," he added.

"No shit?" I said.

"You don't know who I am, do you?"

I knew enough. He was an overly emotional guy who'd just killed his wife and her lesbian lover. A nice guy from what I could tell, unlike the kind I typically fell for. This schmuck sitting next to me had obviously snapped when he found his wife and her lover *in flagrante delicto.* He was handsome, well-heeled, and doubtless had never suffered a broken heart in his life, so I assumed he wasn't used to being double-duped. He must have snapped. Simple as that. So what else did I need to know? Did I care what his name was? He had attached an importance to it as if he was someone special and not just some garden-variety homicidal maniac.

He weakly extended a shaking hand to me. "Scott Boardman, senator from Connecticut and the Democratic Party's hopeful in the upcoming presidential election. But I think I just sank my chances. What do you think?"

I thought he was the hottest guy I'd laid eyes on since my crush on Charles Sewell, chief of police of the Providence Police Department. I wanted to wipe the damp hair from his wolf-pup gray eyes and wrap my arms around his broad but firm waist. I wanted to take over where we'd left off a few minutes before, then, over a postcoital smoke, we could talk over strategy—both political and criminal. But I didn't say any of this because eloquence was not my strong suit, especially when I was sexually frustrated.

"I think you're fucked," I said. "And despite what *didn't* happen between us here tonight, I'm going to have to screw you a little bit more by calling the cops and turning you the hell in."

"Do you have any single malt?"

"You're cut off. Now get your clothes, go into the bathroom, and wash your face while I wake some people up. I'll try to preserve whatever dignity you have left— keep the news off the ticker for at least tonight—but you know you're done politically. Even if your wife jumped off the damn boat and committed suicide, no presidential candidacy can withstand the death of a spouse from anything other than natural causes."

"Miss Lynch, I've been in politics since I was a kid, and I know my career is just as dead as my wife is right now."

He picked up his clothes and retreated to my bathroom while I walked to my landline and dialed Mari,

who was still dining at Al Forno, slurping the last of her
Ligurian pesto pasta. "Call Chief Sewell," I said. "Tell him
we got a high-profile matter that requires his presence
ASAP. Tell him we're bringing in Senator Scott Boardman
as a possible murder suspect, and to keep it zipped until
he gets here."

"No joke, Shannon?"

"No joke. He's here at my place. Meet me in the
garage."

"I *knew* I recognized him," she said. And then, without further ado, she hung up.

I walked to the bathroom door and heard the good-
byes of a conversation Senator Boardman was having on
his cell. I knocked and he emerged clothed and ready to
go. I let him smoke another cigarette by the windows
while I began my cross-exam. "Are you scared?" I asked.
"Cuz I'm a pretty good ally here. I can walk you through
this, and maybe out of it, real quick." I snuck a smooch
behind his ear.

He took another drag of his cigarette and blew the
smoke out fast. Then he came to me and kissed me on
the cheek. "I can't involve you."

I stroked his back once, then perched on my win-
dowsill before I spoke. "That's kind of too late now, since
Brooke Stanford spotted us together in the bathroom
tonight. And who'd you call in there?" I nodded toward
the bathroom. "Your lawyer?"

He nodded. "And Jake Weller, my public relations
man. He was supposed to meet me tonight at the restaurant. He never showed. He needs to know what's going on."

"What'd he say? Your campaign is in the toilet?"

"I didn't get him. He'll hear about this in the god-damn news and have a heart attack."

He walked back over to the bedside table and stubbed out his cigarette. We descended to the garage in silence, where my faithful friends already stood in a huddle awaiting my arrival with the celebrity suspect.

Laurie's head poked up first. "On his way," she said to me without further explanation, referring of course to Chief of Police Sewell.

As Beth was saying "We told him no sirens," an un-marked but unmistakably official-looking Ford Crown Vic pulled into the garage. My very married lover, Charles, aka Chucky, Sewell, emerged from the backseat.

"Hey, Sewell," I said. "How's the wife and kids?"

"What's this about?" he said, wiping the sweat from his brow. "Why am I not home in my climate-controlled house watching the real news?"

Well-bred, but no longer presidential hopeful, Scott Boardman made the introduction. Boardman pronounced his name and extended his hand to Chucky, who under-standably refused to shake hands with a murder suspect. Chuck just nodded at Boardman and then pulled me a few feet away, whispering, "Isn't he the senator from—?"

"You know this bloke?" I said. "He told me he *thinks* his wife and her lover were murdered tonight. The bod-ies should be on some boat in the Newport harbor."

"Cat tails," he said, nodding to himself.

"How in hell did you know they were lesbians, Chuck? Am I the only politically challenged one of this group?"

"His wife's a lesbian?" He almost choked.

"'Cat tails'?" I repeated.

He dropped his head to his shoulder. "Christ, Lynch. You're *thick* tonight. All that booze is rotting out your brain. *Cattails* is the name of his boat. A sixty-eight-footer. Is that where the wife is?"

"A *friend's* boat was what he said."

Chucky left me wavering on the proverbial dock and walked back to Boardman and the rest of the group. "Ms. Lynch here says you made some incriminating statements earlier this evening. Do you care to repeat them now, or do you want a lawyer?"

As if on cue, a dark-suited man with hair damp from a recent shower and looking very much the corporate white-collar defense lawyer strode into the garage.

He exhaled the name "Scott," and caught his breath. "Say nothing." Then he quickly turned his attention to Chief Sewell. "What the hell kind of Rhode Island shuffle is this? It looks like a lynch mob—"

"'*Lynch* mob,'" I repeated. "I like the sound of that."

The dark-suited stranger leaned in close to me. I could smell Listerine on his breath.

"*What* exactly did you make my client say *without the benefit of counsel*?"

"We didn't talk much until *after* we had sex, so his incentive to lie was wholly lacking by then."

"Enough," Scott Boardman said softly. "Let's not make this more of a circus than it already is." He looked at his attorney, who was directing all his attention to Chucky Sewell, assuming that as a man, Chucky was the one in charge.

"I'm Ron Esterman," he said to Chucky. "I'd like to

take Senator Boardman home if I may? Unless you intend to hold him..."

Chucky announced that he actually might not mind
getting a statement as long as the suspect was already in
our grasp. He suggested that Senator Boardman might
like to ride in the police car with him and that Mr.
Esterman could follow in his shiny black Lexus parked at
the curb.

Scott Boardman suddenly became the tough-talking
senator. "I'd like to give my statement later, after I speak
with my attorney."

I walked closer to Boardman, still sympathetic. "Hey,
Scott, you have to go with the chief. You just confessed—"

He backed away, looking at me as if I'd just sprouted
multiple horns from my spike-haired head.

His mouthpiece spoke for him. "Senator Boardman
and I are going to talk for a bit." Then directly to Chucky
he said, "You'll find the Booths' boat moored at Forty-one
Degrees North, a restaurant on Thames Street in Newport.
Endurance is the boat's name. We'll come down to the
station later this evening."

"Who's Booth?" Chucky said.

"Muffie Booth is—was a friend of Mrs. Boardman's. I
believe you'll find both women on the Booth family's
boat."

Chucky nodded to the cops standing around him to
make sure they got the information. "I'd like the senator
to leave his car keys with us if you don't mind."

"I do mind," Ron Esterman said. "At this point we
don't even know that a crime has been committed. We'll
wait for a warrant."

"Ron," Scott said, "I've got nothing to hide. But do what you think is best."

Needless to say, I was a bit shocked. First a naked murder confession, and then suddenly he's got nothing to hide? But Chief Charles Sewell and Attorney Ron Esterman were now in charge of Senator Boardman's immediate legal future, so I bit my tongue and kept silent, knowing professionally when to defer to the proper authority. I'd get my chance at Scotty later.

Ron Esterman handed Chucky his business card. "Call me when—and if—you get a warrant."

Beth and Laurie went home, but Marianna convinced me to raise the mast on my Chevy Suburban to hunt pirate ships on the high seas—or in this case, a multimillion-dollar yacht moored at the harbor of 41° North restaurant in Newport, Rhode Island, where a couple of bloody bodies were just then being discovered by the local cops.

3

DAVY JONES'S LOCKER

MARIANNA'S IDEA OF FUN IS GOING TO THE morgue to visit her victims. She insists she can hear them talk to her. Me? I can take the uncommunicative stiffs or leave them. The smell of death doesn't juice me like it does her. If you ask me, the girl is a *died*-in-the-wool necromaniac. (Yeah, I know I spelled it wrong.)

"You need to come too, Shannon," Mari said to me, pushing me toward my car. "It's personal for you now. We need to find out what happened before you get into this guy any deeper. Or, I should say, before he gets into you." Then she stopped and faced me in a sudden assumption of authority. "Or is it already too late?"

"No, but not for lack of trying. He was too drunk to get it up, I think."

"Or perhaps he was too tired after a double murder."

I didn't argue. Not because I thought she was right (being wrong has never stopped me from a good fight), but because I was too busy planning my escape from the death scene in Newport. "Mar, how is seeing dead bodies going to help? The ME will go and tell us what we need to know. What's the damn point of mucking around in all that blood?" I was now behind the wheel but still stalling as I shoved the key into the ignition. "You take the damn car and go. Leave me home. I've been on trial all day and it's been a long night. I'm frigging wilting from exhaustion."

"Are you wimping out on me, Shannon? Who'd have *thunk* it?"

Truth was, she was right. I don't know why I could look at pictures of autopsy and murder scenes but the real thing always shook me.

I slammed the car into drive and we drove in silence, Marianna backing off, instinctively knowing I was fuming at her accusation that I was a wimp. The problem with close friends and family members is they know your buttons—and push them regularly.

I refocused my thoughts on Boardman and his sudden attitude change once we were out of my sheets and back on the streets. Obviously, the call to his lawyer had been made while he was locked in my bathroom. When and why did he decide to recant his admission? Was it my breath, or had he realized that his amnesia shtick wasn't passing the credibility test? Sure, as soon as he realized I was turning him in to the cops, that's when his memory returned—along with a solid not-guilty plea.

I looked down at my watch. Nine thirty-five p.m. I turned into the 41° North parking lot and found a spot. The restaurant was literally on the docks. There was no inside. The buzz on Newport's newest hot spot was that it was a nondiscriminatory private club where anyone, for a fee, could receive a shiny plastic card in the mail that entitled the holder to eat at the restaurant to the exclusion of nonmembers. Being able to moor your boat off its dock and admire it as you dined was an included plus but not a membership requirement.

We slipped through the entrance without notice (or membership cards) because of the bustle of police activity. Murder is a big-ticket item. On a hot August night, the posh new place was bustling with a drunk and dilatory dinner crowd, but the weather, changing fast from balmy to a nasty nor'easter, was compounding the chaos. Even the deck-length clear plastic panels were fighting to stay in place, slapping in protest against the high winds coming off the water.

Diners were being rustled to other tables as a boat was being cordoned off. Because I wasn't as chummy with the Newport cops as I was with the Providence guys, it took a few of my special tricks to get us close to the action. We flashed our AG IDs at whoever cared to glance our way and I mumbled "Yo" a few times. As long as we didn't slow down to give the younger cops a chance to realize they didn't recognize us, I figured we'd zip right onto the actual finger dock where the *Endurance* was moored.

"Follow me, Mari, and don't look up," I said as I walked down the dock ramp to board the yacht. I was blocked by an outstretched arm as I lifted my leg to board.

"Excuse me, *ma'am*. No one on this boat until forensics gets here—"

I retrieved the big guns from my pocket—Chucky

Sewell's old badge from when he was a street cop—
flashed it in the rookie's face, and before he could read it,
stuck it back in my belt, talking nonstop. "We came all
the way down from Providence, so don't make me go
back and tell the mayor you locals are making your
Providence brethren waste gas at taxpayers' expense,
huh? Lucky Dack's on his way from the ME's. He told us
to stand guard for him onboard."

As I pushed my way through the feeble barricade of
his twenty-year-old mug, I heard Mari behind me giving
him a final zing. "And if you call us 'ma'am' one more
time, I'll shove the pointy end of the apostrophe up your
dick."

I turned around and raised my brows at her.
Marianna had been thrown into overdrive by her last
murder case: a serial killer at a swanky private college.
She had gullibly let the student killer practically sit on
her lap as together they tried to solve the murders. And
the more he killed, the more she took him into her con-
fidence. Since then she wasn't as trusting as she used to
be, and she was belting out zingers whenever the oppor-
tunity presented itself. A barely-old-enough-to-shave
Newport cop was an easy mark.

As we stepped carefully onto the boat, I whispered,
"Hey, Mar, you got to go a little easy on the authority
here. We're not in Providence, so the cops aren't going to
be as solicitous. I mean, I haven't *slept* with any of them."

"The night is young. I have faith in you."

"Yeah, but I can't seem to get my temperature down
from my close encounter with Scott Boardman. Right
now I only have eyes for him, if you know what I mean."

"Well, Boardman's a bit indisposed right now, and you know the old song—if you don't have the keys to his jail cell, love the one you're with."

I had moved to the bridge of the boat, behind the stainless steering wheel, looking for the blood to begin its eerie trail. That's how these damn scenes always opened: Curtain up, the wolf is gone. Follow the blood to Grandma's bed, where she'll be lying faceup, howling at a blood-drenched ceiling.

While Marianna was already peering below to the berths, I stood with my hands deep in my pockets until Lucky Dack, our chief forensic tech, strode toward us from the dock. He caught sight of me and reared his head back in a nod. He boarded and then bowed graciously to Marianna and me. "Ladies, so nice to be here. Cuz heaven knows I wouldn't be in a fancy place like this unless someone died a highly unfortunate and violent death on the premises."

"*Au contraire*, Lucky," Marianna said. "*This* isn't one of *those* kind of places. Hell, they'd even let *me* join and I'm an Italo from Federal Hill."

"Frankly, I was referrin' to the price of the drinks." He gave her a wink.

Of the four of us, Marianna had always been Lucky's favorite. She was sweet with just the right amount of savvy. But Lucky and I enjoyed a special relationship, more like blood brothers; we were similar in height, screwed-up family histories, and predilections for perverted sex: Lucky liked his women cold, but preferably before autopsy.

I moseyed up close to Lucky's ear. Even at my height

I still had to stand on tiptoes to whisper in his ear. "These locals here think we're Providence cops," I said. "So don't blow our cover. Mari wants to go below with you. Personal stake in this one, if you know what I mean."

Lucky looked up at the boat's mast, processing the info I'd just hoisted on him. He was the sly and slow turtle, rarely erring with quick responses. He also knew that he had to be especially cautious with us "ladies" because we were usually doing something slightly left of legal. Lucky always performed quick calculations of how much we were jeopardizing *his* job while we were busy screwing up our own.

"Seems to me you two are doing something dangerously akin to impersonatin' police officers here. I'm no lawyer, but didn't you girls just about almost lose your jobs recently for some other questionably illegal activity—like hightailing it to a bar after witnessing those college murders?"

At the words "college murders," Marianna's ears perked up like a bloodhound at a fresh scent. She choked out, "How'd you find out about that? Only Vince and that miserable twit Jeff Kendall knew."

"Well, let me just say this. Far as I know, *Mr. Piganno* didn't breathe a word of it."

Marianna looked at me. "That's it, Shannon, Jeff Kendall just went on my hit list."

"He's been on your hit list since he practically raped you in his father's wine cellar. I'm sick of hearing it. We got new fish to fry here, so throw the dead ones back. Kendall will end up drowning in his own scum," I said.

As Marianna and I sparred over fish stories, Lucky

had made his decision on how far he would go to help us out. He spoke to the two cops standing guard at the stairway to the lower deck. "I'm going down below. These two fine *officers of the court* can come with me. I've worked closely with them in the past and they're pros. Yes, sir, I kindly appreciate their help. So nice of Providence to send them down here for this."

Lucky saluted the cops and stepped carefully toward the stairs. One tech with a camera was allowed down with us, and the four of us descended the steps to the galley area, where I hung back while Lucky led the way to the forward berth with Marianna on his heels. Even though the ceilings were unusually high in this high-priced tug, six-foot-five Lucky crouched as he advanced carefully to the scene, presumably watching his steps for blood drops or evidence along the way. I crept slowly forward as Lucky used hand signals to keep Marianna and me just outside the entrance to the main berth. He motioned the photographer through to begin his work while I explained to Lucky that Boardman had already confessed to the crime so there was no need to be as thorough as he normally would be.

Lucky spoke as he visually examined the area, touching nothing until the photographer was finished. "Don't be too sure of that, Miz Lynch. Once the defense lawyers get hold of 'em, a voluntary confession turns into a not-guilty plea faster than my granddaddy could get his head out of a noose."

"Jesus Christ, Lucky," I said. "You actually had relatives who were *hung*?"

"Nope, but it sure 'nuff gets your attention, doesn't it?"

"Low. Really low," Marianna muttered.

"Sweet chariot," Lucky retorted as he ducked his head to peer through the overhead beam of the bulkhead at the bodies of two women on the bed. He looked up at the bloody ceiling, then down again at them, as if tracing laser lines from wounds to blood spatter. One woman, a blonde, lay faceup; the other was dark-haired and lay facedown with her head hanging off the side of the bed like a broken doll. The bed was blood-drenched, so it was hard to tell at first glance how the deadly deeds had been done. So much red everywhere made me flash back to Boardman in the bathroom at Al Forno. Why, other than his dirty nails, was he so clean of any blood residue if he'd in fact just left this sanguineous carnage?

I held my arms stiffly at my sides to keep from shivering.

"Head wounds," Lucky said in his short-clipped manner. "Lot of blood still red and wet. But it would dry slower in the salt air. Humidity and all." He looked up and shouted at the guys hovering outside. "Get someone in here to do body temps ASAP!" Lucky continued to visually examine the scene from the doorway, mumbling to himself and taking mental notes. He poked his head up again and spoke to the camera cop. "Any of those guys out there questioning the guests before they all leave for the night? And the help too. Someone musta heard or seen somethin' 'round here about five or six hours ago. Like bloodcurdling screams and a guy running down the docks dripping blood all over someone's fifty-dollar veal chop?"

"Which reminds me, Lucky," I said, "I didn't see any

blood on Boardman, and he told me he'd just come from here."

"He clean up anywhere before you saw him?"

"Not that he mentioned, but then I didn't ask…"

"Could it be," Marianna said, "that you didn't ask Boardman any indecorous and embarrassing questions about the recent butchering of his wife and her lover because you didn't want to endanger your budding relationship with him?"

My body loosened in self-defense. I snapped at her like I was getting ready to toss her body on the bed with the two dead ones. "Hey, *buddy*, watch it! Are you suggesting I was shirking my professional responsibility just because my *suspect* was a hot piece of ass? Do you know how many defendants I've sent to jail that, but for the grace of God, I would have dated if they hadn't just sliced up their last girlfriend? Give me a little fucking credit here."

Lucky ducked into the V-berth and inched closer to the bodies, red and gray, the heat of passion having been snuffed by a presumptive weapon-wielding Scott Boardman.

The windows were shut tight and the enclosure was stuffy, smelling like the grease-encrusted toolbox in the trunk of my father's car—an amalgam of marine engine exhaust, seawater, decomposing blood, and the salty smell of stale body sweat.

As if he could sense my reticence, Lucky told Marianna she could come into the room with him but motioned me to remain by the door (undoubtedly because he didn't want to add vomit to the evidentiary mix). Marianna immediately walked toward what I now discerned was a battered-looking ash blond head, half of which was stained dark brown and unrecognizable as human. I wondered why my dinner wasn't already rushing back up my gut, then I remembered I'd never eaten.

Marianna was too busy visually examining the scene to notice my heavy breathing. That was the trouble with the four of us being so close: I couldn't hide things from them like I could the rest of the intimidated world. Beth was the only one who would retreat when I growled, and I expected that as soon as she went to law school and became a full-fledged JD, she too would soon realize that even if I could slice the wings off a monarch butterfly, there were still some things that rattled me. Like fresh blood from a kill.

Marianna remained focused on the crime scene as she spoke to me. "This Boardman guy was some hot dude you hooked up with in a bathroom, *after which* you found out he killed the wife. Precoital stardust was obscuring your vision when you should have been looking for blood. For all we know, he was using the Al Forno restroom to clean up and floss. In hindsight, we should have had the bathroom closed off to the public."

"Lest we fucking forget," I snapped back, "the guy confessed *after* we left the restaurant." Finally, I thought, I had come to my hard-ass senses and shut her up.

"Lest we also fucking forget," she rallied, "he imported a high-priced criminal defense lawyer shortly thereafter. Doesn't sound to me like a guy too committed to confessing."

I fucking hated it when she was right. "It's times like this, Marianna, I consider our friendship *provisional.*"

Marianna pulled out her cell phone and began dialing the Providence police to have them cordon off the Al Forno restroom. She delivered the message directly to Chief Sewell and then flipped her phone closed. "Well, *provided* you don't make any more slipups with this guy, I'll keep my theories to myself. But I can't be screwing around with my career at the AG's. Don't forget, since my last slipup my *job* is provisional, so I can't afford to be swallowing your errors right now. Vince isn't going to let me off the hook twice in one lifetime."

Marianna was wrong about Vince letting her off the hook. Nay, Vince treated Marianna like the daughter he never had. Not only would Vince let her off the hook, he'd actually fish her out of trouble and put her in a holding tank until her wounds healed. I, on the other hand, was a piranha of another story: Vince Piganno and I couldn't be in the same room together without creating a subduction zone for an undersea earthquake. Just as neophyte Brooke Stanford had stated: Vince liked his girls passive and girlie, and I'm about as passive as an oncoming tsunami.

Marianna's cell phone rang. "She's standing right next to me," she said into it, then handed it to me. "It's Vince."

"Speak of the devil," I said into the phone. "Why didn't you call me on *my* phone?"

"I can't waste my brain cells remembering all your numbers. And shit, how far away can you be from the rest of your conjoined group?"

"Yeah, yeah, yeah...there's two women here, both in Davy Jones's locker."

"Stay out of the cops' way, because you girls will screw up an open can and let the friggin' worms out."

I ignored his tangled metaphor. "Scott Boardman is innocent." I said.

"Lynch, don't start acting like the dumb Irish broad you are. The bum's conferring with his lawyer even as we speak. Now both of you get out of there and get your asses back here to start working the case."

"I am telling you, he's innocent. He may have had a blackout, or maybe he's covering for someone else, but I can feel it in my bones. He didn't kill anybody."

"Well, feel *this* in your *bony* body. You're on unpaid leave unless you get back here quick."

I snapped Marianna's phone closed and dropped it in her bag hanging by her side. "He wants us out of here."

The photographer was flashing away as another forensic cop walked to the threshold of the berth. While I was on the phone with Vince, Lucky was slapping gloves on. "Anything else amiss in the other rooms?" Lucky asked the arriving cop.

"Drawers pulled out. Bunks pulled apart. Maybe someone looking for something special, or maybe just someone looking for anything worth stealing. We'll get prints."

Lucky nodded and went back to his work. "Or maybe someone just trying to make it look like a robbery. I mean, how many people keep valuables on their boats?" He walked closer to the bodies. "Well, looks here like we got two naked bodies on a bed, real close to each other, if you know what I mean. Looks like someone just interrupted some lovemaking between the two."

The brunette's body was on its stomach, the head partially off the bloody mattress. Lucky lifted her and turned her over. "Here it is. Head's been bashed by some blunt object." He moved in closer and then stepped back. "What's this?" He crouched down and lifted the edge of the blanket. Mari went first and knelt next to him, both of them peering under the bed.

"What the fuck is it?" I said. "A gun? A knife? What?"

"A really pretty vase," Marianna said, "with some really pretty blood on it."

She stood and walked past me, then called for another forensic tech to bring a large evidence bag.

Lucky began walking to the other side of the bed. "Okey-dokey," he said. "So that's one murder weapon down. The rest is going to be a cakewalk if this gal was beaten with it too."

The blonde's body was lying on its back with her cheek resting on the mattress and her eyes still open as if she was gazing at the other woman. My already dizzy head swooned as Lucky began examining the blood-soaked back of her head. "Well, what do you know?" he said. "Different MO. This one's been shot in the back of the head. Execution-style."

4

GOOFY AND CICERO

IF I HADN'T BEEN SO EAGER TO GET BACK UP ON deck for air, I would have kibitzed with Lucky about the different MOs. Maybe the same badass bashed in one woman's head and then shot the other in the heat of passion. Armed properly and committed to the cause of extinguishing a couple of lives, I could damn well do both. The vase I could understand. Did Scott Boardman see the two women in bed, get pissed, and throw the first thing at hand? The shooting was the stickier problem. If the shooter *was* Scott Boardman in a jealous rage, why did he just *happen* to have a gun in his pocket that night—unless he suspected he would find his wife cheating on him? I mean, toting a gun with you to meet your spouse smacked a bit too much of premeditation. And of course, premeditated murder entitled one to a longer stay at the state pen than a heat-of-passion, whoops-sorry-I'll-never-do-it-again whack in the skull. But I wasn't ready to reserve Scott his room at the Adult Correctional Institution just yet.

I marched off the boat and into the salty night wind. Ten minutes later Marianna joined me in my car and I began an immediate expostulation.

"It wasn't Scott," I said. "I know you're convinced, but it just wasn't. He was confused when he confessed. He saw it—the blood and shit—and went temporarily schizoid."

"You know, Shannon, I thought *I* was the only one made stupid by love."

I slammed the car into drive. "What's your point, genius?"

"I think you should lift your glance up from Boardman's crotch and start paying attention to what's behind his shallow gray eyes—"

By pounding my fist into the steering wheel, I signaled my preference for a silent ride home. Marianna, in response, banged the dashboard back, and we remained at a silent if not peaceful truce the rest of the way.

I dropped Marianna at her car, still parked at Al Forno, and I headed down to the police station, where I fought my way through the unruly press crowd camped at the front doors. I found Chucky Sewell holed up behind the locked doors of his glass-encased office. He was on the phone. I banged on the door and he let me in, as he always did, no matter what he was doing. Except this time we were both on business and he went calmly back to his phone conversation as he paced the windows of his office, peering out on his flock.

Chucky was big and I loved it. The mere girth of him gave me the chills. Since the age of thirteen, I'd felt like the gawky giraffe in a kindergarten production of *Swan Lake*. Being tall and skinny is good for models and

California girls, but hey, I live on the puritan East Coast, where the average height for a female is five-four, and the last time I saw that height was third grade, and even then I was still a foot taller than the rest of my little friends. I'm always ready for that up-and-down thing strangers do with their eyes. I watch their eyes travel the long, exhausting distance from my feet to my head, as if they've just pulled out a yardstick and are measuring me for my coffin.

And there was my Chucky, a nice hefty six-four, a full head of salt and pepper hair, and the cutest twinkling blue eyes my love-biased gaze had ever seen. And except for that ever-so-slight little belly that he could never seem to shed, Chucky was as fit and tight as the strings on a shiny concert grand. He walked every day, everywhere he could. The guy's legs were like tree trunks; his shins as thick as my thighs, and believe me, I know because I measured them once during a rare weekend together in Martha's Vineyard while his wife was in Boondocks, Virginia, visiting her first, second, and tenth cousins. Chucky's kids, five in all, were grown and out of the house. I'd met them all at one time or another at social functions. One of them had guessed the true nature of our relationship—the youngest boy, about twenty at the time. He actually took me aside at a Christmas party and said, "I can tell by the way you two talk to each other. Dad's eyes go soft when he's standing around you. I never see his eyes like that anymore since my sisters moved out."

I didn't bother denying it. What was the point? Chucky and I fit together like a charm to a bracelet, but he was a good Catholic boy who'd never divorce his wife unless she left him first. And at over two hundred pounds (at least that's how fat she looked to me), she wasn't going anywhere fast enough for it to mean anything serious for Chucky and me. So we just left our relationship where it was: a Hepburn-Tracy-type affair. We'd seasoned into an old married couple without ever signing the papers.

"Vince," Chucky said over the phone, "let's just try to wrap this up fast and let the political fallout settle where it may. Murder. Premeditated. That's my take. You figure out the legal end."

I couldn't hear Vince's end of the conversation, but I knew him well enough to know what he was saying. Vince Piganno was like Marianna; they had these idiotic consciences and thought the Code of Criminal Law was holier than the Bible. Maybe it had to do with being Italian. Like those Romans of yore: *The social system will fail unless we follow a social structure and strict moral codes.* And as far as politics was concerned? Vince said lying is a religion to politicians. *They lie during confession,* he'd say.

So I wasn't surprised when Chucky hung up with Vince and thrust his hands in the pockets of his loose trousers, shaking his head at me as if Vince was somehow *my* responsibility.

"Well, your *boss* wants to draw this out. He started quoting goddamn Cicero to me. Something like 'There's nothing more deceptive than the whole political system.' What Cicero has to do with Boardman killing his wife I'd sure as hell like to know."

I sat behind Chucky's desk and started straightening out papers for him. It was a little-known fact that I was a neat freak. Cleanliness I didn't give a crap about, but if everything around me wasn't in numbered piles, I was a raging lunatic.

Chucky flipped the blinds to his office closed so no one would see me behind his desk, messing with police business. Damned if all the cops didn't know about us anyway, but Chucky was annoyingly careful about not giving anyone any real evidence of our unlicensed and illegal coupling.

"I'll tell you what Vince means," I said, "if you really want to know."

"Nah, what's the point? That man and I are like two guys on the same debate team who speak different languages. We're always disagreeing for some reason or another neither one of us understands, but ultimately one of us defers, because winning is our prime goal."

"Whew, that was a mouthful, Chucky. You're getting intellectual on me. What's up with that?"

He came over to me and fluffed my cropped hair into more of a tangle than it already was. "You're the brainy lawyer, honey. I'm just the testosterone-powered cop, remember?"

"Yeah, yeah, yeah...Well, Vince doesn't believe anything people *say*. That's what he meant with the Cicero quote. Vince'll want to wait for the evidence and the grand jury."

"See what I mean? Piganno and I agree. My gut says Boardman's lying too. And if he's not guilty of killing his wife, he's a politician and guilty of something else, so ipso facto, he's lying about something. And the evidence'll bear me out on this. You just wait, darlin'."

"See, Chuck, now *you're* talking Cicero too. Obtuseness among men in power is obviously a widespread epidemic."

Chucky laughed. He loved playing Gracie Allen to my George Burns, pretending he was the goof and I was the smart one. Of course I *was* the smart one, but I never knew if Chucky really believed it, or if he thought he was just humoring me by letting me think so.

I hate the tangled web of men's mucked-up minds.

"Well, whether you like it or not," Chucky said, "we're looking at the Honorable Senator Boardman as our prime suspect. Dack called me right before you got here. One of the women—I'm guessing the wife—was shot point-blank to the back of the head. That ain't heat-of-passion. So unless the ME comes up with a finger pointing in a different direction, I'm liking Boardman for *premeditated* murder."

Shaking my head, I walked to his door. "That makes me real sad, Chuck, real sad. Because I was kind of *liking* him too, if you get my meaning. He's just my type. Big and brawny." I looked up at him, wide-eyed, as if the thought had just hit me. "He kind of reminds me of you, Chucky Bear."

"Should I be jealous?" he said, tilting his head at me.

With a great big grin I said, "Depends on whether or not you care if you lose me."

I loved dragging my fingers through those finely woven spiderwebs and wreaking havoc on the threadwork of lies that men create for unsuspecting flies. Especially the married spiders like Chucky who've managed quite efficiently to lead double lives. He'd managed to have a wife, kids, *and* a mistress who all coexisted—sort of—

happily ever after. Sure, I was his enabler. Sure, it was my fault for letting it happen. (I was no unsuspecting fly.) And because I was free to walk out on him whenever I wanted, I could never really get angry with him. And the truth is, I'm not sure I'd marry him if he *did* leave his wife. So yeah, I liked Chucky, maybe even loved him—in my weaker moments—but sometimes I hated his guts too.

I realigned my spine cocksure straight and chucked Chuck a kiss. But when I whipped open his door ready to blow into the sunset, I saw a humbly stooped Scott Boardman standing next to his lawyer, Ron Esterman. I'm guessing they were waiting their turn at Chucky.

When Scott Boardman looked up at me, staring for maybe a second too long, Chucky followed me out his office door sans that cute blue twinkle in his eyes.

"Thank you for dropping by, *Miss Lynch*," the now seriously official Chief Sewell said to me. "We'll be in touch with your office."

My cue to leave, so I briefly sized up the two men standing before me—Chief of Police Charles Sewell and Senator Scott Boardman. We were on Chucky's turf, so he was clearly the pack leader of our small group in attendance. I deferred to his authority and stayed quiet. But I zoom-viewed on Scott Boardman's face again, and like a cruise missile flying below radar, his downcast eyes snuck another longing stare at me, telling me something, or asking me something, or just plain looking for a chest to cry into again.

Bedroom confession notwithstanding, I still believed the guy was innocent.

5

OFF-KILTER

SATURDAY MORNING DRIZZLED INTO VIEW AT about seven-fifteen when Laurie woke me by phone.

"We're on our way. We need to talk."

Half an hour later I peered down from my window to the entrance five stories below, where the colorful miniatures of my friends sat against the rainy backdrop of sepia and gray. Beth's red Saab, its convertible top down, was idling by the building's granite steps. Laurie, sporting a yellow rain slicker, rode shotgun, while Beth, her head Grace Kelly–scarfed in apple-pie apple green, was behind the wheel. Marianna was in the rear, her arms splayed across the backseat, a white cigarette hanging from her mouth as Laurie leaned over the front seats and reached for Mari with the car's lighter.

Beth looked up and saw me first, waving enthusiastically like a fragile daisy. I grabbed my keys and wallet and headed out, wondering why they'd decided to ride top down in a goddamn drizzle. But never the one to topple the last pin of an off-kilter decision, I said nothing as Beth pushed the gear into drive. Rarely engaging in superficial greetings, we were on our way in virtual silence. We were as used to each other as the right arm is to the left.

As Beth concentrated on the road, I stuck my face into the wind like a contented golden retriever, but I couldn't clear Scott Boardman out of my head.

"What's this all about?" I finally said, irritated by my own thoughts and the rain drizzling on my head. "Or are we just testing the tires for hydroplaning?"

"Just a breather," Mari answered. "A time out for a resetting of our mental clocks."

"Bullshit, Mari."

I didn't take well to criticism. So when I got the gut feeling they were breaking me in slow like an old horse too long in the wild, I started kicking. Was Marianna being straight with me? Was this just a quiet Saturday morning ride through the Elysian Fields, or did they really have anything new to say—like I was fucking up royally?

Safely parked at the salon, I pitched my Camel butt against the curb and we exited the car and headed for the salon's front door.

Nails Only was a misnomer for a place that in actuality serviced every known external part of a woman's body. The Brazilian waxes? Marcia was a regular ob-gyn when it came to a female's nether regions. The salon was run by Marcia, her sister Pat, and Roxanne, who hailed from Galilee, a salty fishing town in South County, Rhode Island. A Marcia and Roxanne confab over drinks was sure to hit all the high notes in the Whorehouse Dictionary of Obscene and Lascivious Acts Against Nature. Funny thing about Rox though: Unless the woman was drinking, she barely spoke at all.

Our *ménage à quatre* congregated at the entrance door as Marcia rose from behind one of the manicure tables. Despite being four-eleven and tipping in at ninety pounds, she had a mouth as big and loud as mine, and pound for pound was every bit as threatening. Word on the street was that she was a cross between a leprechaun and a Hummer.

She had opened early for us. With barely a hi, she pulled a fresh sheet off the shelf and, snapping it open, let it luff down over the table. "Who's ready for some torture?"

I pulled off my jeans and jumped aboard.

Beth ran to the curtains and pulled them closed. "Who's doing me?" she asked.

Roxanne kicked out the chair from under her manicure table. "Over here," she said in curt response.

Marianna sat in front of Pat's station and laid her hands flat on the table.

"Should I get acrylics this time?" Beth said. "Since I won't be typing much longer?"

"Every time we come, the same damn question," Laurie said, rifling through a magazine. "Get them and be done with it, Beth."

Pat wasted no time diving for the latest AG gossip. "So what's the scoop on this Senator Boardman? It's all over the news. Did he do it or not?"

Sooner than expected, we were launched back into

the Boardman fray. In deference to me, I guess, no one answered readily. They knew my suspicions and were waiting for me to answer first.

"Not," I said from behind the curtains.

"Really?" Pat answered.

Pat was a good manicurist. Like a bartender dishing out questions and weighing your responses, she had the knack of making you think she was deeply interested in your opinion but didn't probe further, scurrying from topic to topic, hoping to spark a priest-worthy confession. French manicures and deep-soul catharsis were Pat's specialties.

"Well, *I* think he's guilty," Pat said. "I'm not buying his alibi." Suddenly Pat commanded my attention as if she'd just touched down from a remote planet far away. Half-plucked, I came out from behind the curtains buckling the top clasp of my denims and strutted to her table, hovering over it like a hungry vulture. "Alibi?" I said.

Pat clucked at the sudden attention and made me wait for her answer. Though now that I think of it, she probably had no idea why four employees from the AG's office were waiting on an answer from a nail tech about a murder suspect's alibi defense when we should have been asking her about the newest OPI nail shades.

"Alibi?" I repeated.

"You don't know?" Pat answered. "It was on the radio just before you came in. Apparently he'd been in his car driving up from Connecticut while the murders were taking place. News report says he *found* his wife and her friend dead, panicked, and left the scene."

I gave myself a few seconds to let it sink in, but before

I knew it, I had suddenly realized why this little Saturday morning soiree had been gathered in my honor. I looked at my three erstwhile friends, who didn't seem at all surprised at the news flash. "You're all shits, you know that?"

Laurie spoke first. " Vince called me earlier. We didn't know before this morning."

Beth remained mum. Or was she catatonically dumbstruck by her hands, which were looking cheaper by the minute? "Can I blow my nose with these," she said to Roxanne, "without poking my eyes out?"

I looked at Beth. "Beth, do you friggin' think that's the *crucial* question of the moment?"

Beth glanced at me, somehow empowered by her three-inch nails. "So Boardman recanted his confession. He's a liar, Shannon. *So what?* If someone just murdered two people, is *fibbing* a moral leap?"

"He lied to *me*," I said. *"Me!"*

I must have sounded insane—like some lover scorned, for Christ's sake—because even Beth felt safe enough to make fun of me.

"Yup," Beth continued. "He brutally killed his wife and her lover and *now he's claiming innocence.* Wow, what a shocker!"

I looked at Laurie and Marianna, both of whom could more fully appreciate the dangers inherent in lying to me, but Laurie got up to take my place on Marcia's waxing table, and Mari was mouth-blowing her nails dry.

Beth shrugged. "I'm sorry, Shannon. But sometimes even *you* can make a mistake."

"Well, does anyone think he *could* be innocent?" I asked. "Maybe—"

"Shannon," Marianna whined pleadingly, "stop! The man confessed to you in bed and then called a defense attorney and recanted. It's classic guilt. And since we are the ones employed to prove him guilty, the only question left is, will Laurie get the case, or will Vince give it to me? Because *you* are clearly biased and don't belong anywhere near Scott Boardman—or this case."

"Here's *my* question," Laurie said to me. "Are you going to the cops with his confession? Or are you going to pretend he never said it? It's evidence, you know."

"Fuck you, Laurie," I snapped. "You think you're so fucking smart. As if *you*—because of your *superior intellect*—could never make a mistake based on stupid emotion like Marianna does all the time. And now you're trying to make me feel like an emotional wimp like her—"

"Wait the fuck a minute!" Mari said. "Am I being trashed here just to save your dumb ass—"

I got up and kicked my chair halfway across the room.

And with that, our Scott Boardman rap screeched to a halt like a car at a cliff with no reverse gear. Beth returned to the knotty issue of her nails, while Marianna and Laurie worked their way back to one of our typical frenetic and classic palavers, weighing the urgent matters of our lives and times: waxing versus shaving, the newest fillers for facial wrinkles, the various novel indications for Botox, including suppression of migraine headaches and intra-penile injections for recidivist pedophiles. I remained coldly silent until it was time to leave.

Once outside, Beth still refused to raise her convertible top for the drizzly ride back to Providence-town but she tooled along with extra-special caution because Marianna and Laurie had decided it would be fun to yowl "Dixie" at the top of their lungs the whole way back and Providence was rife with cops who had nothing better to do than torment the unsuspecting and the innocent.

"Stop!" I screamed.

Beth slammed on the brakes.

"Turn the radio up."

Beth obliged just in time for us to hear Brooke Stanford's high-pitched voice announce that she indeed had accompanied Scott Boardman in the car on his ride from Connecticut to Providence while the murders were reportedly being committed. He was innocent. And she was ready to swear to it.

6

FIREMEN

WHEN I WAS A KID GROWING UP IN THE SUBURBS of South Boston, the evening newspaper was still delivered at three o'clock by a boy on a bike. I remember the summer of my tenth year, the whole summer sitting on the front steps, every afternoon waiting for the paperboy. He'd pedal down the street and directly down our front walkway, drop his sack-laden bike on the lawn, and say, "Can I have a water?" Then we'd go inside and up to the attic. "Show me." He sat facing me on the wooden plank floor.

I wasn't sure what he meant at first. But the look in his eyes, guilty, ready to bolt away down the stairs, explained it. I could have said no, go to hell. I wasn't afraid of him. But because I *wasn't* afraid, I unbuttoned my princess-collared blouse, and through my Carter's undershirt he felt my small breast. Just the nipple at first. It felt good. Good in a way that I knew would feel better if my undershirt wasn't there.

For months, always a little more each time. Another button. His greedier hands. Dark and muffled. The sounds of the cars outside hiding us. I always stopped him early, while he was still breathing hard. I'd abruptly put myself back together, button up, and trot down the stairs to the living room. I'd turn on the TV, never granting him another word or glance as he trudged down and silently snuck out the back door as Samantha Stephens was twitching her nose.

He always seemed to be just pedaling off down the street when my father's Impala rumbled into the driveway. The back screen door squeaked open and slammed shut, and my father's tired hoarse voice would call out, "Shannon, run down the store for some milk and bread."

In many life-shaping ways, I grew up in the attic of our house. I became the kind of woman who doesn't hesitate calling a guy for a date. I had no patience for the Scarlett O'Hara–Rhett Butler routine—pretending to be fighting for my virginity to the last. I invited men into my bed when I was ready, just always making sure I threw the guy out *before* he wanted to go, so he'd always know who was in charge.

The only memory I have of my mother is that she was always asleep in the upstairs guest room, until she just wasn't there anymore. Somewhere between her naps and my sixth birthday, my mother simply disappeared from the radar of my life. When I was seventeen and a senior at Monument High in South Boston, my father disappeared too. The stereotypical chain-smoking chronic alcoholic, he left for work one day, an electrician for some small local construction company, and never came home. What happened to the house after I left for college, I don't know and haven't cared since. I just packed my bags one August and hopped a Greyhound bus to UMass—the only place that would give me a full scholarship. I went to law school on a lark, afraid that if I didn't settle on the right side of the law, I'd end up in jail sooner or later.

If there is a God, he gave me a brain, but he was downright stingy in the parenting department.

MONDAY MORNING I HEADED OFF TO COURT TO get another few minutes of sleep during Jeff's closing argument in the Cohen case. My case had sucked from the start, so I wasn't surprised when Jeff sang breezily to the jury that the state had no evidence against his client. After a brief ten minutes, Jeff finished in a rare-for-Jeff brilliant staccato. I almost applauded. The jury would have no trouble finding reasonable doubt in this case. Shit, even *I* was reasonably doubtful that Micah Cohen was a killer.

Jeff made a last-ditch effort to take the decision away from the jury by making a motion for a directed verdict—asking the judge to make the decision because there was no evidence on which reasonable minds could differ. Judge Ragusta denied his motion and let the jury deliberate Micah Cohen's fate. The judge also cautioned Jeff and me not to stray too far from the courthouse because he was *reasonably* certain that the jury would be ready with their verdict in a *reasonably* short time and that their decision would include the words *reasonable doubt.*

I thanked the judge and sprinted out of court while Jeff basked in the glory of a certain win. I took the occasion of my courtroom hiatus to ring up Scott Boardman at the Biltmore Hotel. He'd taken a suite of rooms there pursuant to the cops' suggestion that he stay in town.

"I'm on my way," I said, leaving him no choice.

To avoid the hotel front desk, I took the elevator to the mezzanine level and buzzed his room from there. He agreed to come down to get me. Minutes later he appeared behind the polished brass doors of the elevator. As the doors hummed closed he pulled me in and pushed me into the corner. He ran his sinewy arms up my back and neck and then through my hair. Not a millimeter between us, he waited for my response, perhaps expecting me to resist. But once again I fell for him, right into his arms, my face smothered into his.

"I missed you," he said in a breathless interval between kisses. Then he pulled a few inches back, away from my face, and traced my mouth with his finger. "What the hell is this thing between us all about?"

By "this" I knew he meant our seemingly uncontrollable animal passion. But damned if I had an answer for him, especially since in the few days since I'd seen him, the whole world, it seemed, had been trying to convince me he was a cold-blooded murderer. That thought should have quelled the burning in my thighs, but it didn't.

"I didn't do it, you know," mind-reading Scott Boardman said as the doors slid open to the twentieth floor. I pulled away from him and walked into the hall, then waited for him to pass me on the way to his room. He inserted a card in the slot and the lock clicked open.

Inside was a formal living room of sorts, with a desk and two couches facing each other. He watched my glance go to the fireplace that flanked the left wall. Again he answered before I could ask. "It's real. Do you like fires?"

I shoved my hands in my jacket pockets and gave him my version of the evil eye. "Talk to me, Scott Boardman. My job is on the line."

"And I thought it was your heart you were worried about."

"My heart doesn't pay the rent."

He called a temporary truce to love by ambling over to one of the couches, sitting, and spreading himself back against the cushions like a satiated lion in the sun. "Would you sit a minute, please?" he asked.

I obliged and sat on the couch facing him, where I leaned back too.

"I'm appointing you my lawyer for the day, so this is confidential, right?"

Slick player, this guy, tying my hands in confidentiality so I couldn't run back and tell Vince what he said. Too bad he didn't think of that the night he confessed to me.

I nodded, giving him the go-ahead, but in truth, if he told me something usable as evidence against him in a murder charge—or worse, confessed again... Well, let's just say I had my fingers crossed behind my back.

"Benzodiazepine and alcohol can cause blackouts and hallucinations. I've been taking some Valium-type pill for sleep problems. I've gotten so dependent on it I keep increasing the dose. I never should have been drinking with it. I quit drinking about four years ago."

"Why the booze that night then?"

"Muffie Booth called me from her boat. Told me she was with Pat and that they wanted to see me. That was it. Just come there. I thought it was going to be about Brooke. That the two of them, Muffie and Pat, had teamed up to lecture me about Brooke and the upcoming election."

"Tell me about Brooke. Was she with you that night or not?"

He bent over and buried his head in his hands. When he lifted it to face me, his eyes were far away as if he were reliving the memory. "I went on the boat alone. Seeing the women both dead threw me. I remember stumbling off the boat onto the dock. I almost fell in the water. There's a side alley to the street. I didn't go out through the restaurant. I was wild, drunk, but after the boat... my wife...all that blood...I sobered up fast. I drove straight to Providence to meet Jake. Jake Weller. He's my public relations guy. I figured he'd take over. I was useless. I don't remember Brooke—until Al Forno."

"Why'd you pick Al Forno to meet this Weller guy? As cool as I am under pressure, I wouldn't meet someone at a posh public restaurant for a champagne cocktail after the carnage I saw on that boat."

"I wasn't thinking clear. He said it would be safer if we got as far away from Newport as we could. He suggested Al Forno."

"And you don't remember if Brooke was with you in the car? Before the boat."

"I saw her earlier—late afternoon. She was becoming obsessed about our breakup. I had to calm her down.

Then I met Leo Safer, my campaign manager, for a drink. That's when I got Muffie's call. During my drink with Leo."

"And you were in Connecticut earlier that day?"

"That's where I live, Ms. Lynch—Shannon. We have a home in Fairfield. *May* I call you Shannon?"

"Only if you're innocent."

"I'm telling you the truth. I'm just not sure if that makes me innocent."

"What happened to Jake Weller? He stood you up?"

"I guess he did...I drove to Al Forno and went into the bathroom. I didn't feel well...That's where you found me. And then I left with you."

"Okay. Tell me about you and Brooke Stanford. She has you on speed dial, or what?"

He looked at me, eyes narrowed, wondering how much to admit. I recognized the look from years of questioning stoolie witnesses.

"Just tell me the truth, Scott. Neither of us has time for a game of poker."

"Brooke is a past indiscretion. I felt bad for her. I got her the job at your office—"

"*You* got her the job?" I could already feel my fingers tightening around the Pig's fat neck.

He shook his head. "What difference does that—"

"To me, a lot. Brooke Stanford isn't a team player. She doesn't belong at the AG's office. Bad decision for Vince, but now it's making some sense."

"Even your boss has people he has to answer to. What's the old Bob Dylan song? Everyone serves somebody." His eyebrows shot to the ceiling. "And Brooke, of course, has charms hard to resist."

"Believe me, Vince is charm-resistant."

"Don't be so sure about that. I know men better than you do."

"Then let's get back to my area of expertise. Lies and alibis. So Brooke followed you to Providence and into Al Forno—"

"No...I told you I left her much earlier. I walked into Al Forno alone. Did she follow me there?" He shrugged. "The whole night is a blur—"

"Why, Scott? Why *that* night did you decide to turn your brain into Silly Putty with drugs and alcohol? So you could have an insanity defense to murdering your wife?"

"Don't be absurd." He dropped his head. "Brooke. I was telling her it was over between us. I got her the job at your office out of guilt—because I knew I was going to end it. She expected more...I told her that day there would be...nothing more. I took her for drinks. Champagne. And then I had a few pops with Leo. I shouldn't have been drinking like that with the other meds."

"You may think you know more about *men* than I do, but here's a lesson in *women*: You take a woman to a place and ply her with caviar and a deluxe cuvée when you're trying to bed her. When you're dumping her, you buy her a hot dog, tell her you're filing for bankruptcy, and then congratulate her for being rid of you."

"I'm nowhere near bankruptcy."

I looked at him silently. Either he was lying or he wasn't, but I didn't have enough evidence against him to support an accusation. He was searching my eyes too, as if he were looking for an answer in them. I was in a holding pattern of noncommittal.

"So knowing all this," he said, "will you see me again? There's a conflict, of course. Especially now."

Yeah, *especially now* that I'd heard even more damning evidence against him. Marianna was right. I was getting stupid in love, just like her.

"I disqualified myself from your case when I fell for your gray eyes, their forlorn look, and the way you suckered me in."

He managed a grimace-tinged smile and then joined me on my couch. Holding my face in his hands, he whispered, "When I bumped into you in that bathroom, neither one of us even knew the other's name. Please don't make it sound as if I planned this—this thing between us. But even then...in the bathroom, I knew under that rigid façade of yours there was a nurturing instinct. I knew when you caught me in the bathroom that you wouldn't let me fall."

All this sweet talk was making me dizzy, and no one who knew me well would offend me with that kind of saucy bullshit. But this guy was either so self-assured he didn't give a crap about rejection, or he knew me better than I knew myself, because instead of bolting away and marching to the door, I let him push me down on the couch and entrap me under the mass of his large body and the comforting smell of a soapy aftershave lotion as he slowly moved his face to mine and grazed my lips with his, thereby giving me one more chance to vomit at his dime-store romance tactics. Instead, I closed my eyes and succumbed to his light kisses while scenes of Vince scowling at me, shaking his head, and calling me a worthless female played in my mind like a preview of coming attractions.

AN HOUR LATER I WAS COMBING MY HANDS through my bed-headed hair as I sprinted up the aisle in Judge Ragusta's courtroom. During the last fifteen minutes of Scott's celestial pronouncements of my "otherworldly" beauty, my cell phone had been screaming for my earthly attention with text messages and phone calls. The jury in Cohen was back with its verdict. Too soon. I knew it was bad news.

"Thank you for joining us, Miss Lynch," the judge said.

I nodded and slinked into my seat, feeling my heart just begin its downward beat into postarousal repose. I took a nourishing breath and let my mind wander back to the Biltmore Hotel.

I couldn't say how long it was before I heard Judge Ragusta's voice roaring in the background of my dreams.

"Wake up, Miss Lynch! This court is still in session."

I bolted out of my chair and looked at the judge, who was peering at me over his reading glasses with the eyes of a worried friend. "Are you all right?" he asked.

"Yeah, uh, yes sir, fine . . ."

"We were all wondering if you have anything to ask of the jury before I dismiss them?"

The jury. I turned my head slowly in their direction. Did I have anything to ask? Yes, I did. I would have liked them to repeat their verdict so I could listen this time.

Instead I just shook my head. "Um, no, your honor. Nothing."

"Thank you, ladies and gentlemen. You are dismissed. Mr. Cohen, you're free to go."

"Free?" I said out loud.

The judge nodded. "That's usually what we tell defendants when they're found *not guilty*, Miss Lynch."

I looked over at Jeff, who was beaming proudly as if he was showing off a new set of dentures. I could see the gums of his bottom teeth.

I stood weakly and slunk out of the courtroom before Jeff could accost me with his bloated smile.

BACK IN MY OFFICE, I FOUND MARIANNA, LAURIE, and Beth powwowed with Mike McCoy. He sat regally behind Marianna's desk and was taking notes in a pocket-sized spiral notebook. They all looked up as I stood in the doorway of the small office.

"Because I'm feeling a little sorry for you right now, I'm not even going to ask where you were while the judge's clerk was calling here for an hour and a half looking for you," Laurie said to me. "I don't want concrete evidence of how stupid you're being."

"*I'll* ask," Marianna said. "Where were you? Huh? I had so much more faith in you, Shannon. You were my hero when it came to men, my idol, because God knows, I'm always picking the wrong ones and messing up my life—"

"Hold on a damn minute!" Mike McCoy stood and pushed his chair back. "Are you referring to me as one of the *wrong ones*? Because I can fix that problem up real fast, babe."

Marianna whisked her hand dismissively. "Oh, shut up, Mike. We've been wrong for each other from the start and you know it." Her attention swerved back to me. "Boardman is a suspect in a homicide investigation, Shannon. And if that doesn't bring you down, Brooke Stanford will."

Mike looked at me and moved from behind Mari's desk to join me in the doorway. Standing eye-to-eye, he put his arm around me like old times and said, "Come on, pal. Let's go to your office and have a little heart-to-heart."

Perhaps while I'd been with Scott in his hotel room, the girls and Mike had cooked up this private tête-à-tête between Mike and me, because no one said a word as he and I walked out alone and went quietly to my office.

"I'm getting tired of people trying to help me, Mike," I said after we both sat and my door was closed tight. "Is that why the girls called you? To tail Boardman and me?"

He smirked in that cowboy way Mike had, a crooked smile and tired eyes. "Even if Mari hadn't called me over, I was still coming. Chuck heard the Cohen verdict was in. And when no one could find you..." He blew air out of his lips and shook his head. "Chuck's worried about you."

"So you came here at Chuck's request. Once a cop always a cop, huh, Mike?"

Ex-cop Mike McCoy had retired early. He'd gotten between his partner and one of the several bullets shot by the partner's angry wife. The partner died, but Mike beat the odds and went to work as head of security for a private college where he and Mari met—and have been fighting ever since. Mike was divorced before he met Marianna, for no good reason other than his wife had left *him*. Chucky's wife, on the other hand, was hanging on to him to the tune of *death do us part*. But deep down I think Mike would have left his wife eventually anyway even if she hadn't left him first. Mike was made of different stuff than Chucky. Maybe because Chucky was Catholic, he had a choirboy's guilt tying him in a marriage knot. Mike's religion was fast cars and a good ball game, and on Christmas and Easter, while Chucky was in church, Mike was praying for wins at NASCAR races.

I whipped my feet up on my desk. "Come on, Mike, Chuck's never been worried about me before. This isn't about my job, or any danger I'm in."

Mike was clearly uncomfortable telling tales on his men friends. Chucky may have sent him to me, but Mike didn't want to be there. He twisted in his chair, staring at the phone, probably hoping it would ring and get him off the hook. "Jesus, Shannon, maybe he's worried about losing you. You know I don't like getting involved in this shit. I feel like a pimp..."

"Because Chuck is married—"

"Yeah, damn. Because he's married, and he should just let you be. He has no hold on you. He should just let you go to have your own life."

Mike was right, of course. But he was being paternalistic. If I really wanted to go—leave Chucky for Tom, Dick, Harry, or Scott Boardman—nothing Chuck did or said could stop me. That's what Mike didn't get. Mike didn't understand my part in the adulterous triangle

Chucky and I had drawn. Mike couldn't accept that women really do have free choice and it wasn't just a mindless mantra that feminists chant while they're folding their husband's underwear.

"What exactly does Chuck want you to do, Mike?"

"The chief thinks you're losing perspective with this guy. He thinks it's because of Boardman that you lost the Cohen case—"

"Last week, when I was trying Cohen, I hadn't even *met* Scott Boardman. 'Losing perspective'? That's what he said?"

"Not exactly. But the chief isn't as eloquent as I am, so let me paraphrase. He said he saw a zing in your eyes when you and Boardman were at the station together. He thinks you're raging hot for the guy and the only way to break the damn spell is to show you Boardman's bloody hands."

"So is that what Marianna likes about you? Your *eloquence*? It must make up for that little bedroom problem."

Mike's eyes were daggers as he laughed the kind of laugh that I imagine a hit man laughs right before he puts the bullet through your forehead. "Oh yeah, Shorty, you can count on it. We're gonna find blood on Boardman's hands all right," he sang. "I'm just afraid by then you'll have it all over yours too."

7

GOOD GRIEF!

VIBRATIONS FROM MY CELL PHONE PREVENTED me from delving too deeply into Mike's suggestion of blood on my hands. Mike tended toward spaghetti-western hyperbole, so his prediction that I was getting myself into some serious trouble in the Scott Boardman fiasco didn't faze me. Trouble kept me from boredom, and lately life had gotten routine. I'd been falling asleep before *Letterman* and rising in the morning before the alarm clock rang—without a hangover and cigarette breath. And how long *had* it been since my last cigarette? Hours? Days? And not only was I not craving one, but the yellow stain between my fingers was beginning to fade. So a tad of trouble didn't scare me. Maybe it's what I needed to catapult me back into high gear and away from this recent tendency to fall in love like I was Lucy in a Charles Schulz colorized joke.

I pointed to my door and said, "Later, bro," signaling Mike to get lost and leave me alone with my cell phone, where Scott Boardman's number was registering as a missed call.

As soon as I heard Mike's footsteps down the hall, I hit redial. Scott answered on half a ring.

"Hey. I miss you already. It's cold here without you."

"What do you want, Scott? You're good, but I wasn't born yesterday."

"My lawyer just called. The autopsies are this afternoon. Do you attend those things?"

"I can, but I don't. What's the attraction for you?"

"I don't know. Maybe if I found out exactly ... maybe then I'll know if it was me ..."

"Oh, please. We're back to that? Make up your mind. Either you *think* you did it or you *know* you didn't. Can't be both."

"I'm asking you. Just go and let me know. And as far as my confession ... If I did it, I'll be the first to own up to it. But if I didn't do it and I confess ... well, then I'll be as guilty in people's minds as if I had done it."

"What makes you think I'm free to tell you what the autopsy findings are? Why do you assume you have an open line to everything I know? Just because I'm hot for you—"

"Stop it, Shannon. I was passed out in a bathroom. I didn't find out who you were until we were back at your place, *already in bed.* Maybe you should have just left me on the bathroom floor at that restaurant."

But that was my real question: Did he know who I was beforehand? But how *could* he have known that three prosecutors from the AG's office would be dining at Al Forno as he left the scene of a murder? How could he have known I'd even *want* to catch him when he fell? In the interstice of my silence, he read my mind.

"Do you think I knew that a lead prosecutor at the Rhode Island AG's office would be a striking blonde, who would just *happen* to be dining at Al Forno, and she would just *happen* to need the bathroom just as I was passing out, and then she would just *happen* to find me attractive enough, in my sorry inebriated state, to actually take me home with her? Even *I* can't plan that well, and if anyone knows strategy and spin, I do."

The stereo knock on my office door was Marianna and Laurie. I disconnected quickly with Scott, promising him nothing but a call later that evening. My two partners in the crime-fighting game were on their way to the ME's.

"Vince actually wants us to go this time," Marianna said like a kid being sent to the candy store. "I'll let you know what we find out."

"If you're both going, maybe I should come," I said.

Almost cross-eyed, Marianna looked at me. "Since when do you go to autopsies?"

She was looking at me—hard—making sure I knew she was serious with her next words. "Everything I know about you is subtly changing," she said. "What's going on, Shannon? Are you sick? Don't be stoic. We'll stand by you. I have three kidneys if you need one—"

"Shut up, Mari. You and Laurie are going, so I'm going. Let's just get Beth and call it a party."

They assumed my suggestion to take Beth was sarcasm. But there's comfort in numbers, and none of them really knew how much I hated death at the morgue.

Murder scenes had life in them; a passion of violence; the blood unleashed and still alive, searching for its lost host. For a brief time, death is warm, and on site the setting of life pretties it up. But take that death to the morgue and slide it into a freezer drawer? The fluids coagulate, oils cool, skin becomes sheathed in a waxy coating, filmy cataract eyes stare open, gray toes are freakishly polished from the last pedicure. A shiver ran up my back. A room of cold dead bodies unnerved me, as if the departed souls in the morgue-dead had left an empty space for the invasion of some foreign thing— a body snatcher. Maybe my distorted fears were from a movie I'd seen as a child, a blocked-out memory, or a dream long forgotten, but I hated the morgue—the systematic storage of bodies—and nothing—no one—ever got me to go there except my shame at admitting the weakness of fear—and now, Scott Boardman's request.

WE LEFT BETH BEHIND AND THE THREE OF US drove up to the back door where the bodies were unloaded. No guest to the place, Marianna was a regular. She practically had a designated parking spot. She knew everyone by first name, and, like the biblical scene of Moses parting the Red Sea, everyone moved aside to let her through when we entered. With a pope's nod she walked into the main autopsy suite, where a fresh-faced young doctor gave her a toothy smile.

"Tim Gannon," Marianna said by way of introduction. "Doc, you know Laurie and Shannon?"

"Laurie and I have met, but Shannon...I don't believe I've had the pleasure." He was busy giving me the up and down while Mari talked.

"Shannon prefers hot bodies," she said. "But I convinced her that your charms warm the place up."

Gannon smiled while reading the chart in his hands. I figured he and Marianna had some professional flirtation thing going on, but what she saw in him I'd yet to discover. He was obviously one of those sociopathic individuals who enjoys sawing skulls in half and then scooping out the brains—a Hannibal Lecter type whose decision to dabble in the barbaric mayhem of body mutilation just happened to settle morally on the right side of the law.

"It's friggin' cold in here," I said. "Can't you turn the heat up?"

"Nah, the smell will only get worse," Marianna said, while she looked around for the one thing missing from this ghostly room. "Who's the first victim?" she said to Gannon, rubbing her hands together, enjoying her infantile double entendre.

"I did the wife this morning. Nothing there but a clean bullet to the back of the head. The Booth woman is coming in now. She'll be a bit messier...."

I had somehow managed to slink to the corner of the room closest to a pair of double steel doors. I hadn't even felt myself moving as I inched backward just in time to hear the crack of metal against metal as a stainless steel gurney came whipping through the doors with the ziplocked body bouncing on top. I darted away as a new smell hit me seconds after the thing rolled past me.

Blood, metal...but something else too. Marianna was watching my face and read its question.

"Body fluids," she said. "We never smell them because they're always locked up inside the packaging. But did you ever floss your teeth and then smell the—"

"Shut the fuck up, Mari! I have had it with you."

Laurie was laughing as she donned a pair of rubber gloves and a mask. Marianna joined her and took a pair for herself, but the cocky bitch wouldn't put on a mask. She was making me feel like a limp-dicked slug.

"You're so cocksure of yourselves," I said to them. "I have fucking issues with this stuff, and I don't see either of you caring a whit about what they might be."

I tried to avoid looking at Gannon and the tech (who was eyeing me suspiciously) as they unzipped the body bag.

Laurie yanked her mask down. "We've known you for six years, Shannon. Maybe your *real* problem is that you keep too much of your past to yourself. As far as I know, you were born six feet tall with the mouth of a quahogger. I always kind of pictured you as some scruffy knock-kneed street kid from a Dickens novel, but you never talk about it. Ever." She looked at Mari. "Am I right or what?"

Marianna shrugged and nodded.

"So how the hell," Laurie continued, "are we expected to be sympathetic to issues we've never been privy to?"

"Okay, ladies," Gannon said. "Let's save the psychology lesson for another time. I got work to do. Those who wish to stay may either don some gloves and come observe or go throw up in the little girls' room."

"Fuck you, Gannon," I said, walking straight to the box of gloves marked Medium and whipping them on. Damn things were too small, but by then I was too friggin' humbled to start trying them on for size.

I looked down at this once-human thing wishing Lucky were there, standing beside me. I'd never been at the morgue unless he was present. And that's when I realized for the first time, there was something about Lucky—who had always been at the morgue the few times I went, and always at the death scenes with us— that had made death tolerable for me. My serenity at bloody murder scenes had something to do with Lucky Dack.

Standing just slightly behind and left of Marianna, Laurie was talking, "... I can't believe this is *the* Muffie Booth, of the Newport Booths." She continued talking with a dry edge in her lockjawed voice. "You know, the goat lady who bought the multibillion-dollar estate so that a gaggle of goats could graze and frolic by the sea?"

Marianna shook her head. "Not *her,*" she said. "*Virginia* Booth is in her seventies. Muffie is the daughter, recently divorced. Not only is a senator's wife shot to death, but we've got a dead Newport billionaire socialite outed as gay. The press is *so* all over this."

"Okay, so right off there are no obvious wounds in front," I heard Gannon say. "Nothing defensive either. Hands are clean of cuts, abrasions. Dack took fingernail swabs so we'll see what that gives us...."

Lucky, I thought again.

"I'm turning her over. Mari, can you give me a hand here?" Gannon said.

I watched Marianna move in close, happy to help. Her gloved hands held the lifeless thing steady so Gannon could move it without pushing it over the lip of the table. Mari, who was emotional jelly, was suddenly rolling this thing around like it was a Thanksgiving turkey she was getting ready to stuff. I watched her face, serious and intent. There was nothing here that frightened her, or made her want to cry, or asked her to analyze it beyond what it was in flesh and blood. Maybe it was all those Italian wakes and funerals. But Christ, I was Irish. We prettied and painted our dead like waxen mannequins, finally letting go after the scotch was drunk and the bottles empty. Laurie was the one who should have been quaking around all these fermenting body fluids. Six feet and twenty-four hours after the last breath was gasped, the Jews said good-bye.

"Whoa," Marianna said. "That's what we saw on the boat. That head wound. How deep you think? And was it done by that heavy vase?"

She leaned in close, with Laurie hovering just over her shoulder. Again I'd managed to inch away from the table as if I were standing on a cloud drifting backward. The dead woman lay still and flaccid as Gannon's fingers burrowed into the hole in her head.

"Looks so. And thrown from a distance with enough force, it would make a mush of the whole area."

"What's this?" I heard Laurie say. She was looking at the woman's head. I forced my legs to step closer. Gannon's hands pushed hair away from the skull. "Another hit to the head?"

"Bullet."

"That makes no sense," Laurie said. "Why a vase *and* a bullet?"

"Maybe to make sure she was dead from the vase," I whispered hoarsely as if I'd been gasping for air. "Or maybe we're looking for two killers. Where's Lucky?"

Marianna took off her gloves and threw them in the trash can. "Why? What's Lucky got to do with this?"

"I don't know. Nothing. I need some air."

And then I took my gloves off, threw them on the floor, and walked back to my office alone.

8

CREAM AND SUGAR

WHEN I GOT BACK TO THE OFFICE, ANDY WAS straightening out the furniture in Vince's office.

"I'd better scoot before Macho Man gets back," he said, eyeing the distance between the chairs in front of Vince's desk. "You heard anything more about him firing me?"

"He can't. The ACLU would be after him faster than the FBI after Whitey Bulger. You're safe as long as you whisk all heterosexual dreams out of your head. Which reminds me, where's the Stanford broad this morning? Giving her hundredth news conference?"

A narrowing of Andy's eyes and a sly tilt of his head gave me all the answer I needed. He went into overtalk anyway. "I told you that little bumblebee was trouble. She's too *gorgeous* to be anything but a fluffy bundle of stingers."

I pulled out one of the chairs Andy had just straightened with the tape measure of his calculating eye, and inched it about two and a half millimeters closer to

Vince's desk. Then I plopped into it, waiting for Vince to arrive. Andy emitted a hyperbolic harrumph at my attempt to best his precision, then sat in the chair next to me, leaning conspiratorially close. "So?"

"*She's* lying and *he* didn't do it."

"Oh, tell me, please, before Vincent arrives and turns me into a pumpkin."

"Well, Andy my eager little pet, here's how I see it. Little Miss Sunshine was with us at the bar in Al Forno, acting very alone and looking like she'd just *love* to join the girls and me in our dinner plans if *only* we'd say the word. There was nothing in her behavior to suggest she was there with someone, namely a famous and powerful Connecticut senator. And knowing Brooke's entrepreneurial self-aggrandizing nature, I'm fairly certain she would have broadcast that information to the entire restaurant if she *had* been there with him. I think Miss Stanford came up with that story after she found Boardman and me in the bathroom and then learned *the next day* that his wife had been murdered."

Andy thought a second and then shook his head at me. "Shannon, light of my day and alter ego supreme, sorry to disappoint you, but Boardman has to be in on this alibi. He's not disputing it, so either it's true, and they *were* together all night—making him innocent, as you say—or he and Cookie Cakes are *both* guilty. So either way, the man lied to you."

I was already ahead of Andy. "Sometimes innocent people are scared, and they lie just because they know how guilty they look. Don't forget, I was with the guy alone for a while that night. He was scared, crying on my pillow."

Andy tossed his blond cropped hair (we went to the same barber) and raised his eyebrows to his hairline. "On your pillow literally or figuratively?"

"None of your business, but the fact is, the man's a mess and susceptible to undue influence right now. He might not be thinking clearly."

"And you intend to save his soul? Isn't that so Marianna-ish?"

"Get out of here, Andy, or I'll tell Vince you were coming on to me."

As if on cue, Vince steamrolled through his office door. "Both of you sexual deviants clear out." He headed straight for the open pack of Merits sitting wantonly on his desk. "Get me coffee," he said to no one in particular.

And no one in particular listened, except maybe Andy, who popped up from his chair and strutted to the door while mumbling under his breath, "Well, at least I'm secure in my own sexual identity."

Before he got out the door, Vince mumbled "Asshole" under his breath, and Andy shoved in the last word on the subject. "Cream in it, boss?" And walked out the door.

I'd have to remember to give Andy a few specialized lessons on Vince Piganno and some general ones on diplomacy, or not even the ACLU could save his job.

"I want him out, Lynch. Do the legal research and find a way."

"Cool it, Vince. Andy's doing a lot for your public image. Think about all the great PR you get by having an openly gay receptionist at the attorney general's office."

"Next time he's blowing me a kiss, I'll keep that

thought foremost on my mind—that, and the gun in my top drawer."

"Brooke Stanford," I said, changing the loaded subject.

"Sit tight, Lynch, she'll be here any minute. I want to talk to *you* first." He'd successfully lit his cigarette, gotten his signature crystal ashtray positioned for optimum ash collection, and then settled himself behind his massive desk that looked to be just about the right size to use as my coffin. He leaned over it and stared at me with beady brown eyes set into his permanent pug-scowl. Vince could hold you hypnotized and speechless for several minutes when he assumed that stance, because you knew something momentous—at least in Vince's mind—was coming up. And though waiting wasn't my forte, I have to admit, I was so emotionally dead tired after the marathon Boardman weekend that even a sit-down with Vince seemed like a vacation under the palms. Just when I thought I was comfortable with Chucky Sewell in our never-going-anywhere relationship, the handsome Senator Boardman from Connecticut had somehow nabbed my hardened heart. Hell, I didn't want kids, and frankly I loved living alone. So apart from the occasional lonely holiday when the girls had families to go to, I was pretty much content and resigned to the fact that Chucky and I would go on forever, or until one of us died, or the wife did, whichever came first. Of course, thinking of dead wives brought me right back to Scott Boardman and that pug-face of Vince's staring at me a few feet away. "What do you want, Vince?"

"First off, you lost a high-profile murder case. I won't beat you up now because I got bigger fish to fillet with you, but don't let it happen again or you'll be prosecuting parking tickets for a year." He leaned back in his over-stuffed leather desk chair. "Now, what have I been hearing about an excited utterance of Boardman's while he was enjoying some of your—let's say—*boudoir* talents?"

Vince looked nauseous, as if just picturing me naked was making his cigarette stale and bitter. Before I could come to my own defense, he stamped it out half smoked and hit his intercom button. "Where the hell's my coffee?"

"Andy's not supposed to be getting you coffee," I said. "I know your old receptionist did it, but she *volunteered* her waitressing services. Andy's different—"

"No joke he's *different*." Again Vince hit intercom, but this time I heard Beth's voice pick up. "Beth honey," he said, "will you get me a coffee? My receptionist has his period today."

Poor Beth. Her final days as a paralegal had turned her into Vince's gal Friday. September couldn't come soon enough for her.

"Look, Vince," I said. "I didn't fuck Boardman the night of the murders, if that's what you're asking. Not that I wouldn't have, but there's something about a weeping man that ruins the moment."

He pounded a fist on his desk. "That's the only part I want to hear about, Lynch. The *crying* part. The fucking other part you can keep to yourself."

"He told me he thought he might have done it—"

"*Thought* he *might* have done it?"

"He's got this drinking problem. And then he took some pills... The combination made him black out or something. That's what he said anyway. But I'm the only one who heard it, so—"

"So we can't very well put you up on a stand to testify to it, can we, *AAG* Lynch?" He bolted up from his desk and walked to his wailing wall—the window of his office that gave him a view of nothing more than a dirty gray Providence morning. "A confession and we can't use it! Why is it you girls always put me in these binds? Why don't the *guys* ever get into this kind of trouble? I'll tell you why, this equality shit is ruining our entire system. Women belong at home or teaching kids their ABC's, because if you let broads use the rest of the alphabet they start spelling *trouble* with it. And with the four of you, I got way too many troubles in this place. And now? Now I got Miss Andy out there. I had to get a guy who *isn't really a guy!*"

Through Vince's cannonball of a voice, I heard soft knocking at his office door. He either didn't hear it or he was too arrogant to let it disrupt his female-as-worthless speech. Beth pushed the door open an inch at a time and breathed a brief sigh of relief when she saw me first. Vince jerked around from his window view and started screaming at the intruder, assuming, I assumed, that it was Andy. "Get the hell out of my office!"

Beth's shaking hand splattered steaming coffee on her legs as she let out a puppy-like whimper. I got up to rescue her. "Beth, buck up, or passing the bar isn't going to be your only obstacle to becoming a prosecutor in *this* office."

She ground her pretty peach-hued jaw and handed me the coffee, turning and walking out Vince's door—leaving it open—without ever having coming through it.

I placed the ill-fated coffee on Vince's desk. "I wouldn't

testify to what Boardman said anyway. I didn't believe him when he said it, and I don't believe it now. I think he's innocent—"

"And that's the other thing with you *girls*. You're a bunch of bleeding hearts. But you, Lynch, I thought you were different. But you're an emotional wet rag just like the rest of them. Just another female."

"I resent that, Vince. I am not a *female*—"

"Well, that settles that, then," Brooke said from Vince's open doorway. "I won the bet."

Vince's shoulders dropped a few inches and I thought I saw his eyes widen the merest tad as if the sun just popped out from a cloud. I stood up to my high-heeled six-foot-two height. With one of my snappy comebacks, I could have chopped her to her knees, but I knew when to indulge in a catfight and when the hefty weight of my senior AAG badge would be the quicker route to demolition.

"Close the door behind you and sit down, Miss Stanford," I said soothingly as if I were singing her a lullaby. "Mr. Piganno would like a chat with you."

She swung her hair to the side and looked at Vince for a quick query of my authority to order her around. He gave her his answer by nodding at the chair next to me. She dutifully sat. I let Vince go first for the preliminary attack. I'd wait to take over myself if Vince disappointed me by becoming prey to her obvious feminine wiles.

Like a scripted role she was playing, she shimmied her butt into the chair, then smoothed her tight straight skirt over her legs, crossing them modestly but leaving just enough exposed thigh to throw Vince into a leisurely downshift. He sat, cleared his throat, and began.

"You were at the police station giving a statement that puts this office in somewhat of a compromising position with respect to the prosecution of the case against Senator Scott Boardman. Would you mind sharing with Miss Lynch and me exactly what you said to them?"

Vince was sounding real professional—and sweet. He didn't usually talk in whole sentences complete with nouns, verbs, and "fuck"-less adjectives, at least not that I'd heard.

"The police told me," she said, "well, Chief Sewell asked me . . . not to give my statement to anyone just yet. Something about protecting the integrity of the investigation. He said the police would provide my statement to whomever is assigned the case here."

Vince remained atypically quiet. He lowered his head. When he spoke again, his voice was textured of smooth velvet, a surprisingly fine fabric in Vince's otherwise crudely fashioned wardrobe of words. "Miss Stanford, you're new here, so let me try to explain simply the problem this office is having with your position—"

"I'm not stupid, Mr. Piganno. You can use big words or legal terms, and I'm sure I'll understand."

He looked up at her and began to tap his silver cigarette lighter on his desk in a slow tropical beat. Had it been me sitting there before him, or any one of the girls, he would have growled his next words and gritted his teeth like a dog ready to pounce. I was afraid to hiccup the slightest intrusion, fairly certain Vince would hop over his desk and strangle me.

"I want to *help* you with all this," he said, "against my better judgment—because a tougher man would just fire you—"

"Vince?" I said.

He pointed at me, silencing me. I sat back, still assured that Vince was holding the big guns armed and ready. But Brooke apparently wasn't worried, perhaps because she had connections higher up the administrative ladder.

Or maybe because at that moment Brooke knew something that I didn't.

"And since this office may be prosecuting Mr. Boardman for murder," he continued, "I think we need to know if he has an alibi for his whereabouts on Friday afternoon and evening. And since you apparently *are* his alibi, perhaps you'd like to tell us what you intend to say to a grand jury."

Perhaps?

Vince stared at her as if they shared a secret. Brooke smiled back.

I was getting tired of this overture. When was the fat man going to sing?

"Vince," I said, "can we get to the finale here? I've got work to do."

"Good idea, Lynch," he said. "Brooke and I can do this without you. Why don't you go back to work."

I was boiling. In the six years I'd known the Pig, he'd never once fallen for pretty thighs and cherry red lips, and this little Brooke twerp, sitting in the hot seat, wasn't breaking a sweat.

"Vince, wake up and smell the perfume. I'm not going to sit here and listen to these lies. Either she talks straight or I bend her Barbie nose out of joint."

She turned to me but spoke to Vince, "Is she going to hit me?"

Vince looked at me, and I at him. He was calm, even though, against some of the best odds on record, we were losing the battle with her. Didn't he see it? I was ready to step in and step on her, but the truth is I still thought Vince knew what he was doing. Vince may have had the mouth of a clumsy street kid made good, but he knew how to cross against the light without getting hit, he knew all the shortcuts in town, and I figured he knew how to beat Brooke by keeping his fists in his pockets.

But for a twenty-eight-year-old novice to Vince's wise-guy persona, Brooke was holding surprisingly strong.

"Well, Miss Stanford," Vince crooned, "for now you'll take a leave of absence. I'd like you to have representation. An ex-AAG, Jeff Kendall. I can give him a call for you. He can guide you through this. Because after this office is finished with Scott Boardman, there's going to be fallout—and I don't want it to hit you."

"Why would I need an attorney, Mr. Piganno? I didn't kill Mrs. Boardman. As a matter of fact I'm not sure you're on solid legal ground by firing me. I think if *you* consulted an attorney—"

I bolted up. "You twit! Get the hell out of here."

"Shannon," Vince warned. "Leave her alone."

Brooke slowly rose and straightened her skirt over those lovely firm legs, at the ankles of which I noticed an expensive pair of Chanel pumps with just the tiniest discreet double-C logo on the heels. Running her hands over her thighs, she said, "I don't know what Scott did on that boat. I only know I was with him on the drive from Connecticut. I stayed in the car. What happened after he went on that boat..." She tilted her head at Vince. "Chief

Sewell said you will get my written statement and I shouldn't say anything about an ongoing investigation. I'm sorry."

"He didn't mean don't talk to us," I said. "And just to clarify your employment situation, you aren't *fired*. I believe Mr. Piganno said 'leave of absence,' which would be appropriate for any one of us who was inadvertently involved in a case this office is prosecuting. It's a matter of course. Consider it a temporary vacation." I smiled.

"Then you should be taking a *temporary vacation* too, Miss Lynch," she said. "Because you're as *involved* with Scott as I am."

As she reached the threshold, I added, "If we find that this alibi statement of yours is in any way inaccurate, neither Scott Boardman nor the president of the United States will be able to get your prison sentence for perjury commuted."

I thought I saw a flash of light in her eyes as if she were calculating damage, but it was nothing more than Vince's phone. All his hold lights were blinking.

He hit the intercom button and i heard Marianna's voice. "Is Shannon still with you?"

"What do you want her for?"

"I've got Chief Sewell's office on hold for her."

Vince ended the call and stood. "Go pick it up in your office," he said to me. "I'll escort Miss Stanford out." He straightened his tie and walked around the front of his desk. "Are there some things you need from your office? Let's go get them…"

I gagged my way out his door.

9

CHEERIO

I MARCHED TO MY OFFICE, TRYING TO BURN OFF some steam and actually looking forward to Chucky's chipper voice. He was always good for a good laugh—and talking me down from a high building when my sniper's gun was loaded and aimed.

"Lynch?" the voice said. "O'Rourke here."

Shit. Just what I needed—an irritating call from itchy Detective O'Rourke, a cop who could get lost on his own beat.

"Not today, O'Rourke. I'm cleaning my gun. Call someone else with whatever it is you're selling."

"Oh yeah? Well, maybe I'll call your boss and see if *he* wants to take my call because you're just *not in the mood.*"

"Don't threaten me, you plague-infested fruit fly, or I'll come over there for practice shots. Better yet, I'll torture you so bad you'll be begging me to pull the trigger—"

"All right, all right, calm down, will ya? The chief told me to call. Says he has something he needs to discuss with you ASAP. But maybe you should come in the side door. Incognito. Sunglasses and baseball cap. *Comprende?*"

"I *comprende* all right. What's the problem? The chief needs a real man over there, so he called me?"

"Hey, I'm just trying to protect your ass," O'Rourke said. "Prance through the front door if you want and right into the chief's office. No skin off my nose."

I hung up with O'Rourke, not bothering to analyze his suggestion for cloak-and-dagger secrecy, and headed out for another brisk walk across town in the viscous air of a sweltering August. At least the metallic smell of blood and body fluids still clogging my nostrils from my recent morgue visit would be snuffed out by exhaust fumes and freshly poured tar.

WITHOUT SO MUCH AS A WAVE TO THE DESK COP, I strutted boldly into the station and straight through to the elevators. The doors slid open to Chucky's floor and he was just rounding a corner when I hissed at him, "Chucky, I hope this isn't about Scott Boardman."

He corralled me into a corner where about a zillion and two assorted criminals and their cop escorts glared at us like they were initiates of an elite social club and Chuck and I were a pair of ousted members.

"Mother of Christ," Chuck said, "will you keep your voice down? I must be crazy getting messed up with you in here."

I stuck my face into his twinkling baby blues. "Listen, Chuck, I'm getting myself in enough of my own trouble with this investigation. You've already screwed my heart into the ground, don't burn my job bridges too."

The man actually looked surprised. Like what, this was news to him? Imagine *me* having a heart and then imagine *him* capable of breaking it.

He lowered his head. "Walk quietly to my office, where we can have a civil conversation without the whole force knowing our business."

"Frankly, I don't care who knows, because I'm not married, Chuck. The adultery charge is hanging over your head, not mine."

Chucky had stopped trying to reason with me. Smart man. He physically reminded me that even though my mouth may have been bigger than his, my strength was genetically limited by meager muscle mass. He gripped me firmly by the forearm and escorted me to his office like I was a Saudi Arabian female who'd left home without her burka.

"Now sit down and shut up for a minute," he said pushing me through his door and slamming it shut.

"Can I smoke—"

"No!"

Chucky hated cigarettes, which is why his skin was still so flawlessly young for a man in his forties whose only grooming effort was a monthly haircut at Frank's Barber Shop for which he paid an obscenely minimal amount—something substantially less than the cost of a four-shot Venti Latte at Starbucks. Of course, as I always used to tell him, he had such a voluminous head of hair he could have shared it with ten bald guys and still had some left over to braid. Maybe it was his morning bowl of all-grain Cheerios and daily jogs, but Chucky was the poster boy for poster boys.

He pulled his chair up close to me, so despite his earlier gorilla posturing I knew this was going to be his stumbling macho version of a Hallmark moment. I slapped his hand away as he tried to take mine, and then, as I expected, he went directly into his you-know-you're-the-love-of-my-life-*but* monologue. The same soliloquy I'd heard enough times that I could recite it by heart. (If I only had a heart.)

"What do you want, Chuck?"

"Jake Weller is an old friend of mine."

Jake Weller? I'd never heard this part of our love story before. What did Jake Weller have to do with our adulterous and deteriorating ex–love life?

"He's Boardman's PR guy. And Jake's singing a slightly different tune than Boardman on this."

That's when Chucky's angle hit me. A clever variation on the love theme: Chucky was trying to turn me against Scott Boardman by proving to me that Boardman was lying and assigning him a minor character flaw that in this case led inexorably to the murder of two women.

I let a smile spread slowly on my lips but said nothing, making Chuck work a little harder for what he was trying to achieve—namely breaking the spell between Scott Boardman and me.

Chucky, intent on burying Boardman, dug his own grave a few feet deeper. "So you see, Shannon, Jake Weller is saying that Boardman called him that same night and told him that he *thought* he killed the wife and her friend but he doesn't remember it. That same bull-shit story he gave you."

As far as my tone-deaf ears were concerned, Jake Weller's tune and Boardman's song were in the same key. I was still waiting for Chuck's sour note.

He stood and walked behind his desk, staring at me, waiting for me to respond: fall into his arms and thank him for saving me from the black-heart Boardman, or, in the alternative, throw my chair at him and storm out. But again I remained mute and with the slightest tilt of my head let Chuck resume shoveling dirt in his own grave.

"And Jake doesn't buy Boardman's alibi either. Apparently, Boardman and this Stanford gal who's giving him the alibi were having an affair. I think Jake's scared of being somehow complicit in these murders, so he's asking me for a favor. Like he knows Boardman's career is over, so Jake's trying to save his *own* ass. You know what I mean? And maybe he wants me to go easy on Boardman. I mean, the poor slob probably *did* kill the wife in the heat of passion. I mean…I'm thinking…what would I do if I found *you* slobbering between the legs of another broad?"

Just for variation, and to keep from falling asleep, I straightened my head and tucked my chin in, because this nonsense Chucky was spewing didn't deserve much more than a yawn. There's no way the Charles Sewell I knew would go easy on some guy who murdered his wife, heat-of-passion notwithstanding and no matter how friendly Chucky was with this Jake Weller guy. And he might suffer a few sleepless nights, but Chucky would rat out his own brother if he knew the guy hurt a woman. But I was bored playing this game with Chucky, so I finally said, "Your buddy Jake Weller is playing with the facts. Scott claims to have called Jake Weller after he got off the boat and found the women dead, and Weller agreed to meet him at Al Forno later that night. And I was at the restaurant. Weller never showed. I don't know what Weller's claiming, but as far as I'm concerned, Scott's telling the truth."

Chucky shook his head at me. He was probably confused. I know I was.

"You're gonna continue with this guy, aren't you? Making up all kinds of excuses for him. You don't care that he's a fucking liar—most likely a murderer—and a dirty politician to boot! I hope you're not doing it just to bust my agates, Shannon, because—"

I stood and walked to the door. "Get over yourself, Chucky. Believe it or not, most of my choices in life have nothing to do with you. I'm not your wife who thinks you walk on water—"

"Leave her out of this!"

"Fuck you," I said calmly. "Marjory's never been out of this. It's always been you, me, and *her*. What did the dead princess say? 'There are *three* of us in this marriage.' Maybe it's time I took *me* permanently out of the equation."

"Shannon, please. I'm just worried about you—"

"My ass you are. Mike McCoy is more worried about me than you are, and he's only worried because Marianna will blame *him* if anything happens to me. You, Chuck? You just don't want to lose. It's about me and Boardman, and the fact that we're attracted to each other, and that I don't think he's a killer. That's what this is all about. So you do what you gotta do, and I'll take care of my own business, which, by the way, is no longer any of yours."

I walked quietly out of Chuck's office and slowly back to mine, thinking hard about what I'd just done—severed my relationship with Chuck Sewell, a man with whom I never fought until Scott Boardman entered the scene. Sure, we'd had our spats—and then the enhanced-by-anger make-up sex after—but was Boardman a catalyst for the real resentment I'd been hoarding for years against Chucky? Was Boardman what I needed to finally dump Chuck and get on with my life (such as it was)?

My anger was regressing dangerously toward an odd feeling of loss, a dark, unfamiliar place that Marianna would no doubt characterize as a "depressive state." Other than the girls, and a pretty good relationship with my mail-man, what exactly was my life? Nothing. It was nothing.

When I got off the elevators to my office, I was actually shaking. This depression crap was *so* not for me. No wonder Marianna was always questioning herself, afraid to make a wrong turn here or a right turn there. I felt a slight paralysis coming on, a weakness in my stalky limbs. Depression was like a car running on empty. Anger was the fuel I needed. So I started looking for a fight. Anyone would do, but I chose Vince, even though he was so insensitive to my assaults that it wasn't even any fun fighting with him anymore. He'd think we were just having our daily chat over the newest cases.

I stomped straight to his office, where I found Andy leafing through landscape design magazines. The place was deserted.

"Was there a bomb scare?" I asked him.

"Honey," he answered without looking up, "I would have been the first one out. Your girlfriends are with the Pig at the Dial-up."

"They went to the Dial-up dump *without me*?"

Andy looked up from his magazine. With narrowed eyes, he said, "Pig's invite. Are you okay?"

Back in the privacy of my office, I sat a minute, critically analyzing the strange tug in my chest. Was it a clinically diagnosable heart attack or was I just mad as hell? I dialed Marianna on her cell for an expert opinion. I felt a new simpatico with her, like we'd caught the same bug—the parasite of self-doubt.

Sure enough, Vince and the girls were having a pow-wow at the Dial-up Modem Diner. They'd had a late afternoon craving for pancakes and eggs, Mari explained, as a defense to their restaurant decision.

"I like pancakes *too*," I said, my voice strangled by a strange choking sensation.

"Are you crying?"

"I don't know, Mar," I growled, "tell me what it feels like and I'll let you know."

Marianna then announced, as calm as a floating glacier, "So, okay, Vince is sending me to Newport tomorrow morning to interview the mother, Virginia Booth."

"Why? Her chauffeur won't come to Providence?"

"Vince is trying to low-key the investigation, so I'm going to her turf. Oh…and…um…Pig said you probably shouldn't come."

"Hey, Marianna, how are your *fucking* pancakes?"

Marianna and I had known each other so long that

even over the wire I knew—without seeing it—that she was grinding her jaw.

"I'll meet you for a drink after," she said, "to fill you in."

"Hey, don't worry about me, okay? All this sudden interest in my welfare is making me claustrophobic."

"Fine, Shannon. But hear this...Andy told us Brooke left the office Friday *at noon.* She had enough time to take a little drive with Boardman. In other words, she could be telling the truth about being with him. And if she knew we were going to Al Forno—just think about this—are you sure that Scott Boardman didn't *plan* on bumping into us—all AAG's—and entangling us in his web to set the stage for a one-act slam-dunk mistrial?"

I hung up on her before she could scratch another word into my wounds.

I had never been barred from a case before, always priding myself on my ability to remain neutral and unemotional—I was the one Vince recruited to finish the job when everyone else (read Mari) was making emotionally rash decisions. And what's worse, I'd hoisted this leprous condition on myself by falling in lust with a murder suspect and then stubbornly refusing to abandon the ill-fated affair. Sometimes life deals you a losing hand, and the meekest of us throws in her cards. I like to think I was made of tougher stuff. In the past nothing could scare me into dropping my jacks with someone just because he was *suspected* of being a bad guy. So my recent dip into the dumps notwithstanding, I was going to pull myself up by the bootstraps and straight into Scott Boardman's lifesaving arms, hell-bent on proving them all wrong.

10

WISEGUYS

THE NEXT MORNING I DROVE MY CAR PAST Bailey's Beach Club in Newport, into which, after a transfusion of blue blood, you *could* be sponsored as a *potential* member. Without the blood transfusion, or a keepsake vomit bag imprinted with the *Mayflower* insignia, you were just another ship at sea as far as Bailey's was concerned.

At 9 a.m. the gardeners, having waited until most of the pretty sailboats and their owners had already luffed out to deeper water, were grooming the New York Yacht Club. Why the New York Yacht Club was sitting in Newport, Rhode Island, I had never before questioned. But since I was presently slumming in its neighborhood, I made a mental note to ask Beth—whose family were members—why in hell it wasn't named the *Newport* Yacht Club since here, in fact, was where it hid behind towering stone walls that were about as inviting to the outside world as a leper colony, except, of course,

Marianna and I, as nonmembers, were the lepers being kept out.

Virginia Booth lived just down the road. I had MapQuested her address but still drove past the ten-foot hedges three times before I saw Marianna's black Jeep pulling into the driveway. Like a spy, I followed, and pulled up next to her as she was jumping from its cockpit.

Having already marked my white Suburban, she didn't bother looking at me as she tendered her loving version of *Good morning.*

"What the *fuck,* Shannon." She was locking her car, still avoiding my eyes.

"Cut the surprise act, Melone. You knew I'd be here."

"Yeah, so I did. And I'm so very sorry about the waste of gas, but when the Pig finds out—and he *will* find out, because you're not in the office this morning where you're supposed to be—he'll think I took you with me—against his direct orders."

"I already called in sick. He accused me of having a hangover and I didn't deny it, so I protected your ass—as usual."

During our whispered discourse we'd advanced to the front door, where a housekeeper dressed in an ash gray uniform and starched white blouse answered our ring and escorted us into a sunroom overlooking the whole freaking Atlantic Ocean. Relatively happy with what life had dished me, I wasn't the green-eyed type, but the view made me so sick with envy I could have used Mrs. Booth's *Mayflower*-embossed vomit bag right about then.

Like two mud-stained kids behind a chain-link fence,

Marianna and I stood at the window staring speechlessly at the infinite heaven of ocean before us when we heard a lilting voice behind us.

"Ladies?"

In the doorway stood a stocky woman about five-ten. Gray hair with a distant memory of faded blond was corralled off her boxy face by a narrow headband. Some kind of printed tent covered her shapeless body. Shit, I didn't know Lilly Pulitzer even came in a size 20.

As I was giving her the once-over, Marianna rushed to make the intros, because this woman was clearly not revealing anything without making us work.

"Mrs. Booth?"

The woman lowered her chin and examined us from behind oversized silver-framed glasses.

"I'm Marianna Melone and this is Shannon Lynch. We're assistant attorney generals for the state. We'll be ... well, *I'll* be prosecuting the Boardman murders. We're so sorry about your daughter."

Virginia Booth raised her chin and lifted one side of her thin lips into a rueful smile. Her eyes remained a cold blue.

"The 'Boardman murders'?" She enunciated clearly as if testing the sound in the air. "Is that what this tragedy is being referred to in the press?"

Marianna answered, "I suppose it sells more papers with the senator's name appended to it."

"Thankfully," she said succinctly. "Please sit."

She directed us to a couch slip-covered in faded linen and stood while she addressed us. "I would like it clarified from the onset that my daughter was married for fifteen years and had just recently been divorced—from a man. Any suggestion that her sexual proclivities bent in any way toward an attraction to Mrs. Patricia Boardman should be immediately put to rest."

I wondered if Virginia Booth purposely chose sibilant words or if they just seemed to be rife with *s*'s, because her words sliced the air, emitting a frigid breeze in their wake.

"Lesbian, indeed," she muttered as she settled into one of the two slip-covered barrel chairs facing us.

Marianna tapped my knee. I would have liked to think she was giving Virginia Booth a little of what Vince would call *agita* by suggesting, ever so slightly, that Marianna and I were gay and that she—Virginia Booth—was full of crap, but I knew Marianna better. She wouldn't stoop as low as I would. She was just warning me to keep my mouth shut because she knew I was champing at the bit to describe in bloody detail the way we'd found her daughter's *heterosexual* naked body in an interrupted state of cunnilingus with the senator's wife.

"Be that as it may," Marianna said, "we're concerned with your daughter's personal life *only* insofar as it relates to any enemies she may have had. It can't be ignored that your daughter may well have been the target, and Mrs. Boardman merely an unfortunate bystander."

Virginia Booth shook her head so violently she had to readjust her headband. "Nonsense! My daughter was too much the emotional philanthropist, trying to help Pat Boardman in an impossible marriage with that philandering husband of hers. My daughter was the innocent bystander, and anyone who thinks otherwise will be wasting her time."

"Well then," I piped in as Marianna threw me a sharp side-glance. (I mean, really, did Marianna think I was going to keep my mouth shut the entire time?) "Is there anyone you can think of who might have wanted to hurt Pat Boardman?"

Mrs. Booth offered us a bigger smile this time, but her eyes still weren't sparkling in concert. "Brooke Stanford, of course. She's been trying to get Scott to leave Pat for years. And Pat knew all about them. Miss Stanford is a twenty-eight-year-old opportunist whose social and biological clock is ticking. She is looking for a quick entrée into a world for which she hasn't been groomed."

Marianna tilted her head. "But Miss Stanford is from a rather prominent family in Connecticut. She doesn't seem to need Scott Boardman's money—"

"She is," the alpha mater continued, "too uncultured and young to understand the concept of family unity. The Boardmans have two grown children. Scott Boardman is an aspiring politician. He was never leaving his wife for Brooke, despite the Stanford family's social superiority to Pat *O'Neil* Boardman. Scott made his marital bed, as ill-advised as it was at the time, and he intended to lie in it until death did them part. I might suspect *him* of hurting his wife if Scott weren't a man who has committed his life to politics. But he could never hope to advance politically by shooting his wife and bludgeoning my daughter to death on the way up, now could he?"

"And how do you know about that?" I asked.

Virginia Booth's eyes blinked once, and her head

pivoted slowly from Marianna to me. Staring at me, she said nothing.

Marianna caught the fastball like a pro. "How do you know the manner in which the women were killed, ma'am? That information hasn't been released to the public."

Then, as if her tone hadn't been clipped enough already, she spoke with a dagger in her throat, growling the words. "I am *not* the *public*, Miss . . . I'm sorry, I didn't quite catch your name," she said to Marianna. "Italian, isn't it?"

Oh shit, I thought. Marianna in the face of an ethnic insult from this woman was like taking a nail file to a fresh scab.

Taking the punch for Mari, I stood. "Mrs. Booth, we don't have time for a poker game. Who told you the COD?"

Virginia Booth, now suddenly crooning Mediterranean love songs, looked to her old paisan Marianna for a translation of "COD." Marianna was done with her good-guy act and said nothing, so I became the wiseguy for her.

"*Cause of death,*" I said. "Who gave you that information?"

Back to me she looked, and none too happy that I was suddenly her main interrogator. "Scott Boardman, of course. He came to me immediately."

"Immediately *when*?"

"He came here and told me he'd just discovered their bodies on the boat. I advised him to spend the night here and deal with the police in the morning. I was hoping to do some damage control—"

"Damage control?" Marianna said incredulously. "Your

daughter might still have been alive and you were worried about damage control? I would think 911 would have been a *mother's* first act—"

"Scott assured me there was no way they could still be alive. And of course now I know why. I have since refined my theories on what happened that night. Scott was disoriented. But he refused to stay here, saying he had a driver waiting outside in the car for him and he was going on to Providence to report the incident to the police personally. Of course, now I realize why he wouldn't spend the night under my roof. Even he isn't so much the hypocrite that he could murder my daughter and then spend the night in her childhood home and freshen up in her bathroom to clean her blood off himself."

"*Blood?* You saw blood on him?" I asked as if there was a jury present.

Her back stiffened in the chair. "I'm assuming . . . But I don't examine my guests' clothing. At the time, I had no reason to believe . . . I really wasn't looking."

Neither of us answered her. Sometimes the silent treatment works well too. Lets the suspect know we aren't buying any of their proffered crap.

Virginia Booth stood and held her head back like a horse ready to run. "I was busy. I was busy dealing with my own shock at the time. I had just been told my daughter was dead. I wasn't looking for a murderer—especially not in Scott Boardman."

The fire in the woman's eyes had informed us that we were nearing the end of our welcome. Marianna stood too. "And *did* Scott Boardman use the bathroom?"

Virginia Booth breathed deeply and clasped her hands

in front of her like a supplicant waiting for the communion wafer. She turned slowly toward the front door. "I'll show you out now. I'm going to call my lawyer."

"We'll be getting a search warrant for this house," Marianna said, following her to the door. "Your *bathroom* will remember if Scott Boardman was bloody."

I followed the two of them, pretty confused. I was glad we'd shaken Virginia Booth's composure, but not too happy about Scott's visit to her house right after the murders, a visit he'd conveniently forgotten to mention. I stifled the urge to snarl at the woman as I walked by her. I waited until Marianna and I got outside to lay the broad flat. "I'm calling the station. You call Vince. We need a warrant to search her house ASAP. Who does she think she is?"

"Virginia Booth," Marianna answered limply. "A billionaire heiress to a canned-ham fortune, who, even if we do manage to get her arrested, will be behind bars as long as Scott Boardman was." Marianna turned her back to me and began unlocking her car door. "So you still think he's innocent?"

When I didn't answer, she turned around to face me but I was looking up at the sky.

"What's wrong with you?" she asked.

I hopped into my unlocked Suburban and revved up the engine loud and strong. I zipped the car around to face the street, and on my way past Marianna, who was still waiting for my response, I rolled down my window. "Scott Boardman wouldn't have killed that woman's daughter and then come here to tell her mother about it, and *then* washed her blood off himself in the mother's house. That's too vile an act even for Satan."

But I drove off feeling my hypocrisy like a hunger pang deep inside. Scott Boardman had asked me to attend the autopsies to learn how his wife and her lover died—when he already damn well knew.

11

BROGUE AND A BITE ON THE LIP

BY THE END OF THAT DAY, VIRGINIA BOOTH'S lawyer had called both Vince and Chucky, demanding to know why Scott Boardman was still walking the streets after he'd killed two people and then had proceeded to sleaze up the Booth name by concocting a bogus story about a lesbian love affair. By Tuesday evening, Vince and Chucky had conspired to further stoke Virginia Booth's fiery rage by sending a team of cops flashing a search warrant to her mansion in Newport. Too late apparently, because all the bathrooms had already been cleaned by her efficient and numerous starched staff. The cops found nothing but a few male hairs on the sink, which, even if they turned out to be Scott Boardman's, proved nothing except that he was there, and that Virginia Booth was telling the truth.

Through her lawyer she threatened a suit for police harassment, but no one at our office even bothered looking at the letter. Almost everyone threatens police brutality or harassment at one time or another. Unless the complaining victim can produce a broken bone or a bloody nose, the suits go nowhere except the circular file under Vince's desk.

EARLY WEDNESDAY MORNING I GOT A HOLLER FROM Mike McCoy. Against his better judgment he'd agreed to stake out the police station and let me know what, if any, Scott Boardman activity was brewing. Poor Mike—out of allegiance to Marianna, and the more pressing fear that she'd throw him out of bed, he was doing double-agent duty by spying on Chucky for me while he was spying on me for Chucky.

Mike, an ex-cop himself, was getting his info from the cop at the reception desk. Mike's newest tip was that Jake Weller, Boardman's PR man, had just walked into the station for a meeting with Chief Sewell. Ten minutes after I got Mike's call, I was skipping up the front steps of Providence Police Station and readying myself for a "surprise" visit to my ex-boyfriend. I'd even brought Chucky Bear a bag of salted almonds as a peace offering, and was ready to lie through my pouting lips that my heart was still pitter-pattering over him and that no one could possibly take his place in my life, not even the handsome, sexy, rich, suave, infamous Scott Boardman.

Of course I assumed Chucky would see right through my candy-coated crap, but he'd still melt at my sophomoric effort to soften him up. He could never say no when I turned on my Irish charm, spiced with a bit of brogue and a bite on his bottom lip.

"Get out of here, Shannon!" he growled when I swung his door open.

Frozen in place, I stared at him until he pulled me into his office and closed the door, pulling those damn blinds closed again.

"Chucky," I said, "closing those blinds is a signal to the entire station that I'm in here with you, since I'm the only one you close them for."

"How the hell do you know that? Maybe I have a different broad up here every day at lunchtime. You think any of my men is gonna say anything about it? They just wink and give me the heads-up."

I sat calmly behind his desk. "Really? Is that what they do when I'm here? Just wink and give you the heads-up?"

"No, they don't like you because you're not afraid of them."

"If you had other women in your life, you wouldn't put up with the daily grief I give you. Try the jealousy route on one of those *other women.* I'm not buying it."

"You think you're so smart? You think I'm so pussy-whipped by you and my goddamn wife that I'll roll over for you whenever you want? Well, you made your bed with Boardman, now go lie in it."

Bed? No one knew about my date with Boardman on his couch at the Biltmore except Scott. Unless he meant the night Scott and I tangoed naked in my bed until Scott burst into tears like a virgin on her wedding night. But Chucky didn't know about that either.

"What bed exactly are you referring to, Chief Sewell?"

"I'm referring to your whole attitude with this guy.

You're his for the asking and you don't even see it. You don't see that you're acting like the simple-ass broads you make fun of all the time. If you haven't screwed him yet, it's only because he hasn't asked—or because he couldn't get it up."

Chucky was surprising me with his sudden astuteness.

"You bastard—" The crisp knock on Chuck's door cut me short.

"What is it?!" he snapped.

A meek-looking O'Rourke (well, of course O'Rourke always looked meek) inched open the door. He attempted a serious expression on his Barney Rubble face. "Sir," he said, and then glanced at me, wondering briefly if he should simply ignore the six-foot blonde sitting behind his chief's desk. "Um...sir...Jake Weller is waiting to see you."

"Hold him at your desk. I'll be out in a minute."

Chucky closed the door softly and then gave me a long piercing stare. "Shannon, you're going to have to make a decision here—well, it's a choice really—it's either Boardman or me, because I don't share. And now the whole fiasco is threatening both our jobs too. And neither one of us wants that."

I stood slowly, suddenly sad that Chucky had been the first of us to act like the responsible adult. He was right. I was jeopardizing not only our relationship, but, far more important, the jobs that we both loved and lived for.

"You're right about the jobs, Chuck, but you're wrong about the other stuff. I don't have to choose, because you

never have. But we've already been through that. I'm
here on business. I want to sit in with Jake Weller. I'll just
observe. Promise."

He shook his head at me because that's all you can
do when you're at the kind of impasse that Chucky and I
were at. "No way, Shannon. No way."

"Hey, Chuck." I pulled the salted almonds out of my
pocket like I was feeding an elephant at the zoo. "Here, I
brought these for you. Come on, let me stay. He's not
here for a formal statement, is he?"

"How do you know?"

I didn't know, but I knew it was the only way he'd let
me stay.

"He isn't, is he?"

"Well, no, but…"

"Come on, Chuckster. I promise I'll sit in the corner
and not say one word. And you can send me out any
time you want. If you think things are getting in conflict
territory, I'll leave."

"What conflict? We're on the same side on this, aren't
we? Or did you take a temporary leave from the AG's office so you could *defend* that hump Boardman?"

"No way. Not me. I'll either be a prosecutor forever or
I'll be selling shoes at Saks for the discount."

I was actually shocked that he let me stay. Maybe it
was a truce of sorts, a peace offering. Maybe he knew beforehand what Jake Weller was going to say and he
wanted me to hear it. And I was disobeying Vince, of
course, by coming into contact with potential witnesses,
but I'm incorrigible, and I had no intention of telling
Chuck that Vince had barred me from witness inter-

views. Let Charles Sewell deal with an angry Vince Piganno. Screw them both. I wasn't giving up anything to help either of them.

Hell hath no fury like a bitch terrier's wrath.

For self-imposed penance in a sham of good faith, I sat on an uncomfortably stiff chair in the far corner of Chuck's office as I lapped up the scowl on his face.

Chuck walked to his blinds and pulled them open, nodding through them to O'Rourke, who, seconds later, accompanied Jake Weller in.

Jake Weller was petite and clean-cut, wearing a navy blazer, khaki pants, and a bold red-and-blue striped tie— American Ivy League. He kept his hair closely cropped, but the amber glow of his large deep-set eyes and a shadowy remnant of his freshly shaved beard made him appear of Mideastern origin. He stood uncomfortably in the middle of the room, waiting for instructions. Even the most arrogant people cower under police authority and the threat of incarceration, and here was Jake Weller amid a bunch of ego-challenged men in their private enclave of power.

His golden eyes were wide, and his breathing short and labored. He looked around at Chuck and me, and then back at O'Rourke. I had been ordered to keep my jaw wired, so I remained patiently silent. Chuck and O'Rourke were giving Weller the silent treatment too, increasing the dew already dotting his forehead.

"Over here, Detective," Chief Sewell said to O'Rourke, pulling out the chair in front of his desk. O'Rourke sat where ordered. Chuck looked at Weller, and then at the empty seat next to O'Rourke, but said nothing before sitting behind his own desk. Without so much as a hello, Chief Sewell had communicated to old friend Jake Weller that he was on his turf. Weller sat in the only empty chair left in the room.

Why was Chuck putting Jake Weller on the defensive? Was he posturing because he and Weller *were* old friends and didn't want to appear biased? Or was it a message to me that any friend of Scott Boardman's was no longer a friend of his?

Jake Weller looked from O'Rourke to me. He must have been wondering why I was there. And rightly so. Who the hell was I, after all? Chuck should have sensed the tension, but he either didn't feel it or didn't care.

I decided to buck Chuck just once more before he threw me out of his office for the last time (and I was pretty sure he would). I dragged my chair closer to Jake Weller's while avoiding the stare of Chief Chucky, who'd just bolted upright in his chair at my slide closer to home plate.

"Mr. Weller, I'm Shannon Lynch, an assistant AG." I extended my hand and he shook it strongly but with a damp palm.

He looked back at Chuck. "I was under the impression this would be a private meeting...between old friends, Chuck. I mean...this isn't being recorded, is it?"

Before Chuck could answer, I said, "No worries. We just want to find out the timeline of events the night of the murders. Just tell us whatever you know, no matter how unimportant you think it is." And then I took a real plunge into the unknown. "Because to be honest with you, Mr. Weller, we think this may have been a hate crime

against Pat Boardman and Muffie Booth...for their...
well...let's just call it their *left-wing* relationship. What
do you think?"

I was praying that Weller would answer before
Chucky slid me out on my ass.

Jake Weller looked down into his lap and shook his
head. He was rolling some type of class ring around on
his finger like it was an amulet that would transport him
out. Or maybe he was just releasing sweat from under
the thick gold shank.

"Scott," he said, shaking his head and still looking at
his knees. "I told Scott the campaign probably couldn't
withstand a divorce but that it would be the best for both
of them *after* the election. Of course, in hindsight, a divorce might have saved Pat's life. I don't think she would
have been with Muffie Booth if Scott had divorced her
peacefully. She was punishing him. Really trying to embarrass him. And Scott lost it when he found the two of
them there like that..."

I chanced a glance at Chuck, who was letting me go
at Jake Weller with abandon. Chucky and I were still a
good team; we'd managed to play good guy/bad guy
without even preplanning the move.

"So you think Scott Boardman killed his wife?" I said.

Weller looked up at me. "I know who you are, Miss
Lynch. Scott told me what he said to you. Do you believe
him? The amnesia story?"

"I believe he meant it when he said it to me," I said.
"But someone coached him *after* that, and Scott recanted. I assume his coach was either you, his campaign
manager Leo Safer, or his lawyer Ron Esterman."

"I didn't see Scott that night. I was on my way to Al Forno to meet him, but when I got there, he was already gone. Ron called me later that night and told me what happened."

"So *you* never spoke with Brooke Stanford?" Chucky asked him.

"No, nor did I get a voice mail or a missed-call message from her."

"Jake? That night. What do you think happened?" Chuck asked.

"Jesus, Chuck." Weller squirmed in his chair. "You *know* what I think. But what I think doesn't matter, does it? You need evidence, and I can't help you with that. My gut feelings are as valuable as a Ouija board."

"Hey, Chief," O'Rourke said. Too insecure to ask a question directly of Jake Weller, he was sending it through the chief first. "Does Mr. Weller here know if Boardman was with the Stanford girl at all that night? I mean his alibi and all?"

Chucky and I looked at Weller for his answer.

"I think they had drinks or something," he said. "Scott was ending it for good. She was out of control. Wanted marriage. I had to have a little *talk* with her once because she threatened to go to Pat and tell her. But when she realized Pat wouldn't care, Brooke gave it up. I explained to her that she'd be ending her own career if she went public, embarrassing herself too. I thought I'd calmed her down. Brooke Stanford was a liability from the get-go." He shook his head again. "Scott never did take advice very well. He has quite an ego. That's why he's in this mess."

No one spoke for a minute as we absorbed the not-so-new information and adjusted our positions vis-à-vis Jake Weller.

Chuck and Jake were suddenly old friends again as Chucky nodded, looking like he was in complete agreement with him. O'Rourke sat stiff as always, and I dragged my chair back to the outfield, speaking pretty much to the back wall when I said, "So you're turning your old pal in, huh? His campaign's over so you might as well send him down the river and save your own ass."

"That's enough, Shannon," Chuck said.

"It's *Attorney Lynch*, Chief Sewell," I said standing. "And the last I checked, I was a *lawyer* with the Rhode Island AG's office—and you're a ... cop. My orders come from Vince Piganno, not you."

Chucky stood down, finally realizing that all that sex he'd gotten from me in the past wasn't worth the fucking he was getting now.

"Scott Boardman is guilty, Miss Lynch," Jake Weller said calmly. "And I'm not the only one who thinks so. Leo Safer told me he had drinks with Scott that afternoon and Scott left him to go to the boat to talk to Pat. Something about an estate being settled. Scott knows what happened on the boat that night. Whether he pulled a trigger or not, he knows what happened. And I'm no lawyer, but that makes him guilty of something, doesn't it?"

I felt my phone vibrating in my pocket. "Yeah, Mr. Weller, it makes him guilty of choosing the wrong people to surround himself with, starting with an unfaithful wife, continuing with the striking-while-hot Brooke Stanford, and ending unfaithfully with a turncoat PR man."

"Hey, I'm trying to help you here—"

"You don't have any useful evidence against Scott Boardman. You said so yourself. 'A Ouija board' is how you characterized it, which is not exactly admissible in court. So why are you here? Just to ramp up the current, I think. To make sure we fry him—"

Jake Weller stood. "Now why would I do that? What's in it for me if you charge Scott Boardman with murder? I should be doing the opposite. Standing by the guy I chose to support for president. Pointing to him as a murderer merely compromises my ability to judge character, doesn't it? Who's going to hire me again after this?"

"I don't know, but at least you'll be walking around free while Boardman's strapped to the chair."

"You think *I* had something to do with this?"

"I wouldn't be surprised if you were acting as some kind of *fixer*. Kill the wife and lover. Ransack the boat. Make it look like a double suicide, or a hate crime. Nice and clean. Scott Boardman's dirty laundry is tossed overboard. And maybe you thought he could be a comeback kid and scoop some sympathy votes after the brutal murder of his wife by a *stranger*."

Somewhere in the back of my consciousness, while I was all hopped up hopping on Weller, I was wondering why Chuck hadn't lopped me off at the knees and stopped my tirade. A quick glance at him gave me my answer. He was loving it. He had a sneaky smile in his eyes, watching me pummel Weller like he was my adverse witness at trial. Again, Chucky and I were tacitly playing good guy/bad guy, deftly changing sides without so much as a wink at the other. I was now the bad guy, and I knew any minute—as soon as I was finished wringing everything I could from Weller—Chuck would stand up and stop me, presumably protecting his friend from my onslaught. What a dirty game we both loved to play.

Jake Weller turned to Chucky. "This is slander, isn't it, Chuck? She's accusing me of murder."

Chucky lifted both hands in surrender. "She's the damn lawyer, Jake, not me. What the frig do I know?"

The bad guy/*dumb* guy routine worked too.

They all looked at me now for the answer to their legal question.

"Unless we beat the shit out of you in here for a confession, whatever is spoken is privileged and we have immunity. So yeah, I'm asking you if you murdered—or had someone else murder—Patricia Boardman and her lover."

Jake Weller tightened his jaw. "I want my lawyer."

Sometimes even I hated lawyers.

That little statement signaled the end to all questioning, so I strutted past Jake Weller and out of Chuck's office and then headed back to mine.

My cell had been vibrating for the last ten minutes of Jake Weller's interview. I knew who the caller was, so I ignored it until I was safely behind the closed doors of my office, where I dialed him back.

He picked up and began talking immediately. "I need to see you," he said. "Friday morning, meet me at the docks at the Newport Shipyard. I'm taking my boat out. We need to talk. In private."

All that, and I hadn't even said hello. The man was fast. He didn't waste words or time. And he knew what he wanted.

I agreed to meet him. I was cocky enough to think that after a day at sea with Scott Boardman, I'd know everything there was to know about him and that fateful night that brought us together. Sure, Vince had warned me to stay away from witnesses. But around Scott Boardman I was safe, not breaking any rules, because Vince didn't consider Scott Boardman a witness. He considered him the killer.

12

PILLOW TALK

EARLY THURSDAY MORNING I WAS WALKING UP the granite stairs to the AG building when a voice stopped me midstep.

"Miss Lynch, isn't it?"

I turned to see Virginia Booth under a wide-brimmed straw hat, standing erect on the sidewalk below. She was dressed in a beige twinset and straight skirt fitted tightly over full hips. Wearing reasonably heeled pumps and pearls the size of eggs at her throat, she looked as if she might be ready for an afternoon at the Newport Horticultural Society annual luncheon under the Rosecliff arbor—if there was such an event—I'd have to ask Beth....

She waited for me to go to her. Of course. I walked back down.

"Is there somewhere we could go...?" She'd already looked away from me toward the street. Providence wasn't her town. She bristled stiffly and grimaced as a sooty breeze from a passing truck blew a ragged part through her hair.

I lifted my cell phone from my bag and dialed the office. As I watched her watch the cars whiz by, I told Andy I would be in a few minutes late. Personal business. Then, after dropping the phone back in my bag, I touched her elbow. Her head whipped toward me and I nodded to the sidewalk stretching ahead. Wordlessly she followed at my side to a Starbucks near the Biltmore Hotel. I would have tortured her with the Dial-up Modem Diner, but I knew she didn't want to be seen with me, nor I with her. At the Starbucks in downtown Providence, no one would know her, and, preferring Dunkin' Donuts, I'd never been there.

We nestled into a table in the corner in front of a fireplace with a perpetual fake flame. "You want a coffee? I'm getting one to pay the rent on this table. Otherwise, this stuff tastes like home heating oil to me."

She shook her head, declining. I guess she felt Starbucks should be honored to have her as their guest and felt no compunction about taking up a space without paying dues.

Five minutes later I slid back into my seat holding a steamed-milk concoction. From the feather-light weight of the cup, I was hoping it was mostly air.

"What can I do for you, Mrs. Booth? They don't pay me to loll in coffee bars."

The woman had been focusing on everything but me. She cleared her throat, staring out the window as she spoke. "Your office sent police to my house the other day.

Distressing, to say the least." Now she looked me full in the eyes. "I'd like to know what they found."

"I'm more interested in what they didn't find."

"I suppose that answers my question. But if they found nothing, it is simply because there was nothing there of any value to their investigation. Isn't that right, Miss Lynch? Someone would have been in touch with me if they'd found something of interest."

"Not necessarily."

She cranked her neck to the side as if relieving a knot. "Miss Lynch," she said with an edge in her voice, "you are being deliberately contrary."

I reared my head back. The sharp pain between my eyes was either Virginia Booth getting on my nerves, or a caffeine punch from the Starbucks sludge I was drinking.

"Uncage the spiders, Mrs. Booth. I'm not Miss Muffet."

"I surmised as much."

"I don't think you have Scott Boardman's best interest at heart—"

"Has he mine?"

"Scott Boardman is no different from the rest of us. He's just trying to save himself. But then again, you must know him better than I do. Your families have a long history. I'm guessing that history includes Brooke Stanford too."

"Brooke Stanford is a very pretty red herring. Gone are the romantic days of yore when men killed over pretty virgins. Not that Brooke qualifies for the part, of course..."

She clamped her eyes shut in self-reprobation for her coarse remark. "This is not about love, Miss Lynch. It's about money. These days it always is, isn't it? About money?"

"Not if you're a Muslim extremist."

She gracefully ignored my comment and continued.

"Before he died, my husband and I disagreed over... well...let's just say over Martha's private life—or 'Muffie,' as we called her. To insure that I didn't punish her by strangling her financially, my husband before he died transferred a majority control of the family trust to her. Under his plan, I'd been awarded a stipend only. With a minimum of effort your office will eventually uncover the lawsuit I'd instituted before Muffie's death to regain control. In retaliation Muffie had begun to protect herself. She had begun to transfer joint control of the trusts to Pat Boardman, before I had a temporary restraining order placed on them."

Virginia Booth looked at me for some reaction. But so far nothing she'd told me gave anyone—other than Virginia Booth herself—a motive for killing Pat Boardman or Muffie Booth. I raised my eyebrows in response. I was still waiting for some link to Scott Boardman as killer. She nodded and continued.

"Pat was leaving Scott—for whatever reasons—I don't concern myself with dirty rumors. Scott was trying to get Pat to stay in the marriage just through the campaign. Keep up the happy marriage front. And that's where my knowledge ends. After I instituted the suit against my husband's estate to wrest control from Muffie, I was cut out of the informational loop. Muffie no longer confided in me. Consequently I was no longer privy to information about Pat and Scott. I'm assuming Pat refused Scott's pleas to remain in the marriage and she was going ahead with the divorce. Something happened between them that night. I'm assuming a meeting was held among the three of them that ended with Pat and Muffie's deaths."

I sat before her, unconvinced. Was I thickheaded and blinded by my lust for Scott Boardman? I didn't think so. But Virginia Booth disagreed.

"Ultimately we all try to save ourselves," she said. "We'd be fools if we didn't. But why do I think Scott has you on his side now? Am I right? Has he added another horse to his stable?"

I don't know why, but saying "Fuck you" to someone like Virginia Booth felt like it would damage me more than her, so I stifled the urge and remained stone-faced.

"Of course he has," she said, her mouth twisted into a smile without mirth. She straightened her back, pulling away from me and looking ready to dismiss me by simply walking away. But then she sighed and gave me another look. "Odd I misjudged you. I didn't take you for a fool. Now, Brooke I would expect it from—"

"Fuck you!"

This time she smiled in earnest, knowing she'd finally penetrated the protective shield of my pride. "I know you're dating him. I'm surprised you still have a job, considering the obvious conflicts. But Scott will take that from you too. You'll lose your job over this. He doesn't take prisoners."

She pushed her chair back and looked toward the door.

"Don't you move a muscle," I said. "I'm not finished."

She looked back at me with heavy-lidded eyes struggling against a current of hate to focus on mine.

"What has Scott done to *you*?" I asked. "This isn't just about a love affair between your daughter and his wife. And it isn't just about money. It's about Scott himself. This is personal."

She blinked her eyes as if they were stuck with glue. A cataract haze covered the sea blue of them like a dense fog obscuring the horizon.

"I guess I'll just have to ask him myself during our little weekend sail," I said. "I'll untangle this little mystery between you and Scott. Because I'm not so sure you aren't capable of murder. I'm not so sure at all."

She smiled at me. "You're like an ignorant child afraid of ghosts, Miss Lynch." And like a sudden unexpected gust of air, she whirled up from her chair and blew out the door.

I WALKED BACK TO MY OFFICE, MY MIND WORKing at the puzzle of Virginia Booth's informational resources. Of course, my actions with Scott hadn't been discreet. Discretion was never one of my priorities. But still, how could my personal affairs in Providence have reached the rarefied world of Newport high society without some kind of special delivery? Brooke was my first guess.

I walked in on Vince as he was uncharacteristically hovering over his desk with his shirtsleeved arms resting over a sea of legal documents.

"Playing lawyer today, Vince?" I said as I whipped through his door and sat before him.

He didn't look up but his balled fists clenched and released in response.

"How do I get hold of Brooke?"

Slowly his glance rose to me. The soft flesh of his face was puckered like punched dough into a grimace of anger and fatigue. The hardened marbles of his eyes were ridged in red.

"Working hard, huh?" I said.

"I got a real mess here, Lynch. And you aren't carrying your weight in this office."

"That's exactly what I'm trying to do. But I need to reach Brooke. She was handling some interrogatories for me and I can't find them," I lied.

He buried his face back into the pile of papers on his desk. "Put Beth on it and leave Brooke alone. And that includes phone, e-mail, text messaging, and smoke signals."

"Why, Vince? Is Brooke too delicate a flower for my thorny ways?"

"I'm on top of Brooke Stanford."

"Everyone seems to be in line for that privilege."

He ignored me, so I flounced out his door mumbling under my breath, "Okay, I'll just ask Scott Boardman what I need to know."

He bolted up and came to his door, following me out into the corridor. "What the goddamn hell did you say to me?" he hollered.

Andy's head snapped up. The book he was reading under his desk crashed to the floor.

Wide-eyed and innocent, I turned to Vince. "I said, 'Good luck with the Scott Boardman case.' Are you going deaf on top of all your other shortcomings?"

Vince's sausage of a thumb pointed back over his shoulder. "Get back in here."

Back I trod to Vince's office and plopped into a chair facing his desk. He followed me, slamming his door behind him.

"Blindfolded, with two hands behind your back and wearing a ball and chain, you should have aced that Cohen case against Jeff Kendall. What the fuck went on there? Huh? What exactly the goddamn-fucking-hell went on in that courtroom that you couldn't get a simple-assed conviction against a guy who blew his wife's head off right after he opened her lawyer's letter suing him for divorce on the grounds that he sucks dick on bowling nights?"

"All circumstantial," I mumbled to his windows and the view outside.

"You've won with less. It's never the evidence with you. It's what's in your gut. Once you decide someone's guilty, the trial's over."

Vince sat silently behind his desk again. Still looking at me, he waited in pin-drop silence for my response, not even chancing the click of a lighter for the Merit that he had removed from its pack and now hung limply between his yellowed fingers.

"That's the answer, then, isn't it?" I said. "I doubted he was guilty."

He nodded. "If you didn't think he was guilty, you should have handed him over to someone else. But you didn't do that either. It's almost like you wanted that case...and you wanted to *lose* it."

"He wasn't guilty, Vince. Why send an innocent man to jail?"

He threw the unlit cigarette down on his desk. It bounced softly to the edge and rolled off.

"Yeah," I said softly, "okay, maybe I should have given the case to Laurie. Yeah, Laurie would have been a good choice. A nice Jewish girl prosecuting a Jewish murderer. No charge of anti-Semitism there, huh?" I was talking to the cigarette on the floor in front of Vince's desk. I didn't dare look up at him, because I knew he wasn't anywhere near laughing. His silence was a scary omen. I got this weird feeling that pity for me was keeping him quiet, but I kept babbling.

"I had already started the trial before I realized I didn't think Cohen was guilty. After the defense rested and I got up to begin my closing argument...something happened to my resolve. I don't know...It was almost as if Jeff's clicking pen was a message...I kept hearing the click of a shotgun trigger like dry practice before you load the ammo. Like trying to get up the nerve..."

Finally he spoke. "And you were in that bedroom with the Cohen women, watching her practice with the gun, before she loaded it up and blew her brains out. Is that what you're telling me? You had a goddamn *vision*?"

Vince was actually pretty calm, considering I was telling him I blew a case on purpose, even though my intent was subliminal. But when I looked up at his face, it was cherry red and as shiny as an overblown balloon.

"You're burning out on me, Lynch. I may have to

bench you for a while. Go get a brain-shrink cure. I'll give you some names. Better yet, go ask Melone. She's probably test-driven every head doctor reachable by Amtrak in the Northeast Corridor."

"A nervous breakdown? Just because I suddenly think a few of the suspects we send to prison for the rest of their miserable lives might be innocent? Just because I think sometimes even *we* can make mistakes—in this office—where you sit like some overblown Buddha declaring people innocent or guilty based on how much trial-worthy evidence we can gather against them?"

"Lynch, you're entitled to your opinion. But when you have these touchy-feely moments about the scum we prosecute, then do me a fucking favor and pass the perp on to someone else in the office, and most important— and this is *really* important now, so listen carefully—*don't jump into fucking bed with them.*"

"Sure, Vince, no problem," I assured him, while I was thinking about what I should pack for my weekend cruise with perp d'amour Scott Boardman, with whom I had every intention of jumping into a fucking bed that very weekend. "Just promise me you'll do the same."

"What the fuck does that mean?"

"I got a feeling you're fluffing up your pillows for Brooke Stanford."

No point waiting for the denial. I walked out, sincerely hoping I was wrong.

13

OFF TO THE POUND

I KEPT MY STARBUCKS CHAT WITH VIRGINIA
Booth stashed in the safe house of my mind. I wanted to
cross-examine Scott first about what I'd learned. About
the few billion clams on their way to his wife's name
from the Booth trust accounts. Then tell him his trusted
public relations man Jake Weller thought he was guilty
as charged. Then I would take the whole package to
Vince Monday morning and let the pieces of my heart
fall where they may. After all, what did love have to do
with the bubbling chemistry between Scott Boardman
and me? Not a damn thing. I could always visit him in
prison and get us a private room by signing in as his
lawyer. No one would bother asking me what *side* I was
on. And sex on a conference table? Why not? The Mile
High Club is so *last year* anyway.

My next decision—to go solo and not tell the girls I
was taking off for the weekend with a murder suspect—
was giving me a queasy feeling. But I considered guilt the

illegitimate second cousin of fear and remorse, so the feeling in my stomach was probably just acid reflux from the Starbucks mud I had drunk. Furthermore, since I'd gone AWOL in the Boardman *affaire d'amour*, I'd suddenly become number one on the endangered species list, and the girls wouldn't go twenty-eight hours without tracking me down to have me spayed.

So Friday morning I was lying to Laurie when I told her I was going up to Beantown for the weekend to visit a dying second cousin thrice removed on my stepfather's side. (I don't have a stepfather and I can't count to thrice.) Laurie tried to trip me up by asking me the remote relative's name. That half second it took me to manufacture the pseudonym almost busted me. Fallon or Fiona or something, I said. So when Marianna called me five minutes after I hung up with Laurie to verify my Irish jig of a tale, I just got angry and used the old offense-as-defense device. I began howling expletives at Marianna, starting at the A's and getting only to the F's before I gave up and started sprinkling cherries on the cake of my assault by reminding her that at least *I* wasn't teaching the alphabet to serial killers while they were carving their initials on the bodies of young coeds.

"That's wearing thin, Shannon," she answered. "And just because I've been stupid in the past doesn't mean you should be. We're all close enough now that we should be learning from each other's mistakes. That's what friends are for, right?"

"Are we done?"

"Keep your phone on at all times."

"Sure thing. No problem, buddy. See ya Monday morning." And then I promptly switched off my phone.

I was breathing a sigh of relief as I drove into the Newport Shipyard. I'd lied like a pro and they'd believed me. I felt like I was getting my old swing back. Depression turned out to be nothing as virile as the flu. I'd managed to dab out sad's last sniffle as I deftly swung my Suburban into an empty spot in the lot next to the now familiar Sebring and looked up at the sky, where it looked like a contented God was blowing smoke rings from his fat Cohiba. Giant puffs of fog were blowing off the ocean, breaking into chunks so solid they dispersed over the land like a brood of Casper's suddenly hatched offspring. Nice. It was a perfect day to get lost at sea in the smoky throes of love—or more precisely, the buzz of that super-fresh sexual tension going on between the Board-man and me.

The last time I saw him at his suite at the Biltmore, we were so hot that Scott said he was leaving a damage deposit for the scorched couch. Of course, we never got to the finale before my phone started vibrating me back to work and reality. A half hour later, hearing the Cohen verdict hadn't even bothered me, I was still so buzzed from foreplay. So as I was driving into the marina lot and spotted Scott's parked car, my temperature started to rise again like the apex of a fever at midnight before it breaks. I could feel my heart speed up, hairs tickling the back of my neck.

Scott was standing on the bow of the boat, removing tarps and loosening ropes, bending over, reaching up. His skin, taut from freshly pumped muscles, had bronzed since last we met. Golden hairs on his legs and arms sparkled in the early morning sun. His hair, too, had gilded at the tips. The sun loved him, even heating up the chilly gray of his eyes.

He spotted me walking toward the boat and stopped what he was doing to smile at me like I was a buoy in a storm. His eyes locked onto mine and I almost heard the whistling of his lips as they pursed and expelled the breath he was holding until I pranced up the dock, where he extended a hand and hoisted me neatly over. I paused for the briefest second and smiled at him. He looked around for prying eyes and, satisfied that we were alone, wrapped me in his arms.

"You might be the one to save me," he said as he held my face in his hands. "And I don't mean from a murder charge."

It sounded romantic, so I left it at that.

"I feel like a kid again with you," he said. "A giddy teenager. I couldn't sleep last night thinking about you."

"Hey, I slept fine last night—after we had sex. But it would have been nicer if you'd been there."

He turned quickly away from me and sent his laughter out to sea. I think he liked the way I talked—my sexual boldness—but I also think that kind of honesty in a woman was new to him. I got the feeling that the women he'd known in the past didn't joke much about banging the flesh and getting down to basics. Intimidated by the famous senator from Connecticut, women probably caved in to his every desire and then thanked him for the honor. Not much of a giver, I was usually the *taker* in relationships. But I think Scott Boardman liked what I was taking from him, and I was hell-bent on using him up until he was spent.

He wasted no time getting us under power and motoring out to the open waters. His plan was to sail up the coast back to Providence, where he was anchoring at a marina for repairs. We couldn't go too far, he'd said, because the boat had a slipped disk, or was it a clogged clamp?

"It'll take a bit over an hour. We'll have some lunch in the city and then head back. We can sleep on the boat tonight if you're game."

Ignorance of this whole sailing experience required that I say nothing in response, because I never spoke unless I knew what I was talking about. But spending the night with him? Yeah, I knew all about that. "Sure," I said. "I'm free for the night."

He kissed my neck. "You ready to go?"

I'd motored around in a few dinghies with Chucky but had never been on a sailboat before. Poverty in South Boston has a way of reversing the engines on that type of hobby, if you get my drift. The closest I got to seamanship in my youth was my rubber duck soap holder that stayed afloat no matter how many waves I made with back-kicks in the tub. So about thirty minutes into our trip, when this Italian stallion of a boat started to pitch and roll like a drunken Irishman, I looked to Scott's face for *his* reaction. I figured if he stayed calm, I could keep sipping calmly on my Schweppes and ignoring the salt splash on my face. And he did look calm...as calm as he could look with me licking my lips at him a few feet away.

He was smiling away at me in hot anticipation, and it wasn't until his Starbucks Doubleshot rolled over on the deck next to his feet and spilled all over the shiny white deck that Scott became a tad concerned over the rising whitecaps just beginning to lick the sides of the boat.

"Christ," he said. "It wasn't supposed to be choppy today."

I leaned as far as I could over the railing and poured the rest of my Schweppes overboard. "What exactly does that mean, Scott? Is this something we need to be overly concerned with?"

"Not a thing," he said. "Come here and hold this a minute. I have to go below."

"Hold what? The wheel? What the hell am I supposed to do with it?"

"Keep it steady and pointing toward that strip of land over there."

I looked to where Scott was looking and I didn't see anything but a drab green New England sea and a line of fog in the distance. "You see a strip of land over there, huh? Because I don't see anything but me throwing up over the side of this boat if it doesn't stop bobbing up and down."

"Shannon, this is nothing. A summer squall. Nothing to worry about... except nausea, of course."

Scott's phone began ringing in his pocket. "Come here and hold the wheel like a good girl. I'll teach you how to steer." He took one hand off the wheel and extended the other to me.

I slid off my perch on the starboard side and tripped into the pilot's well. Before I could stand again, the tip of a wave flopped over the boat.

"Shannon?"

I heard Scott's voice hollering for me and I looked up. He'd taken the wheel again and without further question I crawled to him and pulled myself up by the chair behind him. He took my arm and hooked it on the wheel.

"A rogue wave is all. Just keep it steady until I get back," he said. "I'll take this call below, where I can hear. Keep it steady and don't let it roll."

Sure, I thought, *keep it steady and don't let it roll,* as if I had a freaking clue what that meant and how to implement it.

"Don't hold the wheel too stiff. Let it give a little with the movement, you get it?"

"Scott," I said, "just do what you gotta do and get back here *quick.* Giving me orders isn't going to make up for thirty-five years with a rubber duck."

The strength of the water fighting against the boat felt like riding a wild horse at a rodeo. The boat was steering *me.* Seconds later Scott appeared on deck, holding his cell phone to his ear. The screaming from the other end was so loud I could actually hear the anger over the cracks and groans of the boat and sea as they fought each other for control. Scott's face was as sharp and ugly as the crashing waves. He snapped the phone closed and grabbed the wheel from my grasp.

"Get below. I'll take over."

"Who was that?"

"I'm going to speed her up. Ride should be smoother too."

Frankly, I didn't care at that point who'd been on the phone or what he was planning as long as I lived to complain about it. I held on tight to the railing as I dragged

myself down the stairs to the galley. I decided to pop the
Dramamine I'd taken along *just in case* and lie down in
one of the berths until the war was over. I figured I was
wholly useless as a lifesaving instrument, so I might as
well get out of Scott's way and say my last good-byes to
the girls before sleep or death, whichever came first. I hit
speed dial to Beth, who I figured would be the one most
capable of calmly listening to my swan song without lec-
turing me as a parting sally—as if lectures are any good
to a dying person. I mean, what could they possibly warn
me about now? Misbehaving in hell (where I was reasonably certain I was headed)?

"Hello?"

I heard Beth's tentative voice on the other end. Far
away. She sounded surprised.

"Hello? Is that you, Shannon?" she said again.

"Hey, Beth, listen real good, okay? We might get cut
off. I'm on a boat with Scott Boardman. We're heading to
Providence—"

"Providence?" I heard Beth say as if from a great distance. "Where are you now? Shannon, can you hear me?"

"The water's a bit choppy and the boat's rolling
around like a dog with fleas. Just wanted to let you know
in case…"

In case what? In case I died? What the hell was I going to say to her? That Marianna was right after all? That
this miserable ending of my life was God's punishment
for my immoral acts? (Jesus, I *was* beginning to sound
like her!)

"Shannon! Shannon?" I heard Beth screaming my
name. "I can't hear you anymore."

"I'm here," I managed to say as I lurched forward, losing the phone as I landed on both palms and felt the burn on my cheek skidding against the stateroom's tight Berber-weave carpeting. I felt like an ass grabbing the floor for support. I lifted my head long enough to see my phone under the queen bed and began crawling toward it when I heard the deep shrieking of Scott's voice up on deck. Could he have been cursing the foul weather or was he back on the phone?

I reached my own phone, and, still lying on the floor, I put it to my ear, but alas, Beth was gone. I stood, legs straddled for support, and tried to duck back out of the room to reach Scott, who was still hollering above, but another wave seemed to turn the whole boat around and my head reared back, slamming into the low bulkhead of the stateroom. I thought I was fine—until I wasn't. A second of dizziness and the world went black.

How long I was out I don't know, but I woke up gasping for air as if an elephant was sitting on my chest. I tasted a warm salty substance in my mouth, knowing instinctively it was blood. My breathing was labored and heavy as if my chest were crushed. I sucked in as much air as I could and began screaming.

Lucky Dack rushed over to me from just outside the cabin threshold. He gently lifted the heavy weight off me and then removed a gun from my clenched fingers before I could squeeze the trigger into his face.

"Miz Lynch?" he said. "You all right there, girl? You just blink if you can hear me."

I watched him place the gun on a clear evidence bag

he had unfolded a few feet away and then lean back
to me.

"Shit, Lucky. What are you doing here?"

"Your head's bleeding pretty good in the back. Can
you sit yourself up?"

I dragged myself up Lucky's muscular arms and he
pulled me half-sitting to the bed, where I sat on the floor
against the mattress, staring at a bleeding body. And I
began screaming again in a frightened voice I wasn't
used to hearing.

"Who is that, Lucky? What is it? Is it dead?"

He came back to me and put his hand on my cheek.
"Now, you calm yourself. This is your gun, right? Small
Colt?"

I nodded dumbly.

"Okay then, cuz I got to see to this man here. Make
sure he's not still breathing."

Lucky leaned back to the body. "Shot to the back of
the head. Doesn't look like you coulda done it and then
have him land on top of you."

"I didn't shoot a gun—"

"Hey?" I heard Beth's voice from a distance up on
deck. "Can I come down there?"

Marianna's and Laurie's faces appeared in the cabin
doorway. They ducked inside and knelt in front of me.
As Beth walked in behind them, bits and pieces of memory returned along with the bitter smell of my own
vomit. The boat had stopped the awful lurching and was
calmly undulating in the normal rhythm of a drowsy sea,
disrupted only by the loud voices and heavy feet of busy
men on the deck above me.

"Did I pass out?" I said. "Must have been the Dramamine."

"Boatyard owner found the boat floating near the dock, with Scott Boardman hanging over the side," Laurie said. Then she looked over at the body as the police photographer snapped photos. "What happened down here?"

My head began a slow pound. "We headed out from Newport on our way to Providence. He said the boat needed a repair. And real sudden—the waves picked up. I came down here. I called Beth and hit my head. That's it. All I remember."

Laurie looked at Marianna, and they both looked at Beth. "Are you sure she didn't say anything else on the phone?"

Beth shook her head. "It was a bad connection. Something about coming to Providence. I didn't even recognize her voice. I only knew it was Shannon because of caller ID."

Lucky was looking around the room for evidence with rubber-swathed hands.

"Ask Scott," I said. "He'll know more than I do."

And then a few more lights flickered on in my awakening brain. Someone called the cops because Scott was *hanging* over the side of the boat. I looked up at them for a few more answers.

Marianna was shaking her head. "Alive but not talking at the moment. I told you to stay away from him. I've got a sense about these things."

"Sure," I said. "You have a sense when it comes to other people's fuckups. What about your *own* damn mistakes?"

"Welcome to the classic dilemma," she said with a bold authority. "You never see your own mistakes while you're making them."

Laurie shook her head. "Shannon, *none* of us thought you should be spending time with Boardman—at least not until this whole thing is over."

Marianna moved back with Beth. It didn't take much to offend her; Marianna's ego was as fragile as spun glass. Beth had her arm around her, signaling her disapproval of my insult. Shit, even with a bloody head I wasn't getting any sympathy.

"How long was I out?" I asked them again. "How long were we docked?"

Laurie answered. "The guy who owns the shipyard opened up about noon. He says he found the boat drifting at the dock when he came in. Leo Safer must have boarded while Boardman was docking. When did you leave Newport?"

"Early. As soon as I got there. About eight, I think."

I closed my eyes and thought hard for any memory beyond hitting my head on the bulkhead. Did I hear anything else? What exactly had those angry words above meant when I thought it was Scott screaming at the wind?

When I opened my eyes again, two uniformed cops were standing behind Laurie. "Does she need a hospital?" one said. "Or can we arrest her here?"

I looked up at the one who'd spoken. Youngish, twenty-two at best. Dark spiked hair and a long straight nose. I could picture him out of uniform, wearing a sport jacket over a tight tee, picking up eighteen-year-olds with fake IDs at local bars, and then letting them go after they agreed to a midnight drive in the front seat of his souped-up Corvette.

"Arrest?" I whispered.

"Yes, Shannon," Marianna answered. Her voice was raw, still angry, but something else too. It cracked and quivered as tears strangled in her throat and she sucked in a broken gasp of air. "Arrested for the *fucking* murder of Leo Safer and the fucking *attempted* murder of Scott Boardman, unless he dies too, then it'll be *double fucking homicide.* Do you remember anything *now*?"

The back of my head was bleeding all over the bedspread. I lifted both hands to feel the wound and brought my hands back covered in blood. Then I looked directly at the two rookie cops standing next to Marianna, and I knew what they were thinking as the dark-haired one shook his head at me.

"So much for GSR," he said.

If there was gun residue on my hands, it was now adulterated by the cleansing blood of my oozing head.

"Do you own a Corvette?" I asked. "Or maybe a black Camaro with mag wheels and a spoiler?"

"None of your fucking business," he answered. I read his name tag. Kent.

"I didn't shoot that gun, Kent, and forensics will back me up. What would be my motive for shooting Scott Boardman and his campaign manager? Huh? What?"

"That's not my problem."

Laurie leaned in behind me to examine the cut on the back of my head. "Damn, I hate blood," she said, pushing my hair away from the wound. "Heads bleed so badly. I don't think you need stitches, though. It's already clotting up nice."

"Oh, well thank you, Dr. Stein," Beth said. She had fetched a med technician and was pushing him my way. "Please go look at her," she said to him.

As soon as I was pronounced well enough to be arrested, the asshole cop named Kent hauled me up and locked handcuffs over my wrists before I could get a one-syllable "Fuck" out of my mouth.

In shock, Beth screamed and rushed to slap him. "Get away from her—"

But he was too quick. He blocked her slap and returned his so hard across her face that she fell back against the wall. Laurie went to her and I went straight for the asshole cop, who wrestled me back to the floor and wedged his boot under my chin.

I heard Laurie ministering to Beth as Marianna rushed the cop whose foot was under my throat. "You filthy punk," she said as she kicked his leg from under my chin and they began a tussle that brought Lucky up from under the bed where he'd been poking around. "You hold on one minute," he boomed at Kent, "or I'll take you down with one arm!"

"Then tell her to stop fighting me," Kent said as he released Marianna. He looked at me. "She's going to jail like any other criminal."

He had a smirk on his face like I was a long-term fugitive he'd finally found. Why was this snot-nosed young cop so pissed at me? My answer came swiftly as he yanked me up by the elbow. "Let's go see if the chief can get you out of this one," he hissed in my ear.

He pushed me forward, then walked at my heels so close I could hear the crackling of his stiff leather holster as he fingered his gun in it, a reminder to me of his power. *One false move*, I thought as my blood beat hard in my hollow chest, *and he'll friggin' shoot me.*

When we climbed above deck, a coroner's van was waiting for the body below. Lights off, codes called in, Leo Safer was dead. Scott Boardman, I assumed, was already on his way to the nearest hospital.

I was shuffled to one of the waiting police cars parked at the dock. The girls huddled around me, not speaking, not crying, Marianna clenching her jaw, Laurie looking mean and angry, and Beth still wide-eyed and confused. Did she still want to be an AAG?

Laurie said to me, "We'll follow in Beth's car." Then to the cop, Marianna said, "Be nice, because the enemies you make on your way up are the ones you'll be facing on your way down. And everyone comes down sooner or later."

He smiled and nodded like Marianna had just told him to have a nice day. Laurie held Marianna by the sleeve to calm her down. Beth had finally started to cry.

I was still breathing hard and just about to catch my breath when the stretcher carrying Leo Safer passed to the right of me. The asshole Kent lowered my head into the police car and pushed the door shut, but all I heard was the slam of the van's door as Leo Safer's dead body was closed into it.

Like a dog picked up by the local dog catcher, I watched through the back window of the squad car as my three friends piled into Beth's car. I should have been with them.

14

COFFEE BREAK

AFTER A SILENT FORTY-MINUTE DRIVE NORTH during which I listened to muffled laughter in the front seat, the asshole cop named Kent pulled up to the front door of the police station and stopped where the press had assembled for my red carpet entrance. The flash-bulbs started clicking as soon as the back door opened.

I sneered at my captors, "You called the press from the car?"

"Shut the fuck up," Kent said through clenched teeth. He wasted no time pulling me out of the car and parading me handcuffed in front of the cameras for optimum wide-angled lens exposure.

Through the police station they escorted me. Some of the cops looked on wide-eyed. Others smiled coyly in an abbreviated show of thumbs-up approval. Almost worse than being arrested for murder was the shock of feeling an outcast among the very people I thought were my friends.

They pushed me into an empty cell and within minutes I was retrieved by O'Rourke, who freed my cuffed hands and wordlessly walked me to an interrogation room, where a hot cup of coffee sat on the table in front of me.

"You're shaking," he said. "Coffee's hot."

I didn't know what to say. How do you thank someone you've been mistreating for years? Who'd have thought a hot coffee would humble me to my knees? I was afraid to say anything that would sound disingenuous, something even simple O'Rourke would interpret as too little too late, so I opted for straightforward honesty. Always the best course when you're given only a few minutes to unload a shitload of apologies.

"Hey, O'Rourke, thanks for the coffee. You're a good man.... The chief's not around, is he?"

I already knew the answer, but it was nice to see O'Rourke scrunch up his face in pain and shake his head. "Yeah...well...sorry. He left the building when they said they were bringing you in."

I nodded, my position in the chief's life brought abruptly home to me: I was a weak link in his chain of command. In the real world—outside the bedroom—I could do nothing but bring him down with me—down to where I'd brought myself via that ladder that everyone comes back down sooner or later.

"But Mr. Piganno is sending someone over to see you," O'Rourke said by way of comfort. "Shouldn't be too long. Get you anything else while you're waiting?"

I shook my head and O'Rourke walked out, leaving the door open behind him. I sat alone, wondering why the girls hadn't come to meet me. My answer came in the form of an ex-AAG who stood in the doorway scowling at me like I was a flea-infested dog.

"Didn't figure it'd be you, Lynch," he said. "Melone would've been my guess. Marianna could get herself arrested by a meter maid."

"What are you doing here, Kendall?"

"Vince sent me here to have a little *defense* chat with you. Apparently you need a good criminal lawyer."

"Okay then, let me ask you again. Why are *you* here?"

He ran his fingers through his sandy blond locks as he plopped his briefcase on the table in front of me and pulled out a chair. "As much as I'd like to sink you, Lynch," he said, "this just isn't your MO. If you wanted to kill someone, you'd tear him limb from limb, none of this shoot-'em-in-the-back-of-the-head shit. So save me some time and aggravation and give me something to make this all go away." When he finished talking, he tilted his head at me.

Then I tilted my head back at him. "Get real, Kendall. Whoever shot Safer and Boardman walked off the boat at the dock. There's not enough evidence to even hold me here."

He nodded his head. "But I should let them hold you overnight just to bust your agates."

"Probably not in my best interests to be honest with you right now, but go fuck yourself."

He opened his mouth full of pretty white teeth and laughed heartily. "I probably deserve that, but what people deserve is never the question. The question is, who has the balls to give it to them? And that's what ultimately surprised me about Marianna. That she actually dumped *me*."

Yeah, I thought. She did have balls. And I'd always prided myself on being the strong one, the unemotional one, but maybe I'd been giving myself too much credit. Could it be that angst-ridden Marianna was actually stronger than me? And Laurie and Beth too? Did they derive some inner fortitude from having had a real family life? If I had been conceived in a petri dish and grown in a lab, I might have been nurtured by concerned white-smocked technicians instead of ignored and swept aside by everyone except the paperboy.

"Get me out of here, Jeff."

"Yeah, yeah...okay. Initial forensics and simple-ass common sense says there's no way you shot Safer in the back of his head and then hit your head and had him land on top of you. Plus your gun wasn't shot. The bullets they found in Safer and Boardman weren't shot from it. And no one bothered checking Boardman for gun residue because the dumb cops assumed you were the shooter and he was a victim. So timeline looks like you hit your head first, then Safer comes below, gets shot, and lands on top of you. You didn't shoot Boardman, did you? Lovers' quarrel or something?"

"Why doesn't someone ask *him* who shot him? Is he able to talk yet?"

"Just a graze. But the man insists he doesn't know anything. Says he was reaching over to tie the boat up and he felt a sharp pain in his arm. Thought it was a heart attack until he saw the blood, and then he passed out without ever looking up. For a big guy he's a real wimp. Can I ask you what the hell you're doing with him?"

I was beginning to wonder myself.

"It's not because of the chief, is it?" Jeff asked.

"In what way?"

"Are you trying to get the chief jealous so he'll leave his wife—"

"Hey! Would I do a girlie thing like that?"

"You don't have to tell me what really happened on that boat. And if you want another lawyer, I'll stop—"

"Oh, shut up, Jeff."

I stood and walked to a bulletin board at the rear of the room, pulling out pins and stabbing them back in. "Scott and I went out on the boat, the winds picked up, and I went below, hit my head, and my lights went out. I woke up with a corpse on top of me. That's it. I left out all the adjectives, modifiers, and fucking expletives."

"And you heard nothing? No shots?"

"Scott screaming at someone on a phone. By the time the shooting started, I was out cold."

"Okey-dokey." He stood abruptly. "Does Piganno know you're diddling a murder suspect?"

"Yeah, he barred me from the case."

"Well, the whole AG's office is compromised now. You fucked up royally this time, old girl. Must say, I didn't expect it of you. Thought you were above all that female stuff."

"It's not *female* stuff. It's having a soul, something you lack because in your genetic sequence a heart is considered junk DNA."

"Yup, I'm higher up on the evolutionary ladder, where

hearts and souls are about as useful as an appendix and just as prone to inflammation. Want my advice? Don't cut off your balls to spite your face. Temper the estrogen and start thinking like a guy—the way you used to."

"Can I go home now?"

He laughed. "If I don't keep these charges from sticking, you'll be fired. It's automatic termination if you're even *charged* with a crime. So you owe me, Lynch. *Big.*" He swiped his briefcase from the table. "I'll get you out in a jiffy. Sit tight." Then he left me alone with my cold black coffee.

Jeff was right. All my life I'd repressed that female side, the one that played with dolls and cooed at babies. Why was I getting soft now? Was it my body's way of waking me up to reality: Breed now or forever hold your peace? In the past I would have bedded both Boardman *and* Chucky and never mentioned a word to either of them about the other. Was Jeff Kendall right? Was I pitting Chuck against Boardman in some jealousy game to get Chuck to leave his wife and marry me? I couldn't even think such thoughts without getting physically sick. And could I chance facing the girls with this pink-hued dilemma without forever losing my position as their Darth Vadered fearless leader? Would I ever be able to berate Marianna again for being an emotional wreck, scream at Beth when she was crying, or call Laurie a bleeding-heart liberal—without having them raise their plucked eyebrows at me? For the first time in my life I realized it was *hard* being me. For the first time in my life I suspected that the "me" I thought I was might be a façade, a brick wall slanting ominously to one side.

I would hold the wall up or knock it down. Whatever. But I would do it alone. I could still do it solo.

That's when asshole cop Kent came back into my interrogation room and closed the door quietly behind him. He leaned over the table so close to my face that I could see the early evening stubble just above his lip. He smelled of leather.

"You're going to spend the night with us. And I get to tuck you in."

Every muscle in my body tensed as, in my mind, I stood and kicked the table into his gut.

In real life, I collapsed back into my chair, a prisoner.

He stood and moved to the door, backing against it to block anyone else's entry. "Why aren't you asking for the chief? Don't you want Chief Sewell to save your skinny ass?"

I shook my head slowly. "I'm trying to save your job for you. As soon as the chief finds out what you're doing here, you're not only unemployed, you're dead."

He smiled as a light knock interrupted what I assumed was his comeback threat. His head jerked toward the whisper through the closed door. He opened it and admitted his partner, the other cop from the boat, who slid into the room and stood next to his friend. Waiting.

I remained seated. The table between us my only protection.

A nod from asshole cop, and his partner moved behind me to the barred and frosted window.

"Went home for the night," he said to Kent.

"The chief?" I said. "But he'll be back in the morning."

"Not soon enough for you," Kent said. "And he won't

say anything about this because he's as guilty as you are. Adultery is illegal last time I checked."

Before I heard him, the partner came up behind me and slapped a cuff around my wrist, then jerked my other arm behind me and fastened them together. Kent came behind me as I struggled. He kicked the chair out from under me and I fell, my "skinny ass" bouncing on the floor.

They laughed, but the look on their faces wasn't humor. It was a look of pleasure or relief—like something held too long in their bowels and then released.

"What the fuck is wrong with you?" I backed away on my ass, skittering across the floor like a trapped bug until I hit a wall I couldn't climb. "What do you want? What did I do to you?"

"You're a big-mouth broad who thinks she runs this station because the chief lets you suck his dick. You're no better than the whores we pick up every night in Olneyville, but the chief's letting you—his private whore—have the run of the Providence police force *and we're staging a coup.*"

"You've got to be nuts. I'm an AAG. The chief's going to—"

He kicked my feet closer to the wall. "He's doing nothing, because like I said, he's guilty of adultery and so are you. See, I did my legal research. Just because you're not married doesn't mean it's not adultery for you too. What do you think the press will do with the information? Piganno will give you the needle faster than a rabid dog."

"What do you want from me? It can't be rape, because I have a *skinny ass.* And you're too afraid to let me suck your little lollipops, because you know I'll chew them off. So what do you want?"

Kent looked at his partner and shrugged. "Nothing. I don't want shit from you, bitch. I just want you to know we're all sick of it. We want you to know that next time you walk in this station, you'd better say 'please' and 'thank you' real nice to all my brethren. You think you can do that? Be nice?"

"Yeah. Sure," I said. "I can do that. And I'm *real* sorry if I ever offended you. *Real* sorry."

"That's real nice. *Real* nice."

They yanked me up by both arms and dragged me on the floor to the door, where the partner opened the door as lookout and Kent pulled me to my feet and escorted me back to the cell. It was now about eleven at night and the place was quiet. O'Rourke must have left for the night. Chucky had never returned to the station.

Sometime after 3 a.m. I fell asleep on the cement floor next to the steel bench to which they'd handcuffed me.

15

OUT, OUT,
DAMNED SPOT

"HOLY SHIT, SHE *IS* STILL HERE."

I awoke to the rancid smell of a dirty cement floor and opened my eyes to Laurie's voice. Before I could look up, Chucky was unlocking my cuffs and Laurie was lifting my head from the floor. It was just now pounding from the injury I'd received the day before on Boardman's boat.

"Who did this to you, Shannon?" Laurie asked as she inspected the back of my head.

Chucky removed the cuffs and helped me sit up. "O'Rourke said he left you in a room to wait for Kendall. Who put you in a cell?"

"I don't know," I lied. "I must have passed out. Am I free to go?"

Laurie helped me to my unsteady feet and I saw O'Rourke standing outside the cell. He looked at us in terror, obviously fearing he would get the blame for losing me in the police station all night.

"Not your fault, O'Rourke," I said. "Mine. All mine."

Laurie and I hobbled slowly from the cell. Chucky stood off to the side with O'Rourke, grinding his jaw. "This wasn't Kent, was it? Or one of the guys who brought you in?"

I shook my head and lied, "I didn't recognize him, Chief. I don't know who it was."

"Well, you're going through photos of every goddamn one of my men and you'll pick him out. You're gonna tell me who did this to you, Shannon. You hear me? No one on my watch is going to get away with this shit."

I nodded to him. "Not now. Neither one of us needs any more trouble right now."

"Do you need a hospital?" Laurie asked.

I snickered. Marianna or Beth would have tried to presume control and order me to the nearest ER. Laurie was smart enough to ask first.

"Let's go to the office." A second later, I remembered I was a prisoner. I looked back at Chucky. "I *am* free to go, right?"

"Get out of here," he said.

"Shit," Laurie said. "I've never seen your eyes this wide." Walking me straight again, she said, "Kendall said he got you released last night. We didn't know you'd been here all night until nobody heard from you this morning."

Laurie drove us to the office, where, despite the fact that it was Saturday, Vince was waiting for us. Pacing his windows, biting his lip, and smoking his favorite bad habit. If I was expecting a fusillade of reprimand from him, he surprised me by being real succinct when Laurie and I entered his office.

In a quick five-minute monologue that neither Laurie nor I dared to interrupt, he stated our new marching orders: Not one of us was considered unbiased enough to handle the case, so Vince was taking it over himself; I'd single-handedly soiled all the laundry at the AG's office in a high-profile murder case; and I'd just slimly missed automatic termination, which was only on hold pending further fuckups.

"So," Pig summated, "if I find out that you've seen Boardman *once more* during this investigation, you're fired. If you go near, speak to, or even wave to any of the witnesses in this case, you're fired. If a scintilla of evidence surfaces connecting you to the murder yesterday on his boat, you're fired. If you breathe a syllable of back talk to me over this, you're fired. Now you and your girlfriends may return quietly to your backlog of *other* cases and shut your mouths until this thing is over."

No sooner was I locked away in my office than Scott Boardman rang me up on my cell from his hospital room. We had entered a new stage in our ever-bonding relationship: We were now potential suspects in two different murder investigations. He was getting released from the hospital the next day and wanted to confer with me and—of all freaking people—Brooke Stanford.

"Nope," I said.

Like Vince, I, too, could be succinct, leaving little room for argument.

"Shannon, Leo Safer was a friend of mine. Someone shot him and tried to kill me and maybe even you. That same someone's threatening both our careers, not to mention our freedom, and our lives. We need to work together on this."

"Call your lawyer. I think you dragged me into your nightmare on purpose to screw up the investigation into your wife's murder. I'm out. I've got my own hide to save."

Indeed, in a matter of a week I was a murder suspect; a base contingent of Providence cops had communicated a resentment for me I never knew existed; I was on the verge of alienating my girlfriends—the only family I'd ever had—by threatening their jobs as well as my own; and I was still on the phone with the guy who'd caused it all. Why was I still holding the receiver against my ear? Why did I let him soothe me with his smooth voice and the velvet memory of his skin against my face?

"Please don't leave me now, Shannon. I swear to you I'm innocent. I swear I would never do anything to hurt you. How can I convince you?

"Stop lying."

"Okay. Okay. But I haven't been lying, just not telling the whole truth."

"Leading me down the wrong path is worse than giving me nothing. And since my gut instincts aren't strewn with rose petals, I'd rather go on my own with this."

"I promise on my poor wife's soul."

"If you killed her, what's it worth?"

"She's the mother of my kids."

"That didn't stop O.J. from killing the mother of his kids and then leaving her body where they'd find her in the morning when they went looking for their Frosted Flakes."

"They're releasing me tomorrow. Come to the Biltmore at five. Please? One more chance."

"No sex and no Brooke Stanford."

"But you have to hear about her. She's part of this."

I clicked my cell phone closed and dialed up Mike McCoy. Mike and I would never be friends if it weren't for Marianna. He and I were like two bears always fighting for the same cave. But after some quick math I realized my choices were limited. The girls were so concerned with protecting me that they were denying the bigger picture of saving their own careers. So I left them out and called Mike, agreeing to meet him at the Providence Public Library because neither one of us read books and no one would recognize us. We walked in like concerned parents, smiling at the older woman behind the circulation desk, to whom I offered a quick salutation and comment about summer reading lists, and Mike and I proceeded to the far corner behind a tall book stack. I sank to the floor and sat cross-legged while he pulled a chair from a table.

He looked at me without words. Blank, noncommittal. Marianna wouldn't be happy about our clandestine meeting.

"Mike, as much as I hate to admit this—"

"You need help," he finished.

I nodded. "You don't trust him."

"Boardman's like a guy with HIV. Just because he's nice doesn't mean you take chances."

"I need an emotional condom. Why am I being so stupid with this?"

He shrugged. "Your friends think you're having a breakdown."

"I feel something strong drawing me in, drawing me to him."

As soon as I said it I wished I hadn't. I was making girl noises again. And I knew—especially with someone like Mike McCoy—I wasn't going to convince him of anything if I sounded like a flower child from the Age of Aquarius.

I shook my head hard to erase my last statement from his mind. "Okay, so it's not metaphysical. I just believe him. I don't think he killed the wife. I think he was having an affair with Brooke Stanford. Shit, maybe he still is. She's hot and right up his social alley. But that's not important. I've always been able to share." I took a deep breath as both our minds conjured Marjory Sewell, with whom I'd been sharing Chucky for years. "It's just that I believe him and—"

"So what?" Mike said, sticking his chin out at me. "So you believe he didn't kill two women. So the fuck what? Doesn't mean you have to go down for the count trying to prove it. If he's innocent, let Vince and the cops deal with it. You want to sleep with him, be my guest. Just get your ass out of his bed in the morning and go to work."

"Jesus, Mike, I went on a boat with him for a day. Who the hell knew—"

"That's my point. Slink in his back door at night and out the front in the morning, but don't go with him *in public*."

"In hindsight, the boat trip *was* silly."

"*Silly?* Two men were shot, and you were the one holding the gun. That's quite a minimization of twenty-five-to-life. You keep this up, your friends are going to do an intervention."

"Okay, that's not why I called. I need your help. Was Brooke Stanford with him the night his wife was murdered? Did he go on that boat alone when his wife was shot? And does Virginia Booth know more than she's saying? There's something going on with trust assets—money. Can't you scare her into telling you what she knows?"

"Those kind of people go to the gallows tight-lipped. But I'll see what I can do."

SUNDAY NIGHT, SCOTT CALLED ME AGAIN TO confirm he was out of the hospital and back in his hotel suite. Heeding McCoy's advice, I waited until after dark and drove to the Biltmore, snuck in the door and up the back stairway, and fully expected to slink back out before daybreak. Scott had not, however, heeded my warning about Brooke Stanford, because there she was, answering Scott's door like a well-seasoned mistress—or a soon-to-be second wife. I was tired of acting like an emotional female, so I took it like a man.

"Hey there, Stanford. We doing a threesome tonight?"

She emitted a short gust of air from her windpipe as Scott sailed in from the bedroom, freshly showered and toweled from the waist down. A white gauze bandage was wrapped around his shoulder and up under his arm.

"Cut the Hugh Hefner routine, Boardman," I said, "and go put some clothes on."

He feigned surprise. "I didn't think you'd really come."

"What about Brooke here? Did you think she'd come? Or has she already?"

The sound that came from Brooke was a bit more vocal this time. Like a screeching cat in heat. "I won't put up with this, Scott," she said, as she plopped herself on a couch.

"Give me a minute," Scott said to us both, and ambled back into the bedroom to cover his ass.

I snickered as I moved in closer and sat across from Brooke on the matching couch.

She crossed her long legs and sat back. Today she wore slacks, crisp white linen. A yellow-striped polo and navy blazer completed the look of the perfect sailing companion. I had to wonder whether she dressed that way to subtly point out to me that she, in fact, should have been Scott's sailing companion on the day of the shootings.

But then again, maybe she was. "Shoot anyone lately?" I asked her.

"I could call Mr. Piganno right now and you'll be fired by morning," she said.

"And I'll call Chucky Sewell right now and you'll be in jail by midnight."

"For what?" she snapped.

"They'll lock you up till morning—or until they realize it's not against the law to be dull, bland, and wholly without character."

Little did Brooke Stanford know that if I placed a call to the Providence cops and told them I was with Scott Boardman in his hotel room, I'd be hauled in for questioning long before she would.

"I won't bother asking you anything, Brooke, because from what I've seen you're a pathological liar for whom the truth is a disease of the lower class."

She did a little jump on the couch, her body poised for counterattack, but her mouth was so tightly barbed she couldn't even spit.

So I kept going at her. "Like your compadre Virginia Booth. She thinks the truth is dirty too. But maybe that's just because the truth, as you and she know it, is a filthy lie."

Brooke's heart-shaped jaw undulated, her chest pumped in anger, and Scott walked in dressed in Yale-emblemed sweats with a smile blazing across his shiny clean face. "Anyone for a cocktail?"

Brooke popped up and walked to him. "I have to leave."

She stood by his side and turned to me. I looked at them both and wondered how I'd managed to be cast in this political melodrama. Scott whispered something into Brooke's ear and she dutifully resumed her seat on the couch facing me. Resigned and chastened, she tilted her head to her shoulder at such a steep angle I was afraid her dunce cap would fall off.

Scott, meanwhile, was at the minibar, pouring himself a gilded glass of amber liquid. He positioned himself before one of the faux colonial wood fireplaces of his fifteen-hundred-dollar-a-night instant drawing room, where he appeared ready to give a speech. Would it be his version of "I Have a Dream" that we all could tumble into the next room and have a threesome on his big comfy king bed, or a Nixonesque resignation due to murder, wherein the world wouldn't have Scott Boardman "to kick around anymore"?

"Shannon, Brooke," he began, "both of you in your own special ways have been trying to help me out of an unfortunate jam—"

I stood up for air. "Cut to the chase, Scott. I don't have any *special* ways and you're in the thick of much more than a jam." I forced a burp.

"Shannon, forgive my clumsiness. I've been taught how to speak to many people at once. It's inevitable that someone's sensibilities will be compromised when you speak to the masses."

"The masses?"

He placed his glass on the mantel. "I apologize again. But I think you both needed to hear it from each other's mouth and not just coming from me. So let me just get right to the heart of this." He looked at Brooke. "You did not accompany me from Connecticut that Friday afternoon, Brooke. I was alone in my car. We had drinks in the afternoon, but I was alone when I boarded the boat and found my wife dead." He looked at me now. "Brooke concocted the story to help me when she saw me with you at Al Forno and heard about the murders the next morning. She even tried to convince me that we were together, but I wasn't that drunk or drugged. She simply wasn't there and I have no alibi."

Brooke was staring straight ahead. Her dunce cap had disappeared and she was now sporting an aura of haughtiness, refusing to speak because she would only tacitly acquiesce to Scott's words. She had, after all, sworn out a statement in a police report that she would now be forced to recant. She obviously disagreed with Scott's decision to out her as a perjurer. Her career at the AG's office had been short and sweet, and with a perjured police statement, it was now as washed up as the Dead Sea.

We both let Scott continue his one-man show that so far had only me as an audience. Brooke, I think, had heard this all before in dress rehearsal.

Scott took his drink and joined Brooke on the couch, but his attention was riveted to me. "But I don't need an alibi to swear that I'm innocent. The night I met you at the restaurant, I was still under the influence of pills and booze. I thought—I'd almost convinced myself—that I could have done it. But then I came to my senses. Where was the blood if I'd killed two women—especially considering the violent manner in which they were . . . in which they died. How could I have done that and not be bathed in blood myself?"

Time to raise my hand. "Perhaps you washed it off in one of Mrs. Booth's several bathrooms. Which is why I saw only the faintest bit of blood under your fingernails at the bar at Al Forno. You scrubbed and scrubbed until only the blood trapped under your nails—"

He slammed the scotch down on the coffee table so forcefully that it sloshed from the glass and onto the fresh crease in Brooke's linen slacks. She stood and moved away toward the window.

"Who told you that?" He hammered out his words as if each one could stand alone outside the confines of its lowly sentence. "That is simply not true."

"What part? Virginia Booth's house after the murders?

Her bathroom? The scrubbing? Or the blood under your nails?"

"I checked both women to make sure there was no reason to call 911—to make sure there was no hope for either. So yes, I got blood on my hands. And then I went to Virginia Booth's house. I felt I should be the one to tell her about her daughter. I know what the press can do. She's an old woman—"

"But as strong as the oak and nails she's built from."

"And I was scared. I wanted to know if she knew anything...about the two of them...why had I not known that my own wife was gay—"

"You didn't know? You mean you were cheating on your wife with *her*"—I nodded toward Brooke—"and you didn't know? I thought maybe there was an arrangement. Your wife had *her* girlfriends and you had *yours*."

"Our conjugal life ended a long time ago. Our arrangement was that we would stay together for the sake of the children and my career. But I had no idea she was gay. I assumed she had just lost interest in sex, the way so many married women do."

"Women don't lose interest in sex after marriage. They just no longer need it for bartering purposes."

"Whatever her reasons...Pat knew about Brooke... and others before her." He looked at Brooke, who was reaching the point where she would soon lose composure. Whether it was because Scott Boardman was just now telling her he had no more interest in her than his last orgasm, or that he was saying it in front of me, I don't know. But I think if Brooke had had a gun, she'd have shot Scott Boardman. And possibly me too. Which made me go one step further.

"Did *you* do it, Brooke? Maybe you killed his wife to get her out of your way."

"Pat wasn't a threat to me," she said with a flick of her head. "She was a lesbian."

"But she was still his wife—and you weren't. And couldn't be until she was out of the picture."

She looked at Scott. "Eliminating Pat wouldn't have made me her successor. Scott's all done with me. He was done with me before that night." She looked at Scott with imaginary daggers she may have wished were real. "Am I done now, *sir*? Am I dismissed? Because you're obviously done with me."

He got up, walked to her, and took her small hands in his. "I'll help you with the false statement problem. It won't look good for me, but I feel responsible..."

Brooke hesitated for the merest moment, perhaps weighing words better left unsaid. She walked slowly to the door, opened it, and slid out like an agile cat. I looked back at Scott.

"For one guy you can do a lot of damage."

"I didn't invent the wind. I'm not responsible for storms."

"Or good metaphors."

He resumed his seat on the couch across from me. "I respect you, Shannon. You see something you want, you go after it. And if you screw up, you don't blame the whole damn world for it and then try to eke guilt from others."

Presumptuous but keen observation.

He leaned over his glass as if it held the prophetic grounds of Greek coffee. "You're like a man that way. You move on. Men don't waste time allocating guilt."

"Are we talking about guilt over Brooke or guilt over killing your wife?"

"I'm talking about Brooke. I'm talking about my wife. I'm talking about women and why they'll never rule the world. They get bogged down in emotion."

Scott Boardman was making Vince Piganno noises but without the chest-beating.

"What do you want from me, Scott? I mean besides sex—which you don't really need from *me*, since you seem to be shooting women away like ducks at a carnival."

He squinted at me suspiciously. But with no answer from my empty stare, he flopped back against the cushions and closed his eyes. His hands brushed once through his hair and then he laid them by his sides. "I'm tired. I think I have to stop for a while. Stop being what everyone else expects of me." He kept his eyes closed a second or two longer and then opened them to my silence. "And I'd like to start by being honest with you."

"Tell me about the money."

His jaw jutted forward. "You mean that silly trust. I don't need Virginia Booth's money."

"How much money are we talking about?"

He shrugged.

"I'm assuming it's billions, and 'silly' and 'billions of dollars' just don't belong in the same sentence as far as I'm concerned. What will Virginia Booth say *under oath* about the events that occurred on the night your wife was found murdered on the Booths' boat?"

He didn't even raise a brow over my legally framed question. He was probably surprised I'd waited so long to treat him like the murder suspect he was.

"Virginia Booth thinks that I'm a mediocre father and a worse husband. She thinks I've misled Brooke and countless women before her. She will try to make everyone believe I murdered my wife and her daughter. But she won't say any of this because private grief is preferable to public revenge."

"What *specifically* will she say about your visit to her house that evening?"

"I went to her house after. I told her what I'd found on the boat. And then I collapsed in one of the bedrooms—don't know how long—and then I just up and left and drove to Providence."

"Why did she lie? She said you used a bathroom and left immediately."

He rubbed his eyes like they were some magic lamp from which the truth would materialize. "I used a bathroom and then collapsed in a bedroom. She wasn't around when I left."

"And why would she clean the bathrooms to protect you, if she wants the world to think you're guilty?"

"Virginia Booth's house is cleaned daily top to bottom by an army of live-in maids. It wouldn't even occur to her that a room might hold evidence. She doesn't exist in that world."

"Don't be so sure of that. Her daughter and your wife—both murdered—and neither of you called the police. Neither of you thought to dial 911? What am I missing here?"

"Haven't you ever done anything wrong that you avoided for a while and hoped it went away?"

And then, of course, I remembered the year before, when the four of us girls had been drinking and cavorting in downtown Providence. We witnessed the aftermath of a bloody murder and then we'd taken off. We didn't dial 911 either.

"I think Virginia and I were both stalling," he said. "The entire episode would be aired in the press and our private lives telecast like some reality-TV show. And then my campaign…but of course that was over at the first gunshot."

"And what about Jake Weller? He insists you called him that night and spoke with him. You told me when you called him from my bathroom you couldn't reach him. Who's lying?"

"I'm not going to say he's lying. I had spoken to him earlier. I called him from your place because we were supposed to meet, but I never got him. But leave him out of this. Jake Weller couldn't step on an ant without having sleepless nights over it."

"Who did it then, and why? The physical evidence may be lacking against you, but motive-wise you should be strapped to the chair and lit up like Times Square. Just like Jake Weller says. You *look* guilty as sin."

He smiled. "He actually said that?" He nodded. "Jake's a smart guy but he's always been a scared little man. The press people love his self-effacing ways, but I'm not surprised he'd be quick to cut and run." He looked away from me. "Has he given some kind of formal statement?"

"Who did it, Scott? I got a feeling you know."

"My suspicions haunt me. I would be convinced it was Brooke, but I can't see how she did it and then drove to Al Forno for a wine spritzer." He smiled. "*Your* hide may be steeled enough for such a cold act, but not Brooke's. She'd panic when she saw all the blood, the screaming…well…I assume there was screaming…and then the eerie silence. I never realized how strong the smell of blood is. That was my first reaction when I boarded the boat. The smell. Salty and chemical."

"Don't underestimate Brooke—or anyone else. Murder is a special act. A *private* act. And like most private acts, it's done behind closed doors, hopefully with no one watching. And no one knows what any of us does in the privacy of our secret rooms."

"What about Muffie? It did, after all, happen on her boat. Couldn't she have been the target and my wife collateral damage?"

"Her ex-husband?"

"He's in Ecuador at a polo match."

"No way."

His expression serious and quizzical, he said, "Well, I guess it *could* be Peru…I know he was in the Galapagos—"

"Forget it, Scott. If you've got nothing new to say, I have to go."

"Now? You have to leave *now*?"

"While I still have a job."

"What about Leo Safer? Is someone going to try to shoot me again? Why isn't anyone worried about *my* safety?"

"Because the cops think you're dirty. When you come

clean, they'll protect you. Otherwise they'll treat you like a mobster who has a contract out on his life. You made your bed with thieves, so they'll let you lie in it."

He followed me halfway to the door, where I stood not looking back.

"Wait," he said.

He held me with electric gray eyes and a rueful grimace in his twisted smile. A child who'd spilled milk, standing contrite, asking for his mother's love with the certainty of knowing it was there and always would be. "Don't leave me now, please."

"I'll call you," I said, and walked through the door without looking back. I was certain I would never call him. Confident I'd finally broken the spell between us. The flame had been lit but I had the willpower to simply never call him again.

I reached the lobby and pushed the revolving door to the street side, listening as it whooshed behind me—and twirled me back in.

WHEN I RETURNED TO SCOTT'S ROOM, THE DOOR was still ajar. He was standing just inside, had retrieved his scotch, and was sipping it as he leaned against the wall—waiting for me. He didn't say anything when I slipped back in and stood with my back up against the door, pushing it closed with my foot. I expected him to smile, self-satisfied and cocksure. But he didn't. He stood quietly looking at me as if I'd never really intended to leave, he'd never expected me to return, but was happy I had. Without more than a handful of words, we decided to do something normal—like have a quiet dinner—instead of falling into bed and screwing our brains out. Scott donned a Patriots baseball hat and pulled it low on his head. With his baggy sweats and tattered sneakers, he looked younger, less sure of himself, more ready to trip over the untied laces of his suddenly messy life. We took back alleys and side streets until we stumbled upon a restaurant I'd not been to in years—a romantic French place with formal dining upstairs and a windowless bistro in the basement, to which we descended without discussion.

The downstairs bar at Pot au Feu was a cranky old wood structure surrounded by hundred-year-old stone walls. We sat. Ordered onion soup. But it wasn't until our second beer that Scott started talking.

"Funny how I'm not sad that all this happened. It probably makes me look guilty, but I'm glad in a way. If losing everything got me where I am right now, it's not such a bad thing."

"Your wife is dead, Scott. What are you saying?"

"I don't mean that. I mean my career and the politics. I'm not really sure I wanted to keep going. I felt as if I was on the crest of a wave and if I stopped, I'd drown. I had to keep riding it."

"So it crashed to shore and you fell off."

He nodded into his beer. "And I'm not sorry." He looked up into my eyes. "Do you believe at least *that*?"

"I believe people are either good or bad. Black or white. And I think whatever you were as a child you'll be at death. People don't change. So my question is, which are you?"

"What color is a coward?"

I laughed softly. "Black in my book."

He nodded. "I agree. So I guess I'm a bad person." He found my hand where I had it tucked in my pocket, rolling my little silver cell phone around like a giant worry bead. He pulled my hand out and held it open on the bar. "But you're not a coward, Shannon. That's one of the things I love about you."

"Love?"

"Okay, *admire.* You're right, 'love' is a little ambitious at this juncture." He pulled his hand out of mine and brushed it through his hair. "I could go to jail over all this. Even if I'm innocent."

"Make a deal—a plea bargain—and you'll be out in no time."

He didn't look at me right away. He waited. Picked up his beer and took the last swig. Put the glass down on the bar. And still staring at the liquor bottles on the wall facing us, he nodded. "How long? If I admitted to killing my wife, how long would I be locked up for?"

I played the game with him because I believed we were playing. Scott had already confessed once, he wasn't going to do it again. I shrugged. "Maybe ten years. Maybe less if we can find mitigating circumstances."

"When I got there, Pat drew a gun from the bedside table drawer. She pointed it at me. When I tried to yank it from her hand, it went off." He was still talking to the wall. "How's that sound?"

"Not bad. But there were two bodies, remember. How did they both die from your one gunshot?"

"Pat killed Muffie before I got there. When I arrived,

Pat tried to shoot me, and in struggling to take the gun away, I shot her by accident."

He glanced away from me. A thought remembered? Or a self-defense plea discarded? He was tired. His eyes blinked slowly open, closed, and then open again as he looked at me full-face. "But that's all a lie," he said. "That's not what happened."

Scott paid the check. He took my hand as we walked down the street together, bringing my fingers up to his mouth and kissing them lightly at every corner, where we looked both ways and continued on to the Biltmore, where he wanted me to come upstairs with him. I refused, not for any of the silly reasons, like playing hard to get, or pretending I didn't want to, or suddenly becoming the scrupled girl-next-door, but because I was suddenly afraid of Scott Boardman. Suddenly suspected there really was something in the man that was life-threatening, like he was standing next to a dark hole of mystery I was afraid of tumbling into.

So I sent Scott Boardman up to his suite alone—by the back staircase—and I went to find my car, parked on a side street a few blocks away. I was sorry I'd dispatched Chief Chucky with such little forethought. His would be the perfect arms to fall into and wind around myself to keep me from hotfooting it back to Scott Boardman. But alas, I'd unceremoniously sent Chucky to the benches to sit this one out, so resisting Scott Boardman was something I had to do alone.

16

A FEW LAUGHS

HAVING SPENT THE WEEKEND BY MYSELF, I strutted into my office Monday morning with new resolve, until I got to the threshold of my office door and heard Marianna on my phone. She was sitting at my desk, facing away toward the window, her feet balanced on the trash can.

"That brown shirt and orange print tie? You look like a used-car hawker from Seekonk. Pink shirt, navy blazer… *Yes*, you can wear pink. Don't get homophobic on me, Mike."

I remained just outside the door, eavesdropping on a civilized conversation between two people in a normal relationship. Or at least as normal as a relationship can be between a hypochondriac depressive (Marianna) and a sliver-brained NASCAR enthusiast (Mike). But they sure as hell didn't sound like Scott and me—so far our love spats had revolved around bloody fingernails, who murdered whom, with what weapon, and whether Brooke

Stanford, his unscrewed ex-lover, drove the getaway car. Compared to my relationship with Scott Boardman, the ex-triangle between Chucky, Marjory, and me was beginning to feel like a heartland romance.

Marianna's next words woke me from a rare moment of self-reflection: "Shannon's cracking up. All the years I've known her I never even suspected she was capable of such emotional gaffes.... *Me?* Oh, fuck you, Mike. 'Hot-tempered Italian' my ass. That's such stereotypical bullshit...."

They talked a few more minutes and I listened to the denouement of their love-tangled pas de deux. As Marianna was saying good-bye I revved myself up and walked briskly in, pretending to be slightly out of breath.

"Hey there, Mar, what's cookin'?"

"Your goose, you ass. Where the hell have you been?" She swirled front and forward and popped out of my chair.

"I'm all done with Boardman," I answered. "At least bedroom-wise."

"It's about time," Laurie said, appearing in the doorway. Beth snuck by Laurie and nabbed a seat in front of my desk. "I told you, Mari, if we left her alone, she'd come to her senses."

I was standing by my windows looking at the crew who had appeared in my office as if rappelled in on a military mission: Marianna, standing sentried just behind my desk; Laurie, guarding the doorway; and Beth, seated comfortably in a chair as if waiting for her next undercover assignment. "I hate it when you all think you can read my mind and predict my moves." I looked around at my crowding office. "I need a vacation from this. Just butt out, all of you."

Marianna came around from my desk and faced me. "We can only read the *same freakin' mind* you had last week and the week before, but if it's this *new* mental state you're fogged up in, I'm not so sure that even *you* can predict what you'll do next."

I ignored her and sashayed behind my desk, plopping into the seat that was still warm from Marianna's zaftig ass.

Marianna considered me a minute before speaking. "Jeff called me this morning."

I threw my bag to the floor. "To gloat? The Cohen case sucked from the start. It was a giveaway. What does he want now?"

"He wanted to meet me about Brooke Stanford." Just at that moment Marianna decided to check out her manicure, counting her fingers like maybe she forgot how many she had or something. "But if you want us all to butt out, I guess we can move this meeting to my office."

I began grinding my jaw. "Mar, those ten fingers you're busy counting will be nine or less if you don't start talking."

"Jeff knew Boardman got Brooke the job here. He thinks she and Boardman are still concocting stories—"

"Bullshit. And you know why it's bullshit? Because Jeff wouldn't tell us that even if it were true. Jeff hopes this whole office blows up in a conflagration of incompetence. He can't wait for us all to fuck up. And you're the *last* person he'd call with inside info. He wants *you* to be the fuse that detonates us."

"Right," Marianna said. "I know that, *sweetie*. So I'm reading between the lines here. Which is what you'd be doing if you weren't brain-damaged by recent events."

"You know what, Marianna? You can't break my heart, so fuck you."

"I wouldn't even attempt to slum in the dark chambers of your heart—assuming you had one. It's your brain that's on the blink anyway. It started with the Cohen case. Sure, it was a shit case with no evidence, but in the past you could have been in a coma and won a case against Jeff Kendall. Something about that case knocked you for a loop."

"I'm burned-out—"

"We're all burned-out, Shannon," Laurie said, taking the seat next to Beth. "Go cry it on the mountain and then climb back down to reality."

The chair springs screamed as I flopped back. "The truth is, I thought the Cohen woman shot herself. I didn't think the husband did it."

Marianna, who had been standing by the window, suddenly bolted forward and slammed her fist on my desk in front of me. "See! That's what I mean. In the past you would have told Vince to pass the case off to Laurie or me. Or, failing that, you would have tried to convince Vince to drop the charges. If you thought Cohen was innocent, you shouldn't have taken the case. Falling into Boardman's arms is a symptom, not a cause. You were on a downward spiral before Boardman twirled you in his arms."

I kept my eyes to the ceiling, attempting introspection. Failing that, I was watching a spider who seemed to be watching us back. Marianna interpreted my silence as acquiescence and I had no particular interest in bursting her bubble, or worse, revving her back up into another sermon. I won the stare-down with the spider and he toddled off to his corner web. When I lowered my glance to Marianna, she was still nodding her self-righteous head, waiting for my response.

"You really aren't done with Boardman, are you?" Beth said.

She had a quiet way of interjecting herself into our high-voltage meetings. She spoke softly, almost as if she were thinking out loud.

I gently pushed Marianna's face away and sat up. "Huh?"

Laurie was nodding her head. "Your normally gutter-focused head is still floating around like a helium-filled balloon."

"Midlife crisis?" Mari suggested.

"Too young," Laurie answered.

"Late-onset autism?" Beth said, safely following their lead.

"Too old," Mari said.

"My mother?" I said.

Silence.

"Yeah, it's like a nightmare that I keep thinking about all day. Except there was never any nightmare. I've been thinking about my mother. And I don't know why."

"What's that got to do with Scott Boardman?" Beth asked Laurie, still too timid to question me directly.

"Not a freaking thing, Beth," I answered. "Boardman's in my blood and I can't sucker him out. I think it's one of those things that has to melt down like a candle at its end." I looked back up at the ceiling for my spider. He was still there in his little web of a house. "But you're right. I'm not done with him yet."

"So what should *we* be doing about that?" Beth finally looked me in the eyes.

"I'm not your fourth Musketeer. I can take care of myself."

"Listen up, Shorty," Laurie said. "We can *all* take care of ourselves. We're lawyers and prosecutors to boot." She patted Beth on the back to assure her that her day at the legal bar would be arriving soon. "But isn't it better when you have help?" Laurie's chin was pointing at me. "A few laughs along the way?"

"I haven't heard any good jokes from any of you lately. All I'm hearing is bleak Armageddon scenarios." I leaned forward in my chair again. "Maybe if I find out who killed his wife...I can blow his fucking candle out once and for all."

Marianna nodded. "That's what Mike has been saying all along, but you aren't listening."

"Because Mike's convinced Boardman did it. But what if he's innocent, Mari? What if?"

Marianna lifted her index finger, signaling a request that I give her a few minutes to talk without biting her head off. "I was just talking to Mike about this. He thinks Jake Weller's the way to go. Think about it. Weller came of his own free will to talk to Chief Sewell. What did he say? Can't you find out? Are you still talking nice to the chief?"

"I was there during their meeting. He fingered Boardman but with absolutely no evidence. He was babbling about tarot cards or some such shit."

"Tarot cards?" Beth squeaked.

"Or Ouija boards," I muttered. "Frankly, I think he's a red herring. I'm emotionally up shit's creek without a plunger. I don't know which way to go with this."

"Back to Newport?" Laurie suggested. "Let's try the Muffie Booth connection."

Marianna nodded. Laurie looked at me for approval.

"I like it," Beth said. "Can I come this time? That *is* kind of my territory."

"Yeah, let's take her, Shannon. But how do we get away without Vince missing half his office?" Marianna asked.

"We don't," I said. "You and Laurie stay here and work the cases. Keep fighting with the Pig to keep him occupied and out of my hair. Beth's with me. She and the Newport social crowd can share Yankee Doodle Dandy stories."

Beth cranked her head to the side and looked at Marianna for confirmation of the plan.

Marianna answered me in response to Beth's glare. "We'll be shish kebab on one skewer if Vince finds out what you're up to."

Beth was busy on her BlackBerry checking dates. "We could say we're going to the flower show. No, wait, that was the last weekend in June. How about the American Cancer Society Tuscan Twilight Ball at Rosecliff? That one's held at the end of July—closer to now. Or we *could* say it's the Newport Jazz Festival. That's past too, but I'm not sure Mr. Piganno keeps himself abreast of the latest Newport social events, so perhaps we needn't worry too much about exact dates. Verisimilitude in our lies to him should be sufficient."

I leaned over the table to her. "Why do you clog up your brain with the freaking Newport social schedule?"

"Technically, I don't clog my brain with it," Beth said calmly. "I mean, to me it's not mind-clogging. But then— of course—*I'm* not you."

I looked at Marianna and Laurie for an earthly translation of what she meant.

"I just know certain things by heart," Beth answered. "Like the Lord's Prayer. Don't you remember hearing it so often in church as a child that you had it memorized without any effort at all?"

I shook my head. Not because I didn't know the Lord's Prayer by heart, but because I was shocked at how— though I'd known her for six-plus years—Beth was sitting in front me like some subspecies from Planet Xenon.

"But," she segued without the slightest hesitation, "will Vince *fire* me if I get myself in trouble with you guys before I even get *hired* as an AAG?"

"Beth," I said, popping up from my chair and heading for my door, "break yourself out of automaton mode and wind yourself up. You'll have to learn that Vince Piganno—despite the fact that he has simian ancestors— is a smart man. There's a reason he hasn't fired us through all our years of bold-faced disobedience."

Beth's eyes opened wide and once again she looked

at Marianna and Laurie for verification of my hammered assessment of the Pig.

But Marianna's eyes were drilling through mine as we stood face to face. " 'Simian ancestors'?"

"He's Sicilian, isn't he?" I said.

"No, Shannon, he is not Sicilian. But I still resent that kind of comment coming from a *potato-eating Irish slug* who would still be in a cave if it weren't for the Romans who civilized—"

I waved Marianna's drivel away like a whiff of bad breath. "Beth," I said, "after some of the things we've done in this office—and gotten away with—Vince sometimes looks the other way. Mainly because—well, so far—we've managed to come out on top and he's the ultimate beneficiary."

"I guess so . . ." Beth said.

I whacked her so hard on the back that her headband slid forward over her eyes. "Saddle up."

Marianna was shaking her head. "The other thing Beth has to learn is how to deal with you on her own. You think it's easy dealing with you, Shannon? You're a steamroller with teeth."

"Mari?" Beth straightened her headband and looked at Mari with an expression something akin to nausea.

"She won't eat you, Beth, as long as you don't stand still too long." And with that, Marianna stood and moved past me out the door.

"I'll toughen your hide in two shakes of your little lamb's tail," I said to Beth.

Beth, still unsure, took a few deep breaths as if she were getting ready to make her first skydive from a speeding plane. "Maybe I should just finish the motion I was working on..."

I winked at Laurie as I spoke to Beth. "I'll meet you at the Suburban, kiddo. You have ten minutes." And then I walked out, not quite sure where we were going, but really sure that I couldn't sit around the office and do nothing while the trail to three murders was looming ahead of me and growing cold.

17

THE OMEN

ON MY WAY TO THE AG LOT, I SPIED CHUCKY "THE Chief" Sewell poking around my Suburban.

"You dusting for prints, sweetkins?" I hollered as I strode to him.

He backed up away from the passenger side window and waited for my arrival. The closer I got, the farther back he reared his head, as if we were two magnets approaching each other from the same pole.

"Where're you off to?" he asked.

Lying was a talent that required careful but impromptu planning. I looked at my watch. It was 10 a.m. "A snack," I said. "I'm waiting for Beth."

His eyes narrowed. "You and Beth? Alone?"

"Hey, why does everyone assume Beth isn't safe around me?"

"You aren't taking her to that Red Fez dive, are you? Health Department found rats there on more than one occasion."

"You're worried about me with a few little rats when the biggest one I've ever faced is standing right in front of me? Anyway, I heard the Fez got a cat, so we're all set." I inserted my key into the lock.

"Door's open," Chuck said. "You must have forgot to lock it."

I pulled open the door and stood for a minute, wondering why Chuck was alone. The chief of police always traveled with an entourage. And why was he hanging around the AG parking lot, and more specifically, *my car*?

"You looking for evidence of something?" I asked. "In my car? Stalking me? What's up with this?"

I heard him say something under his breath, talking to the ground, and then like a little kid, he kicked a stone across the lot and looked up at me. "I wanted to apologize."

"Oh yeah?"

"I shouldn't have left you at the station like that. Alone. You know, the police station...it's like a boys' club and...well, there's jealousies. A lot of competition. And a lot of those guys are jealous of you...my relationship with you...well, you know...that you can burst into my office any damn time you want and get away with it. That kind of thing. They get pissed."

I didn't answer him. I was waiting to see if he knew the whole story of what went on that night. Waiting to see if he found out it was Patrolman Kent who kicked me around an interrogation room and then handcuffed me to a bench all night.

"So, what I'm saying is...I'm sorry, is all. I knew all this shit beforehand and I shouldn't have weaseled out on you. I should have been there for you. Regardless of what anyone else thought or said...I shoulda been there."

I gave him a minute to breathe, to decide whether he felt sufficiently cleansed. He was still kicking pebbles around the lot. When I still didn't answer him, he looked up at me for a response.

"No problem, Chuck," I finally said. "No worries. I understand. You just didn't want to make it worse by showing me favoritism as a prisoner. I got it right away. I knew why you'd taken off. Why you left as soon as you knew I was being brought in. I was a prisoner, after all. What would it have looked like if you'd run to my rescue? And I wasn't angry. Because I expected it. Actually, I should be *thanking* you. Yeah, thanking you for showing me your true nature. For showing me that when my *fucking* life is on the line, you'll protect your own back and let my ass swing out in the cold. It's something I always suspected, but it's nice to have it verified that very *special* way. You know...with a few kicks, sleeping on a filthy cement floor, and me almost being forced to *suck* some street cop's *dick* because you were afraid of creating...what'd you call it? *Jealousies* among your men."

Chuck's jaw was undulating so hard I thought he might crack his teeth if I went on for one more word. I almost heard the growl coming out of his throat before he actually spoke. His teeth were still clenched.

"God-fucking-dammit, Shannon. I find out who did this to you and he'll be out on his ass."

I hopped into my car as Beth approached from the end of the lot. Chuck turned his head in the direction I was staring and saw her too. I honked at her and slammed my door shut, thereby avoiding uncomfortable good-byes with Chuck. And I didn't bother looking back at him as I started my engine and drove toward Beth. I felt sorry for him and I hated him at the same time. But one thing I didn't feel was love. I may not have been over Scott Boardman yet, but I was definitely over Charles Sewell.

"What did he want?" Beth asked. She threw her bag in first, then pulled herself up into my Suburban like it was a wall she was trying to scale. "Wow, this is a big car. I don't think I've ever been in it before. We always take my car when we all go together."

"Because you're always the designated driver for the rest of us alcoholic losers."

She settled her small body into the large front bucket seat and fastened her seat belt. "So what did Chief Sewell want? Does he have any news on Boardman?"

"I fucking hate pricks, and if I could have my way I'd lop off the balls of every man I've ever dated."

Beth kept her stare straight out the front window. She seemed to be holding her breath, so I punched her in the side and she jumped and screeched simultaneously. It was kind of funny, so I laughed. "I'm only kidding, Bethster."

"Of course. Obviously I knew that." She turned to me and gave me a prim wooden smile. "So where are we off to?"

"Grandma's house."

"That's another joke, right? Because you could mean Virginia Booth's house, but technically she's not the *grandmother* of the deceased. Although she's probably *someone's* grandmother. But I don't necessarily think that she'll tell us much. It's very possible that Virginia Booth has consulted an attorney already and has been told to hold her tongue—"

" 'Hold her tongue'? What the fuck kind of legal term is that? You ever hear a defendant plead the Fifth by saying, 'Your honor, I *hold my tongue* on the ground that I might incriminate myself'? Jesus Christ, Beth. Grow the fuck up!"

"I'm sorry, I just don't want to sound like a know-it-all when I'm only a paralegal. I'm a little intimidated by you and—"

"Hey, Beth, isn't anyone in your family friendly with the Booths? I mean, don't your families travel in the same social circles?"

"Sure. Mother called yesterday and told me how upset Doogie is over Muffie's death."

I pulled the car over to the side of the road because I wasn't sure I could strangle Beth with one hand and still steer the car. *"Doogie?"*

"That's Virginia's nickname. Her maiden name is Douglas, so they always called her Doogie for short. Anyway, Mom says Doogie's been calling everyone, trying to ruin Scott Boardman's name around town. Well, he's a member of the New York Yacht Club, just down the road from her, you know, and we're members too, so Doogie's trying to get a petition going to get his membership repealed. Nasty business really. Mom wanted my opinion as to whether or not she should sign the damn thing. I say stay out of it. Especially because I work at the AG's office, the very office that would be prosecuting him, if we ever get enough evidence. I mean, how would it look if my own mother signed a petition that presumed his guilt? A real conflict, right? I'm hoping she took my advice. Should I call her?"

"Lesson number one. Never take your family to work. Remember what happened to Marianna's little sister last year? We leave your mother out of it. Now, good old Doogie must have a list of potential signees, no? A list of people she's calling to oust the senator?"

"Well, I assume it's her pals at the club. I can guess who they are. I have them all on my contacts list. I keep all kinds of stuff on my BlackBerry. You should get one."

I pulled the car back on the road and headed down 95 South and Route 4 toward the Jamestown and Newport bridges. If anyone could pry those tight-lipped lockjaws loose, it was Beth—if she would only shut her mouth long enough to let someone get a word in edgewise.

"I'm thinking Bootsie Bergen would be a good place to start," Beth said. "Bootsie's daughter Lolly was great friends with Muffie. I mean, they were older than me, but Lolly and Chip Chase, her husband, had this great lodge in Stratton where we'd all ski winter break, and I remember Muffie from then. I always thought she was a little mannish looking now that I think of it—"

"Why haven't you told us any of this?"

Beth thought a minute. "Well...isn't it Scott Boardman you're interested in? The Chases' ski lodge in Stratton is a leap, isn't it?"

"Honey, Muffie Booth was murdered too. And if Muffie and Pat Boardman had so tight a thing going on

that the Muff was transferring millions in assets to her ...
well, it seems like their little love trysts might have been
going on for a while. Someone has to know something."

"Right, I see. You're taking the whole thing from a different angle. Like Muffie was the target."

"Every angle, Beth. If there's nothing else you're going
to learn in law school this fall, it'll be that there can be
more than four angles to a box. The second most important thing you'll learn is that you need to *unlearn* the
terms *right* and *wrong*. The only side that's important is
the side you're on. I had a law professor in Torts. He
made each one of us take a case and then argue both
sides of it. Lesson being that *both sides are the right side.*
How you argue it just depends on which side of the
courtroom you happen to be sitting on."

I felt Beth looking at me and, from the corner of my
eye, saw her beaming smile.

"I always thought you just intimidated juries and
that's why you win so much in court. But you're every bit
as smart as Laurie. And Marianna's so pretty she doesn't
have to be that smart, but ... I mean ... Mari's smart too."

So it wasn't respect after all. Everyone just got out of
my way because I was as threatening as a Dumpster full
of crap. Did any of my friends take me seriously as a
lawyer? Maybe the Cohen case was an omen.

"Why," I asked Beth, "does everyone just *assume* Laurie
is smart and I'm not? Because she's Jewish? I'm a dumb
drunken Irishman and she's a descendant of Einstein?"

"Shannon, I thought we all made a pact not to trash
each other's ethnic backgrounds unless the trashee was
present."

"Shit!" I picked up my phone and dialed Laurie at the office. "Laur, I just made a Jewish slur. Not only do all Jews think they're brilliant, but apparently they've got the whole fucking world bamboozled too. So what do you have to say about that? Huh?"

"Scott Boardman's here," she whispered. "In with Vince now. He just walked in with his *brilliant* lawyer Ron Esterman—a Jew, I might add."

"Fuck you, Laurie."

"Anything with you and Beth yet?"

"We're working on friends of Muffie Booth. They all have purse-puppy names like Doogie and Bootsie and Lolly."

"Perfect," she said.

I wasn't sure whether she was talking about our leads in the case or the poodle names of the socialite set, but we agreed to keep each other posted and signed off.

"So," Beth prattled on, "Lolly lives in a condominium at Bonniecrest. She'd have been Muffie's closest friend— well, after Pat Boardman—but I guess technically Muffie and Pat Boardman weren't *just friends.* I should give Lolly a call first, though."

Beth made the call from the Newport Bridge, and fifteen minutes later we were in an apartment overlooking the same glass-green waves Marianna and I had seen from Virginia Booth's house. Beth had—on my suggestion—neglected to tell Lolly that she was being accompanied by a friend (as unlikely a pair as Beth and I were). We also agreed to keep Lolly ignorant of the fact that we were there on semi-but-unauthorized official AG business, so of course when Lolly Bergen saw the Mutt and

Jeff team of Beth and me standing on her doorstep, her smile was less enthusiastic than a woman of her manners should be when entertaining for tea.

"Be-eth?" she sang. "It's been ages. So awful about Muffie, huh?" Without a breath she looked at me. "Hi! I'm Lolly Bergen." She extended her cool white hand.

Lolly was Beth's height. Thin and wispy. Her palm green eyes made the brackish New England coastline look like swamp water. A few freckles dotted her cheeks and nose, and the waves of her strawberry blond hair were corralled tightly back in a ponytail at the nape of her neck. She wore those same Jack Rogers flats that Brooke had worn the fatal night at Al Forno, although Lolly's were apple green, and her short skirt was covered in pink and green seahorses.

I tried my best to be subdued, more to convince her that Beth and I were actually close friends than because I didn't want to offend her. These icy kinds of girls always act stiff and proper until you get a few glasses of white wine in them, then they pull out a pack of Marlboro Lights, order a martini, and fuck every guy who winks at them.

"Hi!" I gave her my paw. "Shannon Lynch. Nice place you have here."

"Oh yeah? Thanks. Chip and I bought it ages ago and Newport's suddenly hip again. Chip works in Boston and he stays there during the week. We have a condo there too. Can I get you two something to drink?"

Beth took Lolly by the hand to her kitchen as she spoke. "You know, when I heard about Muffie I wanted to call you immediately, but you know my job and the conflict and all. But I said, the hell with it. Lolly Bergen's been my friend forever and no job is more important than your friends, so I just decided to come right over and throw caution to the wind."

I rolled my eyes and followed the chatty little birds to a kitchen that looked as sterile and steeled as an operating room. It always bugged the crap out of me that rich people—who never have to cook—always have the high-end commercial-grade appliances.

I twirled myself into a counter stool and glanced over the sink through a triple bank of open windows to where the sea crashed and rolled, sending its sweet and salty smell into the room.

Beth without a word had gone to the cupboard and pulled down three long-stemmed glasses. "How about wine? What've you got open?"

Lolly pulled a bottle of Santa Margherita from the fridge. It was three-quarters full. She and Beth twittered catch-up gossip as they coordinated their efforts to pour us each a brimming glass, then they sat together at the white marble counter facing me. I snuck a look at my watch. Half past noon. Cocktail hour for unemployed socialites? But who was I to judge? How many scotch neat lunches had I imbibed at the Red Fez in the middle of the day in the middle of a trial?

Hoping Lolly would have enough alcohol in her system to spill her guts before she found out I was an AAG, I plunged quickly into discourse of the most inane kind.

"So, Lolly, you grew up around here, right? You guys are childhood friends?"

Lolly looked over at her old friend Beth. "Well, Bethy's

a bit younger. I'm between Muffie and Beth in age." Then she remembered Muffie. "Oh my God, poor Muffie. Imagine dying like that. I mean being *murdered*. Do you know how she died, Beth?"

Beth shrugged. "They don't tell me those things," she lied like a true professional. "I'm not a lawyer there yet, you know."

Lolly nodded. "A hate crime maybe? Because of... well, you know...their *thing* together. And I guess it was getting really serious. You heard about Doogie's lawsuit, right? To stop Muffie from transferring assets or something. I think that's what it's all about. Money. Isn't it *always*?"

Beth took a sip of wine. "Perhaps, Lolly, but I hope you aren't thinking Doogie could have murdered her own daughter?"

Lolly's eyes opened wide, bursting with information, but she had the good breeding to make Beth drag it out of her rather than just gossiping outright.

"Spill it, Lolly," Beth said, refilling Lolly's wineglass to the brim and then dashing a bit more in hers and mine in a good-faith show of camaraderie. I'd faked a few sips of mine because wine gave me an instant headache, but if it had been a nice single malt...

Lolly woke me from my dream. "Doogie and Muffie haven't gotten along since...well...practically since Muffie got her first *period*," Lolly said. "I think it was way back then that Muffie kind of knew...that she was different." Lolly took two hefty gulps of wine and stared at the back wall for her next revelation. "Muffie and I actually experimented once. She wanted me to touch her—"

"Okay! So wow, that's cool," I said, stopping the conversation dead. "So Muffie and her mom were, like, at odds since . . . well, for*ever*." I was proud of myself, starting to pick up the WASP jive, drawing out my words with imaginary syllables and fluffing up my sentences with superfluous words.

Lolly nodded deeply. "I mean, she married *just* to make the family happy, but she never had kids and they always traveled separately. The divorce was inevitable. I'm surprised it took so long to end it. But I think it was Pat who finally forced the issue . . . and now Pat and Muffie are both dead. I wonder what will happen to the money now that both Pat and Muffie are gone."

Beth's mouth dropped open as she looked to me for my legal opinion. I was shaking my head slowly, mixing up all the facts and trying a get a clean timeline of events. Trust and estate law wasn't exactly my area of expertise, but any second-year law student could have answered the question. "It depends on what stage the transfer was at," I said. "If Muffie had successfully completed the transfer to Pat before their deaths, then the lawsuit will go forward, and Virginia . . . ah . . . *Doogie* . . . will ask a court to void the transfer and all the assets would revert back to her. But if she doesn't prevail in the suit—if she loses and the court finds the transfer valid— Scott Boardman, through his dead wife's estate, will be a little bit richer."

"And," Beth finished, her eyes wide, "Scott Boardman just got another motive for murder."

18

OVER MY DEAD BODY

BETH AND LOLLY DOWNED THE REST OF THEIR
wine as Beth lulled Lolly into a dreamy discussion of the
latest Newport gossip, none of which netted any further
useful information. But Beth seemed thrilled to be back
in the loop. She was animated with Lolly in a way I'd
never seen her be with us, laughing, gesturing, and by
the time we were ready to go, she and Lolly were practically in each other's arms. I felt like an intruder. I took
my glass to the sink, signaling the end of cocktail hour,
and Beth and I extracted ourselves from Lolly's hungry
need for company.

She walked us to the elevator and we said our good-
byes, Beth and Lolly promising to keep in touch. Before
the elevator door closed, Beth was already making plans.
"Okey-dokey, smokey," she chirped. "Let's go for lunch.
The Cookhouse. I'm famished. And I don't want to go
back to Providence just yet. I love it here. The smell of
the ocean simply gets me high."

"That and sixteen ounces of wine on an empty stomach."

"So, the second-floor bartender at the Cookhouse knows everything about everyone in this town. And they have the best clam chowder on the planet."

Back in the car, Beth buckled herself in, and then suddenly popped up like a jack-in-the-box. "Ooh, let's go see Doogie first! I bet I can get information out of her!"

I started the engine of the Suburban and held off answering her until we were safely out of the lot. "She won't speak to me and I can't send you alone. You'll screw things up."

I expected Beth to be stung by my comment, but she laughed, giggled actually. She was still in hail-fellow-well-met mode, and I was the odd man out.

"Okay then, Kemo Sabe," she said. "On to the Cookhouse."

SETTLED AT A QUIET CORNER OF THE UPSTAIRS bar at the Cookhouse, I ordered us up some chowder and a couple more drinks—scotch and soda for me this time and another Pinot Grigio for Beth—while I tried to apologize for my comment to her in the car about screwing things up. Apologizing was not one of my strong suits—in fact I didn't remember the last time I'd done it. But I should have known Beth would rescue me from my rotten, ill-mannered self.

"You know, Shannon, we've all come to expect that from you—those snipes that are not really well thought

through. I mean, I'm not telling you to change or anything, but...well...it's like having a crutch. I think you
hide behind being brusque and mean-spirited so no one
will want to get too close to you. Because that's exactly
what happens when you lay those punches—people tend
to stay far enough away from you so that when you
throw your zingers it doesn't sting that badly. Does that
make any sense to you?"

"What if I *don't* want anyone that close to me?"

"Well, you can say that if you want, but I don't believe
it." She turned away from me. "I accept your apology
nonetheless."

I was ready to retract my apology when Jake Weller
strolled in and ordered a beer at the other end of the bar.
I moved out of view behind a support beam and kicked
Beth.

She turned to me. "Now what's wrong? Honest to
God, Shannon, you're impossible to figure out—"

"Shh," I whispered as I leaned farther out of sight. I
nodded my head toward Jake Weller, who was busy talking to the bartender. "That's Scott Boardman's press guy."

Beth remained safely anonymous as she pinned her
ear to his conversation, but then he stood abruptly and
walked over to us.

"Shannon Lynch, right?" He extended his hand to me.

I nodded, shook his, and introduced Beth, who
plunged right into conversation with him. "Do you live in
Newport?"

He shook his head. "I'm on my way back to campaign
headquarters in New Canaan. May I sit with you?"

Beth chirped, "Sure," and pulled her glass toward me to make room for his beer. I remained silent.

"I'm from here originally," Beth continued. "I live in Providence now, though, but I still know *everyone* in Newport. I just *so* love it here."

He smiled at her, and then winked, smooth and saccharine, but giving up nothing.

Beth fluttered her eyes and shook her hair in a dizzying rendition of the airhead female. "Sorry, didn't mean to pry," she sang. "And I talk way too much."

He smiled again and then looked over at me. "But this isn't *your* neck of the woods, is it, Miss Lynch?"

I smiled and winked back at him, giving him the same nothing he'd just given Beth.

Beth, on the other hand, chattered away, either knowing she was the buffer to Weller's and my impasse, or just being Beth, who I was now beginning to realize would talk incessantly once she was wound up and set loose.

"...because Scott Boardman, and, well, Pat too before she died, is a member of the NYYC, and I never remember seeing them there. Of course, I haven't been to the club in ages. Mother and Dad still sail but my work schedule is so crazy—"

"And you work with Miss Lynch? An AAG too?"

Beth raised her eyebrows apologetically. "Not yet, I'm afraid. I start law school in the fall."

Weller returned his attention to me. "I guess you think I'm a real jerk, talking the way I did about Scott in Chief Sewell's office? In hindsight, I'm sorry about that."

"You should be," I said. "Because you had nothing to offer, so, frankly, I question your motive."

He shook his head and looked down at his beer. "You girls are around death every day. Violent murders, rapes, mutilations. When I heard about Pat and her friend—brutally killed—you have no idea what effect that has on a middle-class guy like me. I panicked. Went to see the one friend I had in the police, Charles Sewell. I really didn't expect anyone else to be present. I wanted to get the thing off my chest, where it was sitting like bricks. I couldn't breathe."

"Boy, do I understand that," Beth said. "When I first went to work at the AG's office, I was freaked by the crime scene photos. It took me a while…and I still can't go to the morgue. Well, not that I'm required to…yet."

He smiled kind of sweetly now, his coyness gone. "I'm the public relations guy for a very powerful senator. I had a moment of weakness. And as I said, I thought our conversation would be private." He looked away out the window to where rows of yachts rocked at their moorings, their masts swaying like staffs of wheat in a field. "What can I say?" He looked back at Beth and me. "I apologize."

"Hey, no skin off my nose," I said. "Give Scott Boardman a holler and apologize to him."

"You and Scott have become…friends, I hear. He and I have already talked. Settled up. We'll see what happens in the coming days. I can't imagine this investigation will go on too much longer. God knows you must have folders full of evidence from that bloody boat. And you've probably taken fingerprints from everyone who is even remotely suspect, right?"

Jake Weller was smart enough to avoid Beth's and my

stares. Smart enough to throw the statement out but not look to us as if he were expecting an answer. Smart enough to know he wouldn't get any.

"We like surprises at the AG's office," I said. "We let no one know where the evidence is pointing until the handcuffs are ready to be snapped into place. Right, Beth?" I was still looking at Weller.

"Oh my God, yes," she answered. "Remember that college president the police rousted from bed at five in the morning? When he saw himself on the six o'clock news in pajamas and handcuffs, he had a heart attack in the jail cell." She explained to Weller. "He recovered in time for his trial, though, where Shannon sent him to prison for life. He shot his business partner and tried to make it look like a mob hit."

Either Beth had made that whole story up to scare Weller, or I was losing my mind, because I had no recollection of the case. But I was proud of her anyway. Beth was learning how to play with facts, arm them and load them up so they had the most impact. She was promising to make a nice addition to our prosecutorial team.

But then Weller surprised us by taking a different tack.

"I'd like to make amends," he said. "Help you in any way I can. The campaign is on hold indefinitely, so I'm free to sleuth with you. That is what you're doing here in Newport, right? You didn't come all this way for the clam chowder."

Beth pushed her cold unfinished bowl of chowder away and took a sip of her wine. She knew when she was out of her league—not quite ready for the majors.

I looked Jake Weller in the eyes like I was studying a map and making a quick decision which road to take before I passed them both and lost my chance. I emptied my scotch and twirled the ice cubes around in my mouth while I dug into my bag for a card. I flicked it on the bar in front of Jake Weller. "When you have something worthwhile to tell me, give me a call. Otherwise, stop stalking us. I don't like it."

"You still don't trust me."

"Mr. Weller, I doubt your own mother trusts you."

He took my card and nodded good-bye as he slipped off the bar stool and then spun it around. "Maybe Scott's the one you shouldn't be trusting, Miss Lynch." And then he walked out.

"So much for making amends with Scott Boardman," I remarked to Beth. I waved the bartender over for our check. He came to Beth and me and leaned over the bar. "That gentleman paid your tab. It's all set."

I looked at Beth and then back at him. "When was that?"

"As soon as he walked in. He said he was meeting you here."

I shouldn't have let him pay our tab, but he'd already left, and it was too late to undo the deed.

My cell phone began singing "Oh Danny Boy"—the special ring I'd programmed for the chief's calls. "Yeah?" I said into the phone.

"We need to talk. Boardman's ready to plead guilty."

"Bullshit."

"Yeah? Then why did his lawyer just leave the AG's office looking for a deal?"

"And what did Vince say?"

"No freaking way, is what your boss said. No deal. So we need to talk, Shannon. Meet me after work. Boardman's guilty, and I want you to stay away from him. He's a dangerous asshole. Some of us don't take wife-killing too lightly."

"Sorry to hear that, Chuck. You should try it sometime. 'Cause the only way I'm coming there to talk to you is over Marjory's dead body."

19

THE CENTURY LOUNGE

"YOU HAVE TO AT LEAST CONSIDER HE'S GUILTY *now*, Shannon," Beth said as we drove in relative silence back to Providence. "I never thought I'd even *think* this, but with Scott Boardman, you might be blinded by love."

"It can't be love. I don't even know his middle name."

"You require a positive ID for love?"

"You used to be a nice kid, Beth. What happened?"

"I would have to credit you for that."

I felt Beth staring at me as I kept my eyes on the road ahead. She waited for a response to her assertion of my inability to see clearly while in the throes of love. Beth assumed that merely because I was quick to jump into love and even faster to kick the guy out, that I was the love guru, when in fact the only long-term relationship I'd ever had was with the husband of another woman. "So you think Boardman's guilty too? I'm the only putz who's holding out for his innocence?"

"You're the only one who *cares* whether or not he's

innocent. I'm not sure what you believe in your heart of
hearts."

"First of all, stop talking to me like I'm Marianna. I've
never been accused of having *one* heart, let alone several
hidden away like Russian nesting dolls. And I don't know
what I believe anymore. I had a gut feeling that Micah
Cohen was innocent, and I screwed that case up. He
should be hanging right now instead of sucking off his
boyfriend in his wife's bed. So, yeah, I might be wrong
about Boardman. Maybe it's old age—suddenly feeling
my own mortality—but I don't jump to convict anymore
just because I'm a prosecutor. I'm not going to put someone in jail just so I can have another notch in my AG belt."

"What about another notch in your sexual conquest
belt? Being with a rich and famous senator who's making
a White House run is pretty heady. And I bet Chief
Sewell is jealous as hell."

"You're wrong, Beth. I'm not playing the jealousy card
with the chief. I really like Boardman. And maybe he's
hiding something, but I don't think he killed two women.
And then what about Leo Safer? Did he shoot Safer and
then shoot himself to make it look good?"

"Yes, some people are capable of shooting themselves
to cover up a murder. How about the woman who point-
blank shot her three young children in the backseat of
her car and then shot herself to make it look like a car-
jacking gone bad? What I'm trying to say is, you aren't
thinking clearly on this. Is your fuzzy vision a blindness
caused by love for Scott Boardman, or is it a symptom of
a more general malaise that made you lose the Cohen
case too?"

I hated Beth when she was this coolly analytical. Laurie could be like that too—take a thought that was initially seemingly preposterous, and then draw it out into an irrefutable geometric equation to prove her point. But in order to keep our communal friendship whole in the delicate game of constructive criticism, Laurie usually kept her math to herself, whereas Beth was always anxious to count one of us out when one of our lives wasn't adding up. That she could always get to the bottom line while achieving a wholesome balance by not offending delicate sensibilities was a credit to her sweet nature and good intentions. So I stifled my urge to tell her to go pound sand up her ass.

"Beth, do me a favor. Use my phone and get Vince on the line. I don't want to involve you."

She dug efficiently into my bag, found my cell, and dialed the office, handing me the phone when the gruff voice said, "Where the fuck are you now?"

"Boardman wants to plead?" I said.

"Who said he wants to plead? His lawyer was just feeling around. Seeing what's in the air."

"So Ron Esterman must think he's guilty."

"I don't care what anyone thinks. Boardman's my number one squeeze for these murders until someone *prettier* comes along."

"You've been hanging around Andy too long, Vince."

"I told you to stay away from the Boardman case, not take a goddamn vacation. Get back to the office. There are other cases that need attention. Unless you're on a losing streak, in which case hand in your resignation and

I'll find someone else who can fuck things up cheaper than what I'm paying you." And then he disconnected.

Beth and I drove back to Providence in relative silence. Because Beth was technically a lame duck pending her September severance, she wasn't worried about her own neck, but I assured her anyway: "Don't worry. The Pig doesn't know you're with me."

In Vince's office I readied for a heart-to-heart on my erstwhile heartthrob, Scott Boardman, but Vince wouldn't oblige. "What do you want?" he said as I stood in front of his desk still panting from the jog up the stairs. He looked up at me. "Is the elevator broken again?"

"I need the exercise. My lungs are killing me from lack of smoke. You got one?"

He pushed his pack to the edge of his desk, where I grabbed it and slapped the pack until a slim white stick of tobacco peeked out at me.

Vince continued to feign reading the folder he was peering into. At my silence, he looked up at me again. "You want me to light that for you too?"

"What did Ron Esterman say?"

"What did *I* say to you on the phone? It's none of your goddamn business in the first place, and in the second, he was just poking around here trying to find out where we were on this. And frankly I was sweating when I took my hands out of my pants to tell him that we have so much *nothing* on this that I've been playing with myself just to get my spirits up!"

"You *have* been hanging around Andy too long."

"Andy who? I fired the fag."

"You asshole, Vince. When the fuck did you do that?"

"While you've been sunning in Acapulco, or wherever it is you been hiding these days."

"Jesus Christ. What's his number? We've got to hire him back."

"Why? And since when do you make those decisions?"

"Why? Because he's good, and you fired him for no other reason than his sexual orientation. And I have to make decisions when you screw up and expose this office to civil suits from the ACLU and God knows what other organizations set up to protect innocent people from your homophobic, misogynistic, racially challenged thick head."

Vince went back to his folder and began turning the pages as if they were heavy bricks. "Boardman's guilty," he said. "His own lawyer is having second thoughts. So take your broken heart out on someone else. And Andrew Lavigne is history. We got a new *girl* coming in tomorrow. Tell Beth to sit there until she shows up." He glared up at me again. "Where the hell is she anyway? The state's still paying her salary. I want her at work until her classes start."

I took a few deep breaths and decided to light the cigarette that was getting crushed in my hand. The last real smoke I'd had was with Scott Boardman in my apartment that first fateful night. I pulled a seat up closer to Vince's desk as he eyed me suspiciously. Our relationship wasn't the up close and personal kind.

"You got that match now?" I asked.

He threw his lighter across the desk and I lit his lousy Merit cigarette with his excellent sterling lighter. "How can you smoke these things? It tastes like an old butt on the first hit."

"What are you still doing here?" he said without looking up.

"Vince, tell me about Boardman's lawyer—what exactly did Esterman say to you? Because I had almost the same conversation with Scott Boardman about pleading out—"

"When?" he said calmly. "When did you have this conversation? Before or after I told you you were fired if you went near him again?"

"After."

His silence told me I should keep going. If he was going to throw something at me, he'd wait until I was finished.

"After Leo Safer's murder, Scott begged me to meet him in his hotel room. Brooke was there. She recanted her story, he recanted his alibi, and then she left. Then he and I had a hypothetical conversation about his pleading out. I thought it was because he was getting scared, and pleading to a few years was better than taking a chance at trial and going away for life. Three murders... and he's scared. At least that was my take."

"And you advised him to plead?"

I shook my head. "Nope. I was just listening, Vince. Saying enough so he'd keep talking but giving him nothing. But in the end he maintained his innocence."

"Sure, because Boardman was feeling you out the same way Esterman was feeling me out. They're just trying to find out what we have."

I agreed with Vince, and once again I felt duped by

Scott Boardman. I had never been with a man who could outthink and outsmart me—and I didn't like it one bit. The lovey-dovey hand-holding, and the charmed words "don't leave me" and "forever," were like the sprinkling of love potions on an ass's sleeping head. And like a stupid fairy princess, I kept falling for it.

"You're going to drop those ashes on the rug!" Vince yelled.

A precarious two inches of ash was teetering on the end of my half-smoked cigarette. I brought it gingerly to Vince's ashtray, stubbed it out, and then backpedaled my chair into its original spot. "You're right. I'm an asshole. I'll stay away from him from now on. I promise."

"Do us both a favor and don't make promises you aren't gonna keep. You'll be after Boardman now even more than before. Because, bottom line, Lynch? The fact that he broke your heart doesn't hurt half as much as the fact that he broke your balls. Am I right?"

I nodded. "And the fact that you've been right twice in one day just proves beyond a doubt that I'm losing my edge."

"Get the fuck out of here before I start breaking your balls too."

"You already have."

When I left Vince's office, Andy was sitting at his desk bright-eyed and bushy-tailed. "Hey, gorgeous, why so glum?"

"Andy? Vince said he fired you."

"Silly girl. Vince loves me. Underneath? He's a real *man's* man—if you get my drift."

"I wouldn't doubt it, Andy. Homophobes usually are."

IT WAS CLOSE ENOUGH TO CLOSING TIME FOR ME to cash out. I went for a solo drink near my loft and then went home, where I found Jake Weller skulking in his car next to my spot in the parking garage. I zipped into my space and got out. As I was walking to his driver's side window, he rolled it down and immediately began apologizing.

"Hey, I don't want to hear it," I said. "Unless you're going to confess to the murders, just stop stalking me."

"Why would you believe *my* confession and not Scott Boardman's? Because I'm not a pretty senator from Connecticut who was running for president until he shot his wife?"

"You could have stopped at 'pretty.' And I told you, I don't think your own mother believes a word you say."

His eyes looked heavy, like he'd been drinking all afternoon.

"When we left you in Newport, you said you were on your way back to Connecticut. What are you doing back in Providence?"

"Something you said made me change my mind."

"And what was that?"

"That I could help you with the investigation. So I'm offering my help."

"I never said that, Mr. Weller. You told me *you* were free to sleuth. But frankly I don't need your help. It looks like Scott Boardman's going to get away with murder and there's nothing any of us can do about it."

He rolled up his window and removed the key from

the ignition, ready to exit the car. I moved out of the way so he could open the door and get out. Facing me, he said, "I can help. Where do you want to talk?"

I jerked my head toward the street where a block away was the bar I'd just left. He locked his car and we walked in silence to the Century Lounge.

"Great name," Weller said as he pulled on the solid wood door. "What's the significance?"

"I have no clue, unless it's the fact that it's probably been here for a hundred years and keeps opening and closing but retaining its name."

The air turned rancid and stale as soon as the door swooped closed behind us and took with it the meager pocket of air that had stowed away in our clothes on the journey in. Local bands played here every weekend, so the few windows in the place were blacked over and sealed to enlighten the makeshift corner stage just outside the kitchen. It was the kind of place you never wanted to see in daylight, and since none of the bulbs exceeded forty watts, one presumed that even if the broken ones were replaced, the shock of the built-up muck of Fry-O-Lator grease, body oils, and spilled foods would still meld warmly into the background of chipped black walls and taupe gray commercial carpeting.

"It smells funky in here," Jake Weller said.

I had stopped just inside the door, staking my claim to the place like a cowboy waiting for a showdown. "We'll sit at the bar. I never sit at the tables. Too much dried food glued under the tops, and my ass always sticks to the seats." I proceeded on ahead and waited to see if he'd follow me. I purposely hadn't looked at his face, but I assumed he was grimacing. My taking him there was like a baptism. Either he really wanted to talk to me, or he'd bolt out the door and never look back.

I slid onto a bar stool, and sure enough, he'd trailed me. I was hopeful something useful would be gleaned from this meeting, because everything he'd said before now was just so much diarrhea dressed up to look like bullshit.

I ordered a beer from the bartender. "Heineken in the bottle, please, and hold the glass." I looked at Weller. "If I were you, I wouldn't trust the mugs here. They don't have a dishwasher—and I mean they really have *no one* to wash the dishes."

"Make that two," he said to the bartender. To me he said, "You come here often?"

"When I feel like being alone, which is now, so hurry up and talk."

"You already know I think Scott did it, or knows who did. It's just a matter of putting all the pieces together. I figure you've got some of the pieces, I've got some, and the rest we can find out between us."

"The cops have a job. They find killers. I have a job. I prosecute them. What's your job? Public relations. Why do you care so much who killed Scott Boardman's wife?"

"Because I knew she was going to die and I should have done something to prevent it."

No napkins and no coasters, the bartender slammed two glass bottles of Heineken on the bar in front of us. I waited for Weller to pick his up and take his first swig. Then I waited for him to lay it down on the bar. Then I waited for him to look at me, pick up the bottle, and gulp again.

"Don't you want to know why I thought she'd be murdered?" he asked, putting the bottle down on the bar and staring at it like it held the answer to his question. "Because she told me. Because Pat Boardman was afraid she wouldn't live through the November election."

"And you're now going to tell me she was afraid of Scott? She was afraid her own husband would kill her? Absurd." I finished my beer and ordered a Talisker neat, the only single malt scotch on hand.

"I thought you said you don't drink from the glasses here," he said.

"I said *you* shouldn't. My frequency in this place acts like a vaccine."

He drank the last of his beer and ordered another—in a bottle. He kept talking because he knew his time with me was like waiting for microwave popcorn—after one or two seconds of silence, I'd consider him done.

"Scott was furious over the lesbian thing. He had just recently found out—told all of us on the team. He thought she picked crappy timing to be 'coming out.' He thought she should have waited until after the election. I guess her girlfriend—the Booth woman who died with her—was pressuring her to leave him. And then there was the money—the trust that Muffie Booth was fighting with her mother over. The court battle was going to come out in the papers sooner or later, and Pat would be implicated in that too. The whole thing was a campaign nightmare."

"So Pat Boardman thought Scott was going to kill her over it? Bullshit."

"They weren't living together for the past few months.

Did you know that? She'd moved out and was living in Newport with Muffie Booth, who'd just divorced her own husband."

I must have raised my eyebrows—a mistake for a trial lawyer—because he nodded. "I told you I had information you didn't have. Now do you have any for me?"

"Who said anything about sharing?"

"I did, but I guess I didn't hear you agree to it."

"Smart man. What do you know about Virginia Booth?"

"She's a vulture. Actually, she's worse than a vulture. They only attack what's already dead. Virginia Booth is like those fish who eat their young as soon as they spring from the womb."

"How do you know her so well? You aren't even from her part of town."

"From Scott and Pat. That's how Pat met Muffie. Contributions from the Booth family to Scott's campaign. You see how it all gets tidy in a neat little package?"

"And you're opening this gift for me out of guilt over Pat Boardman? Because you should have prevented her death?"

"I guess so, yeah."

"Shit, Weller. You better be more than guessing."

"Pat was a real person, unlike Scott. Don't get me wrong. I think Scott would've made a great president. He's a good senator. But Pat was too human for him. He's an automaton. He sets a path and goes toward it, and if he needs to show some tears along the way to meet his goals, he'll cry for you on command. Pat was crying *all* the time. He cheated on her. He ignored her. And in the end, when he found out about Muffie Booth, he treated her like a piece of garbage, telling her he never should have married her, that she only damaged him politically. He told her that rather than her being an asset to him politically, he'd achieved what he had in *spite* of her. That's how much he belittled her. He's a mean man, Miss Lynch. He may be okay for someone like you, but for Pat Boardman, he was a lethal virus. And now she's dead."

I didn't bother delving into his definition of "someone like me." I was hoping I knew what he meant. I was hoping he meant that I was made of tougher stuff than Pat Boardman. But on the chance that he meant something else—on the chance he meant I was as virulent and ugly as he thought Scott Boardman was—I didn't question him further. Because maybe he was right, and I had no defense.

"I think you're a snitch, Jake Weller. I think you're a man who fucks a woman and then brags about it in the morning. And I think you're a man who rats out his friends."

"I know what you think. And nothing I do is going to change your mind, because the more I defend myself to you, the slimier I look. So I'm not going to get on my knees and beg you to believe me. Take it or leave it." He dug his hand into his pants pocket and pulled out a wad of bills. "How much do I owe you? Here." He threw a fifty on the bar. "That should cover it all. Call me when you hit a brick wall with all this." He stood from his stool and pushed his remaining cash back into his pocket. "Or just let Scott Boardman go free. Pat's dead. Doesn't matter to me anymore what you do."

"Hey, Weller," I called after him. He stopped but didn't turn. "Are you married?"

He swung his head around, questioning me with his eyes.

I shrugged, because honestly I didn't know why I'd asked him.

He walked slowly back to me, hesitating like he was uncertain he wanted to impart any more information. "I wasn't going to tell you this, because you don't believe me anyway, and because I didn't want to besmirch her name any more than it has been, but Pat Boardman was with me before Muffie. If you want my opinion, I think Pat's whole affair with Muffie Booth was experimentation from a woman who'd been emotionally abused by men her whole life. First her alcoholic father, and then Scott Boardman, whose ego is so big it even suffocates him."

Jake Weller looked up at me, because the next words needed eye contact for believability, and if nothing else, Jake Weller was a good PR man. "I loved Pat Boardman," he said to me. "And I think in time she would have come back to me. But she wasn't given that time. And that's why I'm here with you now, drinking bottled beer in this ptomaine-infected dump, letting you talk to me like I'm some lowlife who doesn't deserve to lick your shoes."

He walked out and I let him go in peace, because for the first time since I'd known him, he'd earned some of my respect.

20

NO ROOM AT THE INN

AGAINST ALL NATURAL INSTINCTS, I KNEW MY next call should be to Chief Charles Sewell. What was his relationship with Jake Weller? How far back did they go? I decided to go with an unnatural instinct and call Mike McCoy first. I liked the fact that I could run things by him without any flak. He was the objective observer, the sounding board with no ax to grind, and, because of his loyalty to Marianna, I could be certain of his loyalty to me.

Mike and I agreed to meet at the Dial-up Modem Diner the next morning, where I found him with Marianna and Laurie, having the Heart-i-Man special—an egg-white omelet with dry whole wheat toast.

"What the frig are you doing to this man?" I said to Marianna. "You deep-sixed his egg yolks along with his balls?"

Mike spit his coffee over Laurie, who gritted her teeth

and wiped herself off with a few hundred napkins from the chrome table dispenser.

"He'll be forty-five next year," Marianna said. "He has cholesterol issues."

Mike pointed his fork at Marianna. "Hey, *you* have issues with my cholesterol. I don't have any issues with it." He took the salt shaker and gave his omelet a heavy dose. "You gonna start with my blood pressure now?"

"No, Mike," Marianna said. "Because your blood pressure issues have nothing to do with salt. They have to do with your jaunts to Daytona Beach and the NASCAR races where you gamble half your salary away every month."

"Oh, fuck me," Laurie muttered. "Am I really needed here?"

"You might as well stay," I said, motioning for the waitress. "That way you won't have to listen to Mari complain about it later."

She held up both hands in surrender. "I'm comfortable with my ignorance, Shannon. Sometimes I'm really okay with it."

I ordered a cheese omelet, bacon, and home fries from the waiting waitress, and then burst into the song of my latest woes. "Mike, you look like you could use some cheering up."

He poured the entire pitcher of cream into his coffee and then looked at me with narrowed eyes, ready for one of my typical over-the-top, under-the-table onslaughts.

"No, hey, I think I agree with you, Mike," I said. "I think Scott Boardman might be guilty."

He grunted in approval and looked at Marianna,

who was holding her cup in midair waiting for the rest of what she thought would be my punch line.

"Nope," I said to their collective expectant stare. "I'm serious. I think he did it."

"Hallelujah," Laurie said. "She sees the light."

"Why this sudden change of heart?" Marianna asked. "He stinks in the sack, right?"

I shook my head. "I'm dead serious. He's the only one with motive. Jealousy, rage, a political career that would be ruined...all motives. And for the life of me, I can't think of anyone else except a random killer—but there didn't seem to be anything really stolen. And Muffie Booth had no apparent enemies except her mother, and mothers don't kill kids over bucks."

"They might if it's a few billion," Laurie said.

"Or if it was an accident," Marianna added. "Maybe there was a fight. Virginia Booth has to cover it up and ends up shooting Pat Boardman, the only witness?" Mari shook her head in disagreement with herself. "But then what about Leo Safer? Why shoot him?"

"Maybe he was blackmailing someone," I answered. Then I shook my head. "Nah, too many loose ends and not enough hard evidence. It feels like the Cohen case all over again."

The waitress brought my eggs and bacon, glistening with the golden sheen of melted animal fat and sweet cream butter. Mike was staring at my plate like it was a *Playboy* centerfold. I snapped my fingers in front of his mesmerized eyes. "What do you know about the relationship between Jake Weller and Chief Sewell?" I asked him.

His dreamy stare rose slowly to my eyes and he reared his head back to break the spell. "Ah, yeah...I don't know, Shannon. I didn't even know they knew each other."

"Crap, that means I've got to eat crow and call that black buzzard myself." I ventured another question to Mike, though I was getting the feeling that Marianna had so castrated him that he was becoming useless as anything other than a deflated punching bag in need of a good blow. "How's he doing anyway?" I asked him.

"The chief?" Mike said. "Matter of fact, I had lunch with him yesterday." He looked at my plate. "Can I have a piece of that bacon?"

"Go for it, Mike," I said.

He grabbed the fattiest slice and gave Marianna a sidelong glance, daring her to open her mouth. Then he rolled the slice into a loose ball and popped the whole thing into his mouth. "Not *too* good," he said.

I assumed he was talking about Chuck and not the bacon. "Are you going to tell me why? Or are you boys sticking together like the good little scouts you are?"

"You figure it out," Mike said to me, suddenly tough again. "You're a real smart girl...until recently."

"I hope that bacon gives you gas, McCoy," I said.

"The chief is bereft and lonely without you," Marianna said. "Mike told me last night. He's not doing well."

Mike slapped the table. "That's it! I've put up with this long enough."

"Oh, what's the harm, Mike?" Marianna said. "If she feels bad for him, maybe they'll get back together."

Laurie threw some cash down on the table and stood.

"Why the hell do you want them back together, Mari? The man is married. Let him stay home with his wife or move the hell out. What gives him the right to a double shot? What? Just because he's the friggin' chief of police?"

"Oh, look," I said, "thanks for the thought, Laur, but far be it from me to start moralizing over someone's sex life. I didn't cash out on him because of that anyway. He just has double standards—if you'll excuse the pun. If he can keep Marjory, why can't I have Scott Boardman on the side?"

"I'm out of here," Laurie said. "But before you quit the game altogether, do you think maybe he was just worried about you sleeping with a murder suspect, who—by your own admission—might be guilty?"

"I don't get it," Mike said to Marianna. "Is she telling her that she *should* dump Chuck or that she *shouldn't*?"

"Both," Marianna said. "But for different reasons." And then she looked at me. "She should dump him because he's married but insists on an exclusive relationship from Shannon, but she *shouldn't* dump him if he's just nixing Boardman as her choice of an extracurricular affair because he thinks Boardman's a murderer." Then she looked back at Mike. "You understand?"

"I *understand* that this is last time I eat with you girls. I'm still hungry, I have indigestion, and my head is spinning."

"Come on, Mikey," Laurie said. "Let's blow this nuthouse."

Marianna and I sat silently as they walked out together. When Mike was safely out the door, she let tumble out the rest of her and Mike's confidential conversation vis-à-vis Chief Chucky. "Mike told me the chief and Marjory split up."

I raised my brows.

"Hey, I don't know if it's because you dumped him and he's taking it as some kind of ultimatum, but she's moved in to the family house in Pennsylvania. Trial separation, the chief called it."

I shook my head in disgust. "You know what really bites me about that, Mari? All these years I've been a mensch by not pulling his chain over being married, and he stays married. And when it finally *looks* like I'm acting like a dweeb broad and giving him marriage ultimatums, he decides to 'do the right thing.' Fuck that, huh? The slimy female route works after all."

"Don't look at it that way, Shannon. It's not that *you've* done anything right or wrong. It's men who make us act like jerks, because that's what they respond to. They need to be given boundaries. They *beg* for us to give them limitations, to rein them in, to socialize them. That's what my father always said, anyway. He always used to say, if it weren't for women, men would still be roaming around in packs and living in caves. It's not the Greeks or the Romans or any other nation that gave us civilization. It's *women*."

For the briefest second I allowed myself to envy Marianna. She had a mother who cooked, cleaned, and dispensed love in all directions, and a father who left for work in the morning and arrived home early enough every night to calm his fold by translating the terrors of the big bad world into a few succinct words of wisdom.

Everything I learned about love, family, and life, I'd gleaned on the front steps of my house in South Boston from the evening newspaper, and from the boy who'd delivered it.

MARIANNA AND I WALKED BACK TO THE OFFICE in silence. I left her at her office door and I went off to mine, picked up the phone, and called the chief. I would refuse to discuss our love life, except insofar as the topic included references to Scott and murder. Out of allegiance to Mike, and a genuine desire not to discuss it, I intended to keep my trap shut about his recent split from Marjory. I limited myself to one major mission at a time, and what I needed to determine, once and for all, was whether Scott Boardman was a killer.

"Shannon!" I could hear the sun rise in Chuck's voice when he recognized mine. "Come on over," he said. "I'm busy as hell here, but for you, I'm always free."

But did I want to dance into the police station past Patrolman Kent and wave hello as I twirled into Chuck's office?

My silence flicked the light on in the cluttered attic of Chuck's dimly lit brain. "Um…no, I guess that's not a good idea, huh? How about lunch? I'll meet you at twelve-thirty. What's that French place McCoy and Marianna go to all the time? The one on Hope Street."

"So suddenly we can meet at a fancy *local* restaurant in public?" Before he could answer, I picked the usual spot of our past rendezvous and secret lunchtime dalliances. "The Captain Jaynes House," I said. "Except this time don't bother booking a room." I hung up.

From Providence it took about thirty minutes to get to the inn in Worcester, Massachusetts. In some fairness to Chuck, it really wasn't a bad place. The quaint colonial-era inn had earned its reputation over the past hundred years or so just by withstanding time. Chuck and I always took room number 3—I liked the white four-poster bed—where a hundred and fifty bucks plus tax got us a queen-size bed and a private bath.

At 12:42 Chuck was already posted at the bar with Teddy the bartender. Their attention was glued to an ESPN program where a group of has-been sports figures were still commiserating over the 2008 Patriots' Super Bowl loss after their perfect season.

"Oh, get over it," I said, standing next to Chuck but addressing them both.

"He had this station on when I got here," Chuck said, turning to me and putting his hand on my back. "*This* guy," he nodded at Teddy, "is the obsessed one. He says he put a hole through his basement wall when the Giants hit that final touchdown."

"There's counseling available for that," I said to Teddy. "And give me a cup of coffee over at that booth." I pointed to one of the two tables out on the small enclosed porch. "This big fella and I have to talk in private." I whacked Chuck on his broad back and walked away.

Chuck followed with his beer and waited for me to sit first. He was quiet and tentative and I knew what he was thinking: A private talk between us in this out-of-town venue had to be about Marjory and their recent separation.

When he sidled in next to me on the banquette, he gave me a sheepish smile to which I responded with a furrowed brow. "Don't flatter yourself, Chuckster. We're here to talk about *my* love life, not *ours.*"

While Chuck absorbed the operative pronouns of my statement, Teddy brought me a coffee and resumed his position around the corner at the bar.

"What do you mean by that?" Chuck asked. "If it has to do with you, it has to do with me," he said confidently (and rather sweetly, I might add). "So if it's about *your* love life, it's about *mine* too."

"I guess—indirectly—you're right. Like if I got married tomorrow, you could be sure that you and I would never see each other again. So, yeah, I guess indirectly my love life affects yours."

Chuck looked beyond me out the window at the lunchtime crowd dining under umbrellas on the deck. He took another slow sip from his tall beer glass, and then looked at me. "Go ahead. Say what you came to say. I can take it."

"How long have you known Jake Weller?"

I could almost see the question bounce around in his spacious head, where it obviously came to rest unsatisfied. "What's *Weller* got to do with *us?*"

"Make the big leap, Chuck," I said with a tart sarcasm in my tone. "Weller's got *nothing* to do with us—but a lot to do with Scott Boardman. And Scott Boardman has a lot to do with us."

He nodded but remained silent.

"But before you take that statement and run home with it, let me say this: Boardman has less to do with our problems than you think. He was just a catalyst, a symptom of the underlying disease of this rotten relationship. Like my arrest—when you left me to your wolves—that was the terminal death knell. So let's not skewer Scott Boardman over a couple of broken hearts. If he's guilty, I'll help you fry him, but if he's innocent, I want to know. And none of that has anything to do with us and this diseased relationship."

Chucky, still quiet, began to grind his jaw. "I hate it when you start jogging in circles like this."

"Well, pick up the speed and follow me closely. Jake Weller is convinced that Scott Boardman killed Pat Boardman, Muffie Booth, *and* Leo Safer, and then he shot himself in the arm to make the whole victim routine ring true. So tell me how long you've known Jake Weller, how *well* you know him, and whether you think he's a no-good rotten liar like I do."

Chucky began his answer with a nod of his head followed by a brisk shake. "I've known him a long time... well, since college, but not that well. We went to UConn together. He was a grade behind me but we had the same major. Poli-sci. He was an okay guy. No reason not to trust him. If he's wrong about Boardman, it's just because he's *wrong*, nothing more serious than that. I don't think he knows anything more than the rest of us. He's just scared because he's involved in the whole mess and doesn't want to be implicated in a murder charge. Think about it, Shannon. Even if Jake is totally innocent and knew nothing about what went on that night, if Scott

Boardman goes down for the murders, Jake's reputation is in the toilet too. It's like getting a tattoo when you're asleep—it's still permanent in the morning no matter how much you didn't want it there in the first place."

"So he's just scared. That's your opinion?"

He bit his bottom lip and nodded, looking into my eyes as if he had more to say. "Can we talk about *us* now?"

"No. I'm not finished."

Chuck got up from the table without a word and walked to the bar. A couple of minutes later he returned with a fresh beer and slid back into the banquette. "Go ahead," he said.

"My problem with Weller is I don't see as much of a motive for his lies as you do, but then again I don't know him like you do—"

Chuck waved his hand at me. "I didn't say I necessarily trust him not to lie. I just think these murders have scared the bejesus out of him. Violence is not in his nature. He was always the quiet type, the thinker type… more the kind of guy who would do what he's doing now. Ratting on people to save himself." He put his beer down and looked off into the distance again, and I watched his eyes focus on something outside the window and then beyond it into his past. "See, like, there was this time once, one of the girls in a history class got her hands on a final exam. A few of us used it and aced the exam because we cheated. When the professor realized we'd gotten hold of the questions, he rounded us all up, and none of us would give the girl up—except Jake. And he was really sweet about it and all—he gave this big speech to the professor about our 'complicity' and some such shit—but he still ratted her out." Chuck reeled himself back to the present and looked at me for my reaction. "See what I'm saying here?"

I nodded.

"So, I think he's an honest guy, just not a *stand-up* kind of guy. You know the difference. Right?"

I nodded again, remembering Jake Weller's admission of being in love with Pat Boardman. I believed him—that he truly loved her—but he should have stopped there. Ratting Scott Boardman out wasn't going to bring her back. And I didn't believe his motive for pointing the finger at Boardman was altruistic. I believe it was just fear that he'd wake up in the morning with that tattoo on his chest that would forever brand him as the PR guy for a murderer.

Chuck let me ruminate on my thoughts awhile, but then he pulled us back to the issues he wanted to deal with. "So, can we talk about something else now?"

I snapped myself out of prosecutor mode and into girl-dom. "Listen, Chuck, I don't want to tumble down Heartbreak Road with you. You do whatever is best for you and I'll do the same, and if we meet up at the end of the line . . . well, we just do. That's all. And that's all I have to say."

"Well, that's not fair." He gently but firmly laid his beer glass on the table. "I need you with me on this—"

"Why? Did I ever ask anything of you. Ever? If I hadn't met Scott Boardman, you'd still be happy in our little threesome of you, me, and Marjory. You see, Chuck, I'm not going to be the reason you leave your wife. *You* are. That's between you and her. You and Marjory have to figure it out without me."

He repeated the only words that seemed to come to his lips. "That's not fair."

"And since we're on this topic that we've so tirelessly avoided over the years, does Marjory even *know* about me? Or has she just accepted your double life and is settling for what she's got?"

He shook his head, ready, I thought, to answer at least one segment of my compound question, but instead he avoided my simple yes-or-no questions by switching topics to one more philosophical and much harder to solve. "You don't understand what it's like to be with someone for thirty years. Have kids together, go to funerals, watch each other throw up—those kind of intimacies, day after day for thirty years, it's not love anymore, Shannon. After thirty years, it's family. Yeah, in a way she's like blood to me—a sister or a mother. Marjory and I could get a divorce tomorrow, but she's never going to be out of my life until one of us dies. You gotta understand that."

"Oh, I do understand. Maybe not emotionally, because I've never even had a close family, let alone a relationship with a guy that lasted thirty years, but I get what you're saying. And that's why I never pushed you for anything more than what we had. And I'm not going to do it now. But what *you* have to understand, Chuck, is that I'd be doing what I'm doing with Boardman whether you were married or not. My feelings for him have nothing to do with you and Marjory. If you did 'get a divorce tomorrow,' as you put it, I'd still be dicking around with Scott Boardman."

I could almost see my last statement hit him like a rock. He pulled his head back slowly, absorbing the impact of my words.

I knew I was ripping his heart in half, but truth is, I didn't want him to do something he'd regret and eventually blame me for. And I didn't want Marjory to be hurt as collateral damage just because I was shooting a hole through Chuck's heart. What Chuck didn't understand was that maybe Scott Boardman coming into my life was the best thing that could have happened for all three of us, because I truly believed Chuck and Marjory belonged together. My crime with Chucky wasn't the breaking of his heart, it was the adultery I'd jointly committed with him over the years. And throughout those years, I'd felt honorable that I'd never once asked him to leave his wife for me. I never once demanded him on a full-time basis. But there was no honor in that. It was an excuse to cover the real crime. The crime where Chuck was the perpetrator, I was the accomplice, and Marjory was the victim.

I finished the last of my cold coffee, pushed my hands into my pockets, and sat back. I had nothing else to say.

"So that's it, then?" he said. "You're all done with me?"

I pushed the small table forward and stood. "Stop being so melodramatic."

Chucky rose too. Faced me with his square chin sticking out at me like an ornery bulldog. I gave him a tender punch in the shoulder, hoping we could get past the emotional stuff to a place where we could still relate on a professional level. "So, do you have anything new on the

Boardman case, or is a killer going to walk away after three murders?" I said.

He softened his canine attack position by lowering his chin and turning away from me. "We've got your un-shot gun and a glass vase with no unidentified finger-prints, which means we know all the players, and we got a lot of people lying. It's almost as if the murderer is be-ing protected by people who know who did it. Like a mob hit. You know what I mean? All in the family. So my in-clination is to let them all go rot in hell. If the socialite politicos want to punch each other's lights out, that's fine by me."

"That doesn't sound like a cop talking, Chucky."

"Yeah, well, maybe it's time for me to retire. I'm sick of it all." He poked me softly in the shoulder, mimicking my shoulder jab at him. "You hear me, Shannon? I'm sick and tired of *all* of it."

"Sorry to hear that, *Chief.* Really sorry to hear that. And I'll be sorry to see you go. But we all gotta do what we all gotta do."

I waited as Chucky settled up with Teddy at the bar, and then Chucky and I walked out to the parking lot to-gether, standing side by side in silence while the valet fetched our cars. Mine came first, and Chucky opened the door for me. "You're a good woman, Shannon, better than you give yourself credit for. Any man would be lucky to have you. So don't make any mistakes, huh?"

"You're giving mistakes a bad rap, Chuck. Sometimes they're friendly. Sometimes mistakes are our best teach-ers. Think about it. If you never made mistakes, you would have never been with me."

21

THE PINE BOX RELEASE

I MAY HAVE SOUNDED UPBEAT WHEN I LEFT Chucky, but it was all bravado. The phantom pain in my heart felt more like a very real hole in the pit of my stomach. I was going to miss dialing him up any old time of the day to tell him dirty jokes. I was going to miss cuddling with him on those long weekend nights that he and I managed to steal away while Marjory was out of town. I was going to miss getting drunk with the girls and dragging Chuck bowling with us, where he'd get the slightest thrill from all the female attention lavished on him by my generous friends, who thought they felt sorry for an old guy stuck in a loveless marriage. For some reason they always took Chucky's side in the game of love. I was the tall sexy blonde, single and ready for life's roll in the hay onward and upward, whereas to them Chucky seemed stuck—gummed up in the thickest part of life, where getting free only meant a final roll on the downside of the hill. Whatever feelings of family Chucky claimed to have with Marjory were oddly similar to the feelings I had for him. Maybe because I'd never had anything close to a real family, I'd let Chucky take the roles of father, brother, and husband. It was a mistake, but as I'd said to him, mistakes didn't scare me as long as I could straddle them without permanent injury. So far so good.

It was already past three when I rolled back into the office. I thought it perhaps time to do a little legal work in case Vince decided to ask me why he was still paying me a salary to go running around town working a case he'd barred me from.

I picked up a file and went to the library to do some research on an upcoming trial. Beth was sitting at the long conference table, staring at her cell phone. She looked up at me wide-eyed as if I were an apparition back from the dead.

"What the frig's wrong with you?" I asked her.

"Shannon. Why are you here...now?"

"Shit, Sherlock. I work here."

"Did she call you too?"

I snapped my finger in front of her eyes. "Wake up, Beth. It's only a dream. What the hell are you talking about?"

"Doogie called me."

It took me a minute to figure out the name thing. I still couldn't understand why some people couldn't be satisfied with their birth names and had to make themselves sound like cartoon characters. I decided it had to be some kind of secret membership rite. Maybe a variation of rapper jive: Have silly name—be cool. Like Doogie and Muffie were to Virginia and Martha what Snoop Dogg and 50 Cent were to Calvin and Curtis.

"She wants to see me," Beth continued. "I shouldn't go, right?"

"Virginia Booth called you and wants to meet with you?"

"Lolly called her and told her that you and I were there asking questions about her and Muffie. Doogie freaked when she heard *you* were with me."

"Okay, so let's go see her."

Beth shook her head. "Alone. Doogie wants to see me *alone.*"

"You call her and tell her you're on your way. Don't worry about the rest. I'll figure it out during the ride."

"Are you going to have me wired?"

"No, Beth. I'm going to call up the folks from *Mission Impossible* and have a mask of your face made, and I'm going to wear it to fool Doogie into thinking she's talking to you, when in fact she'll be spilling her guts to me."

"Stop making fun of me."

"It breaks my heart to say this, but if you're going to work in this office as anything other than someone's *assistant,* you'd better grow up and learn how to bend the truth."

Beth lifted a yellow legal pad from the table. "You're on the motion calendar tomorrow in the Rollins case, Shannon. His lawyer filed a ten-page motion to dismiss. I'm preparing your answer now while you run around simultaneously playing detective and footsies with Scott Boardman. So which of us is acting like the real prosecutor? You or me?"

"You're acting like a paralegal. And law school is just going to teach you more of that book stuff that you already know. *I'm* going to teach you how to be a hard-ass prosecutor. I'll wing the motion tomorrow morning whether you write a brilliant answer or not. Now leave your flowered tote bag behind and let's go."

"Just like you 'winged' the Cohen case?" Beth held her legal pad in midair, like if she showed me concrete proof of my negligent behavior it might shock me into letting her go to Virginia Booth's alone. I took the pad from her hand, ripped off the pages she'd written, and folded them up in my back pocket. "I'll read while you drive. Call Doogie. Tell her you're on your way."

She rose slowly from her seat.

"And the next time you want to insult me or hurt my feelings," I said, "don't bother. It's been tried by the best, and the only person who ever came close was a rookie Providence cop when he kicked me across a room while I was handcuffed."

On our way past the girls' bathroom, we bumped into Andy coming out. "Hey, Vincent is looking for you," he said to me. I looked at Beth for verification. She shrugged. Andy continued. "Well, it's something about a trust fund and Virginia Booth. She was suing her daughter to get the trust fund control back. He just found out that the day the court ruled against her is the day the murders took place. *Motive*," Andy sang.

"Ridiculous," Beth said as she walked ahead to the elevator and punched the down button. "Doogie would never...Mothers don't kill their children. At least not where I come from."

"The same day the decision came down?" I confirmed with Andy.

"You betcha, sweet-cakes. M-O-T-I-V-E," he spelled.

The elevator doors swung open and I joined Beth, who was mumbling something under her breath about absurdity and the lack of understanding we had of someone like Virginia Booth. I let Beth mutter away because time would answer the question of what Virginia Booth was capable of. If I had my way, it would be sooner rather than later, because with each minute that passed, emotions cooled, fears subsided, and the edges of truth softened and blurred. I recalled my first encounter with Virginia Booth four days after the murders. She'd vacillated between gracious and jumpy, sharp-tongued and coolly dismissive. The second time we talked, at the coffee shop, she was calmer, more sure of herself. She had found her footing and had tried to knock me off mine— make me another victim of Scott Boardman.

How would this third visit find her? I was hoping the third time would be the charm.

IN HER RED SAAB, BETH DROVE US TO NEWPORT. I pulled Beth's motion response from my pocket, and while she drove, I read it in five minutes.

"Is it okay?" she asked.

"Perfect," I said. "It's a sure win." I tucked the pages back into my pocket and made a mental note to myself to make a *real* note to myself that I had to be in court at 8:00 a.m. the next morning. My biggest obstacle to winning the motion wasn't the state of the law, or how well

Beth had presented it, but whether or not I could make it to court on time.

At a point between the Jamestown and Newport bridges, my cell phone rang. Marianna had tracked us down. She and Laurie were going to the Red Fez after work and wanted company.

"Maybe," I said into the phone. "We're on our way to Newport and I'll fill you in later."

I clicked my phone, ending the conversation. Beth tried to look at me as she drove, sneaking peeks out of the corner of her eye. "Did Mari scream at you?" she asked.

"For what?"

"Doing what we're doing, of course."

"As a matter of fact, Beth, not only did she not scream, but she said she wished she were coming with us. Marianna and Laurie both realize that in this case, sitting around the office waiting for evidence to blow in through an open window isn't going to work, so we got to go out and reel it in."

"But it's not normal. Prosecutors aren't supposed to act like detectives. The police should be doing this stuff, not us."

"Beth, remember the two police officers—Kent and the other one—who arrested me the day Leo Safer was murdered? The two who would have beat the shit out of the *three* of us if Lucky hadn't been there?"

She snuck me another side-glance, afraid to answer, knowing that my memory of that day and night was still as raw as an open wound.

"Well, police officers like those two, and others like

them, are the ones who investigate these cases. Would you trust that kind of investigating if your mother were under suspicion of murder? Or your sister? Or your brother?"

Beth didn't have a brother, but she dared not correct me. Silent, her eyes remained steady on the road ahead.

"This case is special to me because of Scott Boardman. And when I became a suspect in Leo Safer's murder, the case became *personal.* So I'm not leaving anything up to police officers like Kent and his redneck cronies."

"I thought you liked cops ... I mean, you date them all the time."

"I fuck them, Beth. That's different than dating. And they're not all like Kent. Some of them are okay. The ones who shouldn't have been cops to begin with."

"Like the chief?"

Good question. But my answer didn't take long. "Yeah, like the chief. He's a good guy, that's why he made it to the top. The ones like Kent will eventually be weeded out, but not before they've done a heap of bad shit like beat up a few suspects, plant bogus evidence, and skim drugs from a bust and then resell it to select private customers."

"How do you know all this stuff?"

"Pillow talk with the chief of police for the past five years."

TWENTY MINUTES LATER BETH AND I PULLED UP to Virginia Booth's castle on the cliffs. As before, a gray-uniformed maid admitted us to the sun-filled "morning room" (as Beth called it). We had waited for the mistress of the manse for about fifteen minutes when the maid returned and said that Mrs. Booth was indisposed and couldn't make the meeting after all.

"Give her a couple of aspirin and tell her we'll wait," I said.

The lady in gray stalled a minute before finally spinning on her heels and exiting the room.

In the stuffed chintz chair, Beth sat primly with her hands folded in her lap. She directed her statements to the room at large, as if she were delivering protocol to a roomful of guests awaiting a sitting queen. "She'll make us wait another fifteen minutes and then she'll send the maid down again to inform us that she still isn't receiving guests. We can sit here for an eternity, and if she doesn't want to see us, she won't. And after some extended period of time, if we refuse to leave, she'll call the police to *have* us removed. I just want you to know that," she said confidently. "Virginia Booth will win this particular round."

"I'm guessing she won't try to win this one. Because I'm guessing she doesn't want any more cops showing up here. So we'll just give her the fifteen more minutes she requires and see what happens."

During our wait, I'd perused a coffee-table book on orchid forcing (imagine that kind of arrogance?) and Beth walked around the room surveying the furnishings as if she were a buyer from Christie's pricing the goods for auction. Beth was fondling a Chinese jade vase, turning it over to look for a signature, I assumed, when Virginia Booth appeared in the doorway, studying us from a safe distance as if we were bacteria on a slide.

Beth saw her first and gently replaced the vase. "I'm sorry, Doogie. That was unconscionable of me …"

Virginia Booth ignored her apology and turned her head slowly to me. "And you? Why are you here?"

"You left so abruptly from the coffee shop that day … and I thought we were just starting to bond."

This was the first Beth had heard of a prior meeting between Virginia Booth and me. "What coffee shop?" she asked me.

I kept my eyes on Virginia Booth as I explained to Beth: "Mrs. Booth invited me for coffee. But then once we got to Starbucks, she decided she wasn't thirsty." Still watching Virginia Booth, I said to her, "Was it something I said, Mrs. Booth?"

Virginia Booth seemed to fold in half. She held her stomach and sidled unsteadily to the nearest chair, into which she crumbled. Beth ran to her side. "Doogie?"

Virginia Booth held her hand up to Beth. Her skin had paled even whiter than its natural porcelain shade. She spoke to me. "Your police friends came back here again. They showed me the same warrant from the last time. They found something upstairs—they wouldn't say what. They removed it from my house and said they'd be returning within the next few days with another warrant. One for my … *arrest.*" Now she looked at Beth, who was kneeling in front of her. She took Beth's hand that had been resting within reach on the arm of her chair. Ignoring me, she spoke directly to Beth—who was the only one she'd actually invited into her house. "I thought maybe you would understand, Beth … that you would help me understand all this. And that I could explain to

you what happened. And that in turn *you* might understand."

I took a few steps closer to the stricken woman.
"What's all this gibberish?" I said as Beth looked up at
me, horrified. "What happened the night your daughter
was murdered? Was it the trust money? You killed your
own flesh and blood over a goddamn trust—"

"Shannon," Beth said gently. "Let's just let Doogie talk
a minute. Okay?" She turned back to Virginia Booth.
"You want to tell me something? Go ahead. It'll be all
right. I promise."

Virginia Booth shook her head slowly. "No, dear," she
said to Beth. "It will never be all right again. Muffie ruined everything, as I knew she would once Pat Boardman
got hold of her."

"Oh, so now we're blaming Pat Boardman?" I said.

Beth's eyes shot me a daggered glance. I moved away
and sat on the couch Marianna and I had occupied during our first visit. Beth was clearly the director of this
scene, so suppressing the urge to even breathe, I let
Virginia Booth continue her monologue while I bit my
sharp tongue.

"You know, of course, about the outcome of my lawsuit over the trust. Those policemen told me you all
knew. I'd lost the case that day...the day Muffie died. I
know how that looks, as if I had something to do with
her death." She breathed deeply, switching scenes. "And
upstairs, here, they found something, they said, that implicated me." She looked closely into Beth's eyes. "Do you
know what they found? I can't imagine..."

Beth turned a sour look at me and I knew what she

was thinking. But she disappointed me by actually verbalizing her thoughts. "Did they plant something here, Shannon? Would the cops have planted evidence, or just be lying about it to scare her into confessing something?"

Although I knew that Beth inspired the trust that Virginia Booth needed to bare her soul to us, she still had no right to be releasing confidential information to her—information I'd told her in the privacy of a legal setting, a prosecutor and a paralegal discussing bad cops. True or not, Beth never should have opened her mouth about it to Virginia Booth.

"Beth," I said, and shook my head at her.

She pursed her lips and nodded, realizing her mistake. "Doogie, did you see anything? What they took out?"

She shook her head slowly. "They wouldn't say. Didn't tell me. Just told me, very self-assured, that I would be arrested." She dropped her head to her lap. "I need to explain to you, Beth. To someone who will understand when all this is over, what happened...at least part of it...and why."

"What are you talking about?" Beth said. "Start at the beginning."

"May I get some water first?" she asked.

The tide of her attitude had turned full circle. She was now *asking* us if she could get water in her own house. This is where I liked my witnesses—in the solemn state of scared shitless.

"No," I said. "Talk first, and then you can drink."

"Come on, Shannon," Beth pleaded. "Let me get it for her."

Virginia Booth grabbed Beth's other hand. "No, stay

with me." She hung her head again. "I don't need it anyway."

Beth patted Virginia Booth's hand, and she began to talk again.

"My lawyer called that morning—the morning the judge said the trust transfer to Muffie was valid. That decision meant that I was under her control financially, just as her father had wished. The trust held everything we own. It might have been all right—I don't think Muffie hated me that much, to put me out of my own house—but Pat Boardman was so strong an influence on her. Muffie changed after Pat. I don't know why Pat Boardman hated me. Maybe because of Scott. Because our families had been so close. Pat always felt the outsider in our group. And Scott made sure Pat was kept *in her place*, as he was so fond of saying. He was so fond of telling us all how he *married down*." She looked over at me with tired eyes. Raising her eyebrows seemed an effort. "Scott prides himself on keeping women in their place. I tried to tell you," she said to me. "Scott Boardman is not a nice man, and he was a worse husband—"

"Yeah," I interjected. "He said you'd say that. He said you'd say he was a lousy husband and a worse father."

"Only because it's true," she said.

"Go ahead," Beth said to her, patting her hand again.

Virginia Booth looked up at Beth, as if renewing her faith that Beth was someone she could trust. She nodded. "Pat wanted to move into *this* house with Muffie. Her plan was that I would retire to the guesthouse. Imagine? After all these years in my home, to ask me to move to the guesthouse, where the servants used to live."

I felt like telling her that her dump of a guesthouse was twice the size of my apartment, but under Beth's warning stare, I kept my trap shut.

"So I called Muffie—that day I learned the verdict—is that the right term?" She looked at me. "Is it a verdict when a judge decides against you?"

Beth responded. "No, Doogie. Only juries can render verdicts. The judge made a *decision.*"

She nodded. "Well, he *decided* against me, and I called Muffie that very evening. She was, of course, with Pat. They were staying on our boat at the harbor. In view of all those people, they carried on together." She shivered. "At that restaurant they've built on the docks there. Forty-one Degrees North, they call it. Silly name. I went there to talk to her—to both of them—I thought we could come to some agreement—the three of us together..."

"You were on the boat that night?" I said.

Beth warned me again with a slicing glance.

"I had been here, drinking alone. To build courage... the courage to *beg.*"

She seemed to hiccup. Maybe a tear had lodged in her tight and proud throat.

"Go get her some water now," Beth said to me. "The kitchen is back out the way we came in, and then to the far left."

I was reluctant to leave the two of them alone. Would things be said in my absence that Beth wouldn't share? It never occurred to me that I would be the outsider to Beth, or any of the girls. In an implicit and unspoken trust, I never had to share them before. Even Marianna with her close-knit family had always seemed to find a special niche for the four of us that didn't impinge on her family obligations. In short, did I trust Beth as much as I trusted Marianna and Laurie?

Beth felt my reluctance in the few seconds of my hesitation. "Go, Shannon," she ordered. "A glass of water, please." Then she turned slowly back to Virginia Booth. "Do you want something a bit stronger—to calm your nerves?"

Again Virginia Booth shook her head into her lap, and whispered, "Water will be fine."

I rose from the couch and walked slowly from the room, straining to hear whispered words that never came, until I was back at the front door in a large foyer where, as per Beth's directions, I turned left and started down a hall, where a gray-starched maid, a different face this time, met me. She held a basket of fresh-cut flowers to her chest. "May I help you?" she asked.

"Water," I answered. "For Mrs. Booth in that...morning room."

She nodded and turned back to the kitchen, hugging the basket in her arms.

Mission completed, I returned to Beth and Virginia Booth, who were silent at my entrance.

"The maid's bringing it," I said, and resumed my seat on the couch.

Beth looked at me with wide eyes and shook her head almost imperceptibly. Something had been divulged in my absence. Eye to eye, I queried Beth, and she turned back to Virginia Booth. "Tell Miss Lynch what you told me, Doogie. Shannon's okay, really. She's a bit rough around the edges, but you can trust her. *I* trust her with my life. You can trust her."

How generous of the two of them, I thought, to trust the shanty Irish broad with the foul mouth and rough edges.

Virginia Booth refused to look at me, still unsure of me. Maybe she knew me better than Beth did—better than I knew myself. Maybe I shouldn't be trusted. But I wasn't going to sell myself to Virginia Booth. And anything I said would make me sound like a used-car salesman hawking a hot car.

"It doesn't matter," Virginia Booth finally said. "Everyone will eventually know the truth. It might as well begin with *her.*"

Beth, growing uncomfortable in her kneeling position, stood and then leaned in to perch on the arm of Virginia Booth's chair. Beth never let go of Virginia Booth's hand as she began to speak again.

"Muffie and I were never close. She was more her father than me. A carbon copy really. We were always at odds over one thing or another. Even at Christmastime, I never seemed to choose the right toys. Whereas I already had a collection by the time I was her age, she never liked dolls. She was nine that Christmas, and I had gifted her one of mine—a German bisque Kestner with real porcelain teeth. We'd had a cabinet specially built for what I thought would be the beginning of her own collection." The longer Virginia Booth spoke in the past, the more her voice drained of its color until it was so pale and weak that it flattened into a dull monotone.

"Muffie simply had no interest in dolls. As with every-thing else I tried....She never had an interest in any-thing but her father's sports—especially the hunting. She was an expert marksman." She looked at Beth. "You know the Whitmores' hunting plantation? She would go with Brent." Finally humbled by her memories, she looked at me. "Brent was my husband. Muffie's father," she explained.

I didn't dare even nod for fear of breaking her spell of comfort.

"Oh, but this is all so unimportant now, isn't it? So in-significant..." Her voice trailed off as the maid arrived with a tray of ice water in a crystal pitcher and water glasses etched with the family initials. She walked to the table in the middle of the room and, with the tray, pushed aside the stack of gardening manuals I had looked through earlier, then placed the tray on the table. She poured a glass and brought it to Virginia Booth, who released Beth's hand just long enough to take a delicate sip and then returned the glass to the woman's waiting hand.

When the maid had walked quietly out, Virginia Booth began again, refreshed and emboldened, ready to share some cold hard facts. "I went to the boat. An-nounced, of course. I had called first. I would never want to...interrupt anything." She clamped her eyes closed and breathed deeply, the thought of lesbian encounters making her almost physically sick. "But when I got there...they were like that...under the covers..." The tears she had been stoically holding back finally spilled into her lap. With her next words, her voice cracked.

"Purposely, I believe. Muffie staged that scene to shock me. Oh, how much she must have hated me then. Never had I felt her hate so strongly as that moment. I had sued my own daughter—and lost." She pulled her hand from Beth's. The rest of the story had to be told alone; even Beth would not be privy to the sorrow running through her veins and seeping from her poreless skin.

"I don't think she had told Pat I was coming. It was Muffie's hate that bred that vengeful scene—the two of them in bed. Pat looked shocked. Embarrassed. But Muffie laughed at me. That's when my hand rose to whatever was in its reach. A glass vase. So very heavy. And I remember thinking it was not my strength that lifted it from the table, but my anger. My anger threw it. I threw it at them. A glass vase. I don't know that I meant to hit her … or either of them. I was so angry, so hurt; all the years of frustration and loss seemed to well up in that one minute of letting go … my hand around the thing closest to my reach … and then letting it go … and watching it fly across the room … as if it sailed under its own power, and hit, not Pat—who had ducked from its path—but my daughter Muffie, who had turned toward Pat, worried that it would hurt her. Muffie was worried about Pat while I watched the vase crack into the back of my daughter's head. She seemed almost to bounce— bounce across the bed as if she were a child playing on a trampoline. Or maybe that's what I thought I saw—my child jumping on a bed, laughing and playing. Maybe that's not how it was at all. Maybe what I really saw was what seemed to appear moments later when my head cleared of its fury. The bed awash with Muffie's blood and Pat screaming. Bending over my daughter and screaming. I ran out. Off the boat. I ran home, here, and sat quietly, waiting for someone to call. To tell me what I'd done and how to fix it. But no one called. I waited in my room, it seemed like hours, but no one called. Until Scott came. He came to me here, and told me...they were *both* dead."

She looked at me now full-face. "Can you tell me—is that how Muffie died? From me? From what I threw?"

Instead of answering her, I said, "Is that all? You threw something at her and left? Just ran out?"

She looked away. "I did. Just literally ran away from it all." She might have smiled ruefully at that point. But she didn't. Instead she poked her head up as if she smelled a sudden odor. "I have to excuse myself a minute." She looked at Beth. "May I? I'll be right back."

Beth took her elbow and helped her from the chair. She had been drained by her confessional; she was weak, and so much frailer than the last two times I'd seen her. Beth and I watched in silence as she trod unsteadily out on legs not ready for the burden she had taken on and then released to us.

Neither Beth nor I spoke, both knowing that the time for comments would be later, after the police were called, after Virginia Booth was led away in handcuffs and escorted—not by her chauffeur or a maid—but by police officers to a Newport jail cell to await arraignment for the murder of her daughter on the family yacht.

Beth turned her pale and worried face to the windows, walked to them, and stood looking out at the sage old sea that promised answers, but, of course, offered none. The ocean was just another mirage of wisdom—a body of water that so many gazed at, thinking that there lay the answers to all life's mysteries, when, in fact, all those pretty waves were only a calming solace after the bitter truths had already been uncovered. As much as I could, I empathized with Beth, as well as with Virginia Booth, who could have been Beth's own mother after too many gin gimlets, hurling a book or a shoe or a plate in anger, as we've all done, me more often than others, I admit, except this time the instrument in Virginia Booth's second of lost control was a heavy glass vase that hit, as luck would have it, the back of her daughter's head— Muffie Booth's head—and killed her.

I joined Beth in her ocean vigil, watching waves trickle over the craggy shore. The French casement windows were open to the breeze. Why was there always a perfect breeze by the water—nature's oscillating fan set on "perfect flow"? Beth walked closer to the window, looking out and lifting her head to the clean salty scent while I remained where I'd been standing, but we both succumbed to the hypnotic undulation of the sea, until, like the sudden waking from a dream, Beth turned to me, and I read the question in her eyes: How long does a bathroom visit take, or a sip of brandy, or a brief telephone call in private to friends and relatives?

Beth tilted her head at me and our eyes locked.

Muffie and her dad's favorite pastime—those weekend trips to the hunting plantation to escape the smiling faces of those freakish dolls, the embodiment of her mother's disdain—the stifling confines of Virginia Booth's relentless disapproval, Muffie knowing that her struggle

with her mother would continue until their deaths. And
Brent Booth, Muffie's father, knowing sooner than
Virginia Booth that their daughter was different, but ac-
cepting her nonetheless—offering her a father's uncon-
ditional love. Brent Booth rescued his daughter from all
those pretty dolls that Virginia Booth used like punches,
smashing them into Muffie's head like a command that
Muffie simply wouldn't obey.

"Oh my God," Beth whispered.

I rose to my feet. "Where would they be?" I asked.

"Upstairs, in a locked cabinet."

Together we ran to the oak-railed staircase and up,
Beth scampering and me striding two steps at a time.

"Doogie?" Beth called. Then screamed louder, "Doogie!
Doogie!"

Beth was answered by the shot itself, ringing clearly
through the upstairs hallway, and deafening even
through the closed door of the Booths' upstairs study.

I followed Beth to the heavy wooden door and pulled
at the locked handle, while Beth talked through it. But
no amount of Beth's pleading or screaming brought a
sound from the silent room. I kicked, kicked, and kicked
until wood from around the lock began to splinter free.
Beth stood aside, wide-eyed, astonished at my strength.
The same kind of mindless strength that Virginia Booth
had used to hurl a glass vase at her own daughter.
Passion fueled my legs, until the door finally gave way.

The body that used to be Virginia Booth—a body
now faceless from the bullet that had ripped it from
recognition—lay next to an open cabinet from which one

rifle was missing and lay at the feet of her blood-splattered body.

Beth ran ahead to her. I was held back by a sudden déjà vu. I looked around this room at the white-shuttered windows open to a sparkling sea. The looming mahogany bookcases filled with leather-bound books, a few larger volumes splayed on round tables shining from the glow of low-lit Tiffany lamps. A puddle of Virginia Booth's blood worked its way toward the frayed ends of a rich-colored Turkish rug.

But this is the wrong room. The room in my memory is small and dark; the shades are drawn.

The shades were always down in my mother's room. She liked the darkness, especially at the end, when she began to shun the air itself as if it were keeping her alive against her will.

I was downstairs alone. Why was the television off? It was too quiet in the house. It was the quiet that had first drawn me outside myself and into the lives of the two people upstairs—my parents in my mother's room. I heard the clicking sound first. A constant clicking sound. I was too inexperienced then to know the sound of a gun firing with no load. I followed the clicks to the foot of the stairs. Still waiting to hear a voice, his not hers, because hers had lost its sound long before that day. My mother's weak voice would no longer carry outside the tiny guest room where she slept all day next to a table cluttered with pill bottles and dirty half-filled water glasses.

When the clicking stopped, there was a boring si-lence. I waited at the foot of the stairs, and might have returned to the television, but after the crack that made me deaf except for the ringing in my ears, I ran up the stairs, watching my feet hit the steps without sound. My father had gotten to the guest room first. Or had he been there from the beginning? He stood by the bed where my mother lay, blood dripping from her lip.

There were my parents—both of them dead, but one still standing—my father, whose hand by his side held a shiny metal gun.

"She was sick," he said. As if that explained the blood on the headboard. "Go back downstairs and wait."

I sat in the living room until the doorbell rang and I was taken down the front steps of our house by a tall stranger. He crushed my tiny fingers in his large brown fist. He held my hand too tightly, but I knew as he talked to me that he was hurting my hand out of sympathy. He didn't know how strong he was, or how to comfort a little girl who'd just seen her mother shot and killed.

And then another white space of time passed and I was roused from bed one morning in my aunt's house by my father, who was taking me home. It's as if everything that had happened in those empty white spaces of time happened in my absence. And maybe it did.

"Shannon? Shannon!" Beth was kneeling at Virginia Booth's side. Nothing to be done, but she was dialing 911 while looking up at me. I was still standing at a distance by the door. "What's wrong with you?" she asked.

"My mother," I said. "This is how she died."

If Beth's eyes could open wider, they did. The call made, she tucked her phone into a side pocket and stood away from Virginia Booth's body. "Shannon?"

"I think maybe my father shot her, but she was sick. I

remember the smells in the room. Alcohol, disinfectant, and something else—like the smell at the morgue that day of the autopsies—that sweet smell of decay. And Lucky wasn't there," I muttered.

Beth walked to me and took my elbow, much the same way as she'd taken Virginia Booth's in the morning room to help her stand. Beth, holding me by that elbow, led me out and back down the stairway, where at the bottom, two of Virginia Booth's uniformed staff stood waiting for our pronouncement. Beth, still holding my arm, passed them and without looking back, said, "Don't go up. Wait in the kitchen, please."

Beth walked me to a chair and lowered me into it. She took a few steps back and stood in front of me, waiting some seconds before speaking, within which time we heard the approaching sirens. "What happened?" she asked me. "Your mother shot herself? And what does Lucky have to do with it?"

I shrugged. "She was shot in the head, I think. The headboard was splattered red. She was sick all the time. I remember that. My father telling me she was going away soon. Cancer. The police took my father away for a while, because a black police officer took me to my aunt's house. My father never went to jail. I would know if he'd served time. And then one day he came back and got me."

"He did it? Your father shot her?"

I shrugged. "I never wanted to know. I wanted to remember that she'd just died of the cancer."

"Why," Beth said, "would you ever try that Cohen

case? Why didn't you pass it to someone else in the office?"

"I lost Cohen because I didn't think he was guilty. My heart wasn't in it—"

"Your heart is never in your cases, Shannon. That's why you're so good at it. Bleeding hearts mess up the blood evidence at trial. You lost the Cohen case because your heart *was* in it."

Before I could respond to her statement, the knocking at the front door brought the two uniformed maids to us. They didn't want to answer the door without Beth's approval—Beth, who had now, by default, become the mistress of the house.

"Open it," she told them. "And take them in here first."

Police officers, one after another, lumbered into the room like salivating black bears snorting power in a pretty English garden. Beth remained seated, forcing them to hover around her, to lean into her hushed tones as she spoke softly of Virginia Booth's confession in this room by the sea, and then of her self-inflicted sentence in the study upstairs. The officers, taking Beth's cue—and the silent pleas of the elegant room—responded in whispers. Through a thick curtain of childhood memories, I watched Beth spread serenity like a blanket over a fire. But she was just the eye of this storm—the worst was yet to come.

22

HEARTS, FLOWERS, AND NAKED DAISIES

I FELT BETH DARTING GLANCES AT ME AS SHE drove back to Providence. She wanted me to speak but I couldn't. Virginia Booth's suicide had triggered my past, pervaded my present, and threatened to muck up my future, and I couldn't find the words to get myself jump-started again.

"Are you okay?" she ventured to ask about half an hour into the drive. We were almost at the exit to Providence.

I chose the safest present and ignored my past. "Do you think Virginia Booth may have killed Pat Boardman too?"

Beth shook her head. "When someone like Doogie confesses, it's the whole deal. And don't forget, Pat Boardman's death was a different MO. A handgun killed Pat Boardman, not a glass vase or a hunting rifle. And I don't believe for an instant Doogie went on that boat armed with a gun and an intent to kill."

Beth's words seemed right, though I couldn't, at the time, have said why. My head was a jumble, and I spoke just to break the silence and comfort Beth, because I could feel her worry crowding me, removing the oxygen from the car. I opened the window and the climate-cooled air was sucked out into the humidity. "So who did this, Beth? Someone went on the boat after Virginia Booth left. And I know Scott was there after. He did this, didn't he? He killed his wife, and probably Leo Safer too."

"Shannon, are you sure that's what you want to talk about right this minute? The Boardman murders? There's nothing else *closer to home* on your mind?"

"What's the point of rehashing my past? It isn't going to change anything. I only wonder . . . did my father start drinking after my mother died? Or was he a lush first . . . before he decided to *off* my mother?"

"He didn't murder your mother, Shannon. If he shot her, it was euthanasia and you know it. Stop dramatizing it. You're sounding more and more like Marianna every day."

"Poor Mari," I said. "She always gets a bad emotional rap from us. I'm actually gaining a new respect for her— the way she faces this emotional shit head-on. She sticks her head into her heart and mucks around in there until she gets it all cleaned out."

"Or at least tries to," Beth added.

"And I never give her anything but grief for doing it. Push it away, I always say. Jump right over the hearts and flowers. But sometimes getting over it means stepping plop in the middle of it first."

"But you knew what happened? I mean, this isn't like

the movies, where you see Doogie lying there and it all comes back to you in a flash, right?"

"I'm not sure. I would have been about four or five years old at the time. I think I remember it. I think I walked in right after the gunshot, but it could just be a faulty memory—the bloody headboard. Could be that I heard about it in whispers for so long that I just think I was there. Only my father would know that for sure."

Beth remained quiet, waiting for me to segue to the obvious. Would I seek my old man out and query him? She was probably thinking that I was on a rare emotional roll, and the less she interrupted me, the more I'd open up. But I was pretty much done with my past and was already working on the present to determine how it would adversely affect my future with the slippery Scott Boardman.

"I wonder if Virginia Booth confessed to Scott when he went to her house that night. I wonder if he already knew all this...about Muffie Booth...and kept it from me. So what do I do now? Confront him, and see what he has to say?"

"Not me," Beth said. "I wouldn't give him the right time of day. I may have a different way of doing things than you, but I'd let him come to me. I'd stay quiet, Shannon, and let him get a little nervous at your silence. Let him come beg you for information. And he'll know you've got it, because soon it'll be all over the news that you and I were with Doogie when she...died."

Beth was thinking more clearly than me, and I was happy for it. Truth is, I was always worried Beth wouldn't make it as a valuable member of our little AG legal team.

She was proving me wrong, and I was glad. "You're right," I said. "I'm not thinking straight today. This emotional shit is for the birds. It fuzzies up my brain."

" 'Fuzzies'?" Beth said. "Even your language is sprouting little smiley faces. You sure you're okay?"

"It *fucks up* my brain. Is that better?"

"Well, yeah. It makes me feel more secure—especially after what we just witnessed—that the world is still right and spinning on its proper axis."

"Well, then, let me make you even more secure. Scott Boardman met Leo Safer right before the murders. Maybe Scott told Leo he was going straight to the boat to see his wife. Maybe Leo Safer knew more than we think he did and could actually have proved something, so Scotty boy eliminated him on the boat with me that day, and then shot himself in the arm for good measure."

"What about Brooke? Was she with Scott Boardman that night too, or not?"

"Getting that story straight from Scott and her is like picking petals off a daisy. She was with him; she wasn't with him; she was with him; she wasn't with him. But we'll keep plucking away at the flower girl until she's stripped bare and blowing naked in the wind."

Beth smiled. "You're going to be fine, Shannon. Just fine."

About five minutes from the AG parking lot, where Beth was dropping me to pick up my car, my cell phone vibrated a silent ring. "It's Vince," I said, flipping the phone open and bringing it to my ear.

"I just got a call from the Newport cops. Having a busy day?" he said.

"You betcha," I answered back. "You want us in?"

"No, go home, both of you. We'll talk in the morning. Try as I might, I can't see you did anything wrong this time. The Booth woman called Beth for a meeting, right? Of course, you didn't have to accompany her against my orders, but I could see why Beth would want a lawyer on hand."

"Who told you Virginia Booth called Beth?"

"Your buddies, trying to save both your asses. Is Beth surviving?"

"Since when do you give a crap?"

"Your girlfriends are worried. They didn't call you?"

"Matter of fact, no. Which leads me back to my initial question: What do you really want, Vince? Beth's welfare isn't it, and you know I know it."

He answered with another question. "You're going home for the night, right?"

"I was planning on it, but you want to pay me over-time, I'll come up and fill you in."

"Lynch, lately you're not even worth your regular pay. Jeff sent over some paperwork in the Cohen case *you lost.* He gave me some good zingers on my decision to let *him* go last year and keep *you* on. Don't make me change my mind."

"Nighty night, Vince," I said without a fight. "I'm beat."

We managed to hang up on each other simultaneously as Beth pulled up next to my Suburban. I could tell she was preparing some parting speech laced with a missionary's offer of help for my tortured soul, so I cut her off before she dished out an emotional soup of solace and support, whereupon I'd have to beat her back into a pre-Doogie-suicide manner of dealing with me. "Forget about what happened today, Beth. Okay? Don't torture me with it. I'll deal."

"Are you going to tell Laurie and Marianna?"

"Nothing to tell, but I'm sure we'll revisit it over a bottle of Captain Morgan's spiced rum at next year's Christmas party while we're all throwing up in some Downcity alley. Have a good night. See you in the a.m."

IT WAS ALREADY PAST EIGHT WHEN BETH DROVE out of the office lot. I unlocked my Suburban, boarded the driver's seat, and started my engine. The headlights shot on, illuminating the parked and shiny black Cadillac SRX bearing the vain and chimerical license plate "VP."

Vince rarely stayed in the office past six. I switched off the engine and hopped out of my truck. That Vince's car was still in the lot could have meant nothing more than he'd met someone for dinner who'd picked him up and given him a ride. But his car still parked at the office, and the fact that he'd called to pinpoint Beth's and my whereabouts—and told us twice not to come back to the office—led me to suspicions too vivid to ignore.

I unlocked the AG back door with my set of keys. The elevators to our floor were likewise locked. I punched the up button and the doors spread open immediately, whereupon I inserted a special key unlocking only the entry to our office floor and the elevator responded by slamming closed and taking me up. When the doors opened to our floor, I followed a path of light to the conference room door, underneath which a sliver of blue fluorescence escaped into the dark hall. My ear to the door yielded silence, though I thought I heard some muffled breathing that could have been whispering, hushed voices, or the air-conditioning unit sputtering on and off. It also could have been someone working late, but because I was so intimately familiar with everyone on our team, I knew I was on sounder ground by assuming the live presence of something illicit under way, *behind closed doors.*

I didn't try the door, knowing the slightest sound of my hand turning the knob would quiet the already hushed voices within. But I knelt by the narrow opening at the base of the door and listened until my knees gave way and I sat against the door. Boredom was setting in when I heard a woman's giggle, and then another, and then Vince's gruff voice oddly edged in a lilting swirl.

I smelled cigarettes. And then the clink of a glass.

Jesus, was this just one of Vince's dates? Some pathetic female so desperate for attention that she'd let Vince hide her in a conference room because he couldn't or didn't want to be seen with her in public? Was all this private candlelit poppycock just a penned-in soiree between the Pig and his pig?

I was getting ready to rise and leave when I heard the faintest whisper of a familiar name. A name that had been on the tip of my tongue for the past two weeks. A name that kept popping up like a jack-in-the-box no matter how I tried to keep my hands off the crank.

It was Scott's idea, the voice said.

Scott.

I rammed my hand against the door in a vicious rap

and then tugged on the locked handle and turned with all my strength. "Who's in there?" I heard my voice thunder through the dark hall. "Open the goddamn door!"

What did I expect to find? Or more precisely *who*? By then I'd already erased the memory of Vince's car still parked in the lot. Familiar-sounding voice notwithstanding, it couldn't be Vince. Vince was at dinner, of course, not there, locked in the AG conference room discussing an open case with some dingbat broad. This was not Vince's MO. He may have been deficient in socially acceptable vocabulary, good looks, and the proper way to hold a knife, but professional integrity he was full of. Or he was full of shit, and all the privacy, responsibility, and confidentiality crap he'd been espousing and spouting off about for the past six years was just so much... *bull*.

"Open the door," I screamed again to the room, now hushed in a conspiratorial silence. "Open it or I'll break the fucking lock. And it won't be the first door I've kicked down today."

"Lynch," I heard Vince say, "I told you to go home. We'll talk in the morning."

"Vince? Who's in there?"

The female voice giggled and Vince shushed her.

He came to the closed door. "Lynch, go home," he said in a calming conversational tone. And then he whispered, "I'm on top of this."

"I'll just bet you are, Vince. Move away from the door—"

I could hear him move away, his voice more distant. "If you break this door down, so help me, Lynch, I'll fire your ass for good this time."

"I don't think so, Vince. I think once I get in there and knock some sense into you, you'll be giving me a raise."

"Shit," I heard him mumble. "Wait," he said to me, and I heard him walk away, say a few undecipherable words to the lady-in-waiting, and then return to the door and click the deadbolt. Slowly the door opened under Vince's power.

My mouth hung open, speechless again. What was happening to me? Vince could have shot me through the head with his own gun and laid me on a table next to Virginia Booth, who had recently joined Pat Boardman and Muffie Booth in the morgue down the block, because there at the table, leaning back against the stiff-backed conference room chair with her hair tumbling at her shoulders, was the lovely Brooke Stanford, smiling at me as if she were back on the job full-time and had just replaced me as the sitting authority on all things worth knowing.

Vince remained on the threshold, his shirtsleeves rolled to his elbows, a mist of sweat on the ruddy forehead of his flushed face, his tie missing in action, and his shirt opened at the neck, revealing a hideous gold cross dangling amid the dense hair of his sun-deprived olive-green skin. But the gray-specked chest curls tickling the Pig's throat were not my main concern. What grabbed my attention were the red tresses of the girl sitting at the long conference table, whose shoeless feet were tucked comfortably under her silk-stockinged legs, and whose familiar Chanel pumps lay askew on the floor next to her as if they'd been kicked off at separate yet well-timed intervals, either before or after a tickle and frolic from my erstwhile respected if not revered boss, Attorney General Vince Piganno.

If I expected an explanation from either of them, I was sorely disappointed, because the three of us stood rooted in place—Vince midway between Brooke and me, and me still standing just outside the door—until Brooke emitted another of her nauseating little burps of amusement. She leaned over to display a decent amount of unbridled cleavage and retrieved her shoes from their asundered positions on the floor, and then, pointedly flexing her toes ballerina-style, she slipped the shoes on her dainty feet.

"Don't go anywhere," Vince said, looking at me, but somehow talking to someone else. I looked around the room for another participant in the tawdry scene, but it was not until Brooke flicked those high-fashioned shoes off her feet again that I realized Vince's words had been meant for her. I was still the intruder—the uninvited one—the one who deserved no other explanation but the dry and lifeless words that came next from Vince's worried frown: "Go home, Lynch. You've had a rough day. The press will be at our doors first thing in the morning for an official statement. I need you prepared for the damage-control phase of Virginia Booth's suicide."

There are times when explanations are necessary in the very moment they are sought, and there are other times, like the present, that an excuse for one's poor choices could wait for the church confessional, or a witness stand, or just before the executioner's saline drip begins its course through your condemned veins. As difficult it was sans explanation, I backed away from the doorway, knowing instinctively that even if Vince decided to offer an excuse for his inexcusable behavior, it would certainly not be forthcoming that evening while Brooke remained in his presence, shoeless, smiling, and with what I now noticed was a long-stemmed glass of white wine pressed hard against her lipstick-smeared kisser.

I could have buzzed up the girls that very evening during my drive home to apprise them of the Pig's dirty little rendezvous with Brooke Stanford, but with no explanation myself, either from Vince or one I'd conjured up in a spiteful rage, what would be the point in intruding on their evening meal with such nauseating news? On the brighter side, seeing Vince enjoying an evening snack on Brooke in the AG conference room had somehow pushed the day's spine-tingling events at least temporarily to the back of my mind. During the drive to my loft, the phone I'd fought hard to keep tucked away in my pocket, to avoid spreading the newest nasty Vince gossip, began to ring of its own accord. Well, not entirely. Beth had helped it along with her nimble little fingers.

I flipped it open. "Yup?" I answered. And expecting her comforting wish for my good night's sleep, I quickly added, "I'm fine, Beth. Go to sleep. I'll see you in the morning." But before she could sprinkle the sandman's dust into my eyes, "Nope," she answered. "Not so soon."

I was readying to flip my phone closed, regretting I'd answered it to begin with, when another voice took to the airwaves: "Hey," Laurie said. "It's me. The Fez. Now. One nightcap. Bye."

I had free choice. The four of us did—always—with no hard feelings, but I tucked my cell back into my pocket and veered left toward one of the darker Down-city alleys that would take me straight to hell—aka the Red Fez.

23

THE BIG GIRLS

IT HAD BEEN A YEAR SINCE I'D BEEN TO THE FEZ. Nothing appeared changed except the muck that seemed to be burgeoning like a mushroom in the dank, dark place. The Fez walls, once painted a shiny red, had slowly darkened to a bronzed rust, coated by a patina of cooking grease and pre-smoking-ban clotted fumes. The wide-plank pine floor, once pale, was now a neutral shade of gray, with the added virtue of being slip-proof from sticky grime.

The low-watt ceiling fixtures swayed drunkenly against the breeze of a new ceiling fan, and the Fez owners had done away with menus in favor of posting the daily fare on a chalkboard over the bar, requiring diners to leave their seats and crowd the bar to read the nightly specials. But most of the clientele were jaded regulars who'd either memorized the offerings by damned heart or demanded the tired-looking waitress to either recite the information or suffer gratuity deprivation.

My dim view of the place notwithstanding, I knew where to find the girls even in bad lighting. I headed straight to the bar in back, where Joe, another year older but arrested in the prepubescent stage of pockmarked greasy skin, still held the title of managing bartender despite the fact that he was the only one.

I mounted the empty stool at the end, where, without a word to the girls, I ordered a Glenlivet neat. "Open up a new bottle, Joe. I want to hear the seal break."

"It ain't watered down," he said, standing with his head crooked to the side, a slimy strand of yellowed-blond hair falling over the receding hairline of his balding head. Up and down in a nervous tic, he rubbed one of his hands on the side of his apron. "You ain't been here in a dog's age and you walk in here giving me grief right off."

"If it's not watered down, it's stale. Open a new bottle, please, Joe. I've had a rough day."

Marianna threw a twenty-dollar bill on the bar. "That's your tip, Joe, okay? Open it for her, and we'll all have a glass. Except make mine on the rocks."

"And mine with soda and ice," Laurie said.

Joe then looked at Beth, knowing there'd be yet one more change to the order. "I'll have the same as Laurie except with lime . . . and vodka . . . and hold the scotch."

"Oh, come on, Beth," Marianna snapped. "Just this once?"

She shook her head petulantly. "You know I've had somewhat of a bad day myself. I don't see why *just this once* I can't order my *own* drink like a *big girl.*"

I leaned forward on the bar. "She's been acting like

this all day," I explained. "It must be the law school acceptance. She's starting to act like an asshole."

"Like one of us," Marianna added.

"Beth, we thought we knew ye," Laurie said in a Brooklyn-accented Irish brogue.

"Nothing is sacred," Marianna said to Beth. "Tell us about Virginia Booth. Maybe your good nature died with her."

"Some of my innocence did, I can tell you," Beth said. "Doogie was a rock, like that Prudential Insurance ad. She was what everyone refers to as 'good stock.' Doogie was where you went when *you* had problems. And she could usually dispense some good old-fashioned wisdom and you'd come away feeling rooted in something strong and healthy. For her to take her life like that is—well, it's anathema to everything she stood for."

I was assuming, since Marianna's lead question was posited to Beth and related to Virginia Booth's death, that Beth had said nothing about my childhood revelation. In the past I would have expected nothing less from Beth than a single-minded respect of one's privacy. But who knew this new pre-law Beth; who knew what she was brewing to become? She may have held the mistaken belief that copying the three of us was a noble aspiration. Hah!

A few more comments and questions about Virginia Booth's suicide from both Laurie and Marianna, and I was certain my secret was safe: Neither had even alluded to my awakened memory of my mother's death. Not that I had any particular interest in hiding my past from my friends, but it was nice to know the secret was still

mine to do with as I wished. And that Beth was still…
Beth.

"I got a call from Jeff Kendall today," Marianna announced in a brief post–Virginia Booth lull. "He asked
for *you*, Shannon, but Andy sent the call to my line when
he couldn't find you. Jeff said to tell you that all worries
about the Leo Safer murder are over for you—as if you
were ever really worried about being charged—*and* he
claims that Miss Brooke is hiring *him* to represent her in
a potential perjury charge—filing that false police statement. Jeff said Vince sent Brooke to him. Vince has been
recommending Jeff to a lot of people lately. He sent him
for you too, Shannon, didn't he?"

Laurie said, "Vince knows Jeff, so he feels secure with
him. Who better to represent the other side than someone who was once on yours?"

"But why Brooke?" Marianna asked. "Does Vince
even *like* her since she became such an AG liability?"

The answer to that question was a no-brainer. "I
think Vince likes Brooke even more since the false statement problem. Because he can justifiably fire her, and
then be free to fuck her brains out."

The silence that followed was kind of fun. I loved being the bearer of shocking news. Little did I know that
the shock would still be mine.

Laurie raised her brows at Marianna, and they both
leaned over to me. Marianna was the one who spoke.
"Vince and Brooke? I don't think so, Shannon. I think
you need a good night's sleep."

"What the frig does that mean?"

"Between this Scott Boardman thing…and then watching Virginia Booth shot like your mother—"

"You little bitch," I said to Beth.

Beth choked on her vodka soda and slammed it down on the bar. "Me?"

I stood from my stool and stomped over to her. "I actually thought for a minute you'd kept it between us. I actually thought for a goddamn minute you were different from me, not the asshole I am. But you're no better than the rest of us, a rotten little gossip as bad as the day is long. Maybe more so, especially after what I witnessed with you and that little loose-lipped Lolly."

"Lolly?"

"Yeah, you thrive on other people's misery."

Beth's lips were quivering. She wasn't crying, but the agony in her face had turned it beet red.

"Whoa," Laurie said. "What are you ranting about?"

"I didn't…" Beth choked out, "didn't say a word…" She turned away from me and faced Joe, who had come over during the melee to make sure his tip was still safely tucked under our bar tab.

"She told you about my mother and the cancer? How I saw my father shoot her like a lame dog? Fuck!" I said. "You can all go fuck yourselves." I pulled a wad of cash from my jacket pocket and dropped another twenty on the bar. "You know what? I *do* need a breather from you. From *all* of you."

I was marching out the door when Marianna ran after me and pulled me to a stop. "I don't know what the hell happened with you and Beth today, Shannon, but she said nothing. Mike told me about your mother. Mike knew about your parents and the…Your father was charged with her murder and then the charges were dropped. He told me a while ago, and I just assumed you knew that we all knew and never wanted to talk about it. I just never brought it up. That's all there is to it. And after today…I just assumed…"

"Fuck," I said again. "Fuck!"

The consonant-filled word seemed to halt my frustrations like a sudden wrong note in a melody, a black-key sharp to a white flat. I looked back at Beth, who was still turned away from me. Laurie remained at her side while Marianna swung away at me. "You hurled your misplaced rage at Beth like a batter trying to bang a home run. But there is no game. Beth didn't utter a word about it. What exactly happened at Virginia Booth's house today?"

"Fuck, fuck, fuck," I repeated as I looked at my feet. Marianna softened, her shoulders fell. "I'm going home, Mari. Tell Beth what you just told me…about Mike. She'll understand. And she won't be angry with me." I looked up at Mari. "Okay? Dry her fucking tears for me. I gotta go."

"No, Shannon! You do it. Go apologize to her now. Grow the fuck up!"

I swirled around and left the Fez, bumping into Jeff Kendall halfway down the street to my car.

"Hey," he said. "I've been trying to reach you all day. Did Marianna tell you about Brooke Stanford?"

"What about her?" I said, unlocking my door and hoping he'd disappear into thin air like a bad smell in a breeze.

"Vince wants her represented by counsel. He didn't even give her an option."

It was then that I remembered I'd never told the girls about the little conference room tête-à-tête between Brooke and the Pig.

"Is he paying you too? To represent her? Is he paying her fee?"

Jeff was holding on to my door so I couldn't close it. "We didn't get that far. But she can afford me. My family knows hers in Connecticut. I'll get paid."

"Yeah, I bet you're all real cozy. Like Virginia Booth, you know her family too? And Muffie, her daughter, the girl who was shot with Pat Boardman? You know that family too? Fucked up. All of you are fucked up."

Jeff giggled good-naturedly. "Hey, Lynch, we're all of us fucked up. Me, you, Vince, Beth, Marianna. I don't know about Laurie. Jews are so used to being fucked up and fucked over that they're the only ones who handle it without pulling the trigger. But the rest of us? One big bowl of mixed nuts."

"How'd you find me here? I haven't been to this place in over a year."

"I let my fingers do the walking. You think the bartenders in this small city don't know all of you by bra size?"

"So you're going to run and tell Vince again that we're patronizing a mob hangout?"

Jeff laughed again. "That was between me and Marianna. She busted my chops last year, so I zinged her. Marianna's not the helpless little doe you think she is."

"Don't be telling me what I think, Jeff. You're still in

love with her, otherwise you wouldn't still be sniffing after us every chance you get. Why is it so important that we know you're representing Stanford? What's in it for you other than giving you the chance to be around the AG office again, and, more specifically, Marianna?"

"Mari and I are finished. I just thought you might be curious as to why Vince is being so *fatherly* with Brooke when he should be chopping her up for pork feed."

"I'll tell you why. Because Brooke's an AG employee on leave and Vince has to make sure she doesn't embarrass the office. She's a loose cannon who's still hoping to snag Scott Boardman even if it's in a jailhouse marriage. She knows something about the night of the murders that she's not sharing, and Vince knows you have no allegiance to your clients or the code of professional responsibility, so if he makes *you* represent her, you'll ignore Brooke's right to privacy and tell him everything he wants to know as long as he dangles the right carrot in front of you. In short, Vince is playing you *and* Brooke Stanford."

Jeff didn't waste time fighting back. With his hand still on my car door, he swung it closed with such force the car shook. I watched him walk off toward the Fez and waited until he disappeared inside before I hopped in and drove off.

I might have been done for the day—a day that had felt overstuffed with too many hours—but instead I drove by the office once more to see if Vince and Brooke had emptied the bottle of chardonnay (and the lust in Vince's loins). Vince's car was gone. Too tired to make assumptions as to whether Vince had driven Brooke home, or whether he'd *taken* her home, I simply headed home myself while a jumble of discordant facts banged around in my head like a child with a new set of drums.

But sleep wasn't on my to-do list, because Scott Boardman was on my answering machine.

"Call me," the voice said after I hit the flashing button. Seconds later my cell rang.

"Where are you?" Scott Boardman said.

"Home," I answered.

"I just called a second ago."

"I wasn't home a second ago. I'm tired. What do you want?"

"To help you. I think I can help find who did this to my wife. To Leo."

"Are you sure it wasn't you?"

"I'm serious."

"You've been serious since I met you and we haven't gotten anywhere. Why don't you tell me a good joke?"

"I miss you, Shannon."

I hung up on him, turned the ringer off on my landline, and then powered down my cell. I was brushing my teeth when I heard the hard rapping at my door.

"Hey, open up," Mike called. "Your cell is off and you aren't answering your phone. Are you okay in there?"

I spit into the bathroom sink and went to the door. No need to peep through the hole. I recognized his voice. I was wiping smeared toothpaste from my mouth as I unbolted the door.

"Nice look," he said, pointing to my mouth.

"If Marianna sent you, I'm fine. Go home. Wherever the hell *home* is."

Mike's glance fell from my Crest-covered mouth to my toes and then traveled slowly up my bare legs, which were left exposed just shy of my crotch by an old white T-shirt I'd donned for bed.

"You shouldn't be answering the door that way," he said, his glance returning to my lower extremities.

"How'd you get in the downstairs door?"

"An old cop trick," he said. "There isn't a lock I can't pick."

I turned into my apartment. "Mari gave you the keys, huh?"

"Yeah," he said, following me and slamming the door closed.

"If she's so worried, why didn't she come herself?" I asked.

"She said something about you needing breathing space," he explained while he surveyed my loft. "Nice place. What's it run you a month?"

"McCoy, it's after midnight. I'm beat." I pulled a throw from the couch and wrapped it sarong-style around my waist to cover my legs, thereby removing any additional incentive for him to remain—as subliminal as it was.

He walked to my fridge. "You got a beer?"

"McCoy, go the fuck home!"

He ignored me and pulled open the refrigerator door, peering inside and moving things around as if he'd been doing it for years. "Brooke Stanford and Vince Piganno are sharing sheets. Did you know that?"

"Impossible," I said. I pulled the throw off me and rushed him at the refrigerator door. "Get out of my house." I slammed the door closed. "And Vince is just pumping her for information. Nothing more."

"Yeah, he's pumping her all right."

I faced him. Barefoot, I was a couple inches shorter than him. "You want the couch? Because I'm going to sleep."

He walked past me to the windows overlooking Providence. "Hey, look, I'm real sorry about your mother. Marianna told me about the face-off at the Fez. I'm the one who told her. I remembered the story from . . . well . . . someone told me. I heard it before. I shouldn't have said anything."

"You should have come to me first."

"You know it was a mercy thing, right? Your old man couldn't stand to see her suffer anymore. It wasn't murder—"

"Yeah, shit, McCoy. Whatever—"

"Don't interrupt me when I'm talking." He flared his nostrils, then lowered his head like a tired bull. "Give me a break here, okay? I don't do sentiment easy, especially with a broad like you who thinks crying is a four-letter word."

We faced each other—he across the room by the windows and me standing under the harsh overhead kitchen lights—both of us with our metaphoric guns drawn.

"See, Marianna's easy," he said. "She can rip a Band-Aid off a wound so fast you don't feel a thing. But you? Jesus Christ, you *are* the wound. You're a fucking pain in the ass."

"I didn't invite you here."

He nodded. "Right. Because you're also a thickheaded

pain in the ass. And frankly, I don't know why your friends even put up with you."

"Interesting question. I'll sleep on it."

"I'm not going anywhere yet, so sit tight. You don't scare me, Slim." He walked to my couch and sat. "Now bring me a fucking beer and sit down."

I went to the kitchen, pulled a cold Heineken from the vegetable bin in the fridge and popped the top off. I brought the beer to the couch and sat, putting the bottle on the table and pulling the throw back over my legs.

He eyed me a few seconds and winced like he'd gotten stuck with the unfortunate job of cleaning out the elephant cage. "Look, I know about your father. Your friends know too. So, clear the damn air. They'll feel better. You'll feel better—"

"I need sleep. That's all. Just sleep. No point in going backward, you know?"

Mike swiped the bottle from the table, took a gulp, and then slammed it back down. Motionless and staring at me, he refused to relieve the uncomfortable silence between us either physically or verbally. He waited for more from me.

"I got hooked up with some bad people in high school. Did the drug and alcohol thing. A little petty larceny at the local Rite Aid. Nothing big, but on the fast track to the wrong side. One night I ended up in jail for stealing cigarettes from one of those all-night gas stations. I was seventeen and still living at the house pretty much by myself—my father would disappear for long stretches of time. They put me in a cell and tried to find someone to pick me up. After a few minutes some guy in the cell next to me starts talking. 'I'm sorry,' he says. 'I did it for her, but I didn't know what it would be doing to you.' What the fuck? I look over at this guy. He was a mess. Filthy. A three-day-old beard. And skinny. I remember his ropy neck and the bones running up and down his chest where his shirt was open. And shit, if it's not my old man, who I hadn't seen in months. And he's apologizing to me for killing my mother. Not apologizing for pulling the trigger, but for doing it while I was home. He said he should have made sure I was out of the house first. That's what he said. That he should have sent me to my aunt's first, then shot her head off."

Mike sat quietly. I was tired of my confession. Tired of everything. Tired of the emotion that was seeping from my pores like a toxin I was sweating off. "What are you doing here, Mike? *Really*. What do you want from me?"

"How'd you get to law school?"

"Hey, I don't know. It was either law school for three years or jail full-time. And you know me. I don't do things midrange." I shrugged. "I picked law. Maybe I would have made a better criminal, because my legal skills seem to be waning lately."

"You could have been a cop," he said. "Instead of law."

I shook my head. "Cops and criminals use the same tools for their job. And I like guns too much. I needed the safety of books."

"Good point," he conceded. And then he was apparently finished listening to my woeful saga, because he changed keys like a skillful baritone. "Leo Safer killed Pat Boardman," he said.

I took a deep breath. "Leo Safer?"

He retrieved his beer. "And then I think Boardman knocked Safer off. Think about it." Mike took a few hefty gulps, burped, and then continued. "Let's just say maybe Pat Boardman panicked after Muffie got clobbered by her mother, so she called Leo Safer to do damage control. So Safer goes to the scene and finds Muffie Booth dead and Pat huddled in a corner not knowing what the hell to do. Leo Safer thinks fast and slick—like a good campaign manager. If he pulls some drawers out, throws things around—it's just an unfortunate random killing of a woman on an expensive yacht. Except he knows Pat Boardman isn't going to go along with his story, so he puts a clean painless bullet through the back of her head when she's not looking. Now Scott Boardman's campaign can proceed and maybe even prosper with some nice sympathy votes from the public. He just lost his wife in an act of random violence. Maybe Boardman's new position will be let's-get-tough-on-crime kind of thing."

"And under your theory, does Scott know Leo Safer killed his wife?"

"Not at first. But when he puts two and two together, Safer winds up dead. That's the day we found you on his boat knocked out—and Boardman *nicked* in the arm by a bullet. He staged it. It's the Stanford-Boardman vacillating alibi story that causes the problems. One or both of 'em are lying."

"Why? To protect Leo Safer after Scott just *killed* him?" I shook my head. "More likely Scott would try to expose Safer as the murderer."

"Not if Scott Boardman wanted to stay alive politically. He's still a senator. Even if the presidential campaign is now out of reach, this whole dirty mess would have his senatorial constituency clamoring for his resignation."

Mike slugged down the rest of his beer and again slammed the bottle down hard on the glass coffee table. "The answer is in the soup of characters we already have. Stanford has been lying from the start to protect Boardman, but she's doing him more harm than good by changing stories and creating suspicion. But I think after Boardman killed Safer, that's when *he* started to lie."

"And Brooke is innocent of everything except being in love with Scott Boardman?"

"And sleeping with Vince Piganno—"

I covered my face with my hands. The mental picture of Vince grunting on top of Brooke Stanford was too horrific an image to conjure. "So Scott's the only bad man still walking. That's your conclusion? Virginia Booth killed Muffie by accident, Pat was murdered by Leo Safer to protect Scott's campaign, and Scott killed Leo Safer to end the whole sordid affair and cover all the tracks leading back to him and his campaign?"

He nodded. "And unless someone comes up with some new evidence," Mike said, then burped, "Boardman's going to walk for his part in it."

Mike brought his empty bottle to my kitchen. "You recycle here?" He opened the cabinet under the sink and then, giving up, placed the bottle on the countertop. "Look, Mata Hari, I think you got a bad crush on the senator, so feel free to screw his brains out while you're working him for information. But be prepared to give him up to the cops when that sterling moment of truth hits you like the flush from your first kiss."

Mike walked to the door and then turned to face me. He was nodding lethargically with a self-satisfied smirk on his face. How Marianna could stomach the guy, I didn't know, because I felt like forcibly removing his two front teeth with my one right foot.

"So you work on Boardman," he said with his hand on the door handle, "while Piganno *porks* Stanford. Between the two of you I'm sure you'll figure out how to pin the tail on the ass."

"You've got it all wrong between Vince and Brooke Stanford."

"I'm a man," he said. "I know how guys think. And no matter how hard you try, Slim, you're not thinking like a guy this time."

24

FIRE AND ICE

IT WAS HARD GOING BACK TO WORK THE NEXT morning. I went to Laurie's office first. She was gathering up papers for court and had little time to chat.

"Just get it over with, Shannon. Go to Beth and apologize. She'll forgive you before you get to the end of the sentence."

I nodded at my feet. "Bad stuff. My mother and shit. I thought Freud said you're supposed to have some revelation when the truth finally stares you in the face. I don't feel any different."

"Freud's a bunch of hooey. Besides, you always knew what happened with your parents. You just didn't want to dwell on it, so you pushed it to the back of your mind. But whatever damage it did—if it did any at all—was already done when it happened." She looked up at me, ready to bolt out the door. "We are who we are. Knowing all the details of what made us that way doesn't change a damn thing."

"Yeah, sure, you're right. But if I'm an asshole, I should try to change. No?"

"Yeah. *If you're an asshole.*" She walked to the door. "Gotta go. See you later."

I walked like a condemned prisoner to Beth's cubicle in the library. Her bag was slung on the back of her chair, but I felt a coward's relief that the chair was empty.

Back in my own office I found an envelope on my desk, on which, in Beth's private-school scroll, was written my name. I opened it and took a deep breath.

> *Dear Shannon, I know how hard it is for someone like you to deal with emotion. You need to apologize to Marianna and to me to get past this and learn a healthy lesson on friendship. Apologies are difficult, even for someone like me, but once you do it, you'll be a better person....*

I threw the wretched missive down on my desk and groaned. If I could just get through the damn *note,* I'd probably be a better person, but I couldn't even do that without wincing. I took another deep breath and picked it up again, forcing my eyes to journey the length of the high-winded sentences until I got to the end, where a calm sunset lulled me to a peaceful shore of relief:

> *...so there's no need to apologize. I accept it anyway, and so does Marianna. We love you, and will always be here for you if you ever want to talk about it.*
>
> *Always with love, Beth*

I think I would have rather apologized than face Beth after that note, but I suppose one misery was as good as another for bringing me to my emotional knees. I tossed the note in the trash and walked back to the library, where Beth sat huddled in books.

"Hey, Beth," I said. "Nice note. Thanks."

Before she could spread the lovely smile across her face too wide, I changed the subject. "Virginia Booth's funeral is tomorrow at the O'Neill-Hayes Funeral Home on Spring Street in Newport. It was in the obits this morning. I want you to go with me."

"Oh, I guess so. Okay. But maybe we should *all* go."

"I won't torture you. You don't need Marianna and Laurie for protection."

"Oh," she thought a minute. "Well, I wasn't even thinking of that. I thought maybe they'll be able to provide some *help* for us, because . . . well, is it possible you're not thinking with your usual sharp acuity because of your . . . *feelings* for Scott Boardman?"

Considering Beth's and my recent emotional skirmish, I was reluctant to air my feelings about her comment on my inability to remain neutral re Scott Boardman. So instead of saying the first thing that came to my tongue, I stifled the expletives and lied through my teeth: "Great idea. We'll all go together."

And then I exited the library finishing my sentence out of Beth's earshot: ". . . all dressed up and clacking around in high heels, drawing the attention of everyone who knows anything about these murders—and we'll learn *absolutely nothing.*"

———

LAURIE AND MARIANNA HAD INDEED WANTED TO attend the opulent and high-brow Newport funeral, so on the appointed day, I offered the suggestion that we refrain from huddling together and dress as differently as possible. Beth chose the typical Newport mourning style of St. John knit dress and midheel pumps. Marianna would don one of her Kate Hepburn trouser outfits; Laurie a linen-skirted suit; and me, my typical Saturday night whoring outfit of short skirt and bateau-necked skintight top. Everyone knew Beth and me anyway, so what was the point in disguising ourselves?

We agreed to work the scene individually, so we split up after exiting Marianna's Jeep. I knew Beth would be the best of us to accomplish the feat of fitting seamlessly into the crowd and chatting the mourners up. But could she stay tuned on the assigned program and fight the urge to lollygag with her old Newport friends?

Marianna dropped Beth and Laurie off at the door of the funeral home, where, just as I predicted, no sooner had Beth walked up the garden to the front steps than Lolly Bergen snatched her elbow, looked furtively around for the subject of her intended gossip, and then leaned into Beth's ear. The two remained glued together until they disappeared behind the black-enameled front door.

Laurie paused at the garden for a minute, waiting for Beth to go inside. I wasn't certain if Laurie was stalling because she thought it best for the two to enter separately, or because she knew that just inside the doors a highly preserved, polished, and prettied Virginia Booth lay cocooned in a satin-lined box. Laurie didn't think death should be displayed like fine jewelry. I agreed with her philosophically, but my religious heritage argued vehemently against letting the departed depart in peace. The old Irish liked to keep their bodies around until they resembled and smelled like aged cheese.

Marianna and I drove a bit down Spring Street, choosing to park away from the fray of cars and crowds beginning to assemble for the Booth bon voyage.

"You and Beth get through your shit?" Marianna eloquently asked, looking for a parking spot.

"Hard to say," I answered. "Don't park too far away. How far can you walk in those stilts?"

"Are you kidding me? I bought a size too big and stuffed 'em with padding. They're good for a couple of miles."

"Beth's a weird duck," I said. "Can you be *too* normal?"

"I know what you mean. I envy her. And not that she had the most wholesome upbringing either. Her absentee dad was a golf bum who lived off family trusts. Her mother was a pill-popping functional alcoholic. And she had that illegitimate-sister thing going on when she was sixteen."

"It's that 'hearty stock' stuff Beth was saying to me about Virginia Booth, how the last thing she would expect was suicide from a woman who was always counseling others on how to weather storms while wearing flowered hats. You know what I mean?"

"Sort of," she said, not sounding wholly convinced.

"These old Yankees have a healthy attitude about life—and death."

Marianna nodded but remained silent. She paralleled into a parking spot on a side street off Thames, and we exited the car and headed up toward Spring Street in silence until Marianna suddenly stopped and grabbed me by the elbow. "Pig," she mumbled.

It took me a second to register that she was referring to our boss. "Vince?" I said.

"Brooke Stanford," she answered.

Up ahead at the corner, ambling down Spring Street decked in his version of a classy suit, was none other than Vince Piganno arm in arm with Brooke Stanford.

I lowered my head. "Pigs," I grumbled under my breath, knowing the noun's plural usage wouldn't be lost on my bright and witty friend.

"Exactly," Marianna said, nodding. "Different subspecies, but both oinking ungulates."

We silenced our heels by keeping mostly on our toes as we continued walking and rounded the corner onto Spring Street. Ahead of us, Vince and Brooke touched shoulders as they moved down the street. I heard her intermittently giggling and chattering in his ear. Vince, not the giggling type, kept facing forward, but his reception to her girlish charms was evident in the way he'd lean his head into her whenever her mouth came to his ear.

"Altogether, one disgusting sight," Marianna said in a guttural whisper. "Did you know about this?"

"I found them in the conference room last week after-hours. They were drinking wine and losing their clothes one sock at a time."

Marianna's steps slowed to a stop. "You didn't think it was important to tell me?" I stopped but didn't turn to face her as she continued her questioning. "Apart from the ongoing murder investigation, you didn't think Vince banging an employee in the conference room was gossip-worthy?"

I started walking again. "Too much else going on. I forgot."

"Were they really…I mean, did you *see* anything—"

"Through his opened-to-the-third-button shirt, I saw Vince Piganno's bare chest with one of those gold religious medal things around his neck that your people always wear, and trickles of sweat between his surprisingly firm pectoral muscles. Shall I continue?"

A brief glance at Marianna's sickened faced answered my question.

"He's got something planned," she said.

"His plans with Brooke Stanford stop at his zipper. He doesn't know any more about what's going on with this wily crew than the rest of us."

"So are you finally coming around to suspecting Scott Boardman of murder?"

"I've finally come around to realizing that I'm not perfect and I don't know everything."

"You always knew that, Shannon. This is just the first time you've been able to admit it."

We had slowed to let Vince and Brooke, and a few others, enter the funeral home before we walked up the front steps. We followed the discreet signs to the Booth service and entered the double doors. Marianna walked directly to the casket, and I remained just to the side of the door, watching others enter, mingle, visit, and then sit. Like Marianna and me, Vince and Brooke separated.

Brooke joined Beth and Lolly Bergen and what looked to be others of their old chums. I watched Beth receive Brooke warmly. Good girl, I thought. Beth was playing the game well.

Without pause, Vince had gone straight to Chief Sewell, who was standing in the back of the room in a dark gray suit, looking like the funeral director himself. I had neither seen nor spoken to him since giving him the heave-ho at the Captain Jaynes House on Monday.

I watched as Vince and the chief shook hands. Was it love or simple animal attraction that made the chief seem to light up the space he inhabited like a celebrity, a single bright star in an ink-black sky of mourners? He was a healthy head taller than Vince, but both were imposing figures in their crisp suits and immaculate grooming. I watched them do their male dance of conversation, one nodding, the other saying a word or two, while both looked straight ahead and multitasked a surveillance of their surroundings.

The chief finally spotted me where I had remained near the door. His eyes locked on mine. His head rose and his eyes widened. Vince seemed to melt away into the background. We nodded to each other, neither of us smiling, fixing our stares until I felt a soft tap on my shoulder and I watched the chief's eyes move from me to the intruder at my side.

"Hey," Scott said. "Is this like in the movies when the cops go to the funeral of the victim to see if the murderer shows up to gloat at his crime?"

"Virginia Booth's murderer is in the casket with her. That crime's been solved."

"And Muffie Booth's too. I heard Virginia admitted to killing her."

"But your wife's murderer is still out there. And Leo Safer's."

"But they aren't connected. Muffie and Virginia had their own issues to settle. Or do you think Pat and Leo were a consequence of that?"

"Specifically, I don't know, but generally I *do* know that money and jealousy are the two prime motives for murder. Seems to me we have both here."

The chief and Vince had been watching us from across the room. There they stood, side by side yet separate, a phalanx of disapproval. Something in me was pleased by their audience, and even more pleased that they disapproved.

"I want to see you again—away from all this," I said, nodding toward the crowded room. "Somehow I don't think we're finished."

Scott's eyes glistened in a smile. "I was hoping you'd say that. I honestly thought you were done with me."

"I should be, and I reserve the right."

"Tonight," he hurried to say. "I'll call you on your cell when I'm done here."

I saw Scott's head rise out of our huddle. My Chucky had stealthily come upon us. "Senator Boardman," the chief said, thrusting his hand to Scott. Scott reciprocated the courtesy and they shook hands.

"Anything new on the investigation?" Scott asked him.

"Now, Senator," Chucky crooned, "you know I'm not going to answer that, don't you? Until the handcuffs are ready to go on."

"They won't be going on me, Chief Sewell, so don't get your hopes up."

The edge in Scott's voice cut through the somber air. Chuck tilted his head. "Don't underestimate me," he answered.

"That sounds personal," Scott said. "You sure this is about a murder investigation and not about a bruised male ego?" Scott looked at me and winked, and in response, I looked away, trying to remain coolly distant from the animosity I could feel building between the two men.

Chucky's chest began to heave ever so slightly, his rate of breathing increasing. "You're on shaky ground, *Senator*. I wouldn't be smiling if I were you."

"Is leaving someone you supposedly care about in jail overnight on a filthy cement floor *your* kind of humor?"

"Who told you that?" I asked.

"Brooke Stanford."

I glared at the chief. "Your guys must be gloating all over town that they finally tamed me. That's the only way this could have gotten out."

The chief looked at Scott, not ready to share any more information with him, but clearly not done with me yet, he pulled me aside. "Ask Vince who told Stanford. He's on a suicide mission with that broad."

"And how did Vince find out? I'm not so proud of it that I'm spreading it all over the office. Only the girls knew and they would never say a word."

Scott was watching us, intent and focused.

Chuck took hold of my elbow, gently but firmly, trying to pull me farther away from Scott. I forcefully yanked my arm from his grasp, making his hold on me appear more aggressive than it actually was.

Scott moved in and stood between Chuck and me. "Sir, may I ask you what the hell you think you're doing? This is a wake"—he looked up Virginia Booth's body—"and this young woman"—he nodded at me—"has had enough manhandling and mistreatment by the Providence Police Department."

As if the three of us weren't causing enough of a scene, Vince came lumbering over with his chin stuck out to compensate for his diminutive stature among Chucky, Scott, and me, all of whom towered over him. "What's going on here, Lynch? Maybe you'd better get back to the office."

Scott then turned me gently toward him. "May I take you out of here?" he said, always the gentleman, asking me but never ordering. "You don't deserve this."

While Chucky and Vince waited for my answer, both, for different reasons, hoping I'd decline his invitation, I looked over at Marianna, who was busy chatting someone up. Beth was talking to Lolly while watching me, and Laurie had disappeared, probably to the bathroom, the only sanctuary in which she'd be assured there were no embalmed Christians.

I turned back to Scott. "I don't know why I came in the first place."

I twirled toward the door, avoiding the reactions of Chuck and Vince. Scott followed me and then rushed ahead to pull the door open for me when Brooke appeared in front of us like a bolt of lightning.

"Scott?" she whispered. She'd taken hold of his sleeve

as his hand held the door open. "How can you leave
without a proper *visit*?"

"Please, Brooke," he murmured. But she held fast to
his arm. He met her eyes. "What are you doing?" he
asked. "Let go of my arm and don't make a scene."

"A scene?" she said, no longer caring who heard her.
"*You're* the one who has to worry about public scenes,
not me. I've got nothing more to lose."

Scott took his hand from the door and let it close. He
lowered his head and smiled at her. I had backed away
enough to visibly remove myself from their little fracas.

"What do you want?" he now whispered.

Brooke smiled at her success in his discomfort. "I
want you to stay here—with me. And not leave—with
her." Her head made a deliberate move in my direction,
and I floated farther away, resisting Brooke's attempt to
reel me in to their incipient donnybrook.

Scott nodded, still smiling at her. "Let's go outside," he
said to her, now taking her arm as he had mine minutes
before. With his free arm he pulled the door open again.
But Brooke surprised us both by yanking her arm free of
his hold. "It isn't going to work, Scott. Not this time."

Vince had begun to move toward us as I was moving
away. Was he jealous? Did he think he had any control
over Brooke Stanford? Didn't Vince realize that she was
using him as much as he was using her?

"Brooke," Vince said, hurrying the last few steps, "let's
go." Vince now took her arm and Brooke let him keep it.
Her glare remained on Scott as she allowed Vince to lead
her out the door. I looked around the room. Most of the
guests had returned quickly to their hushed conversa-

tions, having the good manners to pretend they hadn't witnessed the ugly scene.

Marianna was suddenly at my side. "What the frig is Vince doing?" she asked.

I was too busy staring at Scott to answer her. He looked confused but still in control. He smiled at me, waited a moment, and walked through the door himself.

"Let's go," I answered Marianna. "I've got a feeling..."

Outside, my feeling proved correct. Vince and Brooke had crossed the street when Scott began walking down the sidewalk to his waiting car. Scott should have waited inside a few minutes more.

"You can't do the things you do and get away with it," Brooke hollered from across the street. "You're a liar, *Senator Boardman*. And I'm going to make sure the whole world knows it before I'm through with you."

Vince was out of his league with Brooke. She was an untameable animal, and Vince was used to instant results. Every time Vince tried to quiet Brooke down by stepping in front of her, she pushed her way around him. "I'm going to fucking kill you, Scott. By the time I'm done with you, you'll wish you were dead!"

Scott took his reprimand rooted in the same spot. He wasn't facing her as she screamed at him from across the narrow street, but neither did he move as she regaled him with threat after threat. She was out of control. So wholly different from her chilling behavior in Vince's office the day he placed her on leave.

Vince had apparently realized she would have to exorcise her demons by screaming until exhaustion. He stood by as immobile as Scott was across the street from her. Finally she seemed to implode from her own pent-up steam and began walking briskly down the street. After giving me a stern warning look, Vince followed her.

"What's Vince trying to say to me?" I asked Marianna. "You know him better than anyone. What did that look mean?"

Marianna, her mouth gaping open, was staring down the street after Vince and Brooke. This was her first taste of the Vince and Brooke show. "I can't believe this," she said. "What the hell is wrong with him?"

"He's in heat," I answered.

"I'm sorry about that," Scott said, joining Marianna and me on the sidewalk. "She's been drinking, I think. Or maybe drugs..."

"Like the drugs you took the night of the murders?" I said.

"Don't be silly," he answered. "Mine were prescribed. I just took them with alcohol and shouldn't have."

"Maybe hers were prescribed too. Maybe you broke her heart so badly that she has to be on megadoses of antidepressants to get over you."

"Antidepressants don't make you crazy like that," Marianna said. "As a matter of fact, they do the opposite. More likely she's *off* her drugs."

I had forgotten that my hypochondriac friend Marianna was a walking *Physicians' Desk Reference.*

"Will you come with me now?" Scott said. "Let's just get out of here."

"No," Marianna answered him. Then she looked at me. "Don't fall into this mess, Shannon. It's a pile of shit.

Look at Vince. He's beginning to look like Brooke's court jester."

"Maybe your friend's right," Scott said.

Marianna began walking toward her car, leaving the two of us alone. I watched her walk off and willed myself to follow her. Tough decision and not my style to take the simple route. I caught up to Marianna and began walking next to her. I came with her; I'd leave with her.

"Don't look back," she said to me. "Want to get a drink?"

"No, I'm going to find Scott as soon as we get back to Providence."

Marianna just shook her head. "Why would I think you'd ever take my advice?"

"Your advice will guarantee me a long and healthy life—but bore me to death in the process."

I DIDN'T WAIT UNTIL WE GOT TO PROVIDENCE. From the car I dialed up Scott on my cell and we formulated our plan to meet at his suite at the Biltmore Hotel. Marianna remained quiet during our brief conversation. The beauty of our friendship was our ability to let each other step into the fires of hell with stiff warnings but gentle farewells, letting the other fall while always keeping an eye out for a quick rescue. So far none of us had burned to death. Emotion was usually the trigger for all ill-advised behavior, and because I was the most in control of my heart—or as Beth would spin it, I was the Tin Man *without* a heart—I was the least flammable of us. Maybe the ignition was lit with the Cohen trial that opened the cauterized wound of my childhood, and, much like a match dropped in a trail of spilled gasoline, the fire was spreading. But whatever the precipitating cause of my present course, I was dangerously near self-combustion.

25

SEX IN A HOTEL ROOM

MARIANNA DROPPED ME AT THE BILTMORE AND I took my usual route to Scott's room. After a few unanswered knocks at his door, I called his cell and heard it ringing inside the door.

"Scott?" I hollered through the door and dialed again. No answer, so I went down to the McCormick & Schmick's bar in the Biltmore lobby for a quick drink while I waited. But somewhere between the first and last sip of my Glenlivet neat, I realized that I'd called Scott's cell from Marianna's car en route back to Providence, and he'd answered it. He'd had the phone with him in Newport, so he was either in the room and not answering his cell, or he'd returned and then left again without taking it.

"Hi, gorgeous. You looking for some action?"

I turned to see Andy rolling onto the bar stool next to mine.

"Hey," I said. "This isn't a good place for you. I'd try

XO's on North Main Street. And Downcity Bar across from the Turk's Head Building has a hot-looking transvestite hostess after five."

"I didn't say I was looking for action, did I?" He fluttered his lashes at me. "I'm delivering a package to Senator Scott. But he doesn't seem to be answering his door."

The bartender came and took Andy's order of an espresso martini. "Beats Starbucks," Andy said. "And in our office, everyone needs a little *help* of the alcoholic variety to get through the day. The boss is zooming around like a deflating hot air balloon since he got back from that funeral."

"Who gave you a delivery to Scott Boardman?"

He shrugged. "Brooke Stanford accosted me outside the office. I figured she and Vincent are pretty tight these days—joined at the pelvis if you will—so I accepted my mission. I just tucked a sealed manila envelope under his door upstairs."

"Is Brooke still sleeping with Scott Boardman too?"

Andy looked at me with one of his typical over-the-top expressions. This time he shrugged his shoulders to the damned heavens and flipped his palms in the air. "I have a hard time keeping up with the bedroom play *inside* our office. But why would he be sleeping with her now?"

"Isn't everyone in love with her? Although for the life of me I can't understand the attraction."

"It's a penis thing. She's lubed, easily insertable."

"Gross me out, Andy, why don't you."

"Sorry, sweet-cakes, but it ain't love with her. Love is

an *emotion*. Brooke is a *thing*. Now, Pat Boardman? She was a different species. Way too good for Scott Boardman."

I sucked down the remainder of my Glenlivet and then turned on my stool to face him. "Spill."

"I'm a fly on the wall of the Newport Social Register. I know what goes on there without anyone *knowing* that I know. It's a gay man thing. We don't register on the Richter scale of importance, but Newport's where I hang all summer, and if I didn't see Pat Boardman at the Black Pearl ten times, I didn't see her once."

"When and with whom? And why haven't you said anything before now?"

"Obviously before she died. I saw her with some guy, and with the woman she was killed with. And who ever *asked* me if I knew anything? Most people value their dogs more than they value a gay man who *isn't* a celebrity or *doing* one. I'm just another useless poke as far as society is concerned."

"Ah Christ, you're right, Andy. What can I say? It's a shit world out there. But tell me about Pat Boardman. Everything you know."

"I didn't say I knew much. Just that she was a busy bee with her love life. She and the man had heated conversations. You know, heads dipped in hushed whispers over the yummy Pearlburgers, feeding each other greasy fries and licking each other's fingers. And then the dead girlfriend. They'd go to Tucker's Bistro. There's a back room." He rolled his eyes. "Need I say more?"

"Pat and Muffie. You actually saw them at this Tucker's place?"

He nodded deeply. "They were having a lover's spat, so they were easy to notice."

"And the man she was with at the Pearl. Same one all the time?"

"Yes, dear. But he wasn't a local, so I have no clue who he was. I just know he wasn't her hubby."

"Can you describe him?"

Andy's glance drifted away to memory. "Kind of thinning hair. I remember the eyes. I kept thinking of that Balzac novel, *The Girl with the Golden Eyes.*"

"Jake Weller."

"Did I just *solve* the case?" Andy said with the tiniest tone of sarcasm in his singsong voice.

"No."

I picked up my cell and dialed Scott's room again. "Hey, you want some food, Andy? Another drink? I'll buy," I said as I listened to the ringing phone.

"Sure."

Scott's phone went unanswered. "I've got to go," I said to Andy. "Order something and have them put it on my tab."

While Andy ordered, I called the Biltmore front desk and had them ring Scott's room. After a few rings, the call went to hotel voice mail and I hung up. "Here," I said, flipping Andy my Amex card. "Just charge it all on this and keep the card till I get back to the office." I whirled off the bar stool. "And stay out of Brooks Brothers."

Back upstairs at Scott's door, I pounded heavily. Still no answer. I dialed his cell again and waited to hear the ring inside the door. No ringing, this time. I called Mike

McCoy, master locksmith and ex-cop. If anyone could get us into this room without publicity or a key, Mike could.

I waited in the lobby, and a brief ten minutes later, Mike appeared with Marianna in tow.

"So much for no publicity," I said to him.

Mike left us and walked to the front desk.

"Fuck you, Shannon," Marianna said. "Since when am I the public?"

"When you start getting all preachy on me. I don't want any more 'good' advice."

"Well, for someone who's so sure she knows what she's doing is right, you've been needing us an awful lot lately."

The three of us took the back elevator to Scott's room. Again I tried knocking, and dialing his cell. No answer and no ringing inside the room. "His phone was in there half an hour ago. I heard it ringing. Then I went downstairs and had a drink with Andy—"

"Andy?" Marianna asked. "What's he got to do with this?"

"I found him in the lobby bar. Brooke had him deliver a package to this room. I had a drink with Andy and when I came back up here I knocked again and dialed Scott's cell. The ringing is gone. He must have come and gone while I was downstairs with Andy."

Mike left us and returned a few minutes later with a master keycard that he inserted in the door. I looked at Marianna. "How does he do that?"

"Badge," she answered. "They never check the date on it."

Mike pushed the door open and the room was eerily

silent. Two glasses sat on the coffee table between the couches. One empty, the other half full. The room had the lingering smell of a woman's perfume...and something else. I raised my nose to the air like a hound after a scent. "What is it?" I asked Mike and Marianna. "What's that other smell?"

Without answering, Mike walked into the bedroom. We followed and the three of us looked blankly at an unmade bed. In this room the phantom smell was stronger, sickeningly sweet.

"Smells like sex in a hotel room," Mike said.

"Lot of experience in that, Mike?" Marianna quipped. "Sex in hotels?"

"Nah, my experience is mostly limited to the backseats of cars."

Mike started rifling around the room and found a manila envelope next to the bed. "Get me a clean facecloth from the bathroom," he said to Marianna.

I moved closer while Marianna retrieved the towel and handed it to Mike. He gingerly lifted the envelope by its end and walked to a desk in the corner of the room. He held the envelope upside down, and out fluttered several black-and-white photos that fell into a serendipitous array of damning evidence.

The three of us stood with heads cocked at varying angles like simpleminded animals wondering at the meaning of some higher order of intelligence.

"Holy shit," Mike said, stifling a laugh.

Marianna remained docilely silent.

"No wonder he couldn't get it up with you," Mike said.

The aura pierced, I popped my head from the huddle

and turned to him. "Who told you that? Who freaking gave you those *false* details?"

"Who cares now?" Marianna said. "The important thing is finding out what all this means."

"It means none of you should have broken into my hotel room," Scott said from the threshold of the bedroom door. "It means now we have a bigger problem than my dead wife and campaign manager."

"And what problem would that be, Scott?" I ran my fingers through my hair. "I keep looking for straight answers from you and all I keep getting are crooked question marks."

"What happened on the boat that night to Pat and Muffie has nothing to do with those pictures. And if they're made public, not only will it do me irreparable damage, but it will lead the authorities on some wild-goose chase for a connection between...what you see there and the murders of Pat and Leo. And there is none. None at all."

"You're sure of that," I said.

Mike growled, "Unless you pulled the triggers on those people, *Senator.* That's the only way you'd be sure of that."

"Who's blackmailing you?" Marianna asked. She nodded at the photos on the desk. "Those are PI-style photos, perfect for blackmail or evidence in court. So either your wife had them taken to support a divorce action against you, or she was blackmailing you. Was it your wife? That's why you killed her?"

"Brooke," I said. "It's Brooke, isn't it?"

Scott breathed a defeated sigh as if he was emptying

the air of his lungs once last time before dying. He dragged his feet to the foot of the bed and sat, his head slumping over his knees like a rag doll. "Blackmail," he said. "I found them slipped under the door."

"Andy just delivered them for Brooke. This is the package he just delivered," I explained to Mike and Marianna.

"Impossible," Scott said, his head still in his hands. "She wants me to marry her. Why in hell would she blackmail me with those? She knows nothing about… that."

"Who *does* know, buddy?" Mike asked. "Who knows you like to diddle guys on the side?"

Scott winced. Gritted his teeth. Shook his head. "Pat knew." He looked up at us. "So that gives me a motive for killing her, doesn't it?" No one answered him. An interrogator's instinct: We all knew that our continued nurturing silence might harvest more ripe admissions. Of course, truth in those admissions was another matter. We could just be getting a shitload of more lies.

"Jake says that's why Pat began her affair with Muffie," Scott said. "To punish me. Jake insists Pat wasn't gay, just confused or angry with me. Jake was in love with her. Did you know that? Jake wanted us to divorce so he could marry her. I should have let her go. She might be alive today if I'd let her go and forgotten about my political career. And was it worth it? I have no career and Pat's dead. We both lost."

I watched the man sitting on the edge of the bed. Still so strong-looking, virile, ready to take on the world. So *presidential* looking. The kind of men we trust—tall, white, and sandy-haired. We use central-casting standards to choose our candidates, and we vote, like Academy Award judges, for the one who fits the part.

"So who killed your wife?" I asked. "Do we get a straight answer this time?"

"The decision in the Booth estate matter had come down the day Pat was murdered. Muffie called me in the afternoon. She said we had to talk—about many things— the estate case was only one. That's what she said. *We had many issues to resolve.* And she wanted them resolved that night. I had a drink with Leo in Newport at about five o'clock. The Black Horse Tavern. I left him to go to the boat—"

"And he knew where you were going?" Marianna asked.

Scott looked up at her as if he'd just realized her presence. He glanced at me, then back at her. "Why does that matter?"

"Senator Boardman," she responded as if he were her witness at trial, "would you *please* just answer the question, yes or no."

"I don't remember if I told him I was going. But he knew about the court decision—that Pat and Muffie wanted to talk to me about it. I just don't recall if he knew I was going to the boat that night."

Marianna shook her head, and I knew what she was thinking: He'd still slipped through the cracks of a straight answer.

Scott continued his narration. "When I got to the boat—it was about six o'clock, I think—I found them. Both women dead. I went directly to Doogie's—Virginia

Booth's—house to tell her. She didn't look well. When she came into the morning room to greet me, her hair was undone—a disheveled mess—so unlike her. Even if she'd just risen from bed, she'd have neatened her hair before coming down. Even in my frantic state, I noticed her odd appearance. And then, when I told her about the women, she almost fainted into a chair." He nodded to himself. "Of course, now I understand why. She knew then that she'd killed her own daughter with the vase, and she may well have implicated herself in the second murder. She asked me only one question, a question I thought was reasonable at the time. 'How did my daughter die?' I assumed it was just a mother's need to know, but of course, it was more than that. It was Doogie's need to know if Muffie died the same way Pat had. Who dealt the actual deathblow to her daughter? Had she actually killed her with the vase, or had someone come in after and killed them both? That's what she wanted to know. I tried to call Leo back that night, but I couldn't find him anywhere. He wasn't answering his cell and hadn't gone home. So I called Jake, the only other person I could trust. I needed to talk to someone...I told him about Pat and the boat. He agreed to meet me...but in Providence. He wanted us to be as far away from Newport as possible."

"And where was Jake Weller when you called him?" Mike asked.

Scott thought a minute and then answered. "You know...I have no idea. I called his cell and he agreed to meet me in Providence in an hour. So he couldn't have been in Connecticut."

"But he didn't meet you, did he?" Marianna said. "He never showed up?"

"Not while I was there." Scott looked piercingly into Marianna's eyes. "But you were there all night. He didn't show up, did he?"

"I wouldn't have a clue what he looked like, Senator Boardman," she answered. "And I wouldn't have been casing the door for him anyway, would I have? Because at that point—as far as we all knew—you were just another fuck trying to get into my girlfriend's pants."

"Stop it, Mari," I said. "That'll accomplish nothing." I moved closer and sat on the end of the bed with him. "Where was Brooke?" I asked. "Was she with you at all that night before you saw her at Al Forno?"

"It was all a lie that she was with me after four-thirty. She didn't tell me beforehand she was going to make such an idiotic statement to the police. I would have stopped her. She must have thought it up after she saw me at Al Forno and then heard the news about Pat and Muffie. She invented that story the next day. I didn't see Brooke again that evening until she showed up in the bathroom at Al Forno."

Marianna and Mike had huddled near the window after I'd joined Scott on the bed. It was a tacit dance we'd done. They were letting me do the careful interrogation. Scott was talking, seemingly freely; no one wanted to break my spell.

He looked over at me. "And the drinking and the pills? That was all true. When I began receiving those"—he glanced at the photos—"I started taking pills, and I'd been drinking with Leo earlier, and with Brooke before that. The combination made me pass out...and I guess the shock of seeing those women brutalized..."

"When did you begin getting the pictures?"

"When I started breaking it off with Brooke. I suspected she was blackmailing me, but she steadfastly denied it in that sweet innocent way she has. And I didn't think her capable. Didn't think she'd know the first thing about hiring a private investigator and resorting to blackmail. Who knows? Maybe it isn't her. Maybe it's politically motivated. Who the hell knows anything anymore?"

"You," Mike said from the window. "The Black Horse Tavern is less than fifteen minutes from the boat. You could have left Leo Safer, gone to the boat, and killed your wife—or maybe you killed her before you met Safer—had a stiff drink with Safer to calm down, and then hoofed it back to Providence to see Weller."

"But I *didn't*," Scott said, regaining some of his old composure. "I was with Brooke until I left her to meet Leo. And you can't prove otherwise."

"So where do we go from here, Scott?" I asked.

He nodded toward the desk. "Those pictures need to be kept quiet—at least for now—please don't turn them in."

"Can't do that. They're now part of a murder investigation."

"Maybe I should take Doogie's road to perdition and just shoot myself."

"Aw fuck," Mike said, straightening his jacket to leave. "I'm not standing around here listening to him cry. You girls do what you need to do with him. I'm out of here."

Mike walked out and I looked up at Marianna, expecting her to leave with him.

"Let's go find Brooke," Marianna said to me. "Let's ask her about those pictures."

I stood and walked to the desk, glancing down at the grainy black-and-white prints, where in the background I now recognized the bed by which I'd fallen the day Leo Safer was killed.

I picked up the picture up by the same towel Mike had used. "These were taken on your boat," I said to Scott. "This is the bed in the main berth. Who were you with?"

"It doesn't matter, does it?"

"Yes, I think it does. Maybe this guy has a motive for murder. You can't ignore any clues."

"The man in those pictures is dead. It was Leo."

26

PAW PRINTS

MARIANNA AND I LEFT SCOTT SITTING ON THE edge of his unmade bed, examining his hands as if trying to read his future in their palms.

While Marianna and I walked across town back to the office, I thought of Scott's words to me the night we first met. "You know what he said that first night?" I said to Marianna. "He told me I was the most sexy yet *unfeminine* woman he'd ever met. Was that why he liked me? Because he's bisexual and I remind him of a guy?"

"I don't believe in bisexuality. I think Boardman's gay but keeps fighting it and sleeping with women to convince himself he's not. Maybe I'm wrong, but bisexuality makes no sense to me."

"With all due respect, Mari, you're not exactly Masters and Johnson on the subject. I mean, Christ, you're sleeping with Mike McCoy."

She stopped in the street. "What does that mean?"

"McCoy reaches the outer limits on the macho meter.

He's so far from gay he probably winces when he looks in a mirror from the waist down."

Marianna laughed out loud. I didn't get the joke.

"He told me his headboard is mirrored," she explained. "I won't even go inside his place to check it out."

"Where the hell does McCoy live, anyway? I wouldn't be surprised if his legal address was a PO box and he sleeps in his car outside the U.S. Post Office."

"He rents a two-bedroom bungalow in Oak Hill just over the East Side border in Pawtucket. Cute from the outside. It has an adorable navy-and-white-striped awning over the front porch. Really quaint."

"Thank God it's a rental so he can't do any permanent design changes. McCoy has the taste of a Doberman pinscher."

"It's a damn good thing my ego is strong and intact today, Shannon, because you are really testing me now."

"What are you getting all huffy about? I've been trying to have sex with a homosexual. I mean, how *off* is my fucking love meter that I should be poking fun at yours?"

We called a truce and trudged the rest of the way in silence until we reached our building. "I'm going to see Vince," I said, jogging up the steps. "I'm sure he knows where his little love boat Brooke is."

Marianna lagged behind and nodded in disgust.

I didn't have to go far to find Vince or Brooke. Vince was stationed behind his massive mahogany desk, wearing, I think, a genuine smile. My uncertainty of the true nature of Vince's dreamy countenance was based in part on Vince's overall and general lack of mirth. His normal everyday smile was sardonic in nature and resembled the dental exhibition of a rabid dog. It was the added sparkle in his beady brown eyes that tipped me off: It could only be Brooke or some newly installed carbon copy that could induce his hot-off-the-griddle authentic glee.

"Where is she?" I asked.

When he saw me in his doorway, he clamped his paw over the mouthpiece of his phone. His face fell to its relaxed state, and the Vince that I knew and loathed returned in the familiar scowl of an aging bulldog. "I'll talk to ya later," he said into the phone, and hung up. "What do you want?" he barked at me. "And don't ever interrupt me again when I'm on the phone."

"Was that Brooke?"

"When it's your business, I'll tell you."

"She's blackmailing Scott Boardman. You may think she's in love with you, or she may think you're in love with her, or the two of you may be mutually delusional, but the fact is, she wants Scott Boardman come hell or the next Hengchun earthquake."

Vince scratched the back of his head, twisting his neck as if he had bugs crawling up his neck. "She's blackmailing Boardman?"

"You betcha. And the goblins'll get *you* if you don't watch out."

"Close my door," he ordered.

"Why? The whole freaking office already knows. Andy is the one who gave me the tip. You're becoming a joke in your own sty. What is it about that little twit Brooke Stanford that has all of you rats following her into the river like the Pied Piper?"

Vince needed to work off steam, so he pushed himself up from his desk and lumbered heavily to his door,
huffing by me like I was a pool of excrement. He slammed
his door closed and walked by again. "Sit, or don't sit. Do
it however you want, Lynch. But tell me what you know."

"Now we're getting somewhere, *boss*." I wanted to be
far enough away in case he threw something across the
room (he had notoriously bad aim), so I pulled a chair a
few yards away from his desk and tossed the envelope
full of photos on his desk. "Brooke made Andy, on a tacit
assumption of authority from you, deliver an envelope
full of black-and-white prints to Scott Boardman's hotel
room. Scott Boardman apparently blows both ways in
the breeze, if you get my multisexual drift."

Vince began an explosion of laughter the likes of
which I'd never seen. I have to admit, I didn't see it coming. I waited. He couldn't stop. Tears were forming at the
outer corners of his eyes. I saw teeth so far back in his
mouth that I almost blushed. If I didn't know better, I'd
swear he still had his tonsils, but what the hell did a ton-
sil even look like? I reserved the right to find out later,
and then rip them from his throat.

His lips finally came together and formed some
words...then a couple more...then a complete sentence: "You were trying [laugh, laugh] to seduce [guffaw]
a *fag*?"

"Stop it, Vince! That's a politically incorrect word and
it's cruel." I lowered my head. "And he's bisexual," I muttered.

"And I bet you almost *did* make it with him. I always
said you were a guy under all that...well, I guess you

really don't have a lot of that girl stuff hanging off you, do you?"

"Let's cut to the chase, okay, big fella? Because being here with you like this hurts me more than it hurts you."

"Look, Lynch, if Boardman's *gay*, then why the hell would someone like Brooke want him?"

"Because Brooke is a wannabe. She wants to be a billionaire socialite from Newport. She wants to be Mrs. Senator Scott Boardman from Fairfield, Connecticut. She wants to be the fucking First Lady of the goddamn United States of America! And if that means she has to be Marilyn Monroe with you, and Rock Hudson taking it up the ass with Scott Boardman, then that's what she'll do."

If nothing else, my little spiel had clamped Vince's trap shut.

"And I'll clue you in on one more thing," I continued. "Scott gave Brooke the royal dump the night Pat Boardman was murdered."

"He was dumping her a long time before that," Vince said. "When he started pulling strings to get her the job here, he was unraveling his ties with her and hooking her up to our lamppost. It was payoff for services rendered. And maybe he was calling it quits with women altogether at that point, but he was letting Brooke down long before Pat Boardman was killed."

"But the day he took Brooke out for a drink to recite the final act of their relationship was the night Pat Boardman was killed."

"I hope you're not suggesting she did it. Whoever

killed Pat Boardman killed Leo Safer too. Same gun. And Brooke was with me the day Safer was shot."

"Jesus Christ, Vince. You're her alibi? This has to be the most pathetic AG's office in the country. Not only can't we find murderers, but we hand out alibis like lollipops at the doctor's office."

"You're not listening to me, Lynch. Brooke is high-strung, high-maintenance, maybe even a bit of a gold digger, but most of these young girls today are looking for Candy Land. This country's moral code is written by the likes of that Britney Spears broad and her entire pre-pubescent pregnant sisterhood. It's easy pickings in the Lolita slush pile for older guys with a few bucks or a little power. What can I say? She's trying to hitch her ass to some powerful rich guy. But she didn't kill Pat Boardman and she didn't do Safer either. She's desperate, so maybe she's blackmailing Boardman." He shrugged. "But that *ain't* murder. And believe me, I've been deep inside the trenches with her, dredging for information."

"Don't make me vomit, Vince. She's been using you, and she's still trying to snag Boardman, and you aren't the least bit angry?"

"Hah." Vince chuckled again, but no jubilant symphony this time. It seemed he couldn't wait to start singing again. "I had some laughs with Brooke, and while I was laughing, she was talking. So I listened. And what she was saying was real interesting. *So* interesting, in fact, that I had a warrant sworn out this morning for Jake Weller." Vince plopped into his desk chair and rolled it back against the back wall so he could hoist his feet up on his desk. "You know Jake Weller, don't you, Lynch?

He's Boardman's PR guy. The guy who was in love with Boardman's wife, Pat. The guy who went to the Booths' boat the night of the murders to confront Pat Boardman about her philandering husband and ask her to divorce Boardman and marry him. The guy who didn't know that the love of his life, Pat Boardman, was *doing girls* until he saw her that night with Muffie Booth and flipped out over it. The same night he *shot* Pat Boardman while her head was up Muffie Booth's twat."

I was speechless. I was nauseous. I was in shock. I was angry. Jake Weller? Why hadn't I seen that?

"How do you know all this? Only from Brooke? No corroborating evidence?"

"Cell phone records show calls between Brooke and Weller. Brooke says she called Weller after she and Boardman had their farewell toast. She admitted being pissed off about Scott dumping her like the morning trash. Weller then tells her to calm down and don't do anything rash, that he's going to the boat to talk to Pat Boardman."

I bolted up from my chair as if hit by lightning. "I'm losing it, Vince. I should get out of this business. I lost the Cohen case, and I was *so* off on this one. Jake Weller *told* me he was in love with Pat Boardman. Why didn't I make the leap—"

"I keep trying to tell you, you let those messy female emotions muck you up. Listen up and I'll give you a quick lesson."

He lit another smoke and took a long smooth drag. No coughing this time. He was as cocksure as a stud bull.

Vince loved to calm his stable of "overemotional" fe-
males with some good old-fashioned male horseshit.

"You see, Lynch, women usually don't kill the object
of their affection, they kill the competition. Men? They
kill the woman if they can't have her, just so no one else
can have her. It's a guy thing. But hey, don't be so hard on
yourself. The chief and I are working together on this. So
I *did* have a little help. And we don't have Weller yet. We
still got a lot of work to do to get him behind bars. That's
where I need you and the rest of this office."

I nodded. Downtrodden. Still sick to my stomach.
"Chucky?" was all I managed to utter. "How is he?" I
asked, looking back up at Vince, who'd lowered his legs
and was already poking his head through another file.

"The chief? He's fine, I guess. I don't ask personal
questions. That's why I can do my job here with clarity—
you know—with a clear head. The chief doesn't ask me if
I got laid the night before, and I don't ask him how the
wife and kids are. Just business. That's all."

"I thought he and Marjory were separated," I said.

Vince looked up at me. "Who the fuck is Marjory?"

I nodded and walked dejectedly out of Vince's office.
I found Marianna back in her office. Beth was going over
a set of interrogatories with her. They looked up at me
standing in the threshold. "Where's Laurie?" I asked.

"Court," Marianna said. "We're letting all the office
work fall behind. What's going on now? Every time I see
you, you look worse than before."

I shook my head, feeling lost. "Scott Boardman is gay.
The Pig isn't really in love with Brooke. Jake Weller killed

Pat Boardman and Leo Safer. And Chucky's back with his wife. And I should be singing in the rain?"

Beth stood and took me by the elbow again, much the same way she'd done with Virginia Booth in her Newport mansion, and then me, later that same day, after Virginia Booth shot herself. Beth led me to the empty chair in Marianna's office and sat me down. No one spoke for a minute or two, after which I heard the bottom drawer of Marianna's desk slide open. She put a bottle of The Glenlivet 21-Year-Old Single Malt scotch on her desk blotter.

"Neat," I said.

27

BLACK, WHITE, AND BLOOD

FOR THE SAKE OF FRIENDSHIP, BETH SIPPED HER scotch. With each swallow, she winced as if she was drinking motor oil, but I was ready to give her some time. Eventually, if she managed to make it through law school and hold down a job at the AG's office for a few years, she'd acquire a taste for bitter brews.

I hadn't said a word yet—hadn't even begun to feel the first warmth of alcohol-induced calm—when Vince's voice came booming through Marianna's intercom.

"Is *she* in there with you?"

Marianna hit the talk button. "Yeah."

"Send her back in here. New case I want her to start working on."

Marianna's finger hit speaker to turn it off, and I placed my Styrofoam cup on her desk and reached for the scotch bottle just as Beth's hand pulled it from my reach.

I tossed my empty in the trash like a basketball in a hoop. "I'm burned-out."

Marianna rolled her eyes and Beth remained silent—an innocent bystander watching the two of us like she should be taking notes.

I peered into Marianna's eyes as I spoke, hoping to see any hint of friendly fraud, the kind friends perpetrated on friends when they were trying to save a life. "Did you have any inkling it was Weller?" Then I looked at Beth, trying to reel her into the morass of my rotting morale. The kid needed to know what she was in for if she wanted to make prosecution a lifelong career. "You, Beth?" I asked. "You were with me when we saw Weller in the bar in Newport. Did you suspect anything? His demeanor? Anything?"

She shrugged. "I'm so busy trying to absorb information that sometimes the important stuff in the details escapes me. I just remember not liking him much. I remember thinking there's no reason for him to be denigrating Scott Boardman. But I guess if he's guilty, that would be his reason, huh? To divert suspicion to someone else."

I stood abruptly. "I'm going home."

Marianna stood too. "Christ, Shannon, you can't just walk out if Vince wants you to start a new file. Go ask him for a few days off. Don't just disappear."

"Fine, I'll tell him, but he's been porking Brooke Stanford. I'm not *asking* him anything."

I walked to the door and then turned to them. "Have you heard anything about the chief? If he's back with his wife? Has Mike mentioned anything?"

"Not to me," Marianna said. "He cut me out of that loop because I gabbed it to you."

I nodded, turned, and walked to Vince's office. As luck would have it, he was away from his desk. "Where is he?" I asked Andy.

"Went over to the police station to see Chief Sewell. He left a file for you."

"Put it in my office, will ya? I'm going home for the day."

As I was walking to my car, my cell phone registered a call from Scott Boardman. I'd had enough. I didn't answer it. He'd begun to remind me of a spoiled child with too many toys complaining of too few hours in the day in which to play with them.

Minutes later my cell rang again. I was behind the wheel by then, swerving out of the lot. "Yeah?" I said without reading the screen.

"I'm free to leave the state," Scott said. "Just got a call from your chief. I'm no longer a suspect."

"You were never under arrest. You stayed voluntarily."

"Sure," he said.

A few silent seconds later, he spoke again. "I'm checking out of the hotel now. Meet for a good-bye drink downstairs? I promise it's good-bye. I won't bother you anymore."

What could he possibly want now? Hadn't he already been exposed enough? I didn't want any more information on Scott Boardman. Frankly, I was sick of him too.

"Why now, Scott?"

"I've probably tested your friendship to its limits and I just want to leave here as friends."

"Look, Scott, I don't hate you. I'm not mad. I'm just tired. Tired to the point of collapse."

"Please? Take your car home. I'll pick you up at your place if you want, and drop you back off. You don't even have to drive."

As by then I was almost to my underground lot, I agreed to let him pick me up.

"It'll take me about fifteen minutes to check out of the hotel and get there. Meet me in front," he said. "Brooke has been calling me here every ten minutes since you left, so I'm out of here as soon as I hang up with you."

I went upstairs to change out of my work clothes and wait for Scott. When I opened my apartment door, I stepped on a manila envelope the same size as the one Andy had delivered to Scott earlier that day. I assumed Brooke had sent me copies of the photos, hoping to curtail any romantic intentions I still harbored for Scott. By then I was dried up as far as Scott Boardman was concerned. No worries there, Brooke old girl. He's all yours, for what he's worth.

I carried the envelope to the coffee table and dropped it there unopened along with my cell phone. My rare forays into the emotional pits were always brightened by a hot shower, so I headed for the bathroom, getting only halfway there before my curiosity got the better of me. I should have opened the package, at least peeked inside the flap. So I retrieved the envelope and took it to the kitchen and then poured the contents out on the counter. The familiar black-and-white graininess and the obscured lens of a cell phone camera initially convinced me they were only duplicates of those I'd already seen in Scott's hotel room, but as my eyes adjusted to one of the pics, the blurred head of a female came into view. And then another female. Two women on a bed, one lay facedown, the other in a sitting position, her face contorted in a howl of pain. It was Pat Boardman alive—and screaming.

I quickly fanned out the other pictures. Picking one up, then another, and one after another, different angles of the same shot: a boat's berth, two women, one screaming, the other presumably dead.

I picked up the phone to call Vince at the office, remembering too late that he had gone to the station to see the chief. As soon as Andy answered Vince's phone, I hung up and began to dial Chucky's cell number. As I waited for him to pick up, the downstairs intercom rang. Scott, I assumed. I hung up Chucky's still-ringing call and buzzed the visitor up. It had been almost twenty-five minutes since we spoke. I should already have been downstairs. I was late. He was coming up to get me—and I didn't want him to see the photos.

I ran to the door and unlocked the deadbolt, then returned to the kitchen to hide the pictures from Scott and dial the police station number to try to reach Chucky on the main line. My doorbell rang. "It's open, Scott. I'm on the phone."

I shoved the pictures back into the envelope, turning to a high cabinet to put them safely out of sight while I held the phone to my ear.

"Providence Police Station," I heard on the other end.

"Hi, Shannon Lynch from the AG's office. I need Chief Sewell immediately."

It was the clattering of the silverware drawer that drew my attention back to the realization that someone had entered my apartment and stood behind me like a shadow.

"Scott?" I turned.

"Scotty's not here," she said. "Scotty's never coming *here* again. He's all done with me...and with you. Did you get those pictures of Pat? I took them with my cell phone camera. Not too good, are they?"

Brooke Stanford was eerily blank-faced, her hair, as if ignited by an electrical storm, was wild and unkempt. I was used to seeing her manicured, made-up, and perfectly coiffed, and there she was, standing before me, no makeup and her hair a mess—devoid of any artifice to disguise the hatred in her eyes and neaten the wind-blown state of her mind.

"Scott's all done," she sang.

And if that were all there was—the outrageous disorder of her appearance and the creepy singsonginess of her voice—I would have simply overpowered her and waited for Scott to arrive, at which time we'd escort her to the nearest insane asylum, where she'd be chained to a bed awaiting arraignment on some charge or another, the exact penal code statute, at the moment, not readily coming to mind. But it was the meat-carving knife she'd rustled from my cutlery drawer and, with an absent-minded stare, was holding breezily by her side that gave me pause to move even a millimeter from my frozen pose.

"Put the phone down," she said.

I realized I still held the receiver in my left hand, the monotone voice of a taped operator droning on, "Please hang up and try your call again.... Please hang up and try your call again...."

I put the receiver softly down. "Scott's on his way," I said. "No point in hurting me. He'll find you here and you won't get away."

She smiled and slit her eyes closed, tilting her head to the side like a sly human cat. "I don't think so," she said. "Scott's dead. I cut him up into little tiny pieces while he was sitting in his car waiting for you to come down. I left his big ego-bloated head in the front seat, and tossed his *gay* legs into the backseat. How dare he." She jerked her deranged head in disgust. "His legs were heavy. I cut them in *two*."

I knew she was lying. She was clean of blood, and the strength needed to accomplish such a surgical feat was beyond her. Even if she'd gotten as far as slashing at him, Scott could easily overpower her. With bleeding wounds and close to death, he could still overpower her before she killed him with a knife.

"Brooke, you have no blood on you, and you just picked up that knife from my drawer. And I spoke with him no more than half an hour ago."

"And he's late, isn't he?" she said. "He should have been here by now, shouldn't he? Why do you think he's so late?"

Good question.

"Put the knife down, Brooke. I'll wrestle you to the floor before you can kill me with it. You may cut me, but I'll kill you with that knife long before you kill me."

She shook her head slowly. "Not if I get you right in the heart. Right where mine's dead, I'll stab yours."

"Your heart isn't hurting, Brooke. It's your ego. You wanted Scott because you wanted to piggyback on his social ladder. You convinced yourself you were in love with him. The man is gay. He was never going to marry you or me, because Pat Boardman was his cover."

"I would have replaced her. I told him I would take him any way he wanted. And I would never have cheated on him the way she did. I just wanted to be with him and I could have turned him around. We'd been together before, I could do it again."

"Where is he? Where is Scott now?"

Why she did it just then, I'll never know. I'd simply asked her where Scott was, and she raised the knife from her side before I even saw it move and sliced it past my chest and then back up over her head.

I looked down at my shirt. She had managed to cut through the fabric, but the slit in my shirt looked to be only that—a slit in my shirt—until the slit began turning scarlet at its edges and the stain began to spread slowly outward until the front of my shirt was a bull's-eye of blood.

I jumped back against the cabinets, and she slashed at me again. My reflexes were sluggish. While I was thinking—trying to understand how I could have let her get in the first stab, and then why I could feel nothing even after the blood began to flow—she slashed at me

again, and then again, until I reached out for the knife
and caught its blade in the palm of my hand, the blade
slicing deep into the flesh of my closed fingers until neither Brooke nor I knew whether the knife was under my
control as it stuck fast into my flesh, or if Brooke could
still wield it out of my impaled grasp. The advantage was
hers. My fingers ached in pain. And just as suddenly as
she had begun, she yanked the knife from my hand and
moved away from me toward the door, leaving me behind.

I breathed and sank to the floor, trying to look
around me, forcing myself to stay awake, but the room
was blushing red as my vision blurred. Had the blood
splattered into my eyes? I heard Brooke's voice in the
background. Was she in the hall waiting for Scott? I
could crawl and lock the door after her. Close the knife
out of my apartment. It was the knife that was strong,
not Brooke. The knife—I didn't realize until it was too
late—was more powerful than me.

"I buzzed him up," I heard her voice say. Brooke was
talking and she was closer than the hall. Still inside with
me. She and the knife were still inside my apartment
with me.

"And when he comes up, I'll cut him into little pieces.
His heart first. I'll cut his heart out."

How silly—I still had strength to think—how silly of
her to think it was easy to break through a man's ribs
and reach his heart. And then to hold the still-pumping
thing in her fist with one hand and carve around it with
the other. How naive of her to think that even hatred

could give her the stomach and strength to cut a man's heart from his chest while he fought to keep it beating.

I lay my head on the cold tile floor, feeling the cool porcelain against my burning cheek. But I couldn't stay there. Just a second, I thought, and I'll pull myself up. Warn Scott. He was on his way up and Brooke still had the knife.

With my good hand, I pulled myself a few inches along the floor until I reached an opening to the living room from behind the kitchen's island. Brooke was standing at my windows, enjoying the view those few seconds before she would continue her mayhem on Scott.

Where had I left my cell phone? I heard a soft knock at the door. "Shannon?"

Brooke walked to the door and opened it, the knife hidden behind her back.

"What's all over you?" Scott asked her.

She started walking back to the windows. She knew he'd follow her. She held the knife in front of her as she walked, hiding it there as he followed on her heels.

"Scott..." I managed a faint whisper. Like in a dream where the screams are muffled by unconscious sleep, I tried to call out, but the harder I tried, the more I breathed, and with each new breath I felt hot liquid spurting from my chest.

"It's blood!" he said. "Where's Shannon? What the fuck did you do?"

Brooke turned slowly to me, and I watched Scott's glance follow hers. Mistake, I thought, don't let your eyes wander from hers. Keep her in your vision.

But my thoughts found no voice in me, and as Scott turned and took a step in my direction she plunged the knife into the back of his neck. I watched him reel in slow motion, falling back against the plate glass window. His head rising to the ceiling and then falling to his chest. He began a slow slump down the glass as blood stained the windows a pretty translucent rose.

She came after him again, and this time the knife went to his chest. Brooke knew where the heart was. She'd been trying to find mine, and I think she hit the bull's-eye with Scott's.

His mouth opened in a guttural scream as Brooke tried to pull the knife from his ribs.

She'd be back to me when she was through with him. She was almost done with her work of butchering him to death. She'd be returning to me shortly if I couldn't move to get away.

She leaned to his collapsed body and began whispering something to him. And I crawled closer, because there on the coffee table—near Scott's crumpled body and Brooke's hovering shape—was my cell phone.

"You didn't love Pat," she said to him. "Why couldn't you just leave her? You *made* me kill her, Scott. You're the reason Pat's dead. You and Virginia Booth."

"Muffie?" I heard Scott say, the fluid already gurgling in his throat.

"Virginia did that. She made it easy for me to do the rest. They'd think Virginia did them both. So you see, Scott, we killed Leo for nothing because I wouldn't have let you go to jail for killing Pat. I would have confessed before that, if you'd only told me we could be together."

I had by now reached the coffee table, where the phone was a mere foot off the ground if only I could lift my burning hand—the broken one bathed in blood—to grab it while with my good hand I held myself up off the floor. I slid the phone to the floor. Brooke heard the crash and swung around. Quickly I hit some numbers, maybe 911, who knows, the keypad was obscured by the blood from my hand, but the voice I heard was Beth's.

"Hey, Shannon, what's up?"

Beth's voice had carried through the silence of the dying room. Brooke's eyes were wild again. She was angry. She had thought she was done. And I was calling her back to action.

"Goddamn you!" she screamed, and ripped the phone from my hand, flipping it shut. I scurried away from her like a ferret from a wolf, crawling low to the floor on all fours. I waited for the stab to my back and prayed she would miss my spine.

Oddly, I felt a pressure; the knife must have penetrated flesh, but my body's natural flow of anesthesia had taken effect. I felt little more than a hard hit to my left side, and I reeled around on my back and looked up at her. "Leo Safer?" I said, as if Leo Safer was my only concern during the last moments of my life. But then, what is there in the end when one's life is as empty as mine was? No children, no siblings, no mother, an estranged father. What else is there but getting answers to a few unanswered questions? An explanation was all I wanted. A closure to my own ignorance for letting an insipid weakling like Brooke Stanford bring me to this horrific end.

"Who killed Leo Safer?" I asked again.

"Scott," she said merrily. "That's why you're still alive. If it had been me, I would have killed you on that boat too. Scott liked you too much. Probably because you look like a man. He was fucking Leo Safer, did you know that too?"

"Leo knew it was you?"

"Oh, no. Leo was convinced it was Scott who shot Pat. Leo told Scott he had the evidence that it was Scott who killed Pat. And he *did* have it. Because I gave it to him. I gave Scott's gun to Leo. The one I shot Pat and her girlfriend with." She shook her head. "I think the girlfriend was already dead, but I shot her too, just to make sure."

"Why frame the man you love?"

She lifted her gaze out my windows and into the sky.

"Don't look to God," I said. "The answers are in the blood you shed. Not God."

She looked down at Scott. Like a freakish sculpture in a wax museum, his mouth had fallen open into a hardened mask. "To regain control," she stated simply. "Scott didn't care anymore about Pat's murder, about his career, and certainly not about me. I'd lost him." She sat on the couch, cradling the knife in her lap. "Leo went to the boat that day you were with Scott. We didn't know you were with him. Leo was going to confront Scott..." She shrugged. "They must have fought for the gun. Leo was shot and Scott got hurt too. That's what Scott told me, anyway—that it was an accident. But Scott was lying about a lot of things, wasn't he? Like the fact that he was gay."

With the last strength I had, I reassessed my opinion

of Brooke Stanford. She had planned the perfect crime and would have gotten away with it had not her "messy female emotions" gotten in her way.

Brooke plopped on the floor next to me, sitting cross-legged, still holding the knife like it was a secret, and we were sisters at a pajama party wondering what silly pranks we should commit next. She coldly recited the details of Pat's murder. How she'd found Pat on the bed screaming over the lifeless body of Muffie Booth, then the shot that silenced her; the hiding of the gun as her security, the framing of Scott Boardman, and the subsequent death of Leo Safer. Brooke stared off into the storybook of her memory like she was telling me about her first kiss with the captain of her college basketball team. She seemed calm. Almost self-satisfied. Perhaps this was the first time in her life Brooke had ever felt successful, worthy, smarter than those of us who'd referred to her as an airhead.

"You're bleeding heavily," she said, finally coming out of her preteen trance. "It's slow, but eventually you'll bleed to death. Does it hurt?"

She looked over at Scott slumped against the glass window. I wondered if anyone outside knew what they were looking at when they glanced up at my floor-to-ceiling windows and saw, through the glass, the back of Scott's body sitting at the end of a trail of smeared blood.

"Scott's dead," she said, hoisting herself up. "And you will be soon. So I should go."

Yes, I thought. Please go before my friends get here. A thought I'd not considered: Brooke still had the knife, and Beth, if I knew her at all, was on her way with help, the rest of my worried friends.

Brooke went to my kitchen. I heard her talking through the running faucet, but I couldn't make out the words. She was washing her hands, or scrubbing her prints from the knife. Did she assume, after Scott and I were both dead, that it would look as if we'd each died in our struggle against the other? I tried to see the evidence as Lucky Dack would. Was Scott's blood on me? Mine on him? We'd never really been together, either in life or death. Lucky Dack would see that, that the absence of his blood on me and mine on him suggested a third person, the one who would be drenched in both our blood. But Brooke was drying her clean hands on her shirt and was rifling through my closet for a coat to cover her bloody clothes. She picked a knee-length black trench coat. Perfect choice, I thought. Black to hide the red, falling midcalf on her, and belted tightly around her slim perfect waist. Perfect. The perfect crime.

She retrieved the knife from the sink with a dish-cloth. Went to Scott's body. She was smothering the knife in his fingerprints. I heard the elevator rumble in the hall. Brooke seemed unaware. Brooke thought she had more time. But I felt the steps in the hall as thuds against my cheek that lay flat on the floor. I could no longer lift my head. My strength had flowed from me into the blood puddle beneath me.

"Who's here?" She looked at me like a frightened child. "Someone's coming? Who called the police?" she asked. "When did you do that?"

At another time I would have laughed at her fear.

Answered her calmly, "While you were stabbing away at the love of your life, I was dialing the phone—you *fucking stupid, insane bitch.*" But I could no longer form words, and I no longer cared. "Fuck you," was all I could say.

That pissed her off. How dare I still be alive? The shock on her face was almost funny. But then, I was dying, so my sense of humor may have been skewed. If only I had the strength to rise...She was momentarily unarmed and went back to Scott to retrieve the knife. Holding it sheathed in the towel, she raised it above her head, coming at me again. "Your skinny neck," she said. "Your ugly skinny neck—"

A hard rap rattled my apartment door and made her jump. She turned quickly toward Scott's body.

"You can't kill him anymore," I said. "Give it up, Brooke."

"Shannon?" It was Beth's small voice. I smiled weakly, turning suddenly cold and feeling the blood drain from my head. I had fainted before. I knew what was happening.

"Didn't think Beth could knock so hard," I whispered to myself. Keep talking. I wanted to stay alive, conscious. I fought like hell to keep breathing slowly. In...Out... In...Out.

"Shannon!" Beth screamed loud this time.

And then a man's voice. "Move! Get out of my way."

Brooke was standing over me now, bringing the knife back to my throat. I pulled my chin into my chest, protecting myself with the only strength I had. She stabbed the knife into the side of my neck, nicking it, while I dragged my leg across her feet and tripped her. But that was all I had. I was done.

I heard Brooke screaming. Or was it Beth? I lay my head back on the floor. Just a quick nap, I thought. I need to rest a second and I'll get back up. I can do this thing.

My cheek against the floor, I watched the door bang open. Feet on the floor pounding toward me. Toward Brooke, who was slashing the knife in the air like a cowboy at a rodeo lassoing a wild horse. A heavyset man reached for a holstered gun. Had I gotten through to the cops? I couldn't remember and didn't give a rat's ass anymore. I just watched the show as if I were no longer in it. A spectator watching a movie. A character in a slasher flick who'd been killed off by the end.

"No, Vince, let me go, please," Brooke pleaded. "I didn't do this. I found them both like this."

"You little bitch," Vince said.

Beth had come to my side. She was punching numbers on a cell phone—her hands shaking and bloody—my blood. Crying. Screaming my name.

"Beth," I whispered hoarsely. "Scott didn't kill his wife. Brooke did."

Beth looked up at Vince. Brooke had backed up to Scott's body.

"Drop the knife, sweetheart," Vince said. "You think I won't shoot you because of a few drunken pokes? You swing it at me one more time and I swear I'll shoot!"

I watched Beth's mouth open in a scream. "Vince!" The sound of her voice seemed far away.

The gunshot took Beth's attention from her shaking

fingers and she dropped her phone. I read the outcome in her wide-open eyes. They blinked closed in relief and she breathed deeply, retrieved her phone, and punched the keys. "Ambulance, police," she said. "In that order! Ambulance now!" She gave them my address.

28

WHEN SHRIMPS LEARN TO WHISTLE

"AH, THIS IS NICE, HUH?" CHUCKY SAID. "SMELL that fresh air?"

"Algae and pond scum," I said. "And are you really going to impale that worm's brain on a pronged hook?"

"Worms don't have brains *or* feelings. And don't ask me how I know that."

"How the fuck *do* you know that, Chucky? I dug for worms when I was kid, and whenever I'd pick one up they'd squirm into a ball and jump out of my hand. Now, how the hell did the worm know I was picking it up if it couldn't *feel* anything?"

"Instinct."

"Something triggered the instinct. If some big gawky kid a thousand times your size picks you up, *you feel it*, and then you protect yourself."

"Jesus almighty God, Shannon," Chucky threw the hook and worm down to the floor of the sixteen-foot skiff, "you can sure chase the sun away."

I looked up at the sky. The sun was still strong, an Indian summer day. The air was a balmy 78 in odd contrast to the leaves already yellowing to gold from the nightly dips in temperature common to early October.

It was two months after Brooke, Scott, and I were carried out of my blood-soaked apartment on stretchers. Brooke and Scott were dropped at the morgue, and I was taken to Rhode Island Hospital, in tough shape but alive. I stayed for three weeks, by the end of which I was getting wine and spicy corn pizzas from Al Forno smuggled in by the girls. The morning I woke up with a hangover and my blood work showing elevated liver enzymes from alcohol consumption was the day they threw me out. The hospital preferred to call it an early discharge, but hey, let's call a spade a spade.

Vince didn't really care exactly how Leo Safer died, whether it was intentional or in a struggle with Scott. It could have been either. I chose to believe it was an accident. I wanted to believe Scott couldn't be a cold-blooded killer. I like to think my assessments of people were still on target. Like the Cohen case; I didn't think Micah Cohen shot his wife, and I preferred to believe Scott was incapable of murder.

The girls and I continued to torment Vince about his dip into Brooke's honey pot, but he, in his typical macho way, just winked as if he'd been the one who'd gotten away with murder. The thought that he'd been sleeping with a sicko murderer didn't seem to faze him. I guess Vince liked a little James Bond in his sex life. Hey, that worked for me.

"Truth is," I said, focusing back on Chucky, who was

slugging down a Miller Lite he'd just popped the tab on, "I really don't like fishing. Never did like the idea of killing things I'm going to eat. Philosophically I'm a vegan, but nutritionally I like my steak still bleeding. It isn't easy being me."

I knew I was making Chucky miserable. He'd told me once that he and Marjory had met at some lakeside camp in Maine when they were teenagers. They married right after high school and spent their honeymoon at a Saskatchewan fishing lodge. (Saskatchewan might be in Canada but don't quote me.) While Chuck was probably comparing me to Marjory, and waxing nostalgic about his lost vacation with her, I was wishing I was on *Cattails,* Scott Boardman's luxurious yacht, on which I'd spent only a half a day before all the shooting started...

"You know what, kiddo?" he said. "I think you like the *idea* of me more than the real thing. Since Marjory and I split up...I think you're scared of being with me full-time. And the truth? I'm not sure I'm enough to make you happy."

I felt a cold chill at Chucky's words. Had I broken up a perfectly good marriage only to find myself reincarnated as Dustin Hoffman in *The Graduate* on the backseat of the bus? Is this all there is?

"And I don't want you to blame yourself for breaking up my marriage," he said. "If things hadn't been bad at home, I never would have gone for you in the first place. So no worries. We can take it real slow if you want."

Well, thank the Lord, I thought. He didn't expect me to walk down any aisles any time soon. "How *is* Marjory?" I asked. "Is she doing okay with you being gone and all?"

He shrugged, tucked his beer can into a cup holder built into his tackle box, and picked up his fishing rod. He thoughtfully chose a fly from the box and tied it onto the end of the fishing line. The worm got to live another day.

"I guess Marjory's okay," he said. "She has the kids visiting her all the time, especially the girls. She got custody of the family and I got you. But they'll come around in time."

But is this what *I* really wanted? A permanent relationship with a guy who would stay with me until shrimps learn to whistle?

Or would I miss that constant flow of pickups in strange bars? The flirtations. The zipless sex, as Erica Jong would say. Yeah, I liked the never knowing. And I guess, like Vince, I liked the danger too. That danger that Jeff had talked about during the Cohen trial: my *payback for saying "Fuck you" to the wrong guy in the wrong alley too late at night after too many vodka martinis.* Yeah, maybe I like the danger of waking up in my bed in the morning and asking the guy lying next to me, *Do you want milk with your coffee, and, oh, by the way, what's your name?*

"Maybe you should go back to her, Chuck. If I told you things would stay the same between us—I mean if I was okay with you being married to Marjory—would you go back with her?"

He threw his line over the side of the boat. "That's what you want, isn't it? For me to let you off the hook? You and the worm? So you'll both stop squirming. Just throw you back in the bait pail so you can keep sliming around with your girlfriends to singles bars and whatnot?"

"That's real low, Chuckster. Real low. But I guess I deserve it, don't I? Once a mistress, always a slut."

"I didn't mean that—"

"Sure you did. And I'm okay with it. I've never pretended to be anything I'm not."

I picked up the rod Chucky had brought along for me. I lifted the worm from the pail and quickly slid the hook through its soft skin. "Is that how you do it? Fast like that so it doesn't hurt?"

"Yup," he said without looking at me, watching the end of his line bob in and out of the water. "You kill him real fast so it doesn't hurt."

I nodded, threw the rod down on the floor of the boat, and then slid out of my white Keds.

"What the fuck are you doing?"

I stood up in the boat and faced the shore.

"Sit down, will ya? You're going to tip us over," he said.

I didn't bother looking at him as I dove over the side of the boat. I was a pretty good swimmer, but I wasn't a gym babe, and sitting on my ass for days on end had taken its toll. Plus I hadn't done a lick of swimming all summer. Christ, even my sex life was out of shape. But as long as I had the stamina to keep a stroke going, I figured I could make it to shore in about ten minutes. And if I didn't? If I got tired and started to falter? Well, I knew Chucky had learned his lesson when he left me overnight at the police station. He wouldn't let it happen again. He'd always be there to save me, no matter how much of an asshole I am.

CELESTE MARSELLA received her B.A. and M.A. from NYU and her J.D. from New York Law School. She is a member of four state bars—New York, Pennsylvania, Rhode Island, and Florida—and has practiced in all except Florida. In Rhode Island, where she lives with her family, she worked in a gritty criminal law firm. Celeste now writes full time and is currently at work on her next novel.